Family history and his storytelling hero, Bernard Cornwell, inspired GILES KRISTIAN to write his first action-packed Viking series. *Raven: Blood Eye* was published to great acclaim. Two further highly praised novels, *Sons of Thunder* and *Odin's Wolves*, complete the bestselling trilogy.

Giles has long been fascinated by the English Civil War – from absorbing the vibrant illustrations in school text books to appreciating the cold efficiency of Cromwell's New Model Army, admiring the flair of the Cavaliers and revelling in the romance of the doomed Royalist cause – and it is this complex and brutal conflict that provides the backcloth to his new historical series, *The Bleeding Land*. The second novel in the series, *Brothers' Fury*, is coming soon.

He lives in Leicestershire, a county that was wrenched apart during the Civil War. To find out more, visit www.gileskristian.com

Acclaim for Giles Kristian's
The Bleeding Land . . .

'A brilliant read. Kristian weaves a colourful, authentic world in which to set his tale . . . and he has done it with confidence and real flair. Full of tragedy and triumph, honour and treachery, *The Bleeding Land* is a thrilling *tour-de-force*'
BEN KANE

'Expertly plotted, full of passion and bloody drama . . . a book that will appeal to passionate, compassionate readers, men and women alike, fans of C. J. Samsom as much as fans of Conn Igulden. Read it: you'll love every page'
MANDA SCOTT

'With powerful protagonists, a gripping story and rollicking action, I can strongly recommend this *tour-de-force*. Outstanding'
ANTHONY RICHES

'In *The Bleeding Land*, Giles Kristian has made an effortless transition from Viking warriors to the often tricky emotional landscape of the English Civil War. Visceral, brutal and genuinely moving, this is historical fiction at its thrilling best'
SAUL DAVID

'Giles Kristian brings to this novel all the trademarks of his highly successful Raven Viking series . . . a great read. More to come, I hope'
DAILY MAIL

Also by Giles Kristian

RAVEN: BLOOD EYE
SONS OF THUNDER
ODIN'S WOLVES

and published by Corgi Books

THE
BLEEDING
LAND

Giles Kristian

CORGI BOOKS

TRANSWORLD PUBLISHERS
61–63 Uxbridge Road, London W5 5SA
A Random House Group Company
www.transworldbooks.co.uk

THE BLEEDING LAND
A CORGI BOOK: 9780552162401

First published in Great Britain
in 2012 by Bantam Press
an imprint of Transworld Publishers
Corgi edition published 2013

Addresses for Random House Group Ltd companies outside the UK
can be found at: www.randomhouse.co.uk
The Random House Group Ltd Reg. No. 954009

The Random House Group Limited supports the Forest Stewardship
Council® (FSC®), the leading international forest-certification
organization. Our books carrying the FSC label are printed on
FSC®-certified paper. The FSC is the only forest-certification scheme
endorsed by the leading environmental organizations, including
Greenpeace. Our paper procurement policy can be found
at www.randomhouse.co.uk/environment

Typeset in 11/13pt Sabon by
Kestrel Data, Exeter, Devon.
Printed and bound by
CPI Group (UK) Ltd, Croydon, CR0 4YY.

2 4 6 8 10 9 7 5 3 1

For James, this tale of brothers

'That country is in a most pitiful condition, no corner of it free from the evils of a cruel war. Every shire, every city, many families, divided in this quarrel; much blood and universal spoil made by both where they prevail.'

Robert Baillie, 1643

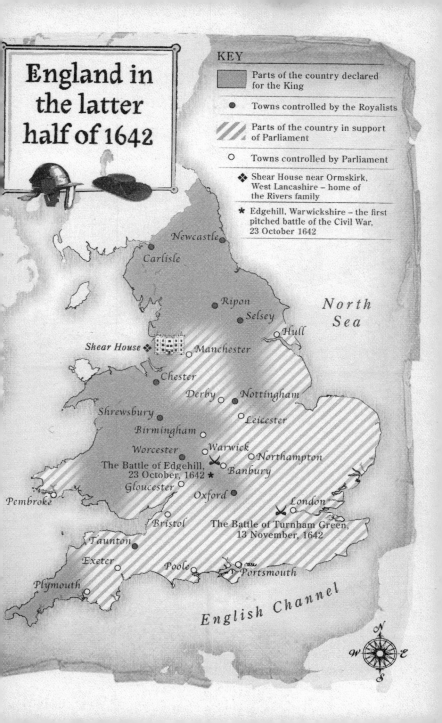

England in the latter half of 1642

KEY

▨ Parts of the country declared for the King

● Towns controlled by the Royalists

▨ Parts of the country in support of Parliament

○ Towns controlled by Parliament

❖ Shear House near Ormskirk, West Lancashire – home of the Rivers family

★ Edgehill, Warwickshire – the first pitched battle of the Civil War, 23 October 1642

North Sea

Newcastle
Carlisle
Ripon
Selsey
Hull
Shear House ❖
Manchester
Chester
Derby
Nottingham
Shrewsbury
Birmingham
Leicester
Worcester
Warwick
Northampton
The Battle of Edgehill, 23 October, 1642 ★
Banbury
Gloucester
Oxford
London
Pembroke
Bristol
The Battle of Turnham Green, 13 November, 1642
Taunton
Exeter
Poole
Portsmouth
Plymouth

English Channel

PROLOGUE

_____

Sunday, 23rd October 1642, Edgehill

IF HE CLOSED HIS EYES MUN COULD ALMOST CONVINCE himself that the great booms were peals of thunder rending the grey October sky. But for the screams. Men did not scream and shriek and wail at thunder, though they did when twelve-pound iron balls ripped off their limbs, smearing the air crimson and leaving splintered bone and mangled flesh in their wake. They screamed then and it was a sound from Purgatory itself; tormented, agonized and hopeless.

Horses whinnied, stamped and snorted, steam rising from their flanks to thicken the fug of men's breath and stinking fear that hung above them all like a veil through which God could not see. Which was just as well, Mun thought, for murder was about to be done.

'There, Hector, good boy. Steady, boy,' he soothed, pushing against his stirrups to pat the stallion's neck where the thick veins throbbed beneath the skin. Hector snorted gruffly in reply and Mun glanced into the throng of restless riders around him, judging his fear against theirs, for they were in the first line of the Royal Horse and it was nearly time. Surely.

For the best part of an hour the cannon had roared their defiance, the fury of each barrage like a bully's bluster, hiding the fear and revulsion that really squirmed in men's guts. For they must be terrified as I am, Mun thought, a shiver crawling up his spine at the sight of thousands of armed men in all their rebellious glory massed thick as briar at the far end of the ploughed field. And there are more of them than us. Damn them.

As for the Horse of the Royalist right wing, in which Mun waited like a man on his way to hang, it was said there were upwards of twelve hundred. Yet Mun felt as vulnerable as though he were naked. His skin crawled at the thought of flying lead being drawn to him like wasps to jam. His guts churned at the vision of wicked sharp pike blades gouging into his flesh. He knew, too, that the passage of so many horses would plough the field again, churn it to a killing quagmire.

And yet, when the order came he would ride at the enemy as though Satan were at his back.

He pulled all two-and-a-half feet of carbine round from where it hung suspended on his right side and checked it was at the half cock, the lead ball snug in the barrel, then made his eyes trace the swirling scroll-work in the polished beech stock. He tried to imagine the craftsman, quietly, carefully etching by candlelight long before this bitter trouble had come to the land. He wondered after the man from whose dead hands he had prised the gun following the fight at Powick, but then a horse screamed nearby, yanking him back to the present.

'At my word we go like Hell's hounds!' Prince Rupert

yelled, vigorously wheeling his mount round to face his men. He wore back- and breastplate over a long buff-coat. His scarlet sash and helmet plume matched the red and gold embroidered saddle cloth and the pistol holsters that lay in front of the fine leather boots that reached his thigh. His black mare tossed her head spiritedly, impatient to charge, but instead the Prince had her perform the Passage, lifting each diagonal pair of legs high off the ground and suspending them in a slow trot.

'Damn beast looks like it's dancing, not going into a fight,' O'Brien growled on Mun's right, leaning over in the saddle and spitting. 'I'll wager the Prince's horse can fence like a bloody French gentleman too.'

Mun knew his father, a master of training and riding horses, a student of manège, would appreciate the horsemanship and he twisted in the saddle, looking for him amongst the three hundred men of the King's Lifeguard whom the Prince had placed in the second line. But he could not see him and turned back.

'A horse will do that for a prince,' he said with a tight smile. In truth, he thought, a performance like that, with the big guns singing to the world, would impress anyone, even a man snagged by the fear of pissing down his own leg.

'You will keep your ranks and let the rebels see your blades!' the Prince hollered, then drew his own sword, which gleamed dully, and held it aloft like a challenge to the heavens. He clung on with one hand as his horse neighed and reared, pawing the air before stamping down and blowing fiercely. 'You will not give fire until we are amongst the enemy man to man.' He grinned and his mare bared her teeth, foaming spittle flecking at the bit. 'In their fright the rebels will give fire too soon, but we shall not. And that is how we will beat them.'

Men cheered and the Prince hauled on his reins and, still waving his sword, galloped along the line, his horse's hooves flinging up great clods of earth as he went.

A foul taste, sour as vinegar, rose in Mun's throat. Fear. He tried to spit but found he could not, for his mouth was dry as saltpetre. Beside him young Vincent Rowe looked as if he was about to vomit, his face ashen as the dead.

'Lord, I am afraid,' Mun muttered, feeling the words on his lips because he could not hear them above the cannon and the horses, the yells of officers and the flat beat of the drums, which had started up again. 'We are all sinners. I more than most men. If I deserve thy retribution, be it a bloody end or maiming, then so be it. But I beg you, Lord. I ask only this. Preserve Tom and keep him from harm. Though we are enemies on this field, he is my brother.' He grimaced because the prayer felt pathetic amongst that gathering maelstrom, like a moth in a rain-flayed, ball-jangling storm, and he suddenly thought he should check his pistols once more. Too late.

He sensed a tremor in the ranks, felt the whole right wing shudder and saw men craning, shifting in their saddles to get a glimpse of the Prince, who was walking his mare back along the line to the cheers of his men.

'Just run, Hector, I'll do the rest,' Mun growled in the stallion's ear.

'For God and King Charles!' the Prince roared, standing in the stirrups, and the words were echoed along the whole Royalist right wing as twelve hundred swords rasped up scabbard throats into the grey day.

'For God and King Charles!'

And then the shouts were not words at all but the senseless clamour of men rousing themselves to butchery, yelling as though to defy the agony that was coming for them.

'Keep him safe!' Mun gnarred at the sky. 'Just do what I have asked.' Then he put his spur to the stallion's flank and rode.

August 1632, Parbold, West Lancashire

The grass in Old Gore meadow had been left to grow long and would have reached the boys' shoulders had they not been mounted. At the end of the summer it would be scythed and dried to provide winter fodder for livestock, but that was a lifetime away. For now it was a wilderness and the Rivers boys were hunting Spaniards.

'Let's go into Gerard's Wood,' Tom piped. 'If I were a Spaniard that's where I'd hide out and plot against the King.' His voice was reed-thin and years from breaking, but the challenge in it was clear as spring water and Mun felt his lip curl.

'It is getting late,' he said, glancing up at the darkening sky. It was stained red, as though the heavens were on fire, and Mun reckoned it would be a fine day tomorrow. 'You know how Father gets when we keep the horses out past dark,' he muttered. It was true that Sir Francis had only recently scolded them for riding at night, saying that it was all too easy for a horse to injure itself on uneven ground and go lame.

Next day, however, and with the boys still numb from their father's wrath, their mother had confided that Sir Francis had been worried for their safety rather than the horses'. There were Godless men and cut-throats abroad after dark.

'But it is not yet dark,' Tom said now through a wicked smile. 'Besides, Father is in London.'

'Maybe tomorrow,' Mun said, tugging the reins to wheel his mount round towards the stream that would lead them south-west and home. Being eleven and the elder by three years, Mun knew he would bear the greater part of the punishment if they stayed out after dark. Their father's riding crop left angry welts that smarted for days after.

'You're not scared are you, Edmund?' Tom needled, weighting his brother's full name the way their mother did when they were in company and Lady Mary was painting a bonny picture of her polite, darling young men. Mun bristled, twisting in the saddle and wrapping his tongue round a grown man's curse. But the words were scattered in a gust and lost as Tom kicked his heels and galloped off through the long grass, sending a kestrel careening up from its kill, crying shrilly at the dusk.

Mun grimaced at the thought of a dozen burning weals peppered up the backs of his legs, then flicked his reins, cursed again and raced after his brother.

Once across the shifting green sea of Old Gore meadow Tom followed the ancient sheep path past clutters of boulders and a few stag-headed Scots pines all cloaked in pale green lichen. It was dusk proper now, the sun having all but sunk far beyond the Irish Sea and the western edge of the world. Over the centuries countless sharp-footed herds had dragged up stones from the soil, so that even Tom slowed his mount to a walk now to lessen the risk of injury. He could smell the woodland beyond the rise – musky, green, rich and damp – and after a little further he wheeled his bay north across a dense scrub of nettles and onto a ridge thronged with bright yellow St John's wort, where he waited for Mun. He had known Mun would follow him. For all his brother's high-mindedness – born of the responsibilities that attended being the eldest – Tom knew that Mun too loved nothing better than galloping across the countryside to fight the imaginary enemies of the King. England needed brave warriors, men who could fight and ride and who feared nothing. What were some hard words and a few lashes of their father's crop compared with the defence of the kingdom?

'I expect we will miss supper,' Mun moaned, catching his breath as he came alongside Tom, who was leaning forward letting his bay crop the yellow flowers.

'Maybe Bess will save us some,' Tom suggested hopefully, suddenly realizing how hungry he was. They had not eaten since waking and nothing whetted the appetite like fighting Spaniards.

A sound brought both boys' heads whipping up. 'Did you hear that?' Tom gasped.

'It came from the woods,' Mun said, nodding towards the mass of beech and oak that sprawled before them, at once both inviting and forbidding.

'Sounded like a girl,' Tom piped, blue eyes wide as he stared towards Gerard's Wood. Sir Gerard had been dead for twenty years and in the absence of an heir the land had gone to the Church, but folk still knew the swath of broadleaf forest as Gerard's Wood. It was a no man's land, a place in which children highborn and low wiled away the summer days confined only by their imaginations.

Mun clicked his tongue and his horse started forward. 'Is your powder dry?' he asked, mimicking the austerity of some of his father's stiff-necked friends who were veterans of the Dutch wars.

Tom clutched at an invisible flask hanging from an invisible bandolier. 'Dry as bone dust, sir!' he snapped with a nod.

'Good man. Then let us round up these Spanish curs.' Mun started down the flower-bright ridge and across another clump of nettles. A flutter of swallowtail butterflies scattered chaotically and Tom grasped for one but missed. 'Don't give fire until my word, you hear?' Mun ordered, looking straight ahead as they passed the first trunks and entered the forest. Again Tom nodded, clenching his jaw and easing his horse on with a stab of heels.

The last shafts of golden dusk light arrowed eastwards through the trees and all around them leaves rattled one against another in the breeze. Tom shivered with the thrill of the hunt and the bay, sensing its rider's excitement, whickered, the sound stifled by the dense cluster of undergrowth. Deeper they delved, through corridors and passageways, across glades and clearings and babbling streams. The forest grew so thick that any sense of direction came only from the nature of the slope. Here, where the evening breeze could not penetrate, the only sounds were the clinks of their own tack, the occasional snort of a horse, and the creaks of boughs rubbing against each other, stretching, twisting as they had over centuries. Until—

'I heard it again,' Mun hissed. 'Over that way.' He pointed towards a stand of beech marked with a clear browse line some six feet off the ground where deer had eaten the twigs and branches as high as they could reach. Nearby, an ancient holm had been savaged into contorted, outlandish shapes. 'We should ride home,' Mun said, though he was leaning towards the sound, ears straining. 'What do you say? Shall we go back?' He twisted in the saddle now and glared at his younger brother.

Tom shook his head, his blue eyes wide and his imaginary carbine still in his right hand. Mun nodded and, clicking his tongue, moved off in the direction from which the noise had come.

Someone was shouting now, cursing in a tone barbed and malicious. Someone else was laughing and then the boys heard the girl's voice again, just as they pushed their horses between a holly briar and a dead beech standing in ruins and perforated by generations of woodpeckers.

'What in Jesu's name do we have here?' a skinny, ashen-pale boy of about sixteen said, brandishing a gnarled lump of oak towards the mounted intruders.

Mun took in the scene: three boys, all with sticks, all bigger and older than he. In the middle of them was Zachariah the cripple. Zachariah's nose was bleeding and his breeches and hempen doublet were filthy and bloodied. And there, standing just behind the ashen-faced boy, her hands to her mouth, eyes round with fear, was Martha Green.

'What offence has he done you?' Mun asked Henry Denton, the boy he knew the best of the three. It was nothing he had not seen before – Zachariah's twisted foot invited the worst cruelty boys were capable of and though Mun had never beaten the boy himself, he had never defended him either.

'Little boys should be in bed,' Henry Denton spat, pointing a stubby finger up at Mun. A stocky youth, Henry Denton was handsome, but a mop of fair hair, clear skin, ruddy good looks and a rich father had made him arrogant too. At least, that's what Mun had heard his mother say.

'Everyone is little compared with you, you fat toad,' Tom said from Mun's left.

'Hold your tongue!' Mun snapped at his brother, keeping his eyes on Henry who was staring balefully at Tom, his lips twisted in a grimace.

'Thomas, isn't it?' Henry said, tilting his head to one side. 'Does your wet-nurse know you are out?' The other two boys laughed and Tom glowered, looking to his elder brother to do something. Anything.

But Mun sat his horse like a statue, legs gripping like a vice, holding the beast still as it snorted and dragged a foot across the ground. Henry shrugged broad shoulders and turned, nodding to his pale, reed-thin companion, who slammed his club between Zachariah's shoulder blades knocking him to the ground. Martha Green screamed and stepped forward but Henry snarled at her to stay back. 'Leave him be, whore!' he said and even the boy with the oak club seemed shocked at that word. The third boy, a fat bully with a face full of pimples, merely grinned, spitting on Zachariah and threatening another blow, so that the cripple dared not rise again. He lay there, face in the forest litter, ruined leg trembling and, Mun noticed, wet.

'You are evil!' Martha cried, her green eyes blazing,

finger pointing. 'God will punish you, Henry Denton. He'll punish you all!'

'You think God cares about one of His mistakes?' Henry asked, lips warping into a smile. 'Why do you care, anyway, whore? What's this cripple to you? Surely he can't screw. He can barely walk!'

'Shut your mouth!' Martha screamed, tears in her eyes.

'Mun,' Tom hissed. 'Edmund.' But Mun was staring at Henry.

'Hobbes, have you got a halfpenny?' Henry asked the pale, skinny boy. 'They say Martha Green will open her legs for a farthing, but seeing as there are three of us, I'd happily stretch to the price of a quart of good ale.'

Without thinking what he was doing Mun dismounted, taking the reins in his right hand and offering them up to Tom, whose eyes were round as coins in a bone-white face.

'Ride home, Tom,' Mun said calmly. 'I'll be along.'

Tom shook his head, glancing at Martha Green whom he thought the most beautiful girl he had ever seen.

'Do as I say or I'll take Father's crop to you myself,' Mun threatened, thrusting his mount's reins into his brother's hand. Tom hesitated a moment, then turned his horse and led Mun's from the clearing, half twisting his neck off his shoulders as he went.

'You mean to fight us, Mun?' Henry asked and, grinning, threw his two foot of beech to the ground.

'They'll kill you, Mun,' Martha warned, hands clasped as Henry's cronies came and stood behind their leader, one at each shoulder.

'I would rather be dead than a coward,' Mun said,

pleased with the way it sounded, though he was terrified enough that his whole body had begun to tremble.

He did not even see the first blow. It crashed against his ear in a burst of white-hot pain, sending him staggering, but before he could fall more blows were raining down, scuffing across his head and shoulders. Mun threw his forearms up, trying to protect his face, but he could do nothing about the kicks that were gouging into his shins and larruping the muscles of his thighs. He was aware of Martha screaming and Henry yelling curses, some of which Mun had never heard before, but mostly he was aware of terrible pain coming from all parts of his body at once. He was certain that one of the boys still had a club and he desperately hoped that the boy would not strike his head, for surely he must know you could kill a man like that.

Then he threw his fists forward, feeling the left one crunch against a nose. A boy yelped and Mun gouged at an eye but then his right leg buckled and he fell to one knee, tasting blood and fearing that they would not stop until he was dead. Another cry, this from Henry Denton perhaps, and then Henry was holding his head and yelling and there was blood between his fingers. Mun called out, blood flying from his lips, his ears ringing so that all sound was muffled. Tom!

Tom was there, wielding his own stick, wild as a boar, teeth bared. He struck Henry again but then the fat boy managed to grab the stick with both hands and yank it from Tom's grasp, turning the weapon on his younger, smaller opponent with a glancing blow that sent Tom reeling.

Mun yelled and charged, half stumbling into the fat boy, knocking the wind from him and falling with him in a tangle of thrashing limbs, and now Martha was amongst the fray too, screaming and clawing at the older boys like a bird of prey.

As suddenly as it had started it was all over. Mun sat against the trunk of an ancient oak watching in a daze a cloud of hornets and moths diving to feed off several glistening dribbles of sap leaking from the tree. This tree is slowly bleeding to death like me, he thought, feeling like a fallen hero, cuffing snot and blood from his nose and smearing it across his cheek. Nearby, little more than shadows in the half light, Martha was nursing Zachariah, who looked like the most wretched thing Mun had ever seen, but then Mun looked down at himself and was unimpressed with what he saw. His doublet was ripped and blood-spattered and his breeches were filthy. As for his face, it felt lumpy and puffed-up and he suspected only his mother would recognize him.

Tom entered the clearing leading both of their horses and wearing a smile. Apart from a slight limp and a sore-looking graze at his temple he appeared quite unhurt.

'Well that put paid to them,' Mun muttered, wincing from a dozen aches and cuts, for Henry Denton and his cronies had gone, vanished into the trees with the last of the daylight. Now the clearing was streaked with the tarnished silver light of a waxing moon. 'We taught those villains a lesson they won't forget,' he added for Martha's benefit. In truth Mun knew they had lost. He suspected that not even Henry Denton would stoop so low as to fight a girl and so it was more likely that Martha had saved them by joining the skirmish. She was the hero, he realized, though there was no need to say as much, especially as his split lip made talking smart like the devil.

'We squashed that fat toad, didn't we, Mun?' Tom said, bringing the horses up to his brother, who rose on unsteady legs and began to brush himself down with his hands, wincing because his knuckles were grazed.

'I told you to ride home, Tom,' Mun said sternly. Zachariah was on his feet now and seemed mostly unhurt, though you wouldn't know it from the way Martha was fussing round him.

'You were outnumbered, Mun,' Tom said, 'and they had sticks.' Then he smiled again, gingerly touching the bloody graze on his head. 'And anyway, we're brothers.'

Mun glanced at Zachariah again, knowing it would not be long before the poor boy took another beating. As for himself and Tom, they would receive one as soon as Sir Francis returned from London. That was as sure as night following day.

'Tell them that we will see them home,' he said, nodding towards Martha and Zachariah.

'But we shall be home very late then,' Tom said.

'Yes, I know,' Mun replied, patting his horse's neck.

Tom grinned and limped across to the others and Mun felt his own lips curl, stretching the bloody split so that it stung awfully. It had been some fight after all and even though they had lost, their cuts and bruises the proof of that, they had stood together until their enemies had fled.

Because they were brothers.

CHAPTER ONE

_____

November 1641, London

TOM RIVERS HAD SPOKEN BARELY A WORD SINCE BREAKING
fast in the Ship Inn. There were too many questions; so
much to say that he feared to start talking now would
be to never stop. And so he kept his tongue still and let
his eyes work, glutting themselves with each and every
wonder they could cram in. And what a feast it was!
At once wonderful and terrifying and like nothing they
had ever known. Besides, though he was amongst more
people than he had ever seen, he knew not one of them
and did not imagine any would be the least bit interested
in anything he had to say.

Standing on the south bank he stared through the
drizzle across the Thames, taking in the sprawled mass
of humanity cloaked in November grey before him. The
western end of the city was topped by the great mass
of St Paul's Cathedral, seat of the bishop of London.
Tom recalled his father telling him that the church had
once boasted an enormous spire, but that had been
destroyed by lightning some eighty years ago – a sure

sign of the Almighty's displeasure with the papists, Sir Francis had said ominously. To the east at the opposite end of the city stood the Tower, England's fortress. Arsenal, prison, government storehouse, royal palace and site of the national mint, its sprawling complex was London's most important centre of state. Cathedral and Tower dominated the city's skyline, but it was what lay in between them that sent Tom's mind reeling, filled his nose with its stench with every gust from across the river. Market areas, wharves, guildhalls, monuments, myriad church spires, houses, and the city gates were linked by a tangle of meandering streets all crammed with people. So many people!

Rag-and-bone men soliciting folks' saleable waste, pedlars crying their wares, woodcutters offering their skills, food vendors transporting fresh victuals. Animals, too, choked the thoroughfares; draught horses drawing carts and coaches, riding horses carrying travellers and messengers, dogs, pigs and poultry running loose in the streets. Then there were the cattle and sheep that were daily driven into the city on their way to rich men's tables. Along with the stench of people and manure, the hearth smoke slung in dirty brown clouds above the buildings added its muscle to this assault on Tom's senses. It was a seething, reeking clutter, a scene of chaos that half intrigued and half terrified him, so that for now he was glad that the sluggish brown river lay as a barrier between him and it.

He took the wide-brimmed hat from his head and shook the water from it, watching a ship trawling for eels, pushing its way against the tide past the Old Swan inn and the Fishmongers' Hall. The Thames was choked with all manner of craft, from the tall ships moored in the Pool of London before the yeomen warders of the Tower, to the rowboats, or wherries as he had heard men call them, and barges that ferried passengers hither and thither.

Yet Tom knew he must soon immerse himself in the flow of folk joining the southern end of London Bridge and make his way along that most important of arteries into the city's beating heart, where he would meet his father and brother. He would leave Southwark behind, passing through Bridge Gate upon whose crown the heads of traitors were skewered as ghastly reminders of what awaited such men. To Tom such barbarity reinforced his image of London as a living thing, an anarchic beast to which sacrifices must be made if some semblance of civilization were to be maintained. Many of the heads were little more than skulls now in which not even the crows would be interested, scraps of leathery skin and wisps of hair stirring in the chill breeze. That morning, when Sir Francis and Mun had left their lodgings early to be about their business in the city, Tom had walked with them as far as the bridge, there telling them he would join them later after he had explored Southwark. But the heads on London Bridge had bound him for a while with their macabre allure. He had simply stared at them, even though he knew such fascination marked him clearly as a countryman. He had stared and wondered what kind of men they had been in life and what offence had led them to that bad end. He'd wondered too how it must feel to cut off another man's head.

Now, peering up through the grey at the pale sun, rain falling softly on his face, Tom reckoned it was approaching midday. Time to cross the bridge then and walk the two miles upstream to Westminster, the other major suburb outside London proper and where, last morning, he had marvelled at the great buildings of Westminster Hall and the royal palace of Whitehall. His father and Mun would be expecting him, for as MP for Ormskirk Sir Francis had privileged access to Westminster Hall and had promised to show Tom its famous roof today, made, Mun had announced proudly, from six hundred and fifty tons of English oak. It irked Tom that his brother knew all these things before him, but that was ever likely, seeing as their father had taken Mun to London several times even before his elder son had become a resident of the Inns of Court.

An appreciation of the complexities of English law was an essential quality in any gentleman, even one owning but a modest acreage, their father had explained when it had been decided that Mun, just turned eighteen, would lodge in London for two years. But this was Tom's first experience of the city and it had not proved disappointing. He drank it in like a parched man. Yet, for all its vibrancy and chaos it was a bitter draught, because Tom knew his fate lay in the Church, where order and hierarchy suppressed instinct and channelled impulse. Such was the lot of many second sons, he knew, young men who could not inherit their father's wealth and power. Mun would get Shear House and its estate and the Church would get Tom. First, though, he would spend four years at Oxford with Homer, Aristotle, Ovid, Virgil and Cicero, honing his skills in grammar and logic, history and mathematics. He would gain the degree of Bachelor of Arts and perhaps even go on to achieve Master of Arts. But all that could wait. For now there was London.

Tom clinched the neck of his coat in a fist and tilted his hat against the rain before stepping back into the road. Then, avoiding two oxen driven by a young man whose face was a mass of pustules, he turned left and made his way towards the bridge.

'How is the debate proceeding, Father?' Tom asked, banging his slipware cup against his brother's before downing a great wash of beer. Pushing through the sopping crowds thronging Westminster had been thirsty work. Sir Francis shook his head and put his own cup to his lips, sipping carefully. His face was gaunt and the reeking tallow candles of the Three Cranes only emphasized the dark pools under his eyes.

'I cannot get a taste for beer,' he said, dragging his hand across his lips, 'I find it too bitter. Let me have my ale and all is well.' Mun rolled his eyes and Tom grinned, drinking again. 'I fear it has gone ill for the King,' their father said, returning to the question and glancing round to make sure he was not overheard. The inn was glutted with drinkers, all types of men so it seemed, and though it thrummed with noise it paid to be discreet about matters to do with the great debate. The Three Cranes being so close to the corridors and alcoves of Westminster Hall, some of those enjoying wine and beer were, Tom knew, bound to be men involved with the Grand Remonstrance in one way or another. 'It's fair to say the Commons is split on the issue,' Sir Francis went on, smoothing his short beard between ringed finger and thumb, 'with many who find it abhorrent that at times like these we should arraign the King and, furthermore, accuse His Majesty of misrule.' He frowned darkly. 'It is preposterous.'

'The Irish rebels must be rubbing their hands at the thought of us all at each other's throats,' Mun put in, shaking his head, so that a damp curl of fair hair fell across his right eye. He took a lump of cheese from the plate between them and bit into it.

'Indeed they must,' Sir Francis said. 'But Pym is persuasive. And determined to boot. Neither does he lack for supporters. Unfortunately. Their strength grows daily and those that are against them begin to fear for themselves.' He shook his head. 'They are all too keen to drag old skeletons from their graves.' At that Tom thought again of the heads spiked on London Bridge. 'Pym would have us believe there are Jesuits lurking in every shadow, waiting behind every tree. The man is a fear-monger and the thing about fear, boys, is that it binds folk. Prevents a man from pursuing his hopes.'

'But what if he's right, Father, and the Catholics *are* preparing to strike?' Mun asked, chewing. 'You only have to look to Ireland. There is no smoke without fire. Don't you always say as much?'

'Aye, perhaps,' Sir Francis admitted. 'And yet, instead of rallying support and raising an army to retake Ireland we are railing against our king.' He scowled as though hit by a foul odour. 'There are those who love chaos. Who would turn the world upside down.' Sir Francis leant closer to his sons, his face tired and drawn; a mask of sharp angles in the dim fug. 'Remember this, boys, fear is the lengthened shadow of ignorance.' He shook his head and grimaced. 'And I am guilty enough. This night we have even stopped a motion that would have seen much-needed arms put in the hands of our brave and loyal men in Ireland.'

'Poor bastards,' Mun muttered, earning a reproving

glance from their father. 'As if it wasn't bad enough them being sent there in the first place.'

Tom had heard it said that Protestants were being savaged in Ireland. Men were being butchered, women were being raped, and children were being skewered with pitchforks and roasted in flames. And fear and chaos, he knew, were very much like fire. They were flames that devoured and spread.

'Aye,' Sir Francis said again, nodding, 'God save their souls.' Mun mumbled a curse as Sir Francis sat back, picking up his cup again. 'And damn Pym for that.'

'If you are too tired, Father,' Tom began, 'we can see Westminster another day. I have already seen so much that I fear I shall not sleep for a week once we return home.' He rubbed his knees, trying to rein in the grin that was running away with his lips. 'Besides, Mother says these days your bones object to London's streets and the flagstones of Westminster's grand halls. She says this is a young man's city.'

Sir Francis's brows arched, bridging bewildered eyes, then he slammed his cup down. 'Nonsense!' he declared. 'I have not begun to patch up this *old* body for Heaven yet, despite your mother's . . . concerns. We shall go there this very moment. What say you, Edmund?'

Mun finished his own beer and belched into a fist. 'Oh if we must,' he conceded, though there was a half smile playing on his lips. 'We cannot have these country folk being entirely ignorant of how the kingdom is run.' He jabbed a finger at his younger brother. 'So long as you get back to Parbold in time to plant the wheat before Martinmas. And we've hogs that need slaughtering before the snows. London is not for the likes of you, young Master Rivers,' he mocked in a quavering voice, repeating the very words their parish churchwarden had used when Sir Francis had first made public his intention for Tom to take the cloth.

'I'll slaughter *you* if you don't watch your tongue,' Tom threatened, presenting his eating knife to his elder brother before stabbing a chunk of cheese with it. Several slices of cured meat lay untouched beside a pot of fruit preserve, but Tom was too excited to eat properly.

'Father, isn't it today that they shall present the Root and Branch again?' Mun asked, thumbing towards the inn's door, which yawned open, vomiting a crowd of drunken apprentices into the afternoon grey. Many such men had been given the day off in light of the furore that gripped the city.

'Root and Branch?' Tom said, feeling light-headed because the beer was strong, of the first water he guessed.

'A petition that seeks the exclusion of the bishops and papists from the House of Lords,' Sir Francis explained soberly. 'Many would take it further still and have us rid of bishops altogether.'

Tom lifted his head, understanding. 'On the way here I heard men protesting loud enough to wake the dead. Though I'll be damned if I could fathom their grievance. Is London always like this?'

Sir Francis shook his head, teeth dragging a small portion of beard across his bottom lip. 'Not like this,' he said, sharing a knowing look with Mun. 'There's a storm brewing, boys, and someone ought to reef the sail before we are all drowned.'

'No fear of drowning around here,' Mun announced. 'I am empty.' He upended his cup, the last drops of beer spotting the rough wooden table. 'Either we go now or I shall have another drink and be damned with Pym and Parliament and their squawking.'

'Edmund!' Sir Francis hissed, glancing around them. 'Do not forget that I am a member of this Parliament you would damn for the sake of a pint of beer.'

Grinning, Tom wagged an admonishing finger at his brother who stood, snatching a last piece of cheese and wrapping it in a slice of ham.

'Come, little brother,' Mun said, producing a shilling from his doublet and slamming it down on the table, 'let me show you where our father and the rest of them spend their days and nights bickering like children.'

Sir Francis sighed, Tom grinned, and the two of them followed Mun, whose broad shoulders cleaved a passage through the press towards the door.

Their father had smelt trouble in the air even before they had threaded their way amongst the crowds thronging the Palace of Westminster, through St Stephen's Porch and into Westminster Hall. Mun had seen him hitch his cloak over the hilt of his rapier, seen his thumb rubbing the swell of the weapon's fluted pommel as they walked, as though to gently wake the sword from its sleep. And though Sir Francis had told them that he expected quite a gathering for the Root and Branch petition, Mun got the impression that even he had been surprised by the multitude. He had said nothing though, and now Mun watched his eyes sift the assembly into types of fellows, that he might deduce what new grievances had bloomed into open protest. Everyone knew that as MP for Ormskirk Sir Francis Rivers felt it his duty to keep one ear to Westminster's ancient flagstone floor, but now Mun suspected their father was beginning to think they should have left the city that very morning. For angry crowds of apprentices swarmed around Westminster, converging on White-hall, and the whisper was that many amongst the nobility had already retreated to their estates. 'Even the King has quit the city for Windsor,' Sir Francis had said. A hot fever was taking a grip of London.

They moved with the tide as folk sought to get to the west end where, in the wash of grey afternoon light from the great arched window, a boisterous horde, their petition presented to a stern-looking official, had taken up a chant against Catholics and popery. The tumult rose, filling Mun's head, weaving with a thousand other voices to cram the vast hall right up to the magnificent hammer-beamed oak roof.

Sir Francis removed his kidskin gloves and turned to Mun through the press, wincing against the din. 'Where is Tom?' he shouted. 'I thought he was with us.'

Mun shrugged, craning his neck for any sign of his younger brother. The great hall was a seething mass of black coats and broad-brimmed hats that gave Mun the impression of a dark, tempestuous sea in which a man could be drowned if he did not keep his wits about him.

'You know Tom, Father,' he said through a smile, as though that was explanation enough, for amongst the Rivers family Tom was famous for having a wandering mind and the feet to match.

But Sir Francis shook his head, brows shadowing flinty eyes. 'This is no time for your brother's games. Find him, Edmund.'

Mun nodded and, hitching his cape back over the hilt of his own rapier, waded into the swell.

*

Tom had not yet set foot in Westminster Hall. Instead, he had let himself get snarled up amongst a knot of rabble-rousers and found himself more or less borne south along Margaret's Street, past the sprawl of ancient chambers, parliament buildings and law courts, like a leaf on the wind. And a bitter wind, too. Several of this band, which was largely made up of apprentices by the looks of their close-shorn heads, eyed him suspiciously, which was hardly surprising, he supposed, given his fine clothes and long hair. One of the louder apprentices, a bullet-headed, stocky man, had even asked if he was a Catholic, to which Tom had replied that he most certainly was not, and this had seemed to satisfy the man, who had given an approving nod and resumed his raillery against papists. For the mob was angry. Many brandished cudgels or balled fists, though none of them so far had threatened Tom as they continued through the pervasive drizzle that thickened the air with the tang of wet wool. So, his heart hammering in his chest, Tom let them and his own curiosity lead where either would.

Which was past the building his father had earlier told him was the Court of Requests, then into the House of Lords chamber, where he was confronted by a wall of uproarious noise that took him aback, making his head spin. Three hundred or more souls, men and women both, had crammed into the chamber, all eager to get near the rails at the east end of the place where the business was being done. A poor view, it seemed, did nothing to blunt their passions and they bellowed, crowed and squawked, their voices making the loudest sound that Tom had ever heard. And yet he would not retreat, not until he had seen for himself the object of the crowd's rage, and so he thrust himself into the maelstrom.

Being the son of a knight and looking like one too still had its advantages, he realized, even in a city where 'the embers of reform', as his father had put it, were beginning to glow, and men instinctively shuffled aside so that Tom was drawn inexorably through the clamorous, damp-smelling array and was soon spat out at the other side. Where he found himself face to face with a grim-looking soldier who hefted his halberd towards him in warning, the wicked-looking, rust-spotted blade gleaming dully in the candlelight. Tom showed his palms, a gesture that said he had no intention of coming any closer. And nor did he. Some of the soldiers were no older than he and nervous-looking, their eyes flicking across the boisterous throng, bloodless hands gripping their halberds a little too tightly. Glancing around, Tom saw scorn and malice twisting every face whether yeoman, journeyman, apprentice, or gentleman. To his right was a woman who had left her head uncovered to show off her elaborate coiffure; Tom suspected she was a beauty but could not be sure with her face warped by the squawking of obscenities that would make a sailor blush.

In sconces along the oak-panelled walls, candles, whose wicks needed trimming, were failing against the dark and miserable afternoon, so that with all the people, smoke and noise, Tom was reminded of the rowdy gaming houses in the Bankside and Montague Close that Mun enjoyed telling him about.

A shoulder struck him square in the back, shoving him forward.

'Stay back, sir!' the soldier yelled and Tom replied

that he would if only he could. Wearing an iron helmet and back- and breastplate over a thick buff-leather coat, the soldier was one of twelve tasked with keeping the crowd from encroaching on the Lords and the man before them: an old grey-bearded priest who Tom perceived was being accused of some crime, though he could not yet say what.

'Who is he?' he asked the soldier, but the man ignored him to glare threateningly – but do no more than that – at an apprentice who had spat a wad of phlegm at the priest. So Tom asked the same question of a man beside him whose face bore the pitted scars of the pox. Like many around him the man was smoking a pipe, its fumes thickening air already acrid with burning tallow, wet cloth and sweat.

'He's a Scot,' the man spat, nodding towards the priest. 'Name's Robert Phillip. He's the Queen's confessor, a damned papist.'

Insults cut through the fug, most of them aimed at the elderly priest, but if they were arrows he was suited in plate armour and seemed oblivious of them.

'This is all because he is a Catholic?' Tom asked, staring at Phillip and straining to hear what the Speaker for the Lords was saying to him.

'It is crime enough if you ask me,' the pockmarked man said, eyebrows arched. Then he pointed the stem of his pipe at the priest. 'But worse than that they say he's the Pope's bloody spy, sent here to spread his filth and pervert His Majesty.'

Tom watched Phillip's lips move but could not hear his words, though whatever they were had the Lords scowling and shaking their heads. 'He looks harmless enough,' he said, wondering how the old man could remain so calm in this bubbling cauldron of hatred.

'That's what makes the bastard dangerous,' his neighbour muttered through tight lips as he drew on his pipe. 'His type are a bloody canker that needs cutting out for the sake of all God-fearing men. For the sake of the country.'

'Bastard's refusing to be sworn on our Bible!' another man yelled, raising a chorus of jeers and taunts.

'Hang 'im!' a man yelled.

'Aye, string the cur up!' someone else bawled. The Speaker for the Lords, a fat man whose red face and sharp black beard glistened with sweat, turned to the throng, both hands raised in an appeal for quiet. Eventually the clamour died, leaving a few late-hurled curses hanging in the pungent air.

'This man is accused of being an agent for the Pope,' he said, 'and of divers seditious and traitorous acts.'

'Give him the whip!' a woman shrieked.

'Furthermore,' the fat man went on, 'he has before this assembly stated his refusal to recognize our Holy Bible.' This provoked another storm and someone threw a fleshy bone, which struck Robert Phillip's shoulder, though he barely flinched as his rheumy eyes glared at the crowd from beneath bushy, unkempt eyebrows.

The Speaker turned back to the Lords, seeming to seek a particular bishop's approval to continue. The aquiline-faced bishop nodded sombrely, his eyes revealing nothing, and the fat man turned once more to the crowd.

'Robert Phillip will be confined to the Tower,' he announced, stirring a chorus of ayes from the Lords and inciting another two dozen opinions for and against the punishment as Tom was buffeted this way and that.

Now Robert Phillip's face flushed as at last he lost a grip on the reins of his equanimity.

'You dare not!' he bellowed in a voice that surprised Tom, for it defied the priest's apparent frailty. Men jeered at his outburst. 'I am Her Majesty's servant! I claim our queen's protection!'

'The Queen is a whore!' someone yelled. Even the Lords were jeering now, some daring to voice their own opinions of their Catholic queen.

'Take him away!' the Speaker commanded the soldiers, and so they formed a guard of iron and steel in which they ensconced the priest that he might make the three miles to the Tower in one piece.

CHAPTER TWO

THE RAPIER WHISPERED UP THE SCABBARD'S THROAT, flashing in the dimly lit hall, and Mun looked along all three foot of slender blade at the man who had come at him with a dagger.

'Stand off, sir!' he said, at which his would-be attacker bared well-worn teeth and spat in disgust. Mun had not seen who had begun the trouble but none of that mattered now, for he was caught in the maw of it come what may.

'You Roundhead dogs grow too bold!' Thomas Lunsford roared at the growing mob that had forced Lunsford's party and Mun and Sir Francis back into the hall's north-east corner, by the stout door that led to the Receipt of the Exchequer. Being similarly attired to Lunsford's men, Sir Francis and Mun had been lumped together with the objects of the mob's wrath and now found themselves outnumbered five to one with the odds getting longer as more apprentices were drawn to the fray.

Having failed to find Tom, Mun had returned just as the one-eyed soldier had swaggered into Westminster

Hall, threatening anyone who dared bawl against bishops. Mun had asked who the man was and his father had told him as they watched Lunsford's men shoving their way through the protesters, their battle-scarred commander riding roughshod through an already volatile situation.

'The King has made him Lieutenant of the Tower,' Sir Francis had said, his tone betraying that even he thought that an odd appointment for a man of Lunsford's dubious qualities. 'That raised Cain in the Commons. Lunsford's a hot-headed fool, a bully and a braggart. Look at him! He's like a child poking a stick into a beehive.'

Many, including Members of the House and others whose curiosity had brought them to Westminster to witness the presentation of the Root and Branch, had slunk off as the mood darkened. Others, city apprentices mainly, who had heard that Lunsford was about the Hall making threats, had come to add their spleen to the growing discord. Any who had come looking for trouble had found it and now Mun and Sir Francis had their swords in their hands and their backs to the wall.

Lunsford will get us all killed, Mun thought, flicking his rapier's point high to deter the fiery-eyed apprentice who had clearly chosen him as a sheath for that dagger of his.

'Keep your guard up, Edmund,' Sir Francis said calmly, 'and cut if you have to.'

Mun nodded, trying to match his father's composure whilst inside his heart was pounding madly. For though he was confident in his skill with the sword – had trained with it most of his life – this had nothing of the art of fencing in it and he feared having to plunge that sharp steel into another man's flesh.

'Bastard Cavaliers think you own us all,' a short-haired apprentice snarled, brandishing a cudgel at Lunsford but keeping his distance from the colonel's wicked-looking blade.

'Have 'im, Daniel!' another apprentice growled, and the mass of them edged nearer, so that Lunsford's men drew closer to one another, presenting an arc of swords to the mob.

Sweat sluicing between his shoulder blades, Mun recalled what he had heard about Lunsford, that he was a cannibal, that he had even on occasion eaten babies, though who could believe such a thing? They also said Lunsford feared neither man nor God, and this Mun suspected was likely true, as he glanced across and saw the twist of a smile beneath the soldier's flamboyant moustaches. He was enjoying this.

'What are you waiting for, traitorous scum?' Lunsford asked this Daniel, who appeared to have appointed himself the mob's captain, with their consent from the looks they gave him. Lunsford's coiffured head was half turned so he could glare at the man with his one remaining eye. 'It will be a pleasure spilling your rancid guts across this stone.' Then he lunged, slashing his blade through Daniel's doublet into the flesh just below his collarbone, and the apprentice screeched in pained surprise, dropping his cudgel. There was a collective gasp and some curses from the crowd, though they instinctively retreated from the colonel's bloodied blade. Lunsford turned and grinned at Sir Francis.

'They whine but they have no bite, Sir Francis,' he

said. 'I'll wager it's been a while since your blade slaked a thirst, hey?'

Sir Francis seemed to swallow the words his eyes betrayed. 'I'd appreciate it, Colonel,' he said, 'if I could get my boy out of here without further bloodshed.' Lunsford laughed, then feinted low at another apprentice's legs but pulled the blade at the last.

Mun had watched the blunt-toothed man's courage bloom and now the apprentice leapt forward, the dagger flashing, but Mun sidestepped neatly and cracked the rapier's knuckle guard into his jaw, dropping him like a rock.

'Your boy looks like a fighter to me, Sir Francis,' Lunsford remarked. 'The apple has not fallen far from the tree, I see.' Then one of the colonel's men slashed another apprentice across his thigh and this was enough to break the mob, so that they parted, giving clear passage to the eleven men who were better armed and clearly not afraid to spill blood.

To Mun's relief, Thomas Lunsford was not so big a fool as to ignore the opportunity to quit the Hall, though he suspected that had more to do with the soldier having already been a guest of Newgate and knowing that the death of one of these petitioners might lead to his calling on the prison's hospitality again. Yet kill one he still might, for some of them were now hurling singlesticks at them as they made for the open door of St Stephen's Porch. Holding his sword arm in front of his face and with his father behind him, Mun followed Lunsford and heard one of the colonel's men yell with pain as something struck his head. Then he was through the door and into the maw of another angry horde. But when these men saw naked swords amongst them they scattered, hurling insults and curses from out of range.

And there, beyond an angry mob of twenty or more apprentices, was Tom.

'What happened to you?' Mun asked as the three Rivers men drew together and Lunsford waded amongst the mob, berating, yelling at them to disperse unless they wanted a taste of what their companions had got inside the great hall.

'They wouldn't let me in,' Tom said, nodding towards another cluster of petitioners who yet lingered by St Stephen's Porch. 'I knew there was trouble but they were not for letting me through. It's time I wore a sword, Father,' he complained, 'then I'd have been able to help.' Sir Francis's arching brows told them what he thought about that, but Tom's attention was elsewhere. 'That's Colonel Lunsford, isn't it? I heard them talking about him.' There was a flash of steel in the dimming light and then a scream as Lunsford cut another apprentice and his men barked madly, waving their blades at any who would not withdraw. Tom was staring, his wide eyes full of something that looked to Mun like admiration. 'They say he eats children,' Tom said. A mob of sailors had turned up now and seemed set to help the apprentices. Some gripped truncheons and others clutched stones and none seemed afraid of Lunsford's band.

'A rumour I'd wager he spawned himself,' Mun said through a grimace, following his father's lead and sliding his blade back into its scabbard.

Two burly sailors looked over belligerently and Mun eyeballed them back, but Sir Francis raised his palms to show the men that they meant no harm. 'Come away, boys,' he said, taking one last look at Lunsford, 'before that bloody fool gets someone killed.' And with that they strode off down Margaret's Street into the gathering dusk, leaving Lunsford and his cronies to the mob.

London's streets made Tom think of spider webs laid one on top of the other and he marvelled at how his father and brother negotiated their complex patterns, turning this way and that until he felt quite dizzy and completely lost. The rain, driving now, bouncing off the streets and flowing in streams along the gutters, did nothing to help him get his bearings and so he followed helplessly as his clothes grew sopping and heavy. The wind had picked up too and had a wintry bite in it, so that it was a relief every time they turned into a street running obliquely to it. At least the weather seemed to have thinned the crowds a little, making progress easier, and with Sir Francis's guidance they soon came to the bridge, where they joined the throng of folk crossing over to Southwark or beyond to the farmlands of Surrey, Kent, Sussex and Hampshire.

'I cannot imagine living here on this bridge,' Tom said, looking up at one of the many grand houses that lined the street running across the bridge. There were shops, too, and expensive ones at that, affirming that the bridge was home to some of the most valuable real estate in London. 'The stench would finish me off.' He raised the back of his hand to his nose. 'It's foul.'

'I suppose you'd get used to it,' Mun suggested, almost stumbling into a beggar who had set up at the busiest part of the bridge, where the multitude had bottle-necked and slowed to a forlorn shuffle. The beggar swore at Mun, who apologized, fishing a copper coin from the waistcoat beneath his soaked doublet and dropping it into the man's empty dish.

London's beggars were another thing Tom thought he could never get used to if he lived here. Many were the victims of disease, but some, including this one, Tom suspected from the missing leg and the bitter dregs of pride in his washed-out eyes, were veterans of the Dutch wars.

They take ship brimming with vainglory, Tom remembered his father saying once, *but they come back empty, broken vessels. And that is war, boys, remember that.* And yet still Tom admired, envied even, men like Colonel Lunsford, because wars happened overseas, meaning those Englishmen who fought in them got to see something of the world. Unlike those who suckled the warm, ample bosom of the Church and never got to taste glory. And that will be me soon enough, he thought sourly.

He pointed out to Mun a yellow-painted shop that sold fine leather boots and another that offered broad hats of felt or, for the wealthy, beaver fur at three pounds. His brother smiled, clearly enjoying Tom's excitement.

'Get your fill of it while you can, Thomas,' Sir Francis said, greeting an acquaintance with a nod and a polite smile. 'We ride home at first light.'

It had taken them nine days to ride more than two hundred miles from Shear House in Parbold to London and Tom was not ready to face the return journey just yet. Furthermore, the weather had worsened since their arrival, meaning it would take longer on the way back.

'I want to stay, Father, at least for another day or two,' he said.

'Out of the question,' their father replied, waving a gloved hand as he marched on.

'I'd keep him out of trouble,' Mun put in, removing his hat to sweep the water from it. His hair, a shade fairer than his brother's, was lank and plastered to his head. 'You could ride home tomorrow and we could follow on once I had shown Tom a little more of London. He ought to see the Tower at least.'

Sir Francis stopped and turned to his sons, glowering, rain dripping from his beaver's brim. The black-caped crowds flowed around them like a dark river past a boulder.

'Listen to me, you young fools,' he hissed like a lit black-powder fuse in a damp cellar. 'London is not safe. Discontentment swells like a boil and will soon grow too large for the surgeon's knife. We do not want to be here when the boil bursts.' Then he sighed, his face softening. 'We came for the debate, did we not? And I did my duty. But now we must get home. Before your mother begins to worry and comes to London looking for us.' He tossed his head. 'Can you imagine her around all this?' he exclaimed, gesturing to the shop fronts with their coloured silks, embroidered fabrics and fine tableware of pewter, glass and silver. 'We would be ruined!'

Mun smiled and slapped Tom's saturated back. 'London will still be here in a few weeks, little brother, when all this has died down and the Puritans go back to snuffing out candles in country churches and sniffing out witches.'

Tom felt crestfallen, but there was nothing he could do and so he nodded as they set off again with the human tide.

Once across the bridge they came to Long Southwark Street, where the crowds dispersed as folk went their separate ways. Some headed west towards the Bankside where, Tom had heard, you could find entertainment in all its forms. Others went east towards St Olave's Street and an area inhabited by lesser tradesmen and craftsmen and, towards its eastern end, the poor. They three continued south along the cobbled way, the stones arranged to slope towards a channel in the centre down which water now coursed, at times red with the blood and waste flung in by butchers. Now and then they were forced to stand aside to let carts and wagons and the public and private coaches rumble past: a luxury Sir Francis did not allow himself, much to Tom's disappointment, even on such a foul day as this. And all the while Tom let his eyes gorge themselves on the sights of the city, which was now falling under night's cloak. The candles usually put out on doorsteps were absent because of the rain, and the air was thick with sweet wood smoke and the dirty, pungent stink of coal. Grey-brown plumes belched from countless chimneys and hung in thick, noxious clouds so low as to obscure the tops of some of the buildings and smear the dark November sky.

Mun smiled, nodding towards the rows of tenements lining both sides of the street, which had commanded Tom's attention for the last fifty paces. 'I expect you must come to know your neighbours very well, eh?' he said. Tom knew his brother was trying to cheer him and felt embarrassed for sulking.

'Some of them must go back eighty feet or more,' he said, shaking his head in wonder. Most were two or three storeys high, the ground floors serving as shop fronts for cobblers, bakers, grocers, butchers, fish-mongers, weavers, tailors, leatherworkers and smiths. Above the shops and clustering in the yards and alleys off the main street were the residential dwellings, home to the rougher sorts, Tom thought, from the looks of the characters lingering under dripping eaves, clouds of grey pipe smoke billowing from beneath tilted brims.

A little further on he tugged on Mun's cape, nodding towards two rakers who, their brimming refuse cart abandoned, were roaring drunk, swinging ale jacks and yelling abuse at passers-by. Nearby, a well-dressed man was paying a black-toothed whore, and in the next corner an old woman, her sopping white hair so thin you could see her sore-covered scalp, sat with her face turned up to the rain, laughing like a lunatic.

'Why does Father stay all the way out here?' Tom asked in a voice Sir Francis, who was striding out in front, would not hear. They were into the commercial heart of Southwark now, where St Margaret's Hill became Blackman Street, from which branched count-less alleys, yards, and dead-end lanes.

Mun shrugged, shaking his head at an urchin who had appeared from nowhere to offer some service or other. 'He says it is his duty as a Member to know the people's mood.' He thumbed at the urchin to be on his way.

'And so it is, boys,' Sir Francis called behind him. 'I already know how rich men think, most of them anyway. I believe I can better serve my king – my country, too, come to that – if I can understand what the common sort are thinking.'

The street urchin was persistent and it took a growled

curse from Mun to finally send him looking for custom elsewhere.

'But the truth is, of course,' Mun said, 'that Father's purse is a little light these days. That's why he boards in Southwark whilst his friends dine on roast veal and venison in the town. He has spent too much money on horses. Isn't that right, Father?' His teeth flashed white in the gathered gloom and Tom braced for their father's anger.

But Sir Francis threw both arms out, palms catching the rain that was lashing down and bouncing off the cobbles and seething in the dark.

'We all have our vices, boys,' he said, never slowing. 'We all have our vices.'

The Ship Inn in St George's parish was nothing special. But it was warm and clean and Sir Francis was a creature of habit. Having lodged there on a friend's recommendation when he first became a Member of Parliament, he'd stayed there at least a dozen times since and told Mun and Tom that he saw no good reason to try another inn. Furthermore, he trusted the landlord's weights and measures, which, he warned them, was not something a wise man took for granted in city or market town these days. Once, some years ago, he had broken with tradition and stayed at the Tabard Inn on Long Southwark where it fed into St Margaret's Hill. It was from the Tabard Inn that the pilgrims in Chaucer's *Canterbury Tales* had set off and this made the place famous, which was why Sir Francis had decided he ought to give it a try. But fame drew crowds and the Tabard took, in Sir Francis's opinion, too many guests, so that the landlord recalled neither his name nor what he drank from one day to the next. He had been relieved when his work was finished and he could go home, leaving the Tabard to the wide-eyed country folk, the French and the endless stream of skilled labourers from the Low Countries who came to London looking for work.

So the Ship it was. Mun knew that some of their father's friends, especially those in the Lords, teased him for lodging in Southwark at all. Surely a man in his position could afford to maintain a residence in London's West End, they said, a mere stroll from the institutions of government at Westminster. But Sir Francis despised those who flaunted their wealth in plain sight of others who had nothing, and Mun admired him for it. Indeed, it was said that Sir Francis Rivers had even warned the King against the excesses of his court, a thing few men would dare. 'You must spend more time at court, Sir Francis,' Charles had supposedly replied in his quiet voice, suppressing his famous stammer, 'and then I warrant you would not be so quick to preach reform. We do things as they ought to be done.' Their father had never corroborated the story, but neither had he denied it, which to Mun was proof enough. He knew their father was proud that His Majesty counted him as a friend, but in truth it was a role that Sir Francis was clearly finding ever more difficult to play, and that afternoon's debacle at Westminster Hall was a case in point. Now, as they sat together eating a pie stuffed with pigeon and rich gravy, Mun sensed the burden of worry in their father. The events of the last days and what it all might mean weighed in his eyes, loomed darkly behind the façade of amusement he had put up at Tom's recounting of London's wonders.

For if his brother had said little earlier in the day, letting his eyes soak up the city's countless extraordinary sights, he was making up for it now, babbling about the endless choice of goods available, the pickpockets he had seen at work amongst the crowds of the Bankside, the stink of the place, particularly the acrid reek of coal fires, the unashamed pleasure-seekers, the heads spiked on London Bridge and the endless parade of beautiful girls that had almost made him forget it was raining.

'I remember my first time walking through the piazza of Covent Garden,' Sir Francis said, eyes glinting at the memory. 'Nearly twisted my damn head off there was so much to look at.' Tom grinned mischievously, then went on relating more of London's wonders, his voice rising above those of a fiddle and two flutes that had struck up somewhere amongst the noisy press. It was a popular tune that soon had folk singing along as Mun sat listening to his brother, feeling a smile warm his own lips. He had once felt like Tom: awestruck and amazed by the city and all it had to offer. It still excited him, but there was nothing like your first trip to London. Now through Tom he was seeing it all afresh. Then Tom came to the part about Robert Phillip, telling of how he had watched the House of Lords committee accuse the old priest of spying for the Pope, how they had scorned his pleas for protection and, worse still, how some of them had publicly insulted Queen Henrietta Maria.

Sir Francis took the napkin from his shoulder and leant forward, dabbing his lips. 'They spoke out against Her Majesty?'

Tom nodded. 'They called her a whore,' he said, wide-eyed.

Sir Francis flicked a hand, disregarding that report.

'Never mind the mob, Thomas, they go where the loudest of them leads and will say anything in the heat. What did the Lords say?'

'I was talking about the Lords, Father,' Tom said, glancing from one to the other.

Mun clenched his jaw, feeling something dark and cold pass through him, like a cloud portending a storm.

'God preserve us,' Sir Francis said, eyes riveting onto Mun's, 'but things are going from bad to worse.'

CHAPTER THREE

'BUILD UP THE FIRE, ISAAC, IT'S GETTING COLD,' LADY MARY said, taking off her thick wool coat and draping it over a chair. Bess did the same, her face stinging now that she was inside.

'Yes, m'lady.' Isaac nodded curtly and limped off to fetch more fuel, leaving them huffing into cupped hands that were red and thrumming with the pain of cold flesh warming. Sir Francis was behind his desk, his quill scratching away busily.

His hand stopped and he looked up at his wife. 'Everything all right out there? You have had them all working twice as hard as they'd like, I shouldn't wonder.'

Lady Mary raised an eyebrow at the implied suggestion of her tyranny and Bess felt herself grin.

'I feel better for knowing that the hedges are mended and the ditches dug clean again,' her mother replied, her eyes watery from the cold. 'And I made sure the men kept their limbs moving so as not to have them freeze and fall off.' She glanced at Bess. 'I think they were grateful, don't you, Bess?'

'It *was* frightfully cold, Father,' she said, refusing to

fully commit to either side. Her father nodded soberly, dipping the quill in the silver ink pot and writing some more.

Despite her father's teasing, Bess knew he appreciated how much it meant to the servants and groundsmen to see either him or Lady Mary out on a bitter day with the rest of them, inspecting the estate and helping where they could.

'So how is it looking out there?' Sir Francis asked, frowning at his writing as though displeased with his work. Bess knew he was writing a letter of reply to a copyhold farmer who had asked to extend the duration of his tenure. The man was a good farmer, albeit folk said he was older than Pendle Hill now, and Sir Francis was pleased to offer him another ten years so long as his son and heir agreed to pay the entry fine on the occasion of his father's death.

'Bleak,' her mother said, rubbing life back into her arms. 'Some of the sheep had got out and wandered almost as far as Gerard's Wood, but we put most of them back. The boys are rounding up the last of them now.' Sir Francis nodded, signing the letter with a neat flourish and then scattering sand across it to dry the ink.

Isaac returned with a faggot and knelt by the fire and Sir Francis waited, patiently watching the servant feed the flames, not speaking again until the thin, silver-haired man had left the room.

'Did you get a chance to speak to him?' he asked, shuffling through some papers and straightening a pile of books.

Lady Mary glanced at Bess, but Sir Francis wafted her concern away with the letter. 'She's his sister, Mary, and likely knows more of it than we do.'

Her mother nodded as though that was true enough, and Bess felt her face flush hotly.

'It wasn't that sort of work,' Lady Mary said, moving towards the fire and holding her hands before the flames, letting the building heat soak through the flesh into the knuckles and joints. 'I did not get the chance.'

Sir Francis made a hum in the back of his throat and sat back in his chair, leaning on one elbow, thumb and forefinger worrying his neat beard.

'It's not going to be easy,' he said. 'You know how headstrong the boy can be.' He looked at Bess, his grey eyes softening. 'Gets that from his mother, of course.'

Mary turned, eyebrows raised as she removed her broad-brimmed hat and the coif beneath, shaking out her long red curls so that they fell past her shoulders. She is still beautiful, Bess thought. 'Well, we will have to say something soon, for Martha's sake as well as Tom's,' her mother said.

Sir Francis nodded resolutely. 'I'll speak with him to-morrow on the way to the village. The pinner has one of our bulls in his pound, so I'm told.'

'Speak to me about what, Father?' Tom said, striding into the parlour and up to the fire, where he stood by his mother, warming his hands. His cheeks were red and the long, thick fair hair that was visible was un-kempt, tousled by the icy wind and the ride.

'Did you recover them all?' Sir Francis asked.

Tom frowned. 'Yes, they're all accounted for.' He took off his hat and ran a hand through his hair, glanc-ing at Bess and their mother, then back to their father. 'Now what is it you want to talk to me about?'

Sir Francis looked at Mary, who gave a slight nod,

then he pushed back his chair and stood, walking over creaking boards to the window. He stood looking out at the bleak day, hands clenched behind his back.

'It is about Martha, Tom,' he began, and Bess wished she had left the room but it was too late now.

'I gathered that much, Father,' Tom said, rubbing chapped hands together. 'What about her?'

'There is no easy way to say this, Thomas, so I shall be direct.' Tom glanced at his mother again, but she kept her eyes on the leaping flames. 'You are not to court Martha Green, nor will you see her any more.'

'Father?' Tom half laughed though the smile never reached his eyes.

'I'm sorry, Tom, but you must not visit her,' Sir Francis said.

'But we are betrothed! We will marry next spring.'

'Betrothed!' Sir Francis blurted, glancing at Bess for any sign that she had known this. She avoided his eye. 'And you have her father's consent?' he asked Tom. 'For you do not have ours!'

'Not yet,' Tom admitted, 'but I intend to call on Minister Green soon.' He turned to their mother now, leaning into her line of sight. 'What is this, Mother? Tell me what is going on.'

'Listen to your father, Thomas,' she said flatly.

Bess felt tears in her eyes but determined not to let them spill onto her cheeks. Tom had made her swear to keep the secret, but now she felt a terrible guilt for indulging the young couple's conspiracy, enjoying it even, when she ought perhaps to have guided Tom with foresight. Was that not her responsibility as the elder sister?

Tom took several steps towards Sir Francis. 'Martha

and I are betrothed and will marry,' he said, sweeping his broad-brimmed hat through the air.

Sir Francis shook his head. 'You must call it off. And you must do it soon.' He turned away from the window, fixing his eyes on his younger son's.

'Why? What has happened?' Tom asked, arms extended, hands reaching for an explanation.

'You know very well what is going on out there!' Sir Francis barked, nodding back towards the window. 'Anyone suspected of being a papist fears for his life. Men are beaten in the streets.'

'Did you know that some poor man was strung up last week in Ormskirk?' Lady Mary put in, her green eyes imploring her son to understand the danger he was in. 'They dragged him from his horse and hanged him from a tree near the market cross.'

'And all because he had the same name as a known Catholic from Bretherton nine miles away,' Sir Francis added, shaking his head at the madness of it all. 'No one is safe.'

'But Martha is no Catholic!' Tom said, hat and empty palm turned to the oak-panelled ceiling. The fire cracked and popped as the flames ate into the hazel's knots.

'And her father?' Sir Francis asked, one grey eyebrow cocked.

'George is a Protestant, Father, you know that! He's a minister, damn it, not some crypto-Catholic!'

'Can you be so sure?' their mother asked, Tom's curse having etched a line across her brow. 'The papists have learned to hide their . . . persuasion.' She touched Tom's arm but he pulled away.

'Of course I'm sure, Mother,' he said.

'That is not the point,' Sir Francis said. He closed his eyes and with both hands scrubbed his face as though wishing to start again, beginning with himself. 'The mob does not seek proof! For them the whisper of doubt is a rallying call. They'll beat the drums and light fires and remind each other of the Gunpowder Treason.' He dipped his chin, glaring at Tom. 'Men have long memories, Thomas.'

Tom looked at Bess, eyes pleading with her to take his side.

'If Tom warns Minister Green then perhaps he can make some public statement,' she heard herself say, 'give a display of his faith so that the people know he is no papist.'

Tom nodded, clutching at the idea, and looked back to their father who walked to his desk and pressed both palms down on it.

'I hear the man refuses to answer these accusations in public?' he asked Tom. 'Well?'

Tom glanced at their mother, then shrugged. 'I have heard him say that he believes men should be free to worship God as they choose, so long as they obey their king and do no harm by it.'

Sir Francis slumped back into his chair, shaking his head. 'Then he is as good as finished,' he sighed. The fire's ill-tempered crack and spit filled the room. The yellow light it gave off seemed brighter and more zealous now, as though it fought the encroaching darkness of the West Lancashire dusk seeping through Shear House. 'You will break it off with the girl,' Sir Francis said in an even, measured voice. 'And we shall keep our heads above this rising water.'

Bess saw Tom's teeth clench, a rampart against

the words that threatened to break through. Then he turned and left the room, and Bess, rather than look at her parents, watched the flames grow fiercer.

As he emerged from sleep's fog, Mun was suddenly aware that Crab had been barking for what seemed a long while. The coals were grey, only their hearts yet glowing with life and heat. Three of the clock? Four? He swung his legs out from the linens and sat on the edge of the bed, gathering his wits and letting his ears sift through the muted sounds coming from downstairs. Thumping at the front door. A woman's voice? Or a young boy's perhaps. Isaac growling at Crab to hush, the Irish wolfhound taking no heed, its deep chest issuing rolling snarls between each salvo of barks. Mun stood and took his breeches from the chair beside his bed, pulling them on just as the bedroom door creaked open and his sister's head appeared round its edge.

'Somebody is here,' Bess hissed, her golden hair burnished by the dying fire's glow. 'Isaac is fetching Father.'

He shrugged his nightshirt back down so that it reached almost to his knees, and grabbed his sword belt, the blade snug in its scabbard.

'Well, let us go and see who is calling on us in the middle of the night,' he said, striding barefoot through the dark.

Bess followed him along the oak-panelled corridor past portraits of long-dead relations, the floorboards squeaking and moaning, then down the stairs. The entrance hallway was a sea of pitch black enveloping a halo of light in which stood Tom, the candle lamp in his hand flickering weakly in a draught, barely holding the darkness at bay. Crab sat obediently at his heel, grey fur ruffling in the breeze.

'What's going on?' Mun asked, coming to stand beside his brother and seeing another face in the shadows.

Tom held up his candle to illuminate a young boy's tear-streaked face. 'This is Jacob Green, Martha's brother,' he said.

Air from the bitter night still swirled through the hallway like an unwelcome guest, causing Mun to shudder.

'You are trembling, you poor boy,' Bess said, 'you must be freezing to death. Did you walk all the way here?'

Jacob shook his head, from which tufts of copper-coloured hair, the same shade as his countless freckles, stuck up messily. 'My horse is tethered, Miss Rivers,' he said, gesturing beyond Shear House's iron-bound double doors. His breathing was still ragged from hard riding. And crying, Mun thought.

'What has happened, lad?' Mun turned to see his father halfway down the stairs, fingers wrapped round a brass chamber stick whose candle guttered as he came, his other hand rubbing tired eyes. His mother followed, one hand sweeping down the polished banister, red hair spilled across her shoulders.

'Tell them what you just told me, Jacob,' Tom said, handing the candle lamp to Mun and striding off.

'Where are you going?' Mun asked.

'To get dressed,' Tom called, bounding up the stairs past their parents.

'Well, young Jacob?' Sir Francis said. 'What in the Devil's name has happened that you would hammer on my door at this hour?' Isaac shuffled around the hallway lighting candles, so that by their blooming light

63

nightshirts, tousled hair and untidy beards were revealed. So too were the fresh tears welling in the boy's eyes.

'Men broke into our house,' Jacob said. 'They attacked Father. They said he is a secret Catholic. That he must answer for his crime.'

'Crime?' Bess said, shooting Mun a worried look.

'All priests who have disobeyed the royal proclamation to leave the country are to be arrested,' Sir Francis said, frowning. 'The King is trying to appease the mob.'

'But Father is not a priest,' Jacob protested, bursting into tears. 'He's not!'

'All will be well, Jacob,' Bess said, stepping forward and hugging the boy to her bosom. But a moment later the lad pulled away, his anguish finding an edge. 'My father is a Protestant, Sir Francis!' he announced fiercely, young eyes raking the folk around him, daring them to suggest otherwise.

'Who are these men? Who has your father?' Sir Francis asked.

'I only knew one of them,' Jacob replied, 'Lord Denton's son Henry. Last year he rode across my father's field in the hunt. My sister says he is a devil.'

Mun shared a knowing look with Bess, neither surprised at Henry Denton's involvement.

'Master Henry struck my father when he refused to go with them,' Jacob said.

'Was your sister there? Martha?' Lady Mary asked, glancing at Sir Francis, who looked back towards the stairs up which Tom had vanished. The boy nodded.

'Have they hurt her?' Mun asked.

Jacob shook his head. 'But she might hurt them,' he said with a brave smile.

'They have the decency not to involve Minister Green's family at least. That is something, I suppose,' Lady Mary said. There was a knock at the door.

'Who is it now?' Sir Francis said exasperatedly, nodding at Isaac to open the door, which the servant did, allowing a blast of frigid air to fill the hall. The candles guttered and the ladies pulled their nightgowns tightly around themselves as a young stablehand named Vincent stepped inside, doffing his hat to all.

'Begging your pardon, sir,' he said to Sir Francis, 'but Master Tom asked me to tell him when Achilles was saddled and ready.'

'And why would Tom want Achilles saddled?' Sir Francis asked.

'I couldn't say, sir,' Vincent replied, hands grasping each other, eyes averted from the women.

But Mun knew why.

'Because I'm riding to the village, Father,' Tom said, striding downstairs. He had dressed in breeches, tall boots, shirt, waistcoat, doublet and thick black cloak. He also wore a sword scabbarded and fixed to a baldrick strapped over his right shoulder.

'You are not!' Sir Francis barked.

'I will not be stopped, Father,' Tom said without breaking stride. 'Are you coming?' he asked Mun.

Mun glanced at Sir Francis, who shook his head, eyes as cold as the air swirling through Shear House.

'Vincent, saddle Hector and bring him up,' Mun said, the words out before he'd had time to think it through.

'Hector is ready and champing at his bit, brother,' Tom said before Vincent could answer. 'I took the liberty of having him saddled.' He shrugged at the question in Mun's eyes.

Mun saw anger in their father fighting to slip its bridle. In his own stomach he felt the butterfly wings of excitement begin to flicker.

'Wait for me,' he said to Tom, walking off to get dressed. 'Do not dare leave without me.'

'We will save your father from these ruffians, do not worry, Jacob,' he heard Tom say as he took the stairs three at a time.

He dressed hurriedly and, taking up his own sword, slipped the baldrick over his head and shoulder as he came back down the stairs. Into the maelstrom of words.

'You will not leave this house, Thomas. And neither will your brother,' their father said, pointing a threatening finger.

'But what about the boy's poor father?' Bess said. 'We cannot leave him to be beaten. Or worse. How could we live with ourselves?'

'It is not our concern, Bess,' their father said curtly, then turned to Jacob. 'I am sorry, lad, but your father should have been more careful. The man is no fool, he knows the dangers.'

Jacob looked up at Tom who was glaring at his father. 'You would leave him to the mob, Father?' Tom asked, fire in his eyes.

'I would,' Sir Francis said.

'Then you are a coward,' Tom spat.

'Tom! Enough!' Mun said, but Sir Francis was already going for his brother, fists balled.

'Francis!' Lady Mary yelled. He halted and turned to his wife, who gave a slight shake of her head, imploring him to hold. He held.

'Martha Green is to be my wife,' Tom said, putting

66

on his hat, 'and I will not abandon her when she needs me. Honour will not allow it.'

'He is right, Father,' Mun said, throwing his cloak around his shoulders. 'It would not be right to stand by and do nothing while a good man, a minister, is so cruelly used. And by the likes of Henry Denton,' he said, the name tasting like dirt in his mouth.

'You would both disobey me?' Sir Francis asked, incredulity twisting his flushing face.

'We must do what is right,' Mun said as evenly as he could, glancing at Bess, who gave an almost imperceptible nod. She looked horrified by the discord around her, for like Mun she had never before had to choose between obedience to her father and her own conscience.

Sir Francis shook his head in bewilderment. 'My father used to say, "God is good, but never dance in a small boat."' He looked at his wife and shook his head. 'Why do our boys insist on bloody dancing?' Lady Mary put her arm around Jacob Green and Sir Francis shook his head again because her silence was all but condonation of their sons' disobedience. He knew he was outnumbered. 'Fetch Priam,' he growled at Vincent. The stablehand turned and was gone.

'You will stay with us, Jacob, until the matter is resolved,' Lady Mary said. 'Isaac, fetch the lad some small beer and something to eat.' Bess ruffled the boy's hair, trying to coax a smile out of him. 'Be careful, husband,' Lady Mary warned, stepping forward to take Sir Francis's hands in her own. 'Bring our sons safely back.' Sir Francis nodded darkly and stormed off to dress. Then Mary leant in to Mun, fixing him with eyes that were suddenly cold despite the candlelight glossing them.

'Do not risk harm for the boy's father,' she whispered, clutching his arm with a grip that surprised him.

He nodded. Then he turned and strode through the still-open door. Into the piercing December night.

CHAPTER FOUR

THEY RODE HARD, THEIR MOUNTS' HOT BREATH TRAILING in moon-silvered tendrils as they galloped across fields of frozen mud and along sunken lanes whose hedgerows clawed at them greedily. Hooves thumped out a breakneck beat, pounding the iron-hard earth. Sword scabbards bounced, saddles and straps creaked, and buckles, metal fittings and tack jingled. The frigid night air scoured Mun's face, dragging tears across his freezing cheeks and biting through his gloves into raw finger bones. And he would have wagered a shilling that even their father, out in front on his noble black stallion, Priam, was finding it exhilarating, that even he was charged with the mad thrill of it. It takes him back to his years at Theobalds House hunting with King James, Mun thought. It reminds him of when he was young.

In the dark the moon-touched sandstone hills loomed, mere pimples compared with their lofty cousins to the east, yet standing like ancient sentinels and made more ominous by night's veil. The Rivers men flew across this darkling countryside, like the shadows of owls

69

sweeping close to the ground after prey. And yet they came to Minister Green's house too late.

'They took him,' Martha sobbed, hurling herself against Tom who wrapped his arms around her as though to shield her from the night itself. 'Those devils took Father.' Her hair, black as a raven's wing, fell about her pale face in soft, tear-tangled curls, and Mun could see plainly why his brother loved the girl, why he had risked their father's wrath by their secret betrothal. Though Tom was still a fool to ask her hand in marriage when he had no means to support himself let alone a wife.

'They hurt him, Tom. They struck Jacob too.'

'Do not worry for Jacob, Miss Green,' Mun said, 'he is safe at Shear House. Our sister Bess will see to the boy.'

'Thank you for coming, Edmund. And God bless you, Sir Francis,' she said, her voice muffled against Tom's chest.

Whilst Tom soothed Martha, Mun glanced about him in the candle-lit murk. The parlour had been much disturbed, with furniture, books and ornaments strewn across the floor. It was a small, modest house and though their father was yet catching his breath after the ride, Mun knew what he would be thinking. He would be wondering at his son's folly in supposing a marriage to this country minister's daughter would ever have received his blessing. For what property could the widowed churchman bring as a dowry to the marriage? And yet Mun could not deny that the girl was a beauty, and a woman's beauty could hold a man in thrall. His father would see that, too. By Mun's reckoning, advanced years had not cooled his father's blood so much that he would not see how a young man could be stripped of sense by Martha Green's full red lips, clear white skin and slender waist.

'They will take him into the village,' Mun said, meaning Lathom, for they were nearer there now than Parbold. 'To stir up the wasps' nest.'

Sir Francis nodded. 'I'd wager they'll ride to the church, too, for they'll be looking for proof of Minister Green's popery. If they don't already have it.'

'Of course they do not have proof!' Martha exclaimed, pulling away from Tom to scowl at Sir Francis, who raised his hands by way of an apology.

'Bolt the door,' Tom told her, gripping her shoulders, his eyes locked on hers. 'We will ride after them and make them give your father up. Do not open to anyone until we return, do you understand?' She nodded. 'Did they put your father on a horse?'

Martha shook her head. 'I don't know. One of them held me as they tied him and took him out. Miles Walton,' she spat.

'Did he hurt you?' Tom asked, glancing at Mun for they both knew Walton. Whenever Henry Denton was throwing his weight around Miles Walton could normally be found nearby.

Martha pursed her lips. 'No,' she admitted, and Mun noticed an expression pass across his brother's face that looked a close relation of disappointment. He means to make them pay anyway, he thought.

'They can't be moving fast if George is bound,' Tom suggested.

Mun agreed. 'And they have their prize thus no reason to hurry. We'll catch them, Martha,' he said, following his father towards the door.

'All will be well, my love,' Tom said, kissing Martha's lips.

'Let's ride, brother,' Mun said, his words prising the young lovers apart, and Tom's jaw firmed once more.

So, leaving Martha Green standing in the doorway, her breath pluming in the frosty night, the three of them mounted sweat-lathered horses and rode west along Briar Lane, their mounts' hooves thundering. Hawthorn, blackthorn and field maple crowded into the well-worn track, shadowy dark masses that threatened to swallow these intruders who dared to be abroad in the dead of night. In Mun's peripheral vision bats swirled and darted above the hedgerows, no more than silent blurs, and amongst the wash of wind past his ears he heard owls hooting and screeching high up in elms whose bare crooked branches were laced with frost and glittering in the moonlight.

And after two miles they found them. Six men, six horses and all of them, man and beast, surprised to see others on the road. They had rounded Briar Lane's last sinuous curve before it came into Lathom village, and there they were, Henry Denton and his companions, half turned in the road and glowering as though the newcomers had interrupted some secret ritual.

'Easy, Achilles,' Tom soothed, for they had pulled up abruptly and now their stallions were whinnying and stamping, indignant at being made to cut short the race. Hector was pulling his head down but Mun held tight on the reins, refusing to be hauled forward.

'Steady, boys,' Sir Francis said, patting his mount's sweat-glossed neck, trying to assuage the beast. 'Remember, no dancing in the boat. You will follow my lead,' he added breathlessly, yanking on his bridle to

72

bring his restless horse back round. 'Thomas, did you hear me, boy?'

But Tom was walking his horse forward, his eyes riveted to Henry Denton.

Henry smiled, a flash of white teeth in the moonlit gloom. 'Have you come to see justice done, Sir Francis?' he called, ignoring Tom, who had stopped a horse's length away. The breath of men and beasts billowed like fog in the freezing air. 'We have pulled this rat from its hole by the tail but I don't mind sharing him with you.' Next to Denton, George Green sat on a piebald mare, his hands bound together across the saddle's pommel.

'Good evening, Master Denton,' Sir Francis said affably. 'What is his crime?' Taking the lead from their father Mun moved into a protective position on Tom's left.

'Why, he is a papist, Sir Francis! A crypto-Catholic,' Henry exclaimed, raising a smattering of curses from his pals. One of them spat a wad of phlegm, which caught in his beard and hung glistening. 'A priest no less. He has been hiding amongst us but we have smoked him out.'

'I am no priest,' George Green muttered through bleeding lips. He looked old and tired, beaten in spirit and weak in body.

'You hear that, Henry?' Sir Francis said. 'He denies it.'

'Of course the bastard denies it,' one of the other young men said, shrugging broad shoulders. 'That's a crypto-Catholic to the quick.'

'That's how they survive to spread their filth,' another man added, talking to Sir Francis but watching Tom. Mun had never seen this man before. He was clean-shaven, hook-nosed and round-shouldered. He sat his horse like a sack of meal for all his fine clothes and the black and silver hilted sword and scabbard strapped to an ornate baldrick across his shoulder.

Henry gestured at this man as though he was some wise sage to whom Sir Francis ought to listen and take heed.

'What proof do you have?' Sir Francis asked, half smiling, still not unfriendly.

'He does not have any proof,' Tom snarled, 'but neither does he seek it. The Dentons think they are above the law.'

Now Henry looked at Tom for the first time. 'On the contrary, it is the law that has commanded all priests to leave the country. Our country,' he added with emphasis. 'If anything we are upholding the law. As should you, Thomas.' He glanced at Miles Walton. 'Unless, of course,' he went on, turning back to Tom, 'you are secret papists yourselves.'

'Hold your tongue, sirrah!' Sir Francis snapped. One of the horses whinnied and a bird clattered from its roost, flapping into the night sky.

Henry raised his hands. 'I apologize, Sir Francis. I have no issue with you. Or your sons,' he added, dipping his head towards Mun. 'But we must be on our way. The rot must be cut out, as any good surgeon will tell you.'

'Does Lord Denton know what you are doing?'

Henry's lip curled. 'What is my father to you?' he asked.

Sir Francis scratched his beard. 'Take my word for it, lad, a father always likes to know what kind of man his son has become.' The words were hooked and

74

baited. 'I am sure he would agree that breaking into a man's house in the middle of the night and tearing him away from his children is not a noble act.' Mun saw his father's right eyebrow hitch. Saw his teeth worry at his bottom lip and the slight shake of his head. All for show. 'I would not be proud of my sons had they done such a thing.'

'Then tell me, Sir Francis,' Henry said lightly. 'Are you proud of your son sniffing round the skirts of this stinking papist's whore daughter?'

Tom's sword rasped clear of its scabbard and he kicked his horse forward but Henry drew his own blade and raised it just in time, parrying a thrust that would have sliced into his shoulder. Steel sang in the darkness and six more blades were hauled naked into the frigid night as Mun and Sir Francis spurred forward to put themselves between Tom and the other four men.

'This is not your fight!' Mun roared, pointing his blade at Miles Walton. He could hear Tom fighting and desperately wanted to help, but he knew they must keep these others out of it or else the night would drown in blood. Sir Francis knew it too, for he was beside him, naked steel glinting.

'Damn you, Rivers!' the heavy-set Walton yelled, coming for Mun. But Mun and his horse had grown up together and they moved as one, the beast side-passing left so that the man's wild swing hit nothing. Hector turned on his haunches and Mun swung, clattering the flat of his blade against Walton's head with a sickening thud. The man's horse walked on and his companions stared open-mouthed as, without uttering a sound, their friend toppled sideward from his saddle. But his left foot snagged in the stirrup, twisted horribly by the deadweight of his body, and for several heartbeats they simply watched as the horse walked on dragging its unconscious master alongside.

Snot Beard yelled and spurred towards Mun, but suddenly Sir Francis was there between them and he whipped his own rapier up, hitting the forte of the other man's blade, then thrust his sword forward, over and under his opponent's in a lightning strike that ripped the weapon from Snot Beard's grasp and sent it flying to clatter on the frost-bitten track.

'I'll kill the next man who raises his sword!' Sir Francis barked and now there were only two armed men facing him and Mun: the clean-shaven man with the hook nose and a nervous-looking young man with small, close-set eyes who was visibly trembling, and they, it seemed, had seen enough to know better than to fight.

Tom was losing this fight and he did not need to see the half grimace, half smile on Henry Denton's face to know it.

You've done well to last this long, was what Henry's sneering expression said, *but you've not trained with the sword as I have. You can ride, maybe, but you have no skill with the blade.*

Tom was aware of other swords flashing in the night, of shouts and movement, but he would not take his eyes off this man whom he hungered to kill. This arrogant devil who was too confident. Too sure of himself . . . as Tom's blade streaked through an opening to plunge into the meat of Henry's shoulder. Henry roared with pain and anger and swung wildly, knocking Tom's blade aside. Too wide, so that Tom knew he could not parry in time. Knew he had lost.

But then Henry's world spun and he with it and for a heartbeat he must have glimpsed the moon; then he hit the ground, the air punched from his belly in a loud grunt. He lay gasping, Sir Francis standing over him, knife in hand, grey eyes glistening like wet flint, and suddenly Tom understood. His father had cut through Henry's saddle girth.

Lord Denton's son climbed to his hands and knees, glaring up at them with hate-flared eyes and trying to curse Sir Francis though he could not get the words out.

'I am taking the minister home,' Sir Francis said icily. The others sat their mounts still as statues, staring.

'I'm afraid that will not be possible, Sir Francis,' Hook Nose said, bringing two pistols out of his thick cloak and pointing one at Tom, the other at Mun. They were wheellock pistols of the kind some of their father's friends had brought back from the Dutch wars, and from what Mun knew of them they could be wildly unreliable. But the two in this stranger's hands were steady and menacing and though Hook Nose had played no part in the skirmish, he had that look in his eye that suggested he had every faith in his weapons.

'Please, sir,' George Green called. Tied and helpless, the minister made a sorry sight. 'For the love of God, do not think of murder.'

'Shut your mouth, rat!' the young man with the small eyes yelped, emboldened now as he jabbed his sword towards Green.

Sir Francis cursed and, holding rapier and knife out wide, stepped back to allow Henry to get to his feet, which the younger man did, wincing because of the wound in his shoulder that was spilling blood down his doublet.

'Who are you, sir?' Sir Francis asked the round-shouldered man, though keeping one eye on Henry.

'You are in no position to ask questions, Sir Francis,' the man answered, his head cocked slightly to the right. He had something of an owl inspecting potential prey about him. 'Now sheathe your blades if you will. This night has enough bite about it already.'

'My father is counted a friend by His Majesty King Charles,' Mun warned the man, gripping Priam's reins in one hand and his own rapier in the other. 'You would not dare give fire.' Nearby, Miles Walton, whom Mun had knocked from his horse, was sitting on the frozen track, groaning and holding his head. None of the others, Tom noticed, had moved to help him.

'With respect, Master Rivers, you do not know the first thing about me and are therefore unwise to make assumptions one way or the other,' Hook Nose said, shadow-browed beneath his broad hat. His mount held still as a rock despite his master gripping pistols rather than reins. Henry and Snot Beard collected their swords while Walton and the younger man with the beady eyes looked at each other uncertainly, clearly perturbed at how the night's events had galloped away with them barely clinging on.

'Do as he says, Mun,' Sir Francis commanded, sheathing his own blades. 'You too, Tom.'

Tom shook his head. 'No, Father, I will not.'

'Do not disobey me!' Sir Francis yelled, spit flying. For a moment Tom eyeballed his father, hot breath pluming in clouds, then his lip curled and he nodded, sheathing his blade as Achilles whinnied his own protest.

'Shoot the whoresons,' Henry gnarred up at Hook Nose.

'Shut your bone box, Henry,' the man replied, pistols still pointing at Tom and Mun.

Henry's eyes bulged. He raised his sword and put it to Sir Francis's neck.

'Stand off, Henry,' Mun snarled, 'or I swear I will kill you even with a bullet in me.'

Henry scowled, moving the point of his blade up so that it trembled a finger length from Sir Francis's eye. The older man did not flinch. If anything he leant towards the blade as though daring Henry to make good its threat.

'Lower your sword, Henry, or I will shoot you,' Hook Nose said, pointing one of his weapons at Henry now.

'What in God's name are you doing?' Henry blurted.

'I am doing what we came to do. We have Green and we will take him to answer for his crimes. I did not come to quarrel with these men.'

'You are too late on that score, sir,' Tom said, simmering with rage.

But Hook Nose ignored him. 'Help your friend, Henry,' he said, nodding towards Walton who had risen on unsteady legs and was peering around himself as though confused as to where he was and how he had got there.

'I will not tell you again,' Hook Nose warned Henry, who shook his head dumbfounded and lowered his blade, stepping back from Sir Francis. 'Thomas Rivers, you will lend Henry your saddle,' he said, then shot Sir Francis a half smile, 'seeing as his own is no longer useable. He may even return it to you.' He shrugged his round shoulders. 'On the other hand, he may keep it as compensation for the hurt you have done him and if you are lucky that will be an end to the matter.'

Henry glowered at Tom and Tom glowered back, then reluctantly he dismounted and began to undo the buckles and straps of his saddle.

'Are we all ready, gentlemen?' Hook Nose asked his party. 'We have wasted enough time with this mummers' play. There is work to be done.'

Tom looked up at the minister, whose bloodied and bruised face was drawn and pale as the moon. 'Have no fear, Minister Green,' he said. 'We will see that justice is done. I give you my word.'

George shook his head sadly. 'There is no justice, Thomas,' he said gloomily. 'Not in this world.' Then his eyes filled with tears. 'Look after Martha, I beg you. Keep her safe. Jacob too if you can. He is just a boy.'

Tom nodded fiercely. 'I will, sir.'

Henry mounted, grimacing with the pain of it, while Hook Nose holstered his pistols beneath the swath of thick cloak across his saddle. Snot Beard yanked on the minister's reins and the small party set off. But then Henry turned his mount in a tight circle, the beast savagely chewing at its bit. 'This is not over, Rivers,' he spat.

'God knows it is not,' Tom replied, the humiliation of their failure thrumming in his voice.

Henry wheeled back round and hooves clopped on the iron-hard track, knocking the peaks off mud that had frozen in low, wind-whipped drifts. As he went, George Green twisted awkwardly in the saddle, the moonlight washing over his miserable face.

'See to my children, Thomas! Give them sanctuary from hateful men. God bless you, Thomas.'

And with that they were swallowed by the night, leaving the Rivers men alone as an icy gust blew down

Briar Lane causing the hedgerows to tremble and the low branches of a nearby elm to rattle bleakly. Somewhere out in the darkness a vixen screamed, the shriek piercing the night. To Mun it was a blood-chilling, taunting sound. It was the Devil's laughter.

CHAPTER FIVE

EVEN CHRISTMASTIDE COULD NOT DISPEL THE GLOOM THAT clung to Shear House as chill as the fog wreathing Parbold Hill behind it. Since the incident on the road to Lathom, a cold, deep sense of uncertainty had lingered round the estate. All the usual traditions were observed. Alms were given to the poor. The grand rooms were adorned with rosemary, bay, holly and mistletoe, and the Yule log blazed in the parlour hearth. Friends, neighbours and relatives were invited to call and Lady Mary ensured that the Twelve Days were glutted with the very best fare they could afford: white bread, turkey, beef, venison, and pickled pork. Plum pudding, cakes and all sorts of sweets were washed down with spiced ale, brandywine and malmsey.

But there was no joy. Mun had only to be in the same room as his father or Tom, or worse still both together, to sense the choler coming off them like waves of heat from a coal fire. Tom's impetuousness and the subsequent fight on the road had put their family at risk, that was how their father saw it. They had been dragged into matters around which they should have taken a wide berth, and that had kindled Sir Francis's ire. As for his brother, Mun knew Tom believed Sir Francis had not done enough to help George Green, that he had been too selfish, or worse afraid, to petition for the minister's acquittal.

'I rode to Baston House, Edmund,' Sir Francis had said when Mun asked if there was anything more they could do for Martha's father, 'and I put it to Lord Denton that the man should be released on grounds of insufficient evidence of his popery.' He was packing tobacco into the bowl of his pipe, thumbing it down. 'Denton and I have never seen eye to eye but I hoped he would put an end to the affair. Instead he threatened me. Us,' he added, looking up at Mun as he put a lit taper to the tobacco and began puffing gently. 'Threatened to go to the law over what Tom did to his son Henry. Gave him quite a cut about the shoulder, it seems.'

'Lord Denton is a damned villain!' Mun had said.

'And one of the most powerful men in the land,' Sir Francis warned, pointing the pipe at Mun, 'which is why this family is better off clear of this whole mire.' His eyes sharpened. 'And Tom doesn't need to know. That I went to see Denton or about the threats to prosecute him for what he did to Henry. I don't want him blaming himself for any of it. I just want him out of it.'

Mun had agreed to say no more about it, hoping that Tom would stay out of trouble, that George Green would be found innocent, and that things could go back to normal around Shear House. His mother had insisted that Martha Green and her brother Jacob stay with them until the matter with their father was resolved. It would be unwise, she said, and unsafe too, for them to remain alone at the minister's house, and Sir Francis had, albeit reluctantly, agreed. And though he understood the reasons for them being there, Mun could not help but feel that their presence was a thorn in Tom's side. How could his brother walk away from the matter with Martha and young Jacob always there to prick his conscience?

Tom's anger festered and Sir Francis's temper simmered until, on Plough Monday, the pot boiled over. The three of them were riding across the estate, calling on each and every tenant as they always did at the commencement of the agricultural year after Christmas. Over the next week every freehold farmer, miller and smith, every copyholder and leaseholder across the sandstone hills or the West Lancashire plain would receive a visit from the Rivers men during which they would be praised for last year's work and reminded of next year's obligations, however small.

They had so far visited three tenant families and Tom had said not a word, a sullen presence on a sullen January day, and there were still another twenty-one tenants to call on. Mun had sensed the storm brewing without seeing any way to avoid it.

'Are we to drag your ill-temper along all week?' their father asked Tom, breaking the heavy silence as they rode across the heath, following the brook eastward towards John Buck's farm. Tom said nothing. He was watching a long ellipse of black shapes jostling across the iron-grey sky: rooks and jackdaws riding a bitter northerly towards their evening roost. 'Open your eyes, lad,' Sir Francis said. 'We can't do any more for the man than we already have. Green knows it, too, and will content himself that Martha and Jacob are safe thanks to us.'

'They are going to kill him, Father, did you know?' Tom said.

Sir Francis took off a glove and huffed into his hand. 'They might,' he acknowledged with a nod, 'and I am sorry for it. You know I am. But no one is safe nowadays. You saw for yourself how they treated Robert Phillip and he is the Queen's friend and confessor. If such as he can be locked up then what chance has a man of George Green's standing? Any of us could be next. Accused of some crime.'

A raven flapped into the sky *kaah*ing angrily at the men and horses that had disturbed its feast: the rotting remains of an old sheep that had not survived the winter, half covered by the brambles thronging the stream-bank and stinking.

'So we are to cower from men such as William Denton?' Tom said through gritted teeth.

'Let it go, brother,' Mun said.

'Aye and not just Denton,' Sir Francis said, 'but the King too. The order for the expulsion of priests came from His Majesty's own lips. Damn it, Tom, I am a courtier! You expect me to go against the King? For the sake of a bloody minister who may even *be* a Catholic? *And* a spy for all I know?'

'I expect you to do what is right, Father,' Tom said.

'Hold your damned tongue!' Mun growled at his brother.

But Sir Francis held up a hand indicating that he still had more to say. 'When you become a man, Tom, you will learn that there is no right or wrong.' He glanced up at the grey sky as though trying to judge if it would be dark when they left John Buck's farm. They had long passed the rotting sheep, but the cold breeze whipped up its stink and carried it after them, so that Priam snorted in disgust. 'There is just survival,' he said, as the cold seeped through Mun's clothes, beginning to gnaw at his flesh. 'Or ruin.'

Martha Green had told no one she was going to Baston House. She told herself that she had not mentioned it to Tom because she had only decided to go that morning and now Tom was somewhere out on the estate with his father and brother. But then neither had she told Lady Mary or Bess or even Jacob and there were no excuses she could think of for that, other than that she already felt herself a burden to Lady Mary and had no wish to burden her further. Instead she had told Lady Mary that she would very much like to ride across the fields up to Old Gore meadow and as far as Gerard's Wood, for Tom, she said, had talked fondly of that route which he had so often ridden as a boy.

'It will be good for you to take the air,' Lady Mary had agreed kindly, 'so long as you wrap up warm. There is a dampness to the air that makes it feel much colder than it is.' With that she had had Vincent saddle one of the smaller, docile mares and Martha had thanked her and headed off, promising to be back soon.

Now, her mount taken off by a stablehand to be watered, she stood in the grand, oak-panelled entrance hall of Baston House while a portly servant went off to fetch Lord Denton. The hall was festooned with tapestries which Martha thought were the most beautiful she had ever seen, and gilt-framed portraits of stern, rich-looking men, which she found intimidating.

Flanking the hall were two enormous wings, one given over to household functions and the other for the entertainment of visitors, and Martha could almost hear the cacophony of feasts gone by, the raucous guests of Lord Denton's ancestors making merry. The sweet smell of burning birch was undercut by the iron tang of fresh meat, and beeswax candles flickered in wall-mounted sconces but could not ward off the oppressive dark of so much ancient oak.

To her right a large door clunked open and a man appeared, holding a glass of dark wine and silhouetted by the glow of flames behind him.

'This is a rare pleasure, Miss Green,' Lord Denton said, raising his glass at her and half bowing. 'Please, do come in where it's warm. It is quite impossible to heat a house like this, you know.' She nodded and entered the parlour. 'My wife, God keep her, used to say that the frigid air is good for the soul. That it keeps our thoughts pure and the humours balanced.'

'And what do you think, Lord Denton?' Martha asked, suddenly aware that her hands were tight knots at her sides. She took off her hat and placed it on the bench beside her.

William Denton smiled, revealing white teeth amongst elaborate moustaches and beard. His greying hair fell in long oiled curls beneath which Martha could see golden hoops hanging from his ears.

'I think I would rather be warm,' he said, closing the door and gesturing towards a tall-backed chair carved from a glossy, rich-looking wood which Martha guessed to be walnut. She sat, hoping she would be offered a drink, for her mouth was so dry, and took in the man before her. Martha had never met Lord Denton before but she could now see from where Henry Denton got his good looks and the vanity to match. Dressed in a fine doublet that was slashed to reveal a purple silk lining, white breeches, silk stockings held up with purple garters, and shoes of soft-looking leather, Lord Denton was clearly a man who liked to be noticed. It came to her then how different Sir Francis was from this man.

'So, Miss Green, have you come to Baston House to admire our famous gardens? If so I am afraid you will be disappointed, for there is very little of beauty to be found at this time of year.' His blue eyes flashed and his moustaches twitched above the hint of a smile. 'Though I would suggest that only makes one more appreciative of beauty when one does come across it.'

Martha forced her own lips into a smile. 'My lord, if I may be so bold, we both know why I am here.' There was no turning back now. 'I believe it was under your orders that my father was taken from his house in the night and imprisoned.'

Lord Denton produced a pipe from the waistcoat beneath his doublet and walked over to a table, lifting the lid of a small, silver dish. 'His Majesty's orders, actually,' Denton said, stuffing the clay bowl with tobacco. 'If indirectly. For it was the King who ordered all priests to leave England.' He held a taper to a candle and took the flame to the pipe, sucking on the stem until the tobacco in the bowl took, at which point he smiled and tilted the thing to show Martha the smouldering contents. 'Your father disobeyed the King. We obey the King.'

'But my father is no Catholic,' Martha said. She opened her hands and saw little crescent-shaped dents in her palms where her fingernails had dug in.

'Ah, but you see he is just that,' William said, pointing the stem of his pipe towards her. 'So say enough of the villagers to make it more likely true than false. An honest tenant of mine says your father would not speak against Laud's reforms. Another said he saw your father perform extreme unction on a dying woman.' He shrugged shoulders that were still broad. 'The people are afraid of Catholic plots, girl, and as their minister George Green has done little to allay their fears. Indeed he has done the opposite. He has inflamed them.'

Martha felt sick. She suddenly understood what was going on, that Lord Denton was simply looking out for his own skin, keeping the common folk happy by giving them the scapegoat they all so desperately needed. Perhaps Denton himself was a Catholic. It was not impossible. But so long as he kept the wolves fed he would have no trouble. The harvests would be gathered, his tenants would pay their dues and all would be well.

'The whispers of frightened people cannot be taken as truth, my lord. You must present proof before you condemn a man.'

'What I *must* do, Miss Green, is preserve the King's peace,' William snapped, a scowl marring his good looks. 'These are troubled times and none of us knows what is coming.' He stood gazing at a tapestry on the wall of a young man hunting on horseback, two dogs trotting obediently behind their master. The man looked strong, long fair hair falling to his shoulders, and Martha wondered if it was Lord Denton himself, immortalized for ever as the young hunter.

'Sir Francis will speak for my father at his trial,' Martha said. It was not true as far as she knew, but she hoped it might give Lord Denton cause to reconsider.

He spun towards her. 'Your protector,' he snarled, 'ought to be helping me keep a hand on the reins, not questioning my judgement. He and those delinquent sons of his ought to consider themselves lucky that I have not brought the law against them. That troublemaker Thomas Rivers set upon my son. Wounded him grievously.' He swept the pipe through the air. 'Slashed him about the shoulder, do you hear?' he said, then put the pipe back to his mouth. 'A perturbing business which I have convinced Henry to put behind him, for which Sir Francis should thank me. Instead he comes here and points his finger at me. Next time I'll whip the man. Remind him of the order of things. If he's not careful the mob will think *he*'s a damned papist. Come banging on his door in the small hours.'

That threat was not lost in the cloud of tobacco smoke pluming around Lord Denton's curled hair and Martha swallowed dryly, her heart hammering in her chest because of what she was about to do. The fire crackled and spat. She felt the weight of eyes staring down at her from the paintings on the walls.

'Please, my lord, I beg you to reconsider,' she said, pleading with her own eyes whilst removing her coif and shaking her head just enough that she could feel her hair tumbling freely to her shoulders. 'My brother is only thirteen years old and our mother died when he was nine. Father is the only family we have.' This was not quite true but true enough seeing as her uncle and cousins had sailed for the New World two years ago. 'Is there anything I can do to prevail on your mercy, Lord Denton?' she asked, feeling tears – they were true enough – well in her eyes. 'Do you have need of a maid? I am a good cook and would ask no pay, just that my father be freed and left alone.'

'And have a papist's daughter under my roof?' William asked, one eyebrow hitched as he exhaled yellow-grey smoke that drifted in lazy tendrils up to the carved oak ceiling. 'Besides, I already have more servants than I need.'

Martha saw something different in his eyes now, something predatory. And so, swallowing the lump that had risen in her throat, she removed her neckcloth, feeling the fire's glow on the bare skin of her shoulders. Her cheeks had begun to burn hotly.

'My apologies, Miss Green,' he said, turning, 'but I have not yet offered you a drink. This tobacco smoke can dry the gills and is even worse for those not partaking. Malmsey?' He was already pouring the dark liquid into a glass.

'Thank you, my lord,' she said. She did not normally drink strong wine but today she would and gladly. The stronger the better. He walked over and offered her the glass, which she took in two trembling hands.

'Now then, I am not an unreasonable man, as anyone that knows me will testify. Let us see if we can come to any sort of arrangement, shall we?' Martha nodded and, putting the glass to her lips, sipped the sweet wine so that its warmth bloomed in her throat and chest. *God forgive me*, her mind whispered.

'What other . . . services . . . can you offer a man in my position?' Lord Denton dared, the thing barely veiled at all now.

Martha let the question go unanswered, which was answer in itself, and Lord Denton went back to the table and laid the pipe on a plate, where it sat smouldering.

'The door is locked?' Martha asked, her whole body shaking now, so that she thought even her soul was trembling.

'No one will come in,' Lord Denton said, assuring her with a smile.

'And you give me your word you will have my father freed?' she asked, fingers fumbling at the lace of her bodice.

'You have my word that your father will not spend another week in that prison.' He gestured for her to stand, so she did, though she feared her legs might buckle at any moment. 'Now take off your skirts, girl,' Lord Denton said, teeth worrying his bottom lip. His forehead glistened with sweat and the firelight danced across his face and Martha thought he was the Devil in human form.

Her skirts fell to the floor and despite the fire's heat she felt a chill breeze across her legs as she pushed down her stockings and took them off, laying them beside her shoes. Lord Denton's eyes flickered hungrily down to her private parts. She saw a shudder surge through him culminating in a twist of his neck that reminded her of a bird of prey.

He went over to the tapestry and ripped it from the wall, then spread it across the floor. Dust caught in Martha's throat but she tried not to cough.

'Now come here,' he said, his voice somehow thickened, and extended a hand down to the floor. 'Make yourself comfortable.'

Martha glanced down at her nakedness, her hair hiding her face for a moment. 'God forgive me,' she whispered. Then she went and lay on the tapestry and closed her eyes.

When Lord Denton had finished he stood and pulled up his breeches, smoothing his moustaches with finger and thumb. He put his fingers to his nose and inhaled deeply, then walked over to the table and filled his glass with wine, turning his back on Martha.

She took the opportunity to stand and found that her legs were weak and would barely support her as she hurriedly put on her skirts, sickened by the man's stink that clung to her, filling her nose and throat. Appalled at the wetness between her legs.

When she was dressed again, Lord Denton turned back to face her and she saw a faint twist of disgust at his lips.

'Are you repulsed by *me*, Lord Denton? Or by yourself?' she dared, lacing up her bodice.

'Get out of my house, girl,' he said through a grimace.

She walked towards him, suddenly terrified that she had upset him. 'I am sorry, my lord,' she said, 'I did not mean to—'

'I said get out!' he barked, so that Martha stopped suddenly, afraid to move at all.

'You will keep your word?' she asked, feeling now more desperate then ever, because of what she had given for that word.

Lord Denton glanced down at the tapestry still on the floor, then glared at Martha.

'Who are you to make demands of me?' he asked bitterly.

'But your word, my lord! You said my father would not spend another week imprisoned.'

'And so he will not,' Lord Denton replied, a grin twitching his moustaches, 'for he is to be executed for his crimes. In four days, I believe.'

'No!' Martha screamed, flying at him. She clawed at him, gouging his face, but William was still a powerful man and he knocked her arms aside and clamped a hand around her throat, using his free arm to fend off her flailing hands.

He's going to kill me, she thought. Then the parlour door opened and Henry came in, his face flushed from riding and his boots trailing mud across the floor.

'Father?'

'Get out!' William yelled, spittle flying from his mouth and spraying Martha.

For a heartbeat Henry took in the scene, eyes wide and mouth hanging open. His gaze flicked down to the tapestry and back up to Martha and his nose twitched as though catching a scent.

'I will not tell you again, boy!' his father growled.

Henry dipped his head and backed out of the room, shutting the door behind him.

'Listen to me, harlot, and listen well. If you do not stop meddling in affairs that are beyond you, I will make it known that you came here and whored yourself.' His grip was strong. She could not breathe. 'I am sure Tom Rivers will be interested to hear that I fucked his dirty little harlot.' Blackness was flooding her vision and she felt hot urine running down her leg.

Then she felt herself fly backwards and hit the floor, where she lay for what seemed like a long time before her senses flooded back in.

'Never come here again,' he said, grimacing at the small puddles on the oak floorboards.

Martha climbed unsteadily to her feet and fled from him, back into the entrance hall where dead faces stared at her accusingly, then out of the great door where she found her horse waiting for her, its reins held by a young boy who would not look her in the eye. She put her coif to her nose and breathed in her own familiar smell, trying to be rid of his because she thought she would vomit. Then she mounted the mare, wincing in discomfort, and rode from Baston House. And she did not see her brother, Jacob, sitting on a chestnut colt among a stand of Scots pine.

CHAPTER SIX

AT FIRST THE SNOWFLAKES HAD CLUNG TO ONE ANOTHER, plunging from the ashen heavens like duck down and melting on the muddied track and on hat brims and cloaks. But now the wind had picked up, scattering the snow into finer flakes that swirled around chaotically, some of them even ascending back into the desolate, wan sky. It was a cold, bleak, hopeless day, but that had not kept the crowds away and now they were gathered, huddled like sheep against the chill. Having come from miles around, men, women, even children stamped feet and huffed into hands, a cloud of freezing breath rising from them along with a constant murmur like that of the sea. For nothing could keep them from an execution.

Most had come up from Parbold, Lathom and Newburgh villages, Bess supposed, following the ancient tracks to Gallows Ledge on Hilldale like so many before them. Like those early pilgrims traipsing up to Golgotha beyond Jerusalem's walls, she thought, wondering then what it was about death that so drew the living. But many, too, had come from farther afield, from Eccleston and Leyland, perhaps even from Preston. Excited folk had traversed fields and woodland on foot or on horseback, tramping over the sandstone foothills of the West Lancashire countryside or through the valley of the River Douglas, wrapped against the day. To watch George Green hang.

They had set off from Shear House before sunrise, arriving in time to see two women executed first, one for being a witch and the other for murdering her husband. The witch had died quickly, thank God, her neck snapping like an old twig, but the other woman had jerked and kicked and fouled herself and it had taken two men hanging from her ankles to break her neck, at which the crowd had groaned and gasped, horrified and thrilled in equal measure.

Her mother had whispered a prayer for the women's souls and her betrothed, Emmanuel Bright, had clutched Bess to his chest at the last to spare her the grisly sight. But to her shame Bess had looked anyway, transfixed by the murderess's lolling tongue and bulging eyes. Now the women, whose chins, forearms and hands darkened as the blood pooled in them, were forgotten and all eyes were turned towards the main event.

'How is he, Edmund?' their father asked, nodding towards Tom who was pushing forward, leading Martha by the hand because she had wanted to see her father, or rather wanted him to see her. Before the end.

'He is angry, Father,' Mun said, the words sounding to Bess's ears like an accusation. To Sir Francis too by the set of his jaw.

'Just make sure he doesn't do anything foolish,' he growled. 'Bad enough that he is with the girl now. In plain sight of this mob.'

'Francis!' their mother rasped. 'The poor girl is about to watch her father hang. Have some pity.'

Sir Francis gave an almost imperceptible nod and cleared his throat. 'You're right,' he muttered. 'It is a thing no daughter should ever endure.' Bess felt his hand cup her elbow and gently squeeze, a father's reassurance that all would be well, and she gave him a smile that merely curved her lips. For Martha Green nothing would be well ever again.

'Still, keep an eye on him, Edmund,' Sir Francis said, eyes fixed on his younger son who was now in the front row. 'He can go on glowering at me until Saint George's Day. That's up to him. But he looks up to you. You'll have to be the one to make him see sense.'

Mun nodded but said nothing, a gust whipping his hair, tangling it with his beard and moustaches as he watched them rig the gibbet. To the right of the gallows three men had scraped a patch of earth clear of snow and now Bess watched them building a pile of furze and sticks.

'Death to all Catholics!' a woman screamed. The crowd cheered this and Bess's eye was drawn eastward to a copse of elms in whose topmost branches a parliament of rooks clamoured raspingly in what sounded to her like a derisive echo of the blood-lusting humans.

Mun nodded eastwards. 'Even the damned birds mock us,' he murmured under his breath, and this, or the cold perhaps, sent an icy shiver scuttling up Bess's spine. This was a desolate place to meet your end.

She looked at the pale faces around them, faces full of disgust and hatred. Full of something else too. Something like greed, as though they hungered for what was coming, their murmured curses stinking of spiced wine as the snow swirled, catching in beards and lashes and melting amongst damp hair. God have mercy on us all, she prayed silently.

Mun pushed forward, putting himself between Martha and a woman whose sombre dress of sad country colours was at odds with her florid face as she shrieked death to all Catholics, brandishing the white bony knot of a hand towards the condemned. But if Martha knew Mun was there she did not show it as she clung to Tom with both arms, as though she would fall without him.

Less than a stone's throw away stood the stout gallows, piling with snow now. A ladder thumped against it, being tested by the executioner whose slab of a face was grim beneath his bird's nest beard. Beside him stood the sheriff Robert Thurloe, two miserable-looking men clutching halberds, and George Green. The minister's uncovered, balding head was bowed, lolling between slumped shoulders, and his hands were bound behind his back. He wore shoes, breeches, a thin linen shirt that ruffled in the icy wind, and nothing more. Even from that distance Mun could see that the man was shivering violently as he awaited the hangman's noose. This cold will kill him before the noose will, he thought.

'Black-hearted bastards,' Tom growled. Mun was about to caution his brother against making his feelings known, when a thin voice sliced through the wind like a knife between ribs.

'Sitha!' Sheriff Thurloe cried, fishing a crucifix on a length of beads from inside the minister's shirt. 'The baubles of a papist!' The onlookers jeered.

'Whottle yer damned trinkets do for thi na, Green?' someone screamed, and some amongst the crowd laughed at that.

'They are not his! You have put it there!' Martha yelled. Tom pulled her against him, protecting her from the eyes that scoured them both, and a fat man lifted his walking stick and pointed it towards Martha, yelling that there was another papist, clear as a boil on a whore's arse.

'Hold your tongue, sir,' Mun snarled, and the fat man shuddered visibly and lowered his eyes, his cane vanishing back into the throng.

Mun could see that Green was speaking now, attempting to address the crowd through the veil of whirling snow. But his voice was too feeble and the people had come to watch him hang not hear him plead his innocence.

'Silence the blasphemer!' a toothless old man barked.

'Stop 'is mouth!' a woman yelled.

'I wish warn burnin' the wratch!' a man chirruped. 'Keep us warm that'd!' And laughter rose on the sour fog of breath as the slab-faced hangman climbed the ladder and straddled the gallows, checking the hang rope's knots with short, sharp tugs. He nodded at Sheriff Thurloe, who gave an order to the other two men at which they lowered their halberds so that the blades were inches from George Green's throat. With that the minister turned and looked up at the gallows and the hangman sitting on it, and someone in the crowd screeched at him to get on with it so that they could all get home to their hearths.

'Got hands cowd as meh wife's heart!' a man yelled, raising his hands to another chorus of laughter. Then, as if in reply, as though he too would be done with the thing, George Green nodded and began to climb. Slowly up he went, his legs trembling, so that the whole ladder shuddered.

Mun felt his hands ball into fists at his sides. 'Don't fall,' he whispered. 'Don't give them the pleasure.'

'That ladder leads to Hell!' a wild-eyed young woman screeched, spittle spraying the cloak of the man in front and turning white as frost.

Mun glanced back and saw Bess bury her face against Emmanuel's chest; he put his lips against her coif, as though breathing in the scent of her hair. Then he caught Mun's eye and gave a subtle shake of his head, an inconspicuous but shared denunciation of what they were seeing. If they have any pity at all they will make it quick, Mun thought. Hoped.

But pity, it seemed, was as scarce as sunshine, and the hangman seemed to take an age to reach down and place the noose around George's neck, and all the while the minister's legs trembled so much that the sheriff himself put a foot on the bottom rung to preserve the execution's decorum. Then, one foot on the ladder and the other in the mud, Thurloe addressed the crowd, declaring the condemned a heretic and a criminal and thanking them for doing their godly duty by coming to witness the King's justice. This was the only time they held their tongues, hanging on his every word, lapping up his praise like proud hounds after the kill. And when Thurloe had finished he took his foot off the bottom rung and stepped back, commanding one of the armed men to turn the ladder and so let the minister fall. But the man would not do it. His lips pressed into a thin line and he shook his head and stepped away, slamming the haft of his halberd into the mud, the weapon proving his role in the play so that no man could rightly expect more.

So Sheriff Thurloe turned to the other man, but he would not turn the ladder, either, and he too stepped back.

The sheriff lifted his arms towards the crowd. 'Someone must turn the ladder!' he called, his breath clouding around his pale face and broad-brimmed hat.

'You do it!' someone yelled and others bayed in accord, but Thurloe shook his head and showed his gloved palms.

'I connut!' he exclaimed. 'But the man must die. We connut leave this Godforsaken place till the sentence is carried out.' He tried to smile but to Mun it looked like a snarl. 'Who will do the thing? Who will earn our thanks?' he yelled.

Mun thought it possible that Green could leap from the ladder himself. End the whole sorry thing. But the minister was clinging to the ladder, his cheek pressed against the gibbet's rough-hewn face, and Mun supposed that even life full of torment and misery was still life, when there was a rope around your neck.

Martha broke away, striding out into the eddying snow.

Tom rasped her name but she was on her way and so he thrust after her and then Mun was walking too, his boots churning the snow and mud, eyes half closed against the growing blizzard.

'Ah, God bless thee, chilt!' Thurloe called, wiping his red nose on the back of his hand, a relieved smile twitching his glistening moustaches. 'Here we have a brave servant of the King!' he announced, sweeping a hand out towards Martha, who was staring up at the gallows. Mun saw that the girl's father's eyes were closed and his face was turned towards the cold sky now, his lips moving in prayer.

'You are too late, gentlemen!' Thurloe called to Tom and Mun as they drew nearer. 'This brave young girl was fust and shall have the credit!' They ignored him and came on and someone in the crowd yelled that three of them would get the job done even quicker, but the sheriff frowned and ordered the two soldiers forward to block their path. Which they did, threatening them with their halberds while Martha approached the gallows unimpeded.

Mun saw her look up at her father, hands pressed against her mouth, a barricade against what fought to be said. And yet perhaps her father somehow heard those unspoken words, for he looked down, his eyes glassy and bereft of all hope.

'My daughter. My precious girl,' he said, and Mun watched as a shade of serenity fell over the minister, like a shroud laid over a corpse, and the trembling left his limbs and he smiled down at Martha, all terror having fled from his face. In its place was an expression that spoke to Mun of acceptance. And love.

'Sleep, Father,' Martha called up to him, cuffing the tears from her freezing cheeks. 'It will be over soon.'

He nodded. 'My precious love,' he said, a tear hanging from his chin before dropping eleven feet to the mud.

'Tell Mother I love her,' Martha said.

'What is this, chilt?' Thurloe said, realizing this was something other than what he had thought. Then George Green turned his face back to Heaven and began to pray once more. Martha gripped the ladder with two hands and pushed, but it would not move, so she placed her right leg against it and shoved again and this time the ladder turned and her father fell, the creak of the gibbet drowned by the crowd's sudden murmur.

'There 'e goes!' a man yelled.

'Swing, yer bastard!' another spectator screeched.

'Get her away,' Thurloe commanded one of his men, but Martha had already turned her back on the gallows and was walking towards Tom, her eyes on his. Only his. The crowd cheered as George Green's legs thrashed wildly and the hangman clung on desperately to the shaking gallows, a grimace splitting his bushy beard.

Martha stumbled and fell to her knees, retching, and then Tom and Mun were there and Tom took off his cloak and put it round her shoulders and Mun saw the girl's anguish reflected in his brother's eyes.

'What have I done?' Martha asked, staring at Tom, then at Mun.

'Get her away from here,' Mun growled. Tom nodded, gently lifting Martha to her feet, then led her off across the field towards Isaac and the waiting horses.

For a moment Mun watched them go, then he turned towards the bellowing crowd, seeking anonymity again, though it was too late for that, as George Green convulsed like a fish on a hook.

'It's done then. One less bloody papist,' a man said flatly.

In the nearby elms the rooks continued their raucous conversation and it struck Mun how much the sound resembled the tumbling tide on a pebbly shore. But there was no ocean here, just bleak rolling hills and muddy trackways and snow that was settling properly now, dulling the edges of all sound. He smelt wood smoke and looked over to see that the men had at last nurtured a flame within the heart of the furze, though it was as yet fragile and could be extinguished by a good gust. He glanced around him at the leering, frozen faces until he found his father, whose eyes were already locked on him. Then Sir Francis shook his head dismally. Because George Green was still alive.

'Show some mercy!' someone yelled. 'Pull on 'is damned legs!'

'No mercy for papists!' a woman screamed in reply.

'Let 'im dance!' a farmer bellowed and Mun recognized the man as one of his father's tenants.

Then, peering through the whirling snow, Sheriff Thurloe called for John Waller to make himself known. A murmur rose from the crowd, some repeating Waller's name, and then, reluctantly it seemed to Mun, a thin, ill-looking man slunk from the throng. One arm shielding his face from the blizzard, this Waller tramped through the thickening mantle, spindly legs making hard work of it as he bent into an icy gust. He had a sailcloth knapsack slung across his back and Mun heard a man announce proudly that Waller had trimmed his hair and beard that very morning.

'I hope you dudn'd pay him,' someone teased.

'I'd not have the fellow near *me* with a razor!' a portly man said. 'I'd fear him dropping dead and slicing me damned neck!'

For Waller was a barber, though it was not for his skill and eye for a good beard-trimming that Sheriff Thurloe had summoned him to Gallows Ledge. Not that he wouldn't have been among the spectators anyway, even on such a day as this, Mun supposed.

George Green had stopped his thrashing, though his legs still twitched now and then and his eyes bulged wildly, accusing everything they looked upon. His mouth was a bloody rictus twist, teeth puncturing his tongue which was horribly bloated. Straddling the gallows above him, his composure regained, the hangman sawed a knife through the taut rope and Green dropped five feet to the snow. There was a collective gasp as Sheriff Thurloe bent and held a hand before Green's mouth to check if he was still breathing. Then the minister coughed and Thurloe started, snatching his hand away, so that the crowd laughed at him and he flushed crimson beneath his snow-covered hat.

'Earn your pay, Mister Waller,' Thurloe commanded with a grimace, stepping back and waving a gloved hand at the man lying still as a corpse in the snow. But not a corpse, Mun knew. Not yet.

The barber nodded and, pulling off his knapsack, took from it a leather bundle, laying it reverentially on the ground. His fingers fumbled at the thong, pulling it loose, then he unrolled the bundle to reveal an assortment of implements, which he pushed to one side of the leather wrapping so that he could kneel on the rest of it to keep his breeches dry. Those instruments, all tooth and wicked blade, reminded Mun of a carpenter's tools. He heard his mother implore God's mercy under her breath, and he peered through gaps in the crowds, looking for Tom and Martha, hoping that they were gone.

'If the lad's got any sense he'll have the girl half a mile away by now,' Sir Francis muttered as though he had read Mun's mind, and Mun nodded grimly. The two soldiers were tasked with kneeling – no layer between *their* breeches and the freezing earth – and holding George Green still so that Waller could commence his work. And grim work it was. The frail-looking barber took up a knife whose blade glinted dully through the blizzard, and put the blade beneath Green's shirt, pulling it up towards his neck, slitting the soaking linen to expose the man's bare chest. Then using the same knife he sliced into Green's belly and the minister jerked and writhed, and though his hands were still bound behind his back it was all the soldiers could do to keep him down. Waller made two more cuts, these down either side of Green's belly as far as the first incision, and then he turned this gory flap up and laid it on the man's chest and steam rose from Green's insides, clouding in the freezing air. A low murmur spread through the crowd.

Waller looked back at Sheriff Thurloe, who nodded, and then the barber shoved his sleeves up to the elbows and plunged a hand into Green, grimacing, his face turned up to the wintry sky as he worked by touch rather than by sight. After a moment he pulled out a piece of liver, which steamed and glistened wetly, spilling blood down the barber's claw-like hand and spindly white arm.

'Jesu, Jesu, Jesu! Mercy!' George Green shrieked in a strangled, tormented voice. The crowd fell silent but for some gasps and muttered curses, because Waller was getting it all wrong.

'His heart, damn you, man!' Mun yelled, stirring a few ayes. In went Waller's hands again and this time he pulled out the man's gut rope, which gleamed bright purple and blue against the white skin and snow, unravelling as in his panic Waller tried to find the beating heart.

Sheriff Thurloe stepped up and bent over the grisly scene. He was growling at Waller, who was tumbling the guts every which way as he delved deeper into the gory hole, blood even soaking his bunched sleeves. Then he took up his blood-slick knife again and raked it inside Green and there was another moan from the crowd as the condemned man convulsed, blood and mucus frothing at his nose and mouth and choking him, so that his cries to Jesus decayed into a pathetic gurgling that made the hairs on Mun's neck bristle. One of the soldiers holding Green down turned his face away from the barber's work then fell on all fours and vomited. The other man watched it all wide-eyed, his face spattered with Green's blood.

'Show some mercy, Sheriff!' Sir Francis bellowed, and men turned to glare at him, though some gave up ayes, for they all knew Sir Francis Rivers – knew him to be a friend of the King – and most respected him. 'He is a man, Thurloe, not a beast! Show some mercy, damn you!' It seemed to Mun that even this crowd's blood-lust had been sated now and more than a few added their voices in support of Sir Francis.

Sheriff Thurloe peered into the throng and when Mun craned his neck he saw who Thurloe was looking at. It was Lord Denton, wrapped in a bear fur against the bitter day, his hat, which sported a bright purple plume, angled so that it partly obscured his face. But that purple feather dipped and Thurloe gripped Waller's shoulder and told him to end it. The barber nodded and with a trembling hand put down the knife, taking up a saw instead. He put its cold teeth on Green's neck and slashed the thing back and forth, and blood sprayed across his face until at last George Green died.

But Waller's work was not done yet. Next, he hacked off Green's genitals and Thurloe made the soldier who had watched it all carry them, grimacing, through the blizzard and throw them into the pathetic fire, where the grisly meat smouldered and blistered and blackened. The barber found Green's heart then and cut it free, holding it aloft triumphantly, but no one cheered and it too was cast into the fragile flames. Lastly, and with no little struggle, Waller cut off Green's head and some at least cheered this. The barber held it up for all to see, his puny, bloodstained arms trembling with the weight of it, then he threw it towards the crowd and a woman ran and picked it up, screaming with delight.

'Let us be away from here,' Sir Francis said and Emmanuel nodded, leading Bess through the press behind Sir Francis and Lady Mary. But Mun stayed a little longer, watching in horror as a group of young men began to kick George Green's head – the eyes still staring – through the snow, cheering and roaring with the thrill of it. In no time there must have been a hundred people running this way and that across Hilldale's uneven ground, kicking their grisly ball about to keep warm.

CHAPTER SEVEN

'I HEAR THERE ARE THOSE WHO EVEN ACCUSE THE KING himself of being a Catholic. It is madness.' Sir Francis thrust the poker into the fire, jabbing at the fuel. The wood crackled and spat, expelling a spray of bright, angry sparks.

'Because his wife is one?' Mun said, tying one corner of a huge tapestry to a rail that he and Bess had moved into the room and set before the parlour door. The bitter draughts that swept through Shear House's entrance hall had slender fingers that eked into every downstairs room despite closed doors, and Lady Mary hoped the old wall tapestry would keep the worst out, enabling them to keep at least the parlour warm. 'By that token, Father, you love the plays,' Mun added, smiling at his mother who smiled back, for Sir Francis was happier in a stable than the theatre, whilst his wife could quote Shakespeare and Massinger and loved nothing more than a skilfully wrought plot.

'There's more to it than that,' Sir Francis said. 'The King has refused Parliament's petition to hang another seven priests and this gives them all the fuel they need to make such accusations.' He stood straight and put a palm on the small of his back, wincing at some deep ache exacerbated by the harsh winter. 'But Charles is not the fool they all take him to be. He knows that once we start to define our nation this way . . . by persecuting its people . . . we walk a very dark and dangerous path.'

Their mother gestured for Bess to lift her side of the great tapestry higher. Woven to show a golden hind and golden birds of all sizes half concealed amid a forest of green fronds, the tapestry was at least a hundred years old and faded. When she judged it straight, Lady Mary nodded. 'Parliament has grown too big for its boots,' she said, the tone accusing.

But Sir Francis did not argue. 'Parliament's holy crusade is getting out of hand,' he admitted. 'But mine is only one voice.' He shook his head. 'There are those who think as I do, but we cannot be heard amongst all that crowing.'

'Do you think it could lead to war, Father?' Mun asked. 'There is talk that it may.' Bess turned to look at her father, her blue eyes wide as he shook his head, carefully leaning the poker back against the side of the fireplace.

'It will not come to that,' he said, keeping his eyes on the roaring flames. 'Englishmen will not fight Englishmen. The very thought is too monstrous. No, Edmund, I cannot think such a thing will happen in this kingdom. These are dangerous days but it is a vast leap from words to war.'

Mun nodded, not sure if what he felt was relief. Or disappointment.

'Come, let us have no more talk of Parliament and

111

the King,' Lady Mary said, clicking her fingers at Bess, who seemed lost in her own thoughts. 'This house has suffered a dearth of joy for too long. Higher, Bess!' she said. 'Or Mun will tie it crooked and your father will never let us hear the end of it.' Mun began to tie the other corner to the rail as the others stood back to examine their work.

'It will, I think, keep out the worst of the chill, but I hope we don't have visitors,' Lady Mary said disapprovingly, opening the parlour door and calling for Isaac to bring her a paring knife. 'This tapestry was old-fashioned when Queen Elizabeth was on the throne, God rest her soul.'

Bess half smiled and it warmed Mun's heart to see his sister shake off, if only for a moment, the weight of recent events. He knew that Minister Green's execution had troubled her deeply. Since that bleak day on Gallows Ledge Bess had not been herself, which was perhaps more noticeable because she had always been the mainstay of the family, her familiar good humour bracing them all against whatever ill winds blew through Shear House. Now she was sombre and not even Emmanuel, the man she would marry, knew how to cheer her. It did not help that she had taken the minister's boy, Jacob, under her wing, for she had wicked the boy's grief into her own being, and though he despised himself for it Mun sometimes wished Martha and Jacob would leave Shear House and take their troubles with them. So that Bess would smile again. So that Tom might forget the girl and so that his anger might no longer taint the very air gusting through their home. But these were selfish thoughts and the better part of him knew that Martha and Jacob needed them, not just for their everyday succour but for the protection the Rivers family could give them from the gangs that might prey on the children of a condemned Catholic and, some said, spy.

'Where is Tom?' he asked, realizing he had not yet seen his brother that day.

'Martha keeps to her room and will not see him,' Lady Mary said, taking the small knife that Isaac offered. 'He and Jacob rode out this morning. Isaac says that Lathom has a bear.'

'Truthfully, Isaac?' Mun said. 'They haven't had a bear for a year. Maybe longer.'

'Aye, Master Edmund,' the servant said, eyes glinting beneath his thatch of silver hair. 'It's a big 'un too, from what I've heard.'

'We haven't had a decent beast hereabouts for five years,' Sir Francis said. He fluttered long fingers. 'Some poor, threadbare creatures that were older than this tapestry, but nothing like we used to see at Kenilworth back in the old days. You remember the last one they set the dogs on?' he asked Mun. 'You were only a boy but I took you to see it. What a sham that was. I'd seen hens with more teeth.' Mun smiled at the memory. The poor beast had had only three claws and no one had bet against the dogs, which had made the whole thing a farce. He had seen proper, dangerous bears in Paris Garden at Southwark, but not in Parbold or Lathom.

'Tom has taken the boy to see it,' Lady Mary said, cutting a loose thread from the tapestry and shaking her head because she'd noticed another. 'It'll do them both good.'

'The poor beast,' Bess said. 'I cannot think why people find such sport in baiting a chained animal.'

'They find sport in worse cruelties than that, sister,' Mun said, thinking of the hanging.

'Aye, they do,' Sir Francis agreed. 'Besides, your mother is right.' Lady Mary raised an eyebrow at that rare admission. 'The ride out will be good for them. A man can outstrip his troubles on a good horse. Let them have some fun before the reformers put an end to every amusement.' He held a hand before the flames, now and then making a fist as the heat sank into flesh and bone.

'Why don't you join them?' Lady Mary asked, turning to Mun.

'Because,' Sir Francis said, nodding towards the tapestry that was swaying slightly in the breeze, 'Edmund knows as well as I do that that hanging is not even close to being straight.'

The bear was a monster. All tooth and claw and fury. Not even its owner dared get close enough to shorten the length of chain that leashed it by the neck to the post set in the middle of Lathom green. As a result, the beast could shamble fifteen feet in all directions and this terrified the crowd. Men, women and children yelled and shrieked. Dogs barked frenziedly and any horses whose owners had been foolish enough to ride too close whinnied and dragged their hooves through the mud agitatedly, for even if they could not see the beast they could smell it.

'The dogs don't look too keen either,' Tom said, feeling a smile twitching at the corners of his mouth. They were mastiffs. Big, coarse-haired, ugly and eager, they snarled and barked madly, whipped into hysteria by the presence of their great, hulking enemy. Jacob

114

stood to Tom's left and slightly behind, his mouth open and eyes wide as half crowns. Clearly the lad had never seen anything like this. Neither had many of the spectators, from the looks of them. An excited knot of men were crowding the bear-baiter's assistant, desperately trying to place wagers even though the fight was under way. Others, their wagers made, stood gripped by the spectacle, women with their hands to their mouths and men all grimace and snarl in bestial imitation of the dogs.

'See how afraid they all are,' Tom said, taking a grim satisfaction from how even chained the bear struck fear into the gathering. 'But you're not frightened are you, Jacob?' he said. 'Not a big strong lad like you.' In truth there was more meat on a mutton leg than on Jacob Green.

'No, Master Rivers,' the lad said, shaking his head, fists balled at his sides. Tom felt the boy tense up and bravely edge forward, but he started violently when the bear roared and Tom realized he was trembling. Maybe I did the first time, Tom thought.

'But there are so many dogs,' Jacob said. Two of the mastiffs lay wounded, one bleeding from a tear to its throat, the other lying all twisted and panting, its back broken. Yet there were still five dogs besieging the bear, lips hitched back from yellow teeth, spittle flying from snapping jaws.

'Go on, arse-biter!' a man yelled at one of the dogs, throwing his own clawed hand towards the bear. And a mastiff leapt, sinking its teeth into the beast's right shoulder, and hung there, its legs kicking the air. The crowd cheered and the bear reared, roaring, and turned towards its attacker, and another dog saw its chance and sprang forward, clamping its jaws onto the creature's left hind leg.

'It must be seven feet tall,' Tom said, 'biggest I've seen,' as the bear reached its full height before slamming its forelegs back down. But somehow the dogs held on and so the bear shook itself furiously and the mastiff attached to its shoulder was thrashed wildly about, its body twisting and writhing as its teeth gripped its enemy's flesh. Then the bear reared again and this time the mastiff's jaws gave out and it was flung through the air and landed in a gnarled twist, its spine snapped. The crowd moaned. Down came an enormous paw, the claws like meat hooks raking the other dog's flank, ripping the flesh open to reveal the gleaming ribs and a gouge of raw, bloody meat. The bear snorted and panted, its pink eyes leering at the creatures that lusted to hurt it, then it lumbered towards the crowd, which shuffled back in terror as the chain clinked taut.

'See how clever he is,' Tom said. 'He knows where his real enemies are.'

'Go on, you bastard curs!' a man yelled at the remaining dogs. 'Go on now!'

'Have 'im, boys!' another screamed, and the crowd indulged their blood-lust with shrieks and flailing arms as one of the dogs bravely went for the bear's face, biting into its maw and letting its own heavy bones and muscles weigh down the bear's head so that its fellows could attack the bear's legs and back.

The bear shrugged and shook, whipping its head from side to side until the broad-skulled mastiff let go in a spray of bright blood, ripping the bear's muzzle and cheek. In pain-filled fury the bear shook its head again, its torn, ragged flesh flinging blood which splattered the crowd, sending them even wilder with excitement. One woman dragged a hand across her mouth, stared in horror at the dark blood smeared across her knuckles, then fainted. No one caught her. Then the bear swiped, quick as a striking snake, and the blow snapped the mastiff's neck like kindling and the bear roared its triumph as the last two dogs backed off, growling but afraid.

'It has won!' Jacob exclaimed, clearly in awe of the creature.

But Tom shook his head. 'They will not let it win,' he said, as a man burst from the parting crowd, dragged through the mud by four hulking mastiffs. 'Not in the end.' The new dogs strained and choked themselves on the ends of their leashes, desperate for the fight. It was in their blood. It was what they had been born for. Tom sensed Jacob's shoulders slump and knew how the boy felt.

'My sister went to Baston House,' Jacob said.

Tom felt as though he had been punched in the stomach. He was silent for a few long moments.

'When?' he asked.

'Before they killed Father,' Jacob said. 'I followed her.'

'Why would she go to Baston House?' Tom asked, never taking his eyes off the fight. And why would she have kept it from him? His mind was reeling, sifting his memories for clues as to why Martha would have gone alone to the house of Lord Denton. That bastard.

Jacob shrugged his shoulders. 'She does not know that I know,' he said.

One of the dogs squealed, a chunk of flesh ripped

from its skull, so that its right ear hung by a slender scrap spraying bright crimson as it shook its head and stubbornly attacked again. Tom turned to Jacob now and grabbed the boy's shoulders, turning him from the growling, bristling chaos of Lathom green.

'When, Jacob? When did your sister go to Baston House?' Tom was sickened by the thought of it.

'Plough Monday. Four days before they killed Father,' Jacob said. There was another yelp from a dog and the crowd moaned. 'You, Master Edmund and Sir Francis were out riding. So I followed Martha.' The boy looked more frightened now than he had been by the bear *or* the dogs. 'I think Lord Denton hurt her,' he said, his eyes welling with tears. And those words were like a blade in Tom's guts.

'Why would he?' he asked, shaking his head, wanting rid of even the idea of Martha being anywhere near William, Lord Denton. 'Why do you say this? What did you see? Do not lie to me, Jacob. They had your father killed and I hate them for it, but do not lie to me about this.'

'But I'm not lying!' Jacob said, cuffing snot from his nose with a raw, chapped hand. 'I swear, Master Tom. I'm not lying!'

'You saw? You saw Lord Denton hurt Martha?'

Jacob looked down at his shoes which were covered in mud, the laces slimy as earthworms, and Tom realized his fingers were digging into the boy's shoulders, so he lifted his hands, spreading the fingers.

'You spied through the window, didn't you?' Jacob's brows arched above big green eyes that settled on Tom's own, and for the first time Tom realized how much the boy looked like Martha. Then Jacob's lips turned down and trembled as the first tears rolled down his freckled cheeks.

'What did you see, Jacob?' Jacob shook his head and Tom grabbed his shoulders again. 'Damn you, Jacob! What did you see?'

'I won't tell, Master Tom,' he sobbed. 'I won't!'

'Tell me!'

'No, Master Tom! You can beat me if you want to, but I won't speak of it. I'll never speak of it.'

Tom cursed under his breath, then let go the boy's shoulders and hugged him into his chest, ruffling his copper-coloured hair. 'It's all right, Jacob,' he said. 'I'm sorry. I won't hurt you.' But inside Tom a fire raged. 'I'm sorry,' he said again, then gently pushed Jacob away and tried to smile at the boy. 'Come. Let us leave before they get their way,' he said, nodding at the mob. 'Before the dogs tear that proud creature apart.'

'Are we going back to Shear House?' Jacob asked, dragging a hand across his eyes, suddenly ashamed of his tears.

Tom glanced back at the fight. Injured dogs were whining piteously but ignored by the crowd. There were puddles of blood in the mud of the churned green. 'You will ride to Shear House,' he said, then turned and strode off to fetch the horses.

'What about you, Master Tom?' Jacob said, hurrying after.

Tom unclamped his jaw and felt the hot fury surge up from his chest into his throat. 'Ride to Shear House, Jacob,' he said. 'And say nothing to your sister.'

He rode hard, his anger like a whip that lashed Achilles, for the beast had always sensed Tom's mood and responded in kind. He was a fine horse, like his brother Hector black as pitch and foaled by an English mare which Sir Francis had bred with a proud Arabian stallion, and there were few creatures on God's earth that could outrun him. But the line between spirit and ill-temper in a horse was as thin as a switch and Sir Francis, who knew horses better than he knew just about anything else, had once said there were few men, maybe none other than Tom, who could ride Achilles. And now together those two raced across the countryside, rider and steed moving as one, eating up the ground, flinging rain-soaked clods of earth in their wake.

It was late afternoon and Tom felt, as much as saw, dark clouds beginning to hood the earth from the north. It was getting colder again, the tawny light of impending snow tinting the air and filling his nose with a sharp, heavy scent. Achilles's hooves thumped in a breakneck rhythm, vapour trailing from his nostrils as he snorted with the effort of impelling flesh, blood and bone along ancient trackways and muddy lanes. Sleet began to dash down haphazardly, like grain tossed onto ploughed earth, and Tom's cheeks and nose prickled as the air turned frigid.

After two miles he wrenched on the reins and spurred Achilles up a muddy bank, leaving the track in favour of a more direct route through tall oak woods. Old crusts of brittle snow lay in rows between the trunks and in dirty rings around their bases, but the last week's rain had washed away the rest, so that horse and rider were confident in their ability to avoid exposed roots and low branches. They sped onwards, Tom trusting Achilles to weave his own way through the woods, only vaguely guiding with a press of a knee or a tug of the

120

reins, until eventually they broke from the oaks. Into a slanting wall of sleet that half blinded them. But they did not slow. If anything, Achilles picked up the pace now that his stride was no longer impeded by trees, and Tom bent lower, almost flat against the stallion's neck, slitted wind-lashed eyes peering through the sleet at the open fields before them.

'Heya!' he yelled through a grimace, his hair flying madly behind him as the stallion galloped on, the beast sweating now despite the cold. On past bristling hedgerows and black copses of elm, and sheep standing still as rocks, and glistening pools of standing water, and now and then a deer that glared at man and horse, seemingly paralysed, muscles tensed and ready to bolt. On across a darkening landscape, as the sleet turned to snow and the moon, just visible through the grey veil of cloud and near full but for a sliver missing from its right, silvered a halo of sky.

'Heya! Faster, boy!' Tom yelled, ice-cold air scalding his teeth, his hands numbing on the reins as Achilles leapt six feet across the Tawd River, rattling Tom's bones when he landed and dug in and tore on. All colour had seeped from the land, leaving nothing but melancholic shades of grey and black that exaggerated the terrain around him. The rolling Lathom hills seemed in the darkness to rise up and meet the sky, so that Tom had the sensation of riding through the bottom of a deep dark gorge, and horse and rider raced on, as though eager to reach the silver tideline of moonlight that marked the higher ground. With true colour absent they could only judge distance by shade and tone, but their senses were heightened in the snow-blurred twilight and Achilles galloped headlong into the dashing flakes, his black mane shattering and flying, as though Hell's hound, Cerberus, was on to him.

Tom caught the fleeting whistles and calls of a shepherd somewhere out in the murk, moving his flock to lower ground perhaps. The sheep's nervous bleats were distant, lost sounds through the snow as Tom rode north-east now, joining a well-worn, wheel-rutted track. And still they did not slow.

'Go on, boy!' he barked, and Achilles screamed in reply as they tore through a copse of stark, snow-frosted oaks. Then Tom hauled the stallion up onto a muddy tree-lined drive that led to Baston House, the freezing air burning his throat and the wind roaring in his ears. He raised his face, filling his eyes with the imposing mass of brick and stone, the house looming against the coming night, windows glowing yellow, its chimneys spewing wood smoke which Tom could smell even from five hundred paces. Only now did he rein Achilles in, knowing that he must dissipate the stallion's wild excitement if he was to have any chance of dismounting at the end of the slushy track.

'Whoa, boy! We're here, Achilles.' The air seared his lungs as he dragged it into his heaving chest. The beast slowed, tossing his head wildly, foam flecking at his bit as he snorted and steamed. Tom glimpsed a stand of Scots pine a stone's throw from Baston House's arched entrance and decided that that must have been where Jacob had concealed himself after following his sister here. But Tom had not come to hide amongst the trees, and Achilles was still trotting when the young man pulled his left foot from the stirrup, hauled the leg over his saddle, and jumped down onto the churned mud and snow within the walled courtyard. 'Stay here, boy!'

he called, striding the last twenty paces up to the huge oak door, his boots cracking wafers of newly formed ice and his fists balling at his sides.

He did not stop to admire the smooth columns or the skilfully carved arch above which was moulded Denton's crest of a rampant gold griffin, but took the three steps in one bound and began to pummel on the door, his breath fogging the porch. No one came. The chimney smoke and the light spilling from the windows did not necessarily mean that anyone was home – in this weather such a house would have fires burning day and night or have ice climbing the parlour walls. But Tom had noticed boot prints in the settling snow leading up to the steps and this told him beyond any doubt that Baston House was not empty. Fine boots, too, by the marks. And more than one pair.

He battered the door again, this time using the heel of his hand so that the last strike was as hard and loud as the first. Then he heard muffled voices within, followed by a moment's silence before the drawing of bolts hammered the expectant air. The oak door opened wide enough for a head to poke out.

'What, sir, is upon the world that you need pound my master's door to splinters?' The face was round and fleshy, ample eyebrows knitted disapprovingly. But the door was no longer locked, which was all Tom needed. He thrust out a hand and strode forward, throwing the door wide and sending the servant sprawling onto the hall floor. 'Where is Denton?' Tom asked, glancing at the faces hung upon the dark oak-panelled walls, his left hand clutching his rapier's hilt. 'Where is your bastard master?' he snarled at the corpulent servant, who was picking himself up and cradling a plump wrist, beady eyes wide with fright.

Then a door opened on Tom's right, leaking firelight into the candle-lit hall and throwing a large figure into silhouette.

'Who the devil wants to know?' Lord Denton said, his teeth flashing like a wolf's.

CHAPTER EIGHT

'IT'S TOM RIVERS,' SNARLED A VOICE FROM BEHIND LORD Denton. William moved aside and Henry stepped from the parlour into the hall, his rapier's blade glinting in the flamelight. His face was a younger version of his father's, handsome yet marred by an arrogance that manifested itself in the eyes and mouth.

'I'll kill you!' Tom yelled at William, his sword hissing past its scabbard's throat. He flew at Lord Denton, but Henry lunged and Tom had to parry, the blades singing before Henry leapt back. Tom slashed but this time Henry blocked and forced the blade wide, stepping inside to smash a fist into Tom's cheek. Tom staggered backwards, stunned by the blow, but managed to catch Henry's sword on his own rapier's forte and turn it aside. Then he threw his arm high parrying a cut that would have cleaved his head down the middle.

'Fetch my sword!' Lord Denton yelled and Tom was aware of the fat servant edging past, his back scuffing picture frames that clunked against the corridor's oak panelling.

'I owe you, Rivers,' Henry spat. Tom answered with

a lunge that was parried, and a reprise that narrowly missed his opponent's neck, but Henry's riposte was good and would have skewered Tom's chest had he not twisted aside at the last. Henry remised but Tom flicked his wrist, getting the debole of his blade across, and was lucky that that weak part of his sword deflected the blow. Both combatants jumped back, gasping, drawing breath for the first time since the fight was joined.

Feet clumped across old floorboards and men spilled into the hall; five in all, roused from their duties and come to defend their master with knives and cudgels. 'Kill 'im, sir!' one of them yelled.

The portly servant was amongst them and he edged forwards, glancing warily at Tom as he delivered his master's sword: a fine weapon, Tom was not surprised to see, its hilt cup and recurved quillons decorated in relief with silver and gold.

'I'm astonished that the little whore told you,' Lord Denton said, circling a finger which his men took as a signal to surround Tom. Then he shrugged his broad shoulders. 'But then, I was surprised by her appetite too.' He smiled at his son. 'She was a wanton little bitch. My cock still chafes.'

Tom sprang forward but Lord Denton circular parried and forced Tom's blade down until both points struck the floor, and in Tom's peripheral vision he saw Henry leap in, saw the path of the sword hilt which slammed against his head, spinning his world in a blur, white light flaring. Then the others were on him, like the low dogs of the pack having waited their turn, and they began to rain blows down on him. He felt his knees give, then he was down, his sword lost, and they kicked and punched and struck him with knife hilts and clubs, and all he could do was clutch the back of his head, his forearms taking blows that could otherwise kill him.

'Enough!' Lord Denton bellowed. 'Stand off!' Tom swiped blood from his right eye and spat a wad of bloody saliva across the dark wood floor as he tried to rise, his pummelled flesh screaming.

'I'll kill you,' he gnarred at Lord Denton, who shook his head in bewilderment, his long grey hair barely out of place and his hooped earrings glinting dully.

'You are an eager young man, I'll say that for you,' William said. 'Almost as eager as that whore.' With one hand he straightened his doublet. 'Seems you've got bigger balls than your father, Thomas, but not even half his sense. At least Sir Francis knows when to walk away from a fight.'

'Let me gut him, Father,' Henry growled. 'He attacked you in your own house. The law will hang him in any case.'

William shook his head disappointedly. 'You have so much to learn, Henry.' He stepped up to Tom and lifted his blade, so that Tom felt its point quivering a finger's breadth from his cheek, as he eyeballed his enemy. 'Look at him.' Tom tensed, ready to knock the blade aside and make a grab for his own which lay four feet away from his right hand. But he did not know if his pain-racked limbs would move as he needed them to. And if they did not . . .

I'll die on my damned knees, he thought.

'This whelp has lost,' William went on. 'His dewy-lipped love came here, lay on my floor and spread her legs like a tavern whore.' He grinned. 'Begged me to save her father even as I fucked her. Whilst young Thomas here, ignorant of Miss Green's . . . appetites . . . then fails to save her father and must watch the man piss his breeches and swing in the wind.' He frowned. 'Reminds me of one of the Greek tragedies,' he said, glancing at his son. Tom could feel Henry's hatred coming off him in waves. 'And now,' Lord Denton resumed, 'the lad comes here with grand ideas of revenge, only to end up on my floor like his woman before him. If it were you or I, Henry, we would *rather* hang, would we not?' Henry seemed to consider the point, then nodded, baleful eyes riveted to Tom. 'If I've learned anything,' his father went on, 'it is not to give your enemy that which he most desires. That is how one wins.'

'So what do we do with him?' Henry asked with a shrug of strong shoulders. The servants glanced at each other, shifting uncomfortably, awaiting their master's orders. They know full well that my father is a friend of the King, Tom thought.

'We finish what the whelp himself started by coming here, of course,' William said. 'Hold him,' he sneered at his men. Tom heard floorboards creak, sensed the knot of men around him tighten. Then each of them moved in, taking a grip of his pain-filled arms and shoulders and clutching fistfuls of his cloak and doublet. He thrashed for a few futile, agonized moments, but it was no use against so many. Grimly he thought of the bear he and Jacob had watched beset by hounds. And he feared this would end the same way.

'Take him outside, Walter,' Lord Denton barked. 'The boy is bleeding all over my floor.' The fat servant nodded, moving to the door and opening it to the freezing night. 'And Henry, fetch my cloak.' He stepped out into the porch and inhaled deeply of the crisp air, for a moment watching the snow plunge down in silent downy flakes.

Then he strode down the steps and stood staring down the long path leading from his estate across the rolling tree-crowned hills towards Parbold village, as they dragged Tom out. The fat servant aimed a soft fist at Tom's face, wincing as he scuffed his knuckles on Tom's temple, so that Tom managed a bitter smile.

'My sister hits harder than you, you swollen pig's bladder,' he growled, glaring at the man, challenging him to do his worst.

'He's right, Walter,' Henry chided with a malicious grin. 'You don't do it like that.' He huffed warm breath into his right hand, then clenched it into a tight knot and stepped up. 'This is how you teach a cur,' he said, and slammed a burly fist against Tom's cheek, cutting it open. Immediately, bright blood began to drip onto the freezing earth. Tom clenched his teeth against the pain, refusing to cry out, his head reeling from the blow. He wanted to insult Henry as he had Walter, to taunt his tormentor. To show defiance. But he knew Henry hit harder than that whoreson servant.

So he held his tongue.

Then, gripping him tightly though he had given up struggling, Lord Denton's men simply waited, their combined breath pluming by moon and starlight, fogging the space between them and their master's broad back. Henry waited too, a half grin nestled on his face as though he was party to his father's intentions, even though Tom suspected he had no more idea than Tom himself as to what was in Lord Denton's mind.

William turned, pointing his rapier down at the ice-crusted mud and suddenly Tom was being manhandled, dragged to the spot and thrust down, his face in the numbing filth, so that he could smell the cold earth. He felt a foot plant square on his back – Walter's foot – as the others squatted around, pinning his limbs to the ground.

'The thing about cold weather,' William said, and Tom heard the rasp as he sheathed his sword, then caught a glimpse of him taking the cloak which Henry offered, 'is that it always makes me want to piss. Must be my age.'

There followed a silence but for the screech of an owl somewhere in the dark and his own breathing made ragged by the terrible pain in his ribs.

'You may want to move your foot, Walter,' Lord Denton suggested, and the pressure on Tom's back vanished as Walter took two steps backwards, his muddy shoes in line with Tom's sight. 'Henry, make sure the papist whore-loving cur keeps still. I've had these boots but barely two weeks.' Tom felt the cold bite of Henry's sword on the nape of his neck and growled a curse. He tried to look up at his enemy but the steel point pressed harder and his exposed flesh instinctively recoiled from it so that his cheek pressed into the freezing mud again. His eyes followed Lord Denton's high, bucket-topped boots as they strode around to his right and there stopped dead still, their water-stained toe ends level with his backside. He brimmed with furious anger, hot as a brazier of coals, but clenched his teeth on the curses that roared to be set free, in case they thought his clamouring born of fear. Do not give them the satisfaction, his mind commanded his body.

Not so long as he was yet master of himself, if of nothing else, and so every muscle and sinew thrummed with impotent rage, at the injustice of it, at himself for allowing them to humiliate him like this.

And then Lord Denton began to piss on him.

The stream of hot liquid seethed, spattering onto his back and head, running across his cheeks and into the corners of his mouth and the cuts in his flesh, stinging like the devil. And now he bellowed, any vestige of pride sluiced away by another man's piss. 'I'll fucking kill you all!' he screamed. The urine was dark yellow and melted the settling snow around his head, the steam from it filling his nose with its foul stink. 'I swear it! I'll kill you! Get off me, you bastards! You're a dead man, Denton! Get off me! God damn you! Let me go!' They were laughing at him as the steaming stream sputtered, came thick again, then petered to the last drops. Some of it had splashed onto Lord Denton's servants but none of them had dared move or lessen their grip. The liquid had soaked through Tom's cloak, doublet and shirt. He felt it as warmth on the skin of his back and he wished he could close his eyes and die, but he knew he could not.

'Do you not need to piss, Henry?' William asked his son, shuddering theatrically as he tucked himself away. Tom strained his neck, trying to glare at his tormentors, his eyes his only weapons. And saw Walter's black-toothed grin and some others watching Henry expectantly. But Henry shook his head, still pressing his sword's point against Tom's neck. His eyes were wide with awe.

Because his enemy lies in the freezing filth, soaked with piss, Tom thought with grim rage.

'That's a young bladder for you, Walter,' William announced, huffing into cold hands. 'When you get to my age, lad, you'll piss three times a night. Five when it's as cold as this.'

He walked back around to Tom's head and stared

down at him, eyes brimming with disgust at the young man's sopping hair and the cloudy vapour rising from it into the frigid night. 'Now then, Thomas Rivers,' he said, rubbing his hands against the chill. 'You have given the impression of being a headstrong young man and while boldness can occasionally serve a purpose, mostly it gets men killed. Much wiser and, more importantly, long-lived, is he who considers the terrain and the enemy before charging ahead.' He glanced at Henry, letting his son know that he was supposed to be listening to this advice too. 'Therefore, boy, try for a moment to think past your hatred.'

Tom looked up, feeling the blade puncture the skin and scrape past his neck bones. 'I'm going to cut your damned throat,' he snarled.

Lord Denton rolled his eyes and shook his head. He squatted and, baring his teeth, grasped Tom's sopping hair, snarling it around his fist, then yanked his head upwards so that their eyes met.

'You're not listening, boy!' he spat. 'My advice to you is to ride away from here and put this whole . . . occasion behind you. Call it youthful abandon. An error of judgement on your part. But leave it alone. Bring your family into this and you'll lament it so help you God. You'll just be heaping shit onto shit. Do you understand?' Lord Denton tilted his head to one side, like a fisherman trying to decide whether to keep his catch or throw it back in.

Tom glared. Said nothing. The hate and the anger writhed in him like poisonous serpents. They churned and soured and boiled in his gut. He felt them twist his face into a grotesque mask, felt their malevolence blaze from his eyes.

Lord Denton stood and dismissed the whole affair with a waft of his hand. 'Let him go,' he said casually and his men looked at each other. They nodded and Walter counted to three and each of them carefully released his hold on Tom before standing and edging back, as a man does from a wild animal which he has caught and is letting go. 'Bring Master Rivers's horse, Walter,' William said as Henry also stepped back, keeping his blade between them while Tom climbed unsteadily to his feet, eyes riveted to the architect of his humiliation.

'You are lucky I did not spill your pus-filled guts tonight, Rivers,' Henry said, gesturing for Tom to mount his horse. 'Go before I change my mind.'

For several heartbeats Tom eyeballed Henry, fixing his enemy's face in his mind, then, ignoring the piss-soaked tresses hanging against his own face, he turned from them all and snatched the reins from Walter. He mounted as smoothly as he could, given his many screaming pains, then dug in his heels and yelled coarsely. Achilles whinnied, snapping great teeth at the cold darkness, then surged forward, breaking into a canter which Tom spurred into a gallop. The stallion's hooves thumped the snow-covered earth and together they sped away from Baston House along the well-worn moonlit path.

Tom roared at the night like a mad man. Like a wounded animal. The anger and the hate entwined, swelling and blooming inside him, threatening to consume his soul. It was hatred purer and blacker than anything he had ever known. And he let it devour him.

*

Bess could not sleep. She never could when there was a full moon; tonight the moon was a sliver from full and still she could not sleep. She lay cocooned in linen beneath a heavy quilted coverlet stuffed with wool, listening to the mice scratching in the wall by her head and, beyond those walls, the occasional shiver of leaves and the creak of branches clenching in the freezing dark. She was aware of the faintest trembling deep in her own limbs, not because she was cold – she was warm enough – but an effect of the moonlight itself she believed. Its cold luminescence soaked through the window drapes, washing the bedchamber in a silver-white light. An otherworldly hue that revealed the room's contents: the brass stick with its stub of candle and the jug of small beer on the bedside table. The chair at the foot of the bed festooned with clothes – linen coif, woollen cloak, smock, long purple skirt and her silk and lace bodice which sat stiffly against the chair's back because of the bone strips in it. The moonlight burnished the dark chest of polished oak drawers upon which sat a washbasin and pitcher. On another table, beneath a sloping ceiling threaded with fine cracks, her precious things glowed dully: the enamelled gold brooch set with pearls that her mother had given her, the emerald ring from Emmanuel which was too big and needed altering, a child's silver-plated hairbrush and an ivory box containing other cherished possessions.

There was something about nights like this that put Bess's nerves on edge, made her feel as though she were meant to be somewhere else – anywhere but lying in her bed listening to the mice in the walls. She was fitful, her muscles and sinews thrumming as though preparing for sudden flight. It was not fear as such, but rather a sense of belonging to the moonlit night. Of being drawn away from human habitation and comforts to the forests and the moors. Like a predator on the hunt for food.

It was a sense that she should be searching for something. Or running from something?

It did not help that Emmanuel was still away in Shevington a day's ride east, where he was overseeing the rebuilding of the house they would live in once they were married. That old ruin would be full of mice and worse things besides, she thought grimly, for the manor had once belonged to Cockersand Abbey as far back as King Henry's time. Before the dissolution. 'That pile of rubble!' Sir Francis had exclaimed when Emmanuel had first intimated his plan to purchase the manor and its outbuildings including a groundskeeper's cottage and a half-collapsed cowshed. 'That relic is older than Noah!'

'But it is big, Sir Francis,' Emmanuel had said with a sparkle in his eyes and a broad smile. And it *was* big. Huge in fact. And Emmanuel had promised Bess and Sir Francis that it would rival Shear House one day, when he took over his father's business. James Bright was likely the richest cloth merchant in Lancashire, employing no fewer than two hundred spinners, weavers, fullers, shearmen and dyers. But James Bright was ailing, which would have been hard on his family and employees alike if he had not a vigorous, well-liked son to take over when death took him.

'I shall be making five hundred pounds a year!' Emmanuel had announced proudly, for he had but recently asked Sir Francis for Bess's hand in marriage and still felt a little like a man on trial, so he had admitted to Bess. A feeling which, she suspected, her father did little to discourage.

'It is a pile of dilapidation, decay, and disrepair,' Sir Francis had announced to Emmanuel's obvious disappointment, earning a reproachful glare from his wife. He had frowned, coughed, made a steeple of fingers, then said: 'Still, I like a man with ambition. So long as it is coupled with good sense, of course.'

But Bess knew her father had grown fond of Emmanuel Bright, whom she loved with all her heart, and even though they did not share a bed – wouldn't until they were married – she missed him being under the same roof.

Bess could not sleep and so she kicked off the coverlets and went over to the window, pulling back one of the drapes and putting herself between it and the glass as though to be closer to the night beyond. Her breath fogged the pane and she shivered now because the window was as cold as ice. The curtain's old dusty smell smothered her as she stared out across Shear House's frosty, moon-silvered grounds, her eyes ranging along the pebble-strewn drive that stretched off into a dark wood of birch and sweet chestnut. Her mind roamed further still, past the woods and the dovecote whose residents she imagined hunched and shivering and cooing softly, and up to the boundary wall with its iron gate guarded by two stone lions. But then something in the near distance caught her eye, some movement that made her start, a sudden intake of breath catching in her throat where it stayed as her senses prickled. She was suddenly aware of her own heartbeat hammering against the windowpane as her eyes strained to sift the moving shape from the surrounding landscape. It was a man on a horse, she realized, but whoever it was was avoiding the path. Instead the rider was making his way across the east lawn. So as not to be heard, Bess thought.

Which did nothing to assuage the sense of creeping dread that was raising tiny bumps on her arms and legs and stiffening the hairs on the nape of her neck. She pressed a palm against the cold pane and part of her wanted to call out, to wake the sleeping household. To warn them. Another part of her, the part that thrummed whenever the moon was full, preferred to watch a little longer, relished seeing without being seen. This was the stronger instinct and so she stayed as still and quiet as death. Watching.

But then the figure suddenly looked up, a sixth sense perhaps, and the moonlight revealed his face as his eyes locked with hers. Tom!

Her brother put a finger to his lips and Bess felt herself nod. She watched him draw nearer, somewhere in the back of her mind wondering why the sight of him had not dispersed the dread feeling. Then she turned and fetched a cloak down from a hook, throwing it around her shoulders over her nightdress, shivering again from the sense of trepidation that gnawed and scrabbled in her guts like the mice in the walls. Carefully, she opened her bedchamber door and stole out into the corridor, then descended the stairs that she had crept down innumerable times as a young girl up to mischief with her brothers.

There was just enough moonlight filtering past the thick drapes that she could see well enough without lighting one of the hall lamps, whose oily smell she feared would drift upstairs and wake someone. She knew Tom would be stabling Achilles and so she gingerly unbolted the main door, then went into the parlour, cringing as the door-hinges squeaked. Inside, sweet-smelling wood smoke still clotted the air, though the room was cold, in large part due to its having three sizeable windows. Bess took a candle from the mantel over the hearth and, with the poker, stirred the ashes of the fire which Isaac had banked before retiring to bed. When a flame licked up from the grey pile she lit the candle and carefully placed some kindling on the embers, hoping to dull the sharp frigid chill that filled the parlour, making her huff into cupped hands. And then, as the sticks quietly crackled and popped, she faced the door which she'd left slightly ajar, and waited.

CHAPTER NINE

BESS SENSED THAT TOM WAS NOT TELLING HER EVERYTHING. he spoke of taking Jacob to Lathom village to watch the bear-baiting that afternoon, and of how, when it was all but over, the boy had admitted following Martha to Baston House. He told her how Jacob had spied through the parlour window and seen his sister engaged in heated argument with Lord Denton. But Bess sensed there was more to that part of it, judging by the way Tom's eyes had slid from hers towards the fire in that part of the telling. He admitted letting his rage get the better of him. Had confessed to riding full of fury to Baston House to confront William Denton and how he had hungered to cut William and Henry down with his sword.

'I wanted to spill their blood, Bess,' Tom growled in the shadows, the small hearth flames dappling his ravaged face with golden tongues. 'I wanted to rip their bastard guts out.' That part was true enough, Bess knew, and she shuddered. 'But his men came at me and there were too many. They beat me like a damned dog,' he spat, the words laced with shame, and Bess knew that part was also true because his face was a bloody mess. Beneath his gore-tangled hair – usually fair but dark now and filthy – his right eye was swollen shut, the taut glistening skin already blackening. His lower lip was twice its normal size and split so that his beard was matted with blood and Bess had to stop herself wincing because it looked so painful.

But he was keeping something back. She was certain of it. He spoke through a grimace, which was understandable given the pain he was in, and his anger. But at twenty-four Bess was proud of her elder sister's intuition and there was more to the set of Tom's bloody mouth than pain and gall. There was a sense of him checking the truth, holding it behind a barricade of teeth. And then there was the smell coming off him, of damp wool and urine, and Bess could have wept at the thought of her brother being so terrified that he had wet himself.

Tom clenched his left fist and ground it into the cup of his right hand. Both were crusted in mud and drying blood. 'He pissed on me, Bess,' he said firmly, looking at his hands because he could not meet her eyes. Bess swallowed hard because she suddenly realized that younger brothers had intuition too and Tom had somehow known what she was thinking. The shameful admission had been preferable to her assumption.

'Henry?' Bess said, her stomach knotting. She was caught between pity and a swelling black rage.

Tom shook his head and looked up into her eyes. 'Lord Denton,' he snarled.

'Who would do such a thing? What kind of man could treat a person so? What kind of monster?'

Tom did not answer that. 'I'm going to kill him, Bess.'

140

The flitting flames were reflected in his one good eye and illuminated the ruin of the other, and Bess knew the right thing was to speak against such a declaration, to try to dissuade him from violent thoughts. But she also knew her brother and so she said nothing. He needed the promise of vengeance. He clings to it, she thought, like a floating timber from the wreck of this night.

'Get out of those clothes,' she said. 'I'll fetch some water and we'll clean you up. We mustn't let Martha see you like this.' She tried to smile but felt the strain in it. 'You'll scare her to death.'

'I watched them hang my father, Bess,' a soft voice said from the parlour's doorway. 'Do you still think me such a feeble thing?' They both turned to see Martha standing at the threshold, a candle lamp flickering in the draughts and casting its weak light on her neck, chin and full lips but leaving her eyes in shadow.

Tom simply stared at her, his ravaged face a dark scowl, and so Bess invited Martha into the room before they roused the rest of the household. If the others were not already awake.

'Achilles woke me,' Martha said with a slight nod towards a curtained window. 'Not that I could sleep properly for wondering where you were. I knew you had not come home.'

There followed a silence into which Martha clearly expected Tom to drop some explanation. But he had none. So Martha came into the room keeping, Bess noticed, a distance between herself and Tom. 'What happened to you?' Martha asked warily, raising the lamp to throw its small light on Tom's swollen, bloodied face. 'You've been fighting.' Her tone was more anxious than accusing.

'I did scant little of the fighting,' Tom muttered, turning his face from Martha's light so that his swollen right eye was in shadow. The sparse kindling was all but burnt out but Tom kept his face turned towards it anyway, watching the last small flames lick out every now and then. A mouse skittered across the floor in front of the hearth, disappearing into a crack at the foot of the north wall. Then a gust rattled a loose windowpane and moaned down the chimney, causing the flames to flare and seethe briefly before dying away. Bess felt a sudden desperate need to escape that room and its silence that deafened her with unspoken words.

'I will go and get some water to clean your face,' she said.

Tom's head snapped up. 'No, Bess. Stay,' he said, fixing her with his good eye. She noticed fresh blood at the split in his lip, though he did not lick it away. 'I am sure you are as eager as I to hear why Martha went to see that bastard William Denton. Why she has cloaked herself in deceit and kept it from me.'

Bess could not help but look at Martha whose eyes brimmed with tears. The hand holding the lamp was trembling, so that the small flame quivered.

'Well, my love?' Tom said, looking back towards the ashes glowing red in the grate. 'Now would be a strange time to play the demure minister's daughter, don't you think?'

'You are hurt,' Bess said to Tom, reaching out to tug a small twig from her brother's tangled hair. 'Surely all this will wait until morning when we have looked to your injuries?' She glanced at Martha and saw that tears were rolling down her cheeks now. 'When we have all slept,' she added, dropping the twig into the fireplace.

'I went to Baston House,' Martha began, taking a deep, tremulous breath, 'because they had accused my father of popery and I hoped I might prevail on Lord Denton's mercy. That he might intercede on my father's behalf.'

'That bastard does not know the meaning of mercy,' Tom blurted. 'You were a fool to suppose otherwise.'

'I had at least to try,' Martha said, looking to Bess for understanding. 'What else could I do? Your father had turned his back on us.'

'My father took you in! Jacob too,' Tom snapped, glaring at Martha with his undamaged eye. The other was darkest purple now, glistening with tiny beads of sweat.

'Hush, Tom, you will wake them,' Bess hissed. Tom laughed at that and it was an empty, bitter sound. Martha seemed to shudder.

'Let them wake,' he seethed. 'They should know that they have a whore under their roof. I know what you gave him,' he said, a drop of blood trembling on his bottom lip.

'Enough!' Bess said, not wanting to hear any more. She felt like an interloper, as though to hear more was to know too much. But she also pitied Martha whatever the truth of it all, for the girl seemed . . . broken.

'Where are you going?' she asked Tom as he strode past Martha to the parlour door. He turned, the hurt etched in his face nothing against the agony in his good eye, and looked at Bess but not at Martha.

'To rub Achilles down. I rode him hard and fear I've cut him.' He grimaced. 'None of this is his doing.'

'Let Vincent do it in the morning,' Bess said. 'Dawn cannot be far away now.'

'I will do it myself,' Tom said, walking out.

Martha looked unwell, her face chalk-white against her black hair. Bess feared the girl might collapse. She wanted to comfort her. She knew that with two steps she could put her arms around Martha and hold her, this poor girl who had seen her father killed, who had even heaved the ladder to make him fall. And that horror after some desperate and dark undertaking which Bess could only guess at but which she knew had been in vain. Some base and futile act which had cost Martha her honour and now, perhaps, her love.

But Bess did not take those two steps. Instead she stood frozen to the spot, unable to offer anything of any worth except for her presence.

Martha muttered something which Bess did not hear properly, nor did she dare ask the girl to repeat it, then Martha walked from the parlour, leaving her alone in the cold. Her breath plumed in the half light and only then in the true silence did her memory untangle Martha's last words.

'God forgive me,' the minister's daughter had said.

The morning was crisp and clear and cold. A fleet of long, tendrillous clouds were being pushed southwards across the roof of the world, white ships in an ocean of brightest blue. Below them, but still way up, rooks tumbled and eddied in the icy gusts, their distant hoarse clamour reminding Mun of the cries of the hound pack in hollow, echoing woods. But those gathering in the forecourt of Shear House, stamping feet and huffing into hands, were not hunting fox today.

'She cannot have gone far,' he said, putting his foot in the stirrup and hauling himself into the saddle. Hector nickered, greeting his master properly now that they were united as one mass of flesh and bone. 'I'll wager we'll find her up in Gerard's Wood, or if not there then gone to the village. But we'll find her, Tom.'

Tom said nothing. He had saddled Achilles and was now cinching the saddle girth, but the stallion was stomping his front hooves and puffing up his stomach in protest. 'Don't test me today, boy,' Tom growled under his breath, patting the beast's withers. Then, as soon as Achilles relaxed slightly, he yanked the girth tight and fastened the buckle, sliding a finger beneath the strap to make sure it was not too tight.

'Mun is right,' Bess said, 'she just needed some time alone.' Bess was mounted too and cocooned in a thick, hooded riding cloak against the chill. She clapped gloved hands together to warm them and her sorrel mare, Artemis, snorted loudly, her breath pluming in white clouds.

'She needed to get away from me,' Tom said sourly, mounting. Achilles snapped at his bit and screeched, ill-tempered at being ridden again so soon. 'She's out there in this damned cold because of me, Bess, and you know that is the truth of it.'

'We'll find her,' Bess said, glancing at Mun as she echoed his words. Mun's jaw ached, having set rigid at Bess's telling of what the Dentons had done to Tom and then having seen with his own eyes his brother's injuries. Mun swore to himself that those haughty bastards would pay for their actions. But first to find Martha and bring her home. Home to a cup of warm spiced wine and a roaring fire, Lady Mary had said whilst rounding up a search party.

'At least it's dry,' Sir Francis announced from Priam's back, looking up at the great swell of Parbold Hill rising into the blue behind Shear House. 'And Martha's a sensible lass. She won't have gone off ill-dressed.'

'I feared you had run off too!' Lady Mary chided Edward MacColla, the butler, who was hurrying down Shear House's steps bearing a tray upon which sat two bottles of sherry – one full, the other a third full – and several small glasses that chinked as he hastened across the forecourt.

'Ah'm sorry, mah lady,' MacColla gnarred, glancing at Achilles who was still biting down on his bit and tossing his black head. The Scotsman was in his fifties, grey-haired, slender as a beanstalk, and had never, to Mun's knowledge, smiled. His mouth was ever a thin line in his lantern jaw and most of the other servants, especially the women, were afraid of him.

'Ah suspected tha one bottle would be lecht so ah ventured doon intae th' cellar fur anither,' MacColla grumbled. Mun reflected on the times he'd heard Sir Francis moan that he must be the only man who kept a butler who disapproved of drinking.

'Well the cellar must be deeper than I remember it,' Lady Mary said, uncowed by the man's prickly demeanour and taking a glass of sherry from his tray. She reached up and offered it to her husband with a nod that implied he should drink it all and be quick about it. And so Sir Francis downed the sherry in one draught before handing the empty glass back and sweeping a gloved hand across his lips and moustaches.

It had been Jacob who had first realized that his sister was not at Shear House. He had been up just before dawn, lighting fires with Isaac as the other servants began their daily tasks. Knowing how much his sister felt the cold, Jacob had taken to bringing her a cup of hot hippocras every morning but this morning he had found her bedchamber empty. Suspecting she might have been in Tom's room, he had gone across to the west wing to warn her that others were awake.

'I was afraid of what Lady Mary would say if she caught them,' he had told Mun. 'My sister said they do not have your father's blessing. That Sir Francis will not let them marry. But Martha wasn't there.' Tom had opened the door and told Jacob that the last time he had seen Martha was in the parlour and that his guess was that she was with Bess.

She had not been with Bess and now Shear House was a hive of activity as they prepared to ride out across the fields in search of Martha Green. As well as Sir Francis, Bess, Mun and Tom, several of the servants had clothed themselves in thick wool, and mounted horses that were now stamping and neighing excitedly, their ears pricked forward and tails lifted. The stable boy, Vincent, was there, as were Owen O'Neill, Peter Marten and Robert Birch, all of whom worked as labourers on the estate. A good bunch, Mun thought, so that they were bound to find Martha before anyone got too cold.

'You will take the Ormskirk road,' Sir Francis said to these men, at which they nodded resolutely. It was market day in Ormskirk and if Martha had gone there, four pairs of eyes would help the chances of finding her amongst the crowds. 'Bess, Jacob and I will try the village and then if there is no sign of the girl we'll ride to Lathom. The boys will ride up to the woods. One way or the other we'll find young Martha before she freezes half to death.' His eyebrows arched. 'And we'll save ourselves some trouble by separating the mares from the others, especially given Achilles's mood this morning.'

There were a few murmurs as the men voiced their own opinions about where Martha might have gone and each of them took their sherry in one tip to put some warmth in their bellies for the ride.

'Well, good hunting!' Sir Francis announced, then pulled Priam's reins to turn the horse towards the south. And with that they all set off into the cold, bright day, their breath and that of their mounts fogging the freezing air. To find Martha Green.

Mun wanted to ask about the fight at Baston House, wanted to know who was there and each man's role in his brother's debasement, but he did not know how to ask, for Tom was in a black mood. He smouldered like match-cord. His bruised and swollen face was clenched in pain and he sat his horse awkwardly, leaning one way and then the other, compensating for unseen hurts. So Mun held his tongue as they rode up the worn track leading to Old Gore meadow, with Parbold Hill looming against the blue sky.

'He's a good swordsman,' Tom said eventually, cuffing away some liquid that was oozing from the bulge of his blackened eye.

Mun did not know whether he was referring to Lord Denton or his son Henry, but he guessed at William. 'He fought in the Low Countries and against the Scottish rebels with Father and grew a reputation,' he said, remembering Sir Francis telling him that though he had no liking for William Denton the man was a good soldier. Brave too.

'I should have taken a pistol and shot the bastard,' Tom said matter-of-factly.

'Then what, little brother?' Mun asked. 'The others would have surely killed you. As it was you were lucky that Denton let you walk away. You attacked him in his own house in front of witnesses. He could have you arrested. I'd wager he will. Have you thought of that?'

'He raped Martha!' Tom spat.

'And he'll pay for it,' Mun said, though he suspected there was more to it than straightforward rape, that the waters were muddier than that. From what he had pieced together, Martha had gone alone to see Lord Denton and had said nothing about it afterwards. The girl was surely aware of her own beauty. She knew the effect it had on men. Might even have wondered what agreements might be made in her desperation to save her father from the noose. If she had gone merely to appeal for clemency, why hide it from Tom?

'You should have taken me,' Mun said.

The crack of a twig echoed in the beech woods up ahead and for a moment neither brother spoke, ears straining and eyes riveted towards where the sound had come from. A fallow deer bounded deeper into the trees, its white tail bobbing. Mun relaxed. They were up on the high ground behind Shear House now, but at least the trees would offer some protection from the icy wind.

'You can come and watch me kill him,' Tom said through the twist of his mangled lips.

They took an old cart path that had been carved years ago by men lugging timber down to the village and Mun instinctively looked up at the overarching skeletal branches that roofed the deep channel, appreciating how much warmer it was in the beech woods than out there among the wind-flayed meadows and rolling hummocks.

Other than the chink of tack and the creak of leather they made relatively little sound as they delved deeper into the woods. Beneath them the soft loam was covered by a thick, springy crust of brown beech leaves and it was this otherworldliness, Mun supposed now, that had intrigued them both as boys. Woods were places apart, where brave imaginations could conjure fantasies. Where boys could play at war.

But they were boys no longer and the time for games had passed.

He glanced at his brother whose long sand-coloured hair, a shade darker than his own, was still blood-stained and would be until it was washed properly. His brother who was talking of killing a man for real. And Mun did not know what else to say.

A little while later they stopped at a thatched wooden farmhouse from whose chimneys sooty smoke spewed into the blue sky. Mun asked the farmer, a thickset, red-haired man named Goffe, if he or his family had seen Martha. Eyeing Tom warily the man doffed his hat and shook his head, saying that he and his boy had only just returned from taking the sheep to new pasture and so would not know if a girl or the King of England himself had passed by. His wife and daughter had set off for the market at Ormskirk at first light so he could not speak for them. But he offered the brothers some broth and warm cider to fortify them against the chill, which Mun gracefully declined, noting the relief in the farmer's face though not surprised by it, for Goffe would have little to say to Sir Francis Rivers's sons. Besides which, Mun had noticed that ever since the discord between the King and Parliament, many tenant farmers and men of simple means seemed more inclined to keep themselves to themselves. As though the problems were none of their affair and conversing with landowners and the like would only bring them trouble.

So Mun and Tom went on their way, riding at a trot along the old paths until, after another mile or so, Mun shook his head and pulled up, calling for Tom to stop. 'She cannot have come so far in the time,' he said. 'Not on foot.'

'None of the mares was missing,' Tom said, shifting in his saddle, the dark scowl twisting into a grimace at some pain.

Mun shook his head and scratched his bearded cheek, then stood in the stirrups and scanned the bleak landscape across which the low winter sun spilled light that looked warm but was not. 'Where do you two go to be alone?' he asked.

Tom frowned. 'We are not children,' he said, scowling, 'or star-crossed lovers from one of those plays Bess and Mother love so. We have shared a bed.' This admission came with a defiant glint in his good eye. 'Damn Father and his disapproval, but we shall not sneak around like mice around the cat.'

Mun raised his palms. 'All right, little brother, calm yourself,' he said, then frowned like a man looking for another way round a quagmire. 'Where did you and she . . . use to go? When you *were* children,' he said, half smiling, 'and you didn't want Minister Green to know that his daughter was rolling in the hay with a Rivers boy.'

Tom glowered at him for a heartbeat and seemed

about to object again, but then his swollen lips curled just a touch. 'The bridge,' he said. 'We used to meet at the bridge.'

Or underneath the bridge more likely, Mun thought. For Mun had met girls at the old stone bridge that crossed the wide part of the Tawd many times. Had even, one summer's day when he was fourteen, etched Agnes Waite's name into one of the voussoirs, though he'd never told Tom that. He had been beguiled by the effect the crumbling stone arch had on their voices and had wondered if that was how his father sounded when he spoke in the grand buildings of Westminster or London. Time in that dark, hidden place on the riverbank had seemed to stand still, which was what you wanted it to do if you were with a girl who would have to be off home before she was missed. He wondered if boys still took girls to the old bridge thinking it their own secret place.

'She won't have gone there,' Tom said glumly. 'I dare say she won't want to be reminded of me.'

'Any other ideas where to look?' Mun asked. But Tom shook his head and with a flick of the wrist turned Achilles south-east towards the Tawd, towards the place where the Ormskirk road crossed the burgeoning river.

And it was there that they found Martha Green.

Tom had gone off at the gallop, perhaps eager to prove that searching at the old bridge was a bad idea, or maybe just to avoid having to talk. Together they had spurred down from the high ground, Shear House on their right, across wide fields in which plough teams laboured, breaking up the weeds and the remains of the last harvest and turning them under the soil to feed the next crop. They had raced past orchards busy with women preparing the trees for the next fruit season, and skirted copses of oak, maple and hazel in which pigs rooted noisily. And it was past midday when they came down from the fields and pastures to an ancient drovers' path that followed the meandering Tawd. The low winter sun cast them and their mounts in nightmarish shadow forms before them, long spindly legs ranging along the sunken way that was still laced with last night's frost.

On rounding a thicket of bare alder and ash they came to the bridge and slowed their mounts to a walk. Achilles whinnied and snorted, breath gushing from flared nostrils to cloud the crisp air. There was no sign of Martha.

'I told you she wouldn't come here,' Tom said through a grimace, patting Achilles's strong neck. The horse squealed again and stamped his feet and this time Tom growled at him. Then Hector snorted and tossed his head.

'Easy, boy,' Mun soothed. Tom had already turned Achilles round so that the pale sunlight fell on his ravaged face, and there he sat glowering, waiting for his brother. But Mun did not turn. For some reason he did not fully understand himself, Mun gave Hector a touch of heel, urging him forward. Perhaps it was to satisfy a sense of nostalgia, to recall simpler times when this had been a magical place. Or perhaps it was some other, darker sense that impelled him to get a closer look at the old bridge, a curiosity piqued by the stallions' strange behaviour.

Whatever it was it led him along the bank of the murmuring river. And that was when he saw it: a woman's body hanging by the neck from a rope tied to the remains of the worm-holed wooden rail atop the bridge. Before, it had been hidden behind the pier and the curve of the arch, but now there it was, swinging gently in the bridge's cold shadow, a dark pendulum against the blue eastern sky beyond. It was Martha.

Mun's stomach lurched and he yelled his brother's name as he spurred Hector up the bank and onto the bridge, hoping they were not too late but knowing that they were. Then he was dismounted, calling Martha's name and leaning over the low wall to get closer to her, desperate for some sign of life. But there was no life, just a corpse hanging on a rope, a face that had been beautiful, so beautiful, now blue and grotesque, its tongue bulging from a rictus mouth.

'Damn it! Help me!' he roared, not knowing whether to pull her up with the rope or try to lower her into the river. Surely the river was too deep there to wade in, but the idea of hauling her up by her neck disgusted him. 'I don't know what to do!' he yelled. 'Help me!' But Tom was still below on the bank, dismounted and staring at Martha, his face clenched in its own rictus of horror. So Mun took a grip on the rope which he supposed was a tethering rope from their own stables.

Then he braced his shins against the cold stone and began to heave. The girl was surprisingly heavy but Mun was strong, and once he had enough of the rope he put it across his broad shoulders, bracing the weight so that his arms could do the hauling. Then the weight was as nothing and he realized that Tom was there too, and together they pulled Martha up until Tom was able to lean over the edge and grip her under her arms. He hefted her over the low wall and laid her on the ground and for a long moment the brothers looked at her.

Mun could not help but stare at Martha's neck which was clearly broken and now so unnaturally, horribly stretched. Then Tom bent double and vomited.

Mun said nothing for fear that to unclamp his own jaw was to void his stomach, too. He took off his riding cloak and laid it over the girl's dead body, feeling guilty as he covered her up. Yet relieved, too. Then, half stumbling, he went back to the low wall and slumped against it, looking up at the blue sky and the gulls whose arched white underwings reflected the pale golden light of the freezing day.

Because Martha Green was dead.

CHAPTER TEN

MUN KNEW THEY MUST HAVE BEEN AT THE BRIDGE FOR at least an hour. Perhaps closer to two. During that time he had tried to think of what he might say to his brother. Nothing had come to mind, besides which, anything uttered into the silence now would, by its conspicuousness, take on an import at odds with the words themselves. Anything ventured would blunder and fail, he knew, and so he kept his silence and watched his brother's heart break. Tom sat slumped, had barely moved a muscle the whole time. He had thrown Mun's cloak off Martha but then, seeing that her skirts were wet, he had replaced it leaving only her face uncovered. Martha lay on her back, her head cradled on Tom's legs and her arms by her sides as he hunched over, staring into her face, his hands smoothing her raven-black hair back from her forehead over and over again. But no one would mistake the scene for two young lovers sharing a moment of intimacy. They would see the girl's swollen tongue protruding from blue lips. They would notice her bloated red hands that had filled with blood. They would not see the young man's face for he was slouched over the girl, but they would feel the agony coming off him, sense the torment twisting his soul like a weighted rope.

Eventually Mun rose on stiff legs and walked over to the couple, standing silently for a long moment, loath to interrupt. 'Let me take her,' he said gently. Tom did not look up, did not break the rhythm of his hand stroking her hair as he whispered tenderly, as though they two were the only people left on God's earth. 'She can ride with me,' Mun said, placing a hand on Tom's shoulder, which made him flinch. Tom's eyes locked on his, though they were glazed, somehow unseeing. Far away.

'We should get back. Take Martha home. Mother will know what to do.' Tom blinked slowly but said nothing, then bent to Martha's bloodless face once more and continued whispering words Mun could not hear. So Mun waited a while longer, watching flocks of rooks and jackdaws sweeping into a distant field. They came in widely spaced drifts like flurries of black snow, settling behind a man and boy plough team to pillage the turned soil. 'We must go, Tom,' he said at last. Though he did not know why they must go. In truth they could have stayed on the old bridge until dusk and still made it back before dark. And even then, what? Yet he itched to be away, to shrug off the black cloak of the thing. To stay was to indulge Tom's pain, to let it seep deeper into his own soul where the weevils of guilt began to feed. Guilt for not helping Martha when she must have been desperate. Guilt for not standing beside Tom against the Dentons. For not being with his brother when Tom needed him.

'I will take her,' Tom said, swallowing hard. He did not move.

Mun shook his head. 'Let me do it.' For a heartbeat Tom glared at him, but then the younger man's eyes softened, which Mun took to be assent. And so, carefully, more carefully than he had ever done anything in all his life, Mun bent and took the dead girl into his arms, trying not to look at her face.

The ride back to Shear House seemed to take for ever. But he had thought it unseemly to gallop with Martha's body lying across Hector's rump and he knew his brother thought the same, though neither had spoken of it. So they had walked, each adrift on the darkling sea of his own thoughts, as the bright day dimmed and turned colder still. There was no wind to talk of now and yet he could smell wood smoke on the air when they were still half a mile from home. He guessed the others would be back from their respective searches by now. He imagined Bess and Jacob standing in the forecourt waiting for him and Tom to arrive, expecting to see Martha mounted behind Tom, arms circling his waist. But when they passed through the main gateway under the scrutiny of the majestic stone lions on their plinths, and eventually came within sight of Shear House, Mun saw no one waiting in the cold gloom. He did not know whether that would make the thing harder or easier.

'I want to carry her this last part,' Tom said. Mun nodded, stopping to dismount, understanding his brother's need to take responsibility. For draped over Hector's rump Martha was somehow less human. More like the prize kill after a hunt. So Mun watched Tom take Martha carefully into his arms whilst he took their mounts' reins, and then, side by side, they walked towards the house which loomed before them in the purple-tinged dusk.

Of the family, Lady Mary was the first to realize what had happened. She was in the hall when Isaac opened the door to her sons. When she saw Martha in Tom's arms her hands flew to her mouth and she shook her head as though refusing to see what her eyes were showing her. Then the parlour door opened, spilling flamelight into the lamp-lit hall, and Bess was there. When she saw the girl's body she called on God and stumbled, flailing, gripping the doorframe to steady herself.

Mun glanced at Tom and saw that tears were spilling down his cheeks and so, swallowing down the lump in his own throat, he took it upon himself to explain how they had found Martha at the bridge. That there had been nothing they could do, for the deed was long done by the time they arrived.

'My poor boy,' Lady Mary said, wringing her hands, 'my poor, poor boy. Francis! Take Martha and lay her in the parlour. Isaac, have Edward bring some hippocras for the boys. And make it strong,' she called after the servant.

Sir Francis stood behind Bess, one hand on her shoulder, the other still gripping a fire iron he had been using a moment before. He stood the poker against the wall, firmed his jaw and nodded, moving towards his younger son, his arms out in readiness to take the burden from him.

'Get away from her!' Tom yelled, glaring at Sir Francis, who recoiled, startled.

'Let your father help you,' Lady Mary said, eyebrows lifted, the skin beneath them stretched. But Tom ignored her and, tears soaking his face, carried Martha past them all into the parlour.

Sir Francis looked to Mun who shrugged, and they all followed towards the parlour just as Jacob appeared from behind the screen which ran along the hall towards the kitchen. His thick copper hair stuck up in tufts and his eyebrows met in a suspicious frown as he took in the scene. Bess nodded at Mun to follow their father, then went over and took the young boy's hand, leading him off towards the dining parlour to break the news of his sister's death. Mun cursed under his breath because the poor boy now had no family at all, then he closed the parlour door from the inside.

'Let us help you, son,' Sir Francis said, his arms out towards Tom who had laid Martha on the floor and now knelt beside her, head bowed. The dead girl lay on her side, her body making a grim crescent for it had stiffened, bent as it had been over Hector's rump. Flamelight played across her face, the warmth raising a stink from her fouled skirts. A knotty log cracked angrily in the grate and Lady Mary nodded at Sir Francis as though he should repeat his offer of help.

'Let me take her, Thomas,' Sir Francis said softly, stepping closer. Tom's dishevelled hair hung either side of his face, so that Sir Francis leant in awkwardly, trying to meet his eye. 'Your mother will wash the girl and—'

'I said get away from her!' Tom screamed, launching himself at his father, driving him back and sending a table and two glasses flying as he slammed Sir Francis against the wall.

'Tom!' Lady Mary exclaimed. Then Mun was hauling on his brother's shoulders as Sir Francis stood wide-eyed, his arms flat against the wall behind him.

'Let him go!' Mun barked. 'Step back, Tom!'

'He's the reason she's dead!' Tom yelled, spittle flying

from a mouth twisted in fury, his broad shoulders trying to shrug off Mun's grip. 'If he'd spoken up for George Green none of this would have happened!' He was glaring at Sir Francis. 'He's a coward!'

'Stand off!' Mun roared.

'Coward!' Tom spat into his father's horrified face.

Mun wrenched Tom's right shoulder and Tom let go of their father, twisting and flailing with his arm, but Mun blocked with his right forearm and slammed his left fist into his brother's face, sending him staggering. Now it was Tom who looked shocked to his very marrow as he stared at his brother from his good eye, the split in his still swollen lip glistening with fresh blood.

'He could have saved her father,' he said, smearing blood across the back of his hand. With the other hand he pointed accusingly at Sir Francis, and that hand was trembling. 'Instead that bastard Denton raped her and she could not live with the shame of it.'

'Your father could not have saved the minister!' Lady Mary said. The parlour door had opened and Bess and Jacob stood there transfixed, both of them weeping.

'I had to keep my family safe,' Sir Francis said, stepping out from the wall. 'I could not risk the consequences of going up against Lord Denton and his kind. Don't be a fool, Thomas.'

Tom turned back to Sir Francis. 'You are a coward!' he spat.

'Hold your damned tongue!' Mun heard himself yell, feeling his fists become hard knots. 'He is our father!'

'He is a bastard coward and no better than Denton,' Tom snarled, the words dripping venom even as his lip dripped blood.

Mun strode forward and threw up an arm, and the next thing he knew Tom's throat was in his grip, his brother's good eye glaring with hate.

'No, Edmund!' Sir Francis yelled. 'Let him be.'

'Let him go, Mun! Don't hurt him!' Bess screamed like the cry of a hawk, still clasping Jacob's hand, and that cry cut through Mun's rage and he felt himself jerk as though he had been the one struck. He let go of Tom and stepped back, raising his palms to show Bess he meant their brother no harm.

Tom cuffed blood from his lip and turned to Lady Mary. 'See her buried, Mother,' he said, tears of heartbreak and rage gleaming in his good eye and lacing the puffy slit of his injured one.

Lady Mary nodded, frowning. 'Of course we will, Thomas,' she said, glancing down at Martha's corpse, at the blue lips forced apart by the bulging tongue.

Then without another word Tom strode past Mun, a shoulder knocking him aside. Bess and Jacob stepped out of his way as they would for a passing carriage and Tom stormed from the parlour.

Lady Mary made as if to follow him.

'Let the boy go,' Sir Francis growled, 'let him go. Thomas needs some time to gather himself.' Then he turned to Mun. 'You should not have struck him,' he said, straightening his shirt and doublet as though to shrug off the whole sorry incident. He dipped his chin and looked accusingly at his elder son. 'That was grievous, Mun. He is your brother.'

'I'm sorry,' Mun murmured, flexing his right hand to check that none of his finger bones was broken. He wanted to blow across his swelling knuckles, but the hot pain blooming in them was the least he deserved,

162

he thought, eyes resting on Martha Green. Whom poor Tom had loved.

'Fighting as boys is one thing, but to strike your brother as a grown man? It is inexcusable,' Sir Francis went on. 'You will apologize to your brother when he is himself again.'

'And will you, Father?' Mun heard himself ask, his eyes riveted to his father's now, daring to hold that steely gaze.

'Mun!' Lady Mary exclaimed, her eyes wide. 'You forget yourself!' Sir Francis coloured, crimson rage flooding his cheeks. Mun looked away, readying himself for a barrage that never came. Instead Sir Francis glowered and said nothing, his steel grey eyes puncturing Mun's defiance, which was worse, Mun thought, than if he had bawled at him.

'Bess, take the poor boy away.' Lady Mary broke the moment, steering all eyes to Jacob who had not left Bess's side. The boy's scowling face glistened with tears and snot, clenched in confused anger as though he was desperate to understand why Martha had left him, whilst despising her for it.

'Come with me, Jacob,' Bess said, swallowing hard with a resolute nod. And taking his hand in hers she turned him from the grotesquely bent figure on the parlour floor. 'Let us go and find out what's keeping Edward with the hippocras,' she said, catching Mun's eye before leading Jacob off.

'O'Neill and Marten are not back from Ormskirk yet,' Lady Mary said to Mun, bailing the silence that was trying to flood in. 'Knowing those two they'll still be searching the taverns, looking for Martha in the bottom of their ale cups. I want them back here

163

tonight, not staying in town at your father's expense.'

O'Neill and Marten were good men and Mun doubted they would be shirking their responsibilities, but he kept his mouth shut and waited for what he knew was coming next.

'We'll be lambing before we know it,' his mother went on. 'I want the animals pastured closer and the ewes looked after as though they belonged to the King himself. I will not lose as many lambs this year,' she said, almost accusing Sir Francis, 'I simply will not.' Then she turned back to Mun. 'If you go now you'll reach town before nightfall. Bring the men back if you find them easily. If not, bring them back first thing in the morning.' Mun nodded. 'We shall deal with the poor girl,' Lady Mary added without looking down at the body.

'He shouldn't ride in the dark,' Sir Francis put in, taking a pitcher and glass from a table and pouring himself some wine.

'There'll be enough moon to see by,' Mun said to his mother, for he knew her scheme was less about retrieving O'Neill and Marten than it was about putting some distance between her husband and her sons. Which was no bad thing, he supposed.

'And three of us on the road have nothing to fear,' he went on. 'O'Neill's face would put the fear of God into anyone of ill-intent.' Sir Francis conceded this with an arched brow and Lady Mary seized the advantage, telling her husband to move Martha Green away from the hearth. Because the girl begins to stink, Mun thought, despising himself for not being oblivious of it.

So his father bent to the task and Mun turned his

back on them and prepared to go back out into the freezing dusk. To bring back O'Neill and Marten.

Three days after Martha hanged herself Tom arrived in Manchester and there spent two nights before moving southward again. Two weeks after leaving Shear House he found himself in London, in a stinking, dingy hostelry on Long Southwark. And he found himself drunk; undoubtedly more drunk than he had ever been. He had considered lodging at the famous Tabard Inn, which his father had spoken of, but then the fact that he'd learned of the place from Sir Francis was reason in itself not to stay there. Besides which, in his haste to flee Shear House he had not considered practicalities and the purse tied to his belt was not nearly heavy enough for the Tabard. It contained half-pennies, pennies, shillings and crowns amounting to a grand total of a little over one pound, roughly a day's income for a man such as his father. A hostelry like the Tabard and its associated pleasures would leech that money away in no time and so Tom had taken a room at the Leaping Lord, a grubby, run-down place that stank of human waste. A fine drizzle had urged him off Long Southwark's greasy cobbles and through an archway fronting on the street big enough to accommodate wagons, and there, surrounding a court-yard littered with the rotting scraps of vegetables and scurrying with rats, stood the Leaping Lord and its lodgings. Telling himself he would grow accustomed to the stench, and supposing biting fleas had been the reason for the lord's leaping, Tom had paid up front for a room for one week and now, feeling the purse against his right thigh, he wondered how long one pound would last him in London. Not long if I keep pissing it away, he thought grimly.

He took another long draught of beer, nodding in solidarity to another lone drinker across the noisy, fug-filled room. He had brought few belongings from Shear House. He had the clothes on his back and his thick wool cloak that still carried the scent, though faint as mist now, of Martha. He had a rapier scabbarded at his left hip, the inscription on the blade *FOR MY CHRIST RESOLVED TO DIE* hiding unseen in the dark. Made by the renowned German blademaker Johannes Kinndt, the sword was worth at least ten shillings, perhaps more. The cup around the blade was decorated in relief with the heads of King Charles and Queen Henrietta Maria and its recurved quillons were ornamented with fine threads of gold and silver.

And he had two pistols: a fine pair of firelocks twenty-six inches long, eighteen of those inches comprising the octagonal barrels, with long slender butts terminating with a flare for good grip. These he had left in his bare room, wrapped in calfskin and bundled in a spare shirt and jerkin. They were his father's weapons and he felt a tinge of guilt at having taken them from Sir Francis's armoury the night he had ridden from Shear House. But only a fool would take the road unarmed, especially on a horse as fine and expensive-looking as Achilles. A horse like that would fetch ten pounds at market. The stallion was stabled a stone's throw away, feasting on the best hay Tom could buy. He had also paid for fresh stall bedding, so that he suspected of the two of them Achilles had the finer lodgings. The horse deserved it. Achilles had been a faithful friend. He is all I have now, Tom thought, catching a serving girl's eye and lifting his cup. The girl was plump and golden-haired and almost pretty and she perfected a well-worn coy smile as the beer splashed into Tom's cup, and three rough-looking men on the next table jeered and winked, sharing their expert opinions that Tom could get a fuck out of the girl later if he had the legs to follow her. But Tom ignored them and nodded his thanks to the girl, then tugged a piece of his cloak up to his nose – the cloak that smelt faintly of Martha – and breathed in.

CHAPTER ELEVEN

23rd April 1642

COME ST GEORGE'S DAY TOM WAS STILL LODGING AT THE
Leaping Lord inn. He no longer noticed London's stink:
the coal smoke and the sewers, the iron tang of blood
from the slaughter yards and the stench of massed
humanity. He barely flinched at the rats that scurried
across his path when he walked the thronging streets,
and he'd grown almost fond of the mice that shared his
damp room, scurrying hither and thither through the
old straw.

His money was gone, long pissed away during dark
weeks of self-pity and bitterness and the furious need
to forget. Yet he still had a room and one meal a day
and Achilles still had a stall, because Abiezer Grey,
who kept the Lord, had offered Tom work in exchange
for food and board. Tom had bridled at the offer when
Grey, with whom he had never spoken more than ten
words, proposed it. Tom had been not quite drunk and
Grey had thumped a bowl of mutton stew and a slab of
cheat bread in front of him and before Tom could say

he had not ordered the food the landlord had issued the terms as though he cared not at all what answer came back.

'You think I am a pauper, sir,' Tom had slurred, 'that I require employment in this flea-bitten, cow's arse of a hole?'

Grey had shrugged broad shoulders. 'Two weeks past you were drinking ale of the first water. Now you are making small beer last the hour,' he said in a voice characterized by his flat nose that looked to have been broken more times than even Grey could likely remember. 'Can't drink if you can't pay.' The landlord shrugged again but this time at Ruth Gell, the almost pretty serving girl who was watching the exchange from a boisterous thicket of drunken apprentices. Then Grey turned his back on Tom and pushed into the press of bodies and was gone. Tom craned his neck and Ruth gave him a curt nod before flashing her smile at a handsome youth whilst simultaneously slapping another man's hand off her rump, and Tom turned back to his beer, cursing under his breath. He had been sharing Ruth's bed on and off for a week or so and he knew that it must have been she who had persuaded Grey to make him the offer. He could guess how she'd persuaded him, too, for Tom knew Grey shared Ruth's bed as often as, if not more often than, he did. But Ruth had a good heart and had shown him kindness, more than once leaving a bowl of left-over pease porridge or mutton stew outside Tom's room when he had retired for the night, having not eaten. She was a hard worker, too, and there was not a man or woman – other than Tom it seemed to him – could sit at a table in the Leaping Lord if they were not drinking or eating, smoking Abiezer Grey's tobacco or resting from a visit to one of Grey's girls who were, to Tom's eyes, rough as rope but undeniably cheap.

'But where will you go when your money runs out?' Ruth had asked later that same night, pulling up a stool and sitting at Tom's table. 'Abi is a good man but he will not let you keep your room and drink for less than a shilling a night.'

Tom had leant back against a greasy, faded tapestry, scratching his cheek and eyeing the room. He had allowed his beard to grow unkempt and he knew it made him look older than he was but did not care.

'I will find something,' he said.

The only patrons left at the tables now were either too drunk to make it back to their rooms or else sat still as the dead and wreathed in tobacco fog, having smoked themselves into oblivion.

Tom lifted his mug and drained it, then dragged his hand across cracked lips. 'I will find something,' he repeated, blinking at the heady, yellow smoke that stung his eyes. Several smouldering pipes sat abandoned on tables, adding to the fug of sweat, meat stew and the sour stench of old ale.

'I worry for you, Tom,' Ruth said, habit making her snatch up the empty mug and stand to take it away. She glanced around, then with her free hand yanked her bodice a little higher over her plump bosom. No one left worth impressing, Tom thought.

'That's a shiny, pretty thing,' she said, nodding at the signet ring on the third finger of his right hand. 'Gold?' Tom looked at the thing. A gift from his father, its round face was embossed with a lion's head. Mun had one exactly the same. He'd not even thought about it, but now supposed he could sell it, if it came to it. 'Or you could sell your horse,' she suggested. 'He's a fine animal by the looks of him.'

But Tom could never sell Achilles and so the next day he had accepted Abiezer Grey's offer and now he worked for his room and board, clearing tables, hefting barrels, making sure the rakers cleaned the horse dung from the street outside the Lord and took the inn's refuse away. He drew water from Long Southwark's wells and pumps to save Grey paying men to bring it in tankards on their backs, and he oversaw the cleaning of the privies at night, ensuring the jakes farmers earned their pennies. He had thought he would detest the work because he was the son of a knight and had a right to privileges and finery. But he did not detest it. If anything the labour made him forget who he was, and for this he was thankful. He worked hard, drank much, filled his belly and sometimes, at the end of a long day, he shared Ruth's bed.

And he met Matthew Penn.

Penn was one of a gang of men who met regularly in the Lord to rail bitterly and loudly against the King's advisers and did not seem to mind who heard. Not that they need fear many of the King's men lodging or drinking in the Leaping Lord. Everyone knew that in February King Charles had placed Queen Henrietta Maria on a boat to Holland with their daughters and the crown jewels. Charles himself had ridden to York and most of London's nobility had fled the broiling anger round Westminster and Whitehall for their country estates. Now, in the absence of any real voice of opposition, dissent had grown bold and Tom had heard the *vox populi* turn, sure as the Thames tide, against the King. He worked and he drank and he listened to men such as Matthew Penn, an apprentice lawyer, reading and distributing inflammatory pamphlets, inciting men to take up arms for the sake and safety of all Englishmen, with whom the King had broken his contract. Some clamoured against the clergy and some against the King's courtiers. One of Penn's associates, a slab-faced, bald-headed Puritan named Will Trencher, would tremble viciously when proclaiming that King Charles himself was orchestrating a Catholic plot that would see an Irish army sweep through the land butchering all God-fearing folk whether man, woman or child.

'Parliament has issued the Militia Ordinance to preserve us from malignant threats!' Trencher had blazed to the drunk and nearly drunk, 'and it is our duty, gentlemen, to sharpen our blades!'

But the whetstone upon whose edge Penn sharpened his ire was the gentry and highborn who, he regularly announced, used their position to intimidate and oppress others. Men such as Colonel Thomas Lunsford, whom Tom had watched assaulting the crowds outside Westminster the first time he had come to London.

'I for one will rise in General Skippon's new army of the people,' Tom had heard Penn vow, 'and I shall teach haughty bastards like Lunsford a rare lesson. I'll whip that one-eyed whoreson from Westminster to London Bridge and there we'll string the bastard up and watch him dance like the devil he is.'

For men had begun to whisper of war between Parliament and the King. At first it had seemed impossible but now the trained bands and militias were beginning to form. The craftsmen and tradesmen of London were laying down their hammers and chisels and the clerks their pens and their papers. The brewers and leather-makers of the Boroughside, the glass-blowers and soap-makers of St Saviour's, the dyers of the Bankside and the cloth-makers of St Olave's were arming themselves. The bakers and the vendors of fruits, flowers and vegetables were locking their shops and being drawn into companies.

Tom was in the midst of it all. At first he had felt completely alone, helpless and unmoving as a rock around which the waters were beginning to rise and roil. Yet he watched and he listened to the likes of Matthew Penn and Will Trencher and eventually their zeal began to seep into his own being. Their passions and their fury ignited the embers in his own soul. For Tom was angry. Somewhere deep within him, in his stomach and his heart and in the marrow of his bones, baleful serpents writhed and sought release to deliver their venom.

And when Tom listened to Penn rail against men such as Lunsford, in his mind he saw Lord Denton.

22nd August 1642

'I met some unsavoury fellows last night,' Emmanuel Bright said, slapping his mare's rain-slick neck. The beast snorted, spraying water. 'Mercenaries from the Low Countries and base villains to a man. One of them actually told me he cared nothing for the cause but only for His Majesty's half crowns and our handsome women.' The look on Emmanuel's face told Mun that he was perhaps as impressed by these foreign soldiers as he was appalled.

'War attracts such men as a corpse brings crows,' Sir

Francis muttered, looking up to the slate-grey sky for signs of blue. There were none.

'I have seen such fellows too,' Mun put in, watching those armed with pike or musket or nothing at all gather to the desultory beat of a lone drum, swelling the nevertheless contemptible throng before them. 'They squawk loudly enough to anyone who will listen.'

Emmanuel ignored Mun's suggestion that he indulged the mercenaries and their glory-adorned tales of war. 'It would appear His Majesty's divine right to rule his people holds no sway with such types,' he said, 'but rather that profit – a thing as changeable as the wind, it seems to me – is their only master.'

'Take my word for it, such men are as dangerous as those now massing against us under Essex's banner,' Sir Francis said, nodding southwards. 'I would rather be without them.' His lip curled. 'And yet we need them,' he admitted.

Mun had ofttimes heard his father criticize the profligacy of the Court, had even heard him talk disapprovingly of the King, and in the days before they had ridden from Shear House Mun had looked for signs in Sir Francis that he wavered in his enthusiasm for the cause. There had been doubts, Mun sensed, but doubts about war itself as a means to set things straight, rather than questions of his father's loyalty to King Charles.

'War is a horror beyond the man's imagining who has not seen it with his own eyes,' Sir Francis had said.

'But you believe the crown was put on the King's head by God, Father?' Mun had asked. 'So we shall have God on our side if it comes to war. Our cause is right.'

'I fear God does not sully Himself in men's wars,' Sir

Francis had replied. 'And neither does war decide who is right. Only who remains. In some ways I cannot blame those in Parliament who seek to limit the King's power, to dismantle the instruments of his Personal Rule. They wonder why they should support Charles's financial expedients whilst he ignores their grievances.' He cocked an eyebrow. 'I can even accept that some believe the Reformation was a job only half done and would see the Church rid of the rags and patches of Rome. Though the Puritans are too zealous for my liking.' He puffed life into his pipe, the tobacco releasing a languid curl of white smoke. 'But we have made our place in this world, with no little help from the Crown, and I would protect that place.' He frowned. 'We shall do what we must.'

'But if we lose shall we lose Shear House?' Mun said, as much to himself as to his father. The thought, which had struck like lightning out of nowhere, horrified him. He had never considered what would come after this conflict. If indeed it came to war. *The young do not see beyond the morrow*, he could almost hear his father say.

'Those who seek reform would not be reined in,' Sir Francis did say, confirming Mun's fears. 'They would shake the world like a hound shakes a fox, and only the strongest would eat the scraps of what is left.'

Mun had been struck by this revelation that his father marched – would fight – more out of duty to his king and a desire to preserve the world's natural order than out of a belief that their cause was necessarily just. But then it made perfect sense, he realized, for if the rebels won, the Rivers family would likely lose everything. As for his own future, what would that hold if there were no estate to inherit? No land to manage, no farms to maintain? No rents to collect? So they would fight for their king. And the rebels be damned.

And now Mun was soaked to his very bones. He was not alone; four thousand others who had come weary out of Warwickshire to Nottingham were waterlogged too, including the King of England himself. Perhaps it should have cheered Mun a little that King Charles appeared as miserably wet as he, but it did not. It was a pitiful force that had come out for their king and the column's leaden progress through the kingdom had drawn a veil of melancholy over them all. A few days earlier the King had been denied entrance to Coventry. His progression through Newark and Leicester had met with a less than enthusiastic response and even here in Nottingham, a wealthy trading town, Mun sensed the disquiet of folk who resented having the cost of quartering the King's army on the common laid at their door.

'Damn this pissing rain,' Emmanuel said, one hand on the reins and the other a tight fist gripping the cloak at his throat. 'It's keeping folk indoors when they should be here to receive their king.'

Mounted on Hector beside him, Mun stared straight ahead through the rain that dripped rhythmically from his broad hat and through the vapour rising from their horses' muzzles and flanks despite its being high summer. On the field before them King Charles and his nephew Prince Rupert and divers other lords and gentlemen of His Majesty's train stood in a soaking knot, shoulders slumped and talking in low voices amongst themselves.

''Tis not the rain that keeps them away,' Sir Francis

said, patting Priam's thick neck. The stallion nickered softly. 'Men are more keen to bring in the harvest than go to war.'

'Then we shall have to drag them from the fields, Father,' Mun said, ashamed of the gloomy rabble of men, women and children who had gathered to greet their king. Given its central position within the kingdom and its intersecting trade routes Nottingham had seemed to Mun the perfect town for the muster. The King would raise the Royal Standard against the Westminster rebels and thousands of loyal men would rally to form an awe-inspiring army. But it had not happened like that. Mun glanced around, taking in the glum faces, framed by bedraggled, dripping locks and broad-brimmed hats, of the mounted men around him. There were perhaps two thousand cavalry there on that sloping field beneath the great castle wall. Opposite them on the other side of the King's party were, Mun reckoned, no more than six hundred infantrymen who had marched from Yorkshire and whom he'd heard one of Sir Francis's friends refer to as the scum of the county. They did not look much standing there, drawn loosely into companies, with their assortment of pole-arms, clubs and muskets. They stank too, of stale sweat and wet wool, and Mun was reminded of his times in London with its thronging streets and its odorous masses.

'Do you recognize any of them, Sir Francis?' Emmanuel asked, for he knew that in his days at court Sir Francis had met many men who had fought in the Low Countries for money or honour or both.

'A few. Not many,' Sir Francis admitted. 'But I'd wager the Earl of Essex is looking at his lot and thinking just the same as us. Devereux is an experienced soldier, but he is cautious. He won't move against us until he is sure of having the advantage.'

'They say he has already prepared his coffin and takes it with him wherever he goes,' Mun said, smiling at the thought. 'Not the actions of an optimistic man.'

'Not optimistic perhaps, but well prepared nevertheless,' Sir Francis said grimly.

All men knew that the earl was strongly Protestant, but during one of Mun's sojourns in London he had heard the rumour that Essex was one of the Puritan nobles in the House of Lords. Now he asked his father if the rumour was true.

Sir Francis removed his hat and with his hand brushed off the rain that had pooled on its crown. 'The man tends towards the zealous,' he admitted, 'frowns on gaming and drinking and, I dare say, fears for his soul.' He put his hat back on and coughed into a fist. 'Yet I maintain hope that he would not go as far as those whom he serves. The King's right to rule, divine or otherwise, is one of the moorings of society which not even Essex would see severed.' But to Mun's eyes his father did not look convinced.

Parliament had wasted no time in choosing Essex, one of the few English nobles with any military experience, to lead their army, commissioning him to the post of Captain-General and Chief Commander. And neither was the man alone amongst the peerage and greater gentry to have apparently sided with the rebels, though such were few in number so far as Mun could gather.

'Yet he is friends with the troublemaker Pym,' Emmanuel said.

'Aye, who holds the pursestrings of the army raised

against us. We face capable opponents and must seek to put such men back in their place at the first opportunity.' Sir Francis scowled. 'Or else risk the flame of war spreading to ignite the whole country.'

As if to prove his fears well founded, a cheer went up as the infantry company split and six men appeared from the mass carrying the Royal Standard, which they had fetched down from Nottingham Castle.

'This is war then,' Mun said under his breath, half terrified, half exhilarated by what he was seeing. Then the small party stopped before the infantry and there waited whilst His Majesty, Prince Rupert and several other dignitaries walked with great austerity across the churned earth to take their places beside the banner, which looked to Mun no different from those hung with city streamers used each year at the Lord Mayor's Show.

The procession came forward with the standard and Mun stood in his stirrups to get a better view. The King was smaller than Mun had imagined him. Wrapped in a sodden black cloak and with a purple feather plastered to his hat Charles cut a pale, gaunt, sorry-looking figure. In contrast, his nephew Prince Rupert was remarkably tall, six feet and four inches men said. A most striking man, he was well built and handsome, causing Mun to muse that if one did not know better one might be forgiven for presuming that of the two men Rupert and not the other was the King of England. But for the solemn authority that clung to Charles even more determinedly than the rain-sodden cloak. Mun had never seen anyone look more vulnerable. And yet dignified.

'Ground's too bloody soft,' Sir Francis mumbled

under his breath. Two soldiers had been summoned forward and were now on their knees digging into the earth with knives and clawing handfuls of mud from the hole. 'If they don't go down at least three feet the thing will blow over in the first gust.'

Up went the Royal Standard and Mun felt the hairs on his arms and the back of his neck bristle. At its top hung a flag with the King's arms quartered and a hand pointing to a crown.

'What does it say, Father?' Mun asked, for below that image were written several words but there was not enough wind to unfurl the flag and reveal the motto. 'You must have seen it before.'

'It says "Give Caesar his due",' Sir Francis replied, arching his back and wincing at some stiffness.

One of the lords barked an order and two sorry-looking trumpeters stepped forward and put their instruments to their lips but were forestalled with a raised hand belonging to King Charles himself, who was reading the proclamation he held in the other.

'Pen and ink!' the King called, throwing out an arm but not taking his eyes from the parchment. Someone hurried forward with a pen which the King accepted with a curt nod before seeming to strike out some parts of the text and make his own additions here and there. At last satisfied, he handed the parchment to a herald who proceeded to read, with some difficulty it seemed to Mun, the proclamation which declared ground and cause for His Majesty's setting up of his standard, namely to suppress the rebellion of the Earl of Essex, in raising forces against him. The King required the aid and assistance of all his loving subjects to put down the traitors with all haste. When the herald finished he glanced nervously towards but not at the King, who nodded resolutely and waved his hand in small circles at the trumpeters. The fanfare sounded and an officer of the infantry flung his hat into the air, at which hundreds more did the same with cries of 'God save the King! God save King Charles!'

An officer of the cavalry beside Sir Francis lifted his own hat from his head and yelled, 'Hang up the Roundheads!'

Mun grinned at Emmanuel and together they took up the shout. 'Hang up the Roundheads!' they called, rain spraying from their lips, their horses whinnying at the sudden clamour. Mun waved his sodden hat in the air and shivered with the thrill of it all.

Because he was going to war.

CHAPTER TWELVE

———

THE ROYAL STANDARD WAS BLOWN DOWN THAT SAME NIGHT it was put up and could not be planted again for several days because the ground was too soft, and a storm raged, scouring the Royalist camp and making horses skittish and men whisper of ill portents. There were murmurs that even King Charles himself saw the gloomy ceremony as ominous, for he was by all accounts a man for whom solemn ritual was the foundation upon which authority rested firm. But if the King *was* faint-hearted Mun had seen no sign of it as he had watched for three consecutive days His Majesty bring forth the standard to the field. Mun listened each time the proclamation was read aloud, straining to catch every word that was borne off by the wind, so that in the end he could have repeated it verbatim.

'By God we shall teach the rebels!' Emmanuel had said through a grin on the third day, patting one of the new Dutch wheellock pistols holstered on his saddle. A gift from Sir Francis, their polished ivory butt-caps gleamed in the pink dawn light. 'We'll send them running back to London with their tails between their legs.'

Mun had laughed at the image of the rowdy London apprentices as whining hounds seeking to win back their master the King's favour, having been scolded. But then he had thought of Tom, whom none of them had seen for almost eight months. His brother should have been with them, witnessing the King make ready to whip his errant hounds. But where was Tom?

'What has become of you, brother?' he whispered. He could understand why his brother had run off the night of Martha's death, especially after what had passed between him and their father, but they had all thought he would come back after a day or two, been certain he would. They had been wrong. They had even looked for Tom in London, but found no traces. Now all they could do was hope and pray that he was all right and that he would return to Shear House. To his family.

'We need more men,' Mun said, stating the obvious but wanting to say something, hoping conversation might edge thoughts of Tom out of his mind. The wind's fury had abated and the day promised to be hot and dry. A good day. A new day.

'They'll come, Mun,' Emmanuel said. 'Their king has called them and they will come.'

King Charles turned his back on his army and, accompanied by his officers including Sir Francis, made for the castle.

But the men they so desperately needed did not come, not enough of them anyway, which was why Sir Francis, lately made a Colonel of Horse by King Charles himself, had ordered Mun and Emmanuel, yet to be placed in a troop, to ride out amongst the nearest towns and villages and gauge the mood of the people.

'Better to use a neat hammer and strike the nail

true than a rock and see it bent,' Sir Francis had said, meaning the two of them would have a better chance of perceiving men's willingness to fight than would a company of infantry marching through the streets beating the muster drum.

So on the fifth day, Mun and Emmanuel rode some seven miles north to Hucknall Torkard. Lying in a valley on ground rising towards the north and west, sloping south-east and watered by a lively brook flowing to the River Leen, Hucknall Torkard was typical of those towns that still clung to the open-field form of farming. Champion lands bristling with crops and thick with woodland surrounded a great cluster of habitation that could potentially field, according to the King's officers, at least five hundred good fighting men, perhaps more still.

It was Friday and market day and Mun hoped also to get some measure of what quantity of provisions the town could rightly be expected to yield up for His Majesty's army. Certainly there was plentiful grain from the looks of the carts laden with golden sheaves that were coming in from the fields.

They rode leisurely along the main thoroughfare up towards the town square, keen to appear at their ease and thus observe Hucknall Torkard in its natural state rather than to agitate folk who must be every day expecting the King's men to come recruiting. They had dressed simply, too, for the same reason, though both were armed, Emmanuel with his wheellocks and Mun with his prized possessions: a fine pair of pistols whose lock-plates were engraved with the name of their maker, the renowned London gunsmith William Watson. They had been a gift from his mother the night before he,

Emmanuel and Sir Francis had left Shear House for York to answer the King's call. The pistols were similar, Mun knew, to another pair that Sir Francis had owned, a pair of man-killers twenty-six inches long which had gone missing around the time of Martha's death. And though none had spoken much of it, Mun knew full well who now carried those weapons. Wherever he might be.

They wore swords too, slung from buff-leather baldricks so that their hilts rested against their left thighs. Perhaps the folk of Hucknall Torkard did not fear these two strangers had come recruiting for King Charles, but they did see their fine mounts, their weapons and the other accoutrements of highborn gentlemen, and so they doffed their hats and some of the women curtsied, and all scrambled out of their way, as far as was possible on market day. For the streets were thronging with townsfolk, swelled further by those come from nearby villages. Mun felt the warm August air itself – thickened and hazed as it was by floating chaff from the threshing – thrum with the excitement of the market. Cobblers, tailors, coopers and leatherworkers plied their trades from open-fronted stalls. Wool-merchants, fruit-sellers, fishmongers, butchers and bakers yelled in lilting, sing-song voices, entreating folk to examine their fragrant wares. Dogs yapped and fought over scraps, children ran wild, threading nimbly through the crowds, released for a few hours from the grain harvest, and livestock lowed and bleated, excited to be turned out onto the common fields to feed on the stubble and leavings.

'Sir Francis was right,' Emmanuel said, his dark eyebrows arched above kindly hazel eyes, 'these folk are too busy making money to think of making war.'

Mun rubbed Hector's poll just between his ears and the stallion snorted contentedly, for they had pulled up to wait behind a wool cart that had spilled seven or more of its bales. The merchant and his two young sons were frantically trying to reload the cart, ignoring the insults some hurled their way, yet clearly nervous to be holding up two armed and mounted gentlemen.

'Reports have it that the rebels have left London,' Mun said, raising a palm affably towards the merchant to show that he was in no rush. 'These folk and others like them must be brought to the King's standard without delay else we run the risk that they will go over to Essex.'

One of the oxen yoked to the cart was bellowing furiously, its ill-temper likely to have caused the accident in the first place, Mun suspected.

'They would not dare,' Emmanuel blurted as though the very idea was preposterous.

Mun thought about it, then shrugged. 'Maybe not,' he admitted. 'But Father says that if we can raise a proper army, twenty thousand or more, it may be enough to win without a shot being fired. The rebels would piss their breeches and beg His Majesty's forgiveness.'

Ahead, the boys hefted the last bale back onto the pile and the man gave a 'Heya!', yanking on the reins to get the oxen moving again.

'But we don't want the rebels to abandon their treachery, do we,' Emmanuel said through a mischievous grin, 'not before we've bloodied their noses. A disobedient dog must be beaten.'

Mun half smiled but said nothing. In truth he was not sure what he wanted. Certainly there was part of him that welcomed this fight. He had trained with sword and pistol from a young age. Under Sir Francis's guidance he had become an excellent horseman and knew he could outride most men. The thought of riding against His Majesty's enemies thrilled him. He could just imagine Essex's apprentices fleeing for their lives before a full-blooded cavalry charge. And yet there was another part of Mun that knew war was no game, that it maimed and ruined men. That it brought destruction and despair.

And so he decided to do what his mother would surely do were she, like him, caught in two minds. He would ask God.

'That looks to me a good place to start,' Emmanuel said, nodding across the street beyond a noisy crowd that was gathering to watch a cockfight, and Mun guessed his friend was referring not to the smoke-belching smithy or the brewhouse, but rather the Dancing Bear alehouse that sat between them. Two buxom women with loose curls falling to their pale, half-covered bosoms stood outside hefting cups which they swept after by-passers, inviting them to taste 'the sweetest ale in all of England'.

'There is somewhere I must go first,' Mun said, 'but buy me a pint of that if it is good and cold and I'll be there soon.'

Emmanuel frowned and for a heartbeat Mun resented having to explain himself, but then, Emmanuel would be family soon. So he nodded ahead, drawing his friend's eye above the bustling crowds before them. 'I must visit the church,' he said. Three hundred yards away, overlooking the thronging town square and its commerce like a silent witness to Man's greed, stood the church of St Mary Magdalene. 'I've heard it said that the tower was built in the eleven hundreds,' he added, the implied reason for his wanting to visit preferable to the truth.

But Emmanuel did not take the bait and smiled knowingly. 'If there was ever a time to make amends,' he said, rolling his eyes Heavenward, 'it's now. Before the fighting starts. Say a prayer for Bess and me,' he said, then hoisted an invisible mug into the air, 'and I'll make an offering to the old Roman gods. Just in case.' And with that he pressed with his right knee and flicked the reins, wheeling his mount off the road, towards the Dancing Bear. 'Make it a good prayer!' he called, still holding the invisible libation.

'Aye, I'll pray that that ruin of a house you're building doesn't fall in on your heads,' Mun called after him through the warm, clamour-filled August air.

At the church, Mun dismounted and gave a boy and girl a farthing each to look after Hector, then he stood in the shadow of the tower, allowing his eyes to be drawn up to the narrow pointed window arches, higher still to the merlons and crenels of its crown and then the bright blue sky beyond. Then he lifted the latch on the ancient oak door and went inside, closing it behind him so that the sharp noise of the chaos beyond faded to an ocean's murmur.

The church was cool, dark and empty, the last hardly surprising on market day. It had stood here for five hundred years. And will be here when the merchants, traders and craftsmen pack away their goods and take down their boards, Mun thought. It will be here when we are all in the grave.

If he had not been alone Mun might have removed his weapons and left them outside. But then leaving

Hector with strangers – children at that – was one thing. Giving them charge of his pistols and sword was quite another. Besides which, he had come to talk to God about war and a righteous war too, and so in some ways it seemed to him fitting that he should come to the Lord's House bearing the arms he might soon use to discharge his duty; to protect his king whose right to rule derived directly from God's will.

He walked down the nave and chose a stall on the north aisle that was partly washed in pale light from a small window, and there he knelt, letting the light bathe his face, his clenched hands resting on a low shelf in front of him. For a moment he let the radiance warm his eyelids, then he opened them. Beside the window was a fresco the likes of which the Puritans had been defacing all over England. But this one was perfect and when Mun recognized the scene it portrayed, a shiver of portent ran up his spine. It showed the Prodigal Son returning to his father. The son was kneeling, his hands stretched up to his father whose arms were open to receive him. And yet, far from joyful, both faces looked full of sorrow.

'Where are you, brother?' he whispered, watching motes of dust shimmer and swirl within the shaft of light crossing his gaze. Then he put his forehead to his knuckles, closed his eyes and prayed. He prayed to God to give him courage to do his duty if it came to a battle. He prayed that his father and Emmanuel would come through unscathed. He prayed that it might not come to battle at all, but even in the weaving of the prayer he felt the snag of that thread, knew the Lord could see through the tapestry to the man beyond. For, deep in his heart, faint enough that Mun hoped God might not hear it (yet knew that He did), beat the drum of war.

For a while he lost himself in his thoughts, some of which had strayed from the path of prayer, for which he felt vaguely guilty, but then something hauled him back to the present so that he felt the cold stone flag beneath his knees and the indentations in his forehead made by the bony knots of his fingers. A sound. Or rather a change in the sound. The ocean murmur of the market of which he'd been only faintly aware had altered in pitch, like a pot of water rising from a simmer to a rolling boil.

Mun cocked his head, his ears straining to untangle the sounds that were louder yet nevertheless dampened by the thick dressed stones of St Mary Magdalene's church. Screams, he knew with chill certainty. Women. But horses too.

Surely it was not possible that Essex's army could have come this far north already! He strode back down the aisle, his boots scuffing loudly against the cold flags, and lifted the latch, pulling the big door open and stepping out. Into chaos.

Men and women were running in all directions. No, not all directions, he realized, but north and south mainly, into the messuages, the residential plots and gardens, and up the alleys between, to get off the main street. Market stalls were toppled and fruit and vegetables, cups and platters and countless other goods littered the ground. Then he saw what was making the folk of Hucknall Torkard scatter and flee like mice from a swooping owl. Riders, and lots of them, coming up the main street at a trot, blades unsheathed and glinting in the late afternoon sun.

Hector was waiting where he had left him, tossing

his head nervously at the commotion. The young boy, it seemed, had run away but the little girl with the fiery red hair, no more than twelve years old, had not. She stood wide-eyed, one small white hand clutching the stallion's bridle, the other stroking his muzzle to soothe him.

'Thank you, my lady,' Mun said, affecting a bow and smiling as he took the reins from her. 'Now run home,' he said, scooping another coin from his purse and pressing it into her little palm. She grinned up at him, delighted more by his bow, he knew, than the farthing, then she curtsied neatly, turned and ran fleet as a hare up a narrow street between St Mary's and what Mun guessed was the minister's house.

When he turned back the riders had reached the north side of the town square and there they swarmed in a mass of horseflesh, blades and bright feathered plumes, skilfully weaving their mounts between the traders' stalls and each other.

'Not Essex's men,' Mun murmured, judging their attire far too rich and their horses too well bred for them to be the apprentices and trained bands of London, Surrey and Middlesex. And yet, some men of substance *had* thrown in their lot with Parliament. Nobles such as Henry Mordaunt, Earl of Peterborough, William Russell, Earl of Bedford, Edward Montagu, Viscount Mandeville, and more besides.

A hail of pistol and carbine fire shredded the hazy afternoon as some of the cavalry discharged their weapons at the blue sky. Mun glanced across the street to where men and women were pouring from the Dancing Bear, but he did not see Emmanuel.

'Who are these wild gentlemen?' someone beside him

asked in a voice reed-thin with alarm. He turned to regard a lean, elderly man whose bushy silver brows arched either side of a long pointed nose.

'The King's men,' Mun said, sure now that the riders could be no other.

'The answer to your prayers by any chance, young man?' the minister – for Mun was sure that's who the man was – asked suspiciously, removing his hat to run a claw-like hand through some stubborn strands of sweaty grey hair that lay across his peeling, liver-spotted scalp. So Mun had not been alone in the church, he realized.

'Nothing to do with me, rector,' Mun said, though the minister looked far from convinced.

'A man brings pistols into my church, then soldiers ride into town firing their carbines and scattering my flock . . . and you, sir, expect me to believe that you and they are not in league?'

'Get inside your church, rector, and lock the door,' Mun said curtly, for some of the riders were spurring their mounts towards them. And those riders had not sheathed their blades.

'I will do no such thing!' the minister replied. 'The people of Hucknall Torkard have nothing to fear from His Majesty! You may be assured of that, young man.'

Mun glanced round to see that they were no longer alone. A dozen or more of the townsfolk had gathered around them. Men and women, merchants and farm labourers clustered anxiously, clutching their hands, frowning, asking of their neighbours what was happening, or giving of their own ideas. Mun knew they had been drawn to their church, or their minister, or both, for their symbolic authority. Their protection. And whilst he admired them for not vanishing like musket smoke as the others had, he thought them fools, too, for there was much to fear from armed strangers who would wilfully disrupt a royally granted market. Men who thought nothing of wasting powder and ball on the empty sky.

Of the ten or so riders who had come as far as the church, one walked his enormous chestnut mare right up to them and took a cursory glance at the tower's apex behind them, then sheathed his sword. He was proud-looking, verging on haughty, and his curled locks and coiffured moustaches and beard were perfectly formed despite the afternoon's exertions.

'Why have the men of this town ignored the summons of His Royal Majesty King Charles?' the man asked through a twist of lips. 'We are at war, damn your eyes! And yet you hold your market? Are you traitors?'

'We are no traitors!' a man exclaimed, stepping out from the crowd on Mun's right. A leatherworker by the looks of the tools in the sack slung across his hips, he was short and ruddy-faced and either brave, or a fool.

The rider glared at the leatherworker and Mun saw blood-lust in his eyes, knew the man for a hunter who sought his kill at the chase's end.

'The folk of Hucknall Torkard have never broken our faith with the King! Not this king or his father before him!' the man shouted, stirring a chorus of ayes from the crowd which was growing bolder now, inspired by their new spokesman.

'We are loyal subjects,' the minister agreed, 'and you trespass, sir! You break the law by threatening honest folk exercising their right to hold a market here in this town.'

'Threaten?' the horseman clamoured. 'You count a few shots into the sky threats, rector?' He smiled but there was no joy in his eyes. 'This, sirrah, is a threat!' And with that he spurred his mare forward and the crowd edged back in panic, but for the minister and the leatherworker. And Mun. The rider swung his blade, smacking the flat of it against the leatherworker's head, and he dropped like a stone to the baked clay earth.

Mun wanted to move, to either run or fight, but he could not. His muscles gripped his bones, paralysing him, and he stood there uselessly, his right hand clutching Hector's reins, his left gripping the rapier's hilt at his hip.

'How dare you attack us?' the minister challenged the cavalry officer, even daring to step closer to man and beast. 'What is your name, you devil?'

Some of the other riders laughed at this, seemingly enjoying the fear on the faces before them. Their horses neighed and whinnied, their blood running hot.

'My name is Captain Nehemiah Boone,' the officer announced proudly, 'of His Highness Prince Rupert's Royal Horse. And you, sir,' he spat, 'are a traitor!'

'I say again we are no traitors!' the minister declared. No one had dared move to the aid of the leatherworker who lay motionless. But still alive, Mun was almost sure. 'I will answer His Majesty the King myself. Let him judge what we are,' the churchman said.

Nehemiah Boone seemed to consider this for a moment, then he glanced at one of his men who still brandished a carbine that was cocked and ready to tear a hole in a man.

'Silver plate,' Boone announced. 'Bring me what you

have and I will speak favourably for . . .' he looked around at the abandoned stalls, 'this nest of vipers.'

'You are here to pillage God's House?' The minister was incredulous, his brows knitted together, mouth hanging open.

'The King's army needs arms. Powder and shot,' Boone said tiredly, as though he'd had to explain this numerous times before. 'Loyal men need food in their bellies to fight the rebels. Horses need fodder. Who should pay for the defence of the realm if not the people it protects? You who prosper in the munificent shadow of your sovereign lord.'

Through the gaps that opened and closed as these riders controlled their mounts Mun could see the rest of Boone's men. They had dismounted, some holding the horses whilst others scavenged amongst the deserted stalls, stuffing all manner of goods into sacks. It was an odd sight to Mun's eyes, these gaily plumed gentlemen rapaciously plundering vegetables and grain, linen, leather and iron work; buckles, strap ends and spring clips.

Their curiosity having to some extent overcome their fears, the folk of Hucknall Torkard had been drawn back to the fray and now watched helplessly from the edges of the market.

'You are common thieves!' the minister said, trembling with rage now, his hat clutched over his chest. 'You shall not enter my church, Nehemiah Boone. For you are a disgrace to your master. You are a coward, sir!'

In the shadow of his broad hat Boone's eyes bulged and his lips pulled back from a predator's teeth.

'Hold your tongue, traitor!' one of Boone's men

yelled, drawing his sword and spurring his mount forward. The minister shrieked and raised his arms across his face just as Mun stepped in front of him and grabbed the beast's bridle, twisting it down and to the right. The horse screamed and sidestepped and came crashing to the ground, trapping its horrified master. He was screaming now, his leg likely broken, and some of the other riders dismounted to help their friend whilst Boone hauled his belt-hung carbine up from his right side and pointed it at Mun.

'Holster your carbine, sir!' someone ordered. It was Emmanuel, who stood behind Boone pointing both of his wheellocks at the captain.

'No, Emmanuel!' Mun yelled, too late, as another of Boone's men came up behind Emmanuel and smashed a sword hilt into the back of his head. Emmanuel staggered and fell to the ground, one of the pistols discharging harmlessly.

'On your knees, dog!' a massive corporal with a bright yellow feathered plume yelled beside Mun. The Hucknall folk had seen enough and were scurrying off, like rats from a kicked nest. Then a grey-haired, raw-boned soldier stepped in and rammed the butt of his carbine into Mun's stomach, doubling him over. Desperately Mun tried to suck air into his screaming lungs, then Yellow Plume cracked a fist against his temple and all of a sudden blows were raining down on him and it was all he could do to keep his feet as he clasped his fingers at the back of his head, his forearms taking some of the blows aimed at his face. But then hands gripped his arms, hauling them wide, and instinctively he dropped his chin to his chest as a fist hammered against his forehead and he heard finger bones snap. The next fist slammed into his mouth, bursting his lower lip in a spray of blood.

'This is a fine horse, Captain,' a soldier said, taking hold of Hector's bridle and patting his thick neck.

'Take your hands off him,' Mun snarled, blood flying from his mouth.

'Shut your mouth!' Yellow Plume said, ramming a fist into Mun's tortured guts.

'Teach the cur what we do to enemies of the King!' someone hollered.

'In the name of God, stop!' the minister yelled despite the wicked point of a rapier that was wavering an inch from his throat. 'Show some mercy, you devils!'

Something struck Mun behind his knees and his legs buckled but he did not hit the ground because someone still gripped him by the shoulders.

'Don't go down,' a big man growled into his ear, 'they'll kick you to death.' Yet, he was too weak to try to stand again and so sagged pathetically against this soldier's huge chest, dazed and bleeding and beaten. He was hazily aware of Nehemiah Boone dismounting and striding towards him, removing his riding gloves, which he clasped in his left hand whilst balling his right.

'Turn him round, O'Brien,' Boone commanded, at which Mun was brought face to face with the man.

Boone stood before him and glared for several heart-beats, then grinned savagely, drew back his arm across his chest and released it, cracking the back of his open hand across Mun's right cheek. No breaking of knuckles for Captain Nehemiah Boone.

A flash of white-hot light filled Mun's world, then scalding pain that made his head spin.

'You're a bloody fool, Captain,' he spat, 'if you think

this is the way to bring men to the King's army.' Behind Boone two of his men hauled Emmanuel to his feet and restrained him, though he looked barely conscious.

'And what would you know, sir?' Boone sneered, raising his hand to strike again.

'Knock the cur's head off, Captain,' the big corporal growled, gripping a shortened but wicked-looking halberd.

'Hold, Captain!' someone yelled from the back of an enormous mare that was white as fresh snow and trotting neatly up the market square towards the church. A large hunting poodle, as white as the mare, ran alongside yapping orders of his own. 'Stand off, Captain Boone!'

Boone spat on the ground by Mun's feet, then stepped away, gesturing for the men holding Mun to do the same. They did and Mun fell to his knees; his head sagged so that phlegmy blood dangled in strings from his nose and mouth to his chest. He wanted to curl up on the ground, to cradle his pain-racked body and address each hurt, giving each the attention it craved, but his pride would not let him. And so he grimaced and climbed to his feet, expecting another blow.

'Who are you?' the newcomer asked, gesturing at Mun to lift his chin so that he might see his face better. For some reason he did not understand, Mun obeyed and lifted his head, locking eyes with this handsome rider whose curls and feathers mirrored his horse's elaborately luxuriant mane. And then, despite the pain and humiliation and the hunger for revenge, Mun laughed, at which Boone and his men looked to each other with confused frowns and shrugs.

'You find something amusing, sir?' the man on the

white horse asked, a half smile playing at his own lips.

'I am sorry, Your Highness,' Mun said, 'it's just that I had not thought I would meet you quite like this.' He dragged a sleeve through the wet gore on his face, his tongue probing for broken or loose teeth.

'You know me?' the handsome man asked, cocking his head to one side.

'Your Highness, yes I know you,' Mun said, relieved that he had lost no teeth. 'You are Prince Rupert of the Rhine, Duke of Cumberland and General of His Majesty's Horse.'

Prince Rupert smiled. 'My family call me Robert le Diable. Rupert the Devil,' he said, his accent German in the main but cut with other flavours too, 'which is altogether much less of a mouthful. A soldier's name. For a soldier.'

'Your Highness's men have acted most dishonourably,' the minister announced, 'no better than common brigands. They are thieves and scoundrels.'

Prince Rupert waved the accusation away with a gauntleted hand. 'Save your hyperbole for the pulpit, sir. We are at war,' he said, glancing at the unhorsed man who had been dragged off to the side and was being plied with wine to numb his pain. 'What should be of more concern to you is my uncle's disappointment that so few of your townsmen have come to help him put down this vile rebellion. If you are slow to do your duty, we who obey our king must take matters into our own hands.'

'Your Highness!' the minister blurted, but was silenced by the Prince's raised hand.

'Well, sir,' Prince Rupert said, turning back to Mun, a note of intrigue playing across his lean, long face.

Mun guessed the Prince was but a year or two older than he. 'Who are you and why did you attack one of my men?' Those lips that seemed to be fixed in a knowing smile twitched again. 'I dare say it was you that unhorsed that poor fellow. Or was it your friend with the wheellocks?' He thumbed back towards Emmanuel, who was bleeding from his head. 'I will not believe the good minister here put a King's man on his arse.'

This day has not gone as planned, Mun thought, beginning to wish he had forgone his prayers for a few pints of cool ale in the Dancing Bear.

'My name is Edmund Rivers, Your Highness,' he said, 'and my father is Sir Francis Rivers, a friend of His Majesty the King your uncle, and recently made a Colonel of Horse. He serves in the King's Lifeguard.' The Prince's keen, intelligent eyes widened then, but in his peripheral vision Mun saw Captain Nehemiah Boone scowl.

'My uncle's show troop,' the Prince said. 'Fine-looking soldiers.'

Mun ignored the barely veiled insult. He had had enough trouble for one day.

'MacCarthy's leg is broken, sir,' Boone said. 'This . . . gentleman took hold of his bridle and pulled his horse down upon him.'

Prince Rupert's dark eyebrows arched. 'Did he indeed?'

'That man was about to strike me down,' the minister put in, pointing at the trooper with the broken leg whose pain-racked face was sheened in sweat. 'This young man, Edmund Rivers, saved my life.'

'He broke MacCarthy's leg!' Boone protested. 'Could have killed him.'

'Nevertheless, Captain, a neat trick to bring down a

horse of that size. But then my uncle has spoken of Sir Francis Rivers's mastery of manège,' he said, looking back to Mun. 'It would appear the son has inherited the father's gift with horses.'

'It takes but little skill to lie a horse down,' Mun replied, thinking how unlikely it was, though not impossible, that word of his father's love of manège should have reached the Prince's ear. 'I am sure Your Highness knows horses as well as any man,' he said, tasting blood but not wanting to spit in the Prince's presence.

'It is true I have inherited my mother's affinity for animals,' the Prince said, glancing at his white dog, which was sitting obediently, looking up at its master. 'Did you know, Edmund Rivers, that I have domesticated a hare and taught it to follow me at heel?'

'If only your men showed such dutifulness,' Mun dared, glaring at Captain Boone.

'Insolent dog,' Boone snarled.

The corner of the Prince's mouth twitched, his brown eyes fixed on Mun.

'Perhaps you could demonstrate whatever skill you do possess, Master Rivers,' he said, gesturing over to Hector who was still in the custody of one of Boone's men.

'Your Highness?' Mun said, wincing at the pain in his side that sharpened with each breath. He would have put money on it that that damned carbine butt had cracked a rib.

'You have robbed me of a good man, Rivers,' the Prince said. 'If you prove yourself as good as or better than MacCarthy, I will take you into my troop as recompense. You will serve under Captain Boone. I shall arrange it with your father.'

'I don't want him, sir!' Boone blurted.

Again that flap of the royal hand. 'Well, Rivers? Will you show us some rare horsemanship? Or have Captain Boone's . . . attentions left you too sore to ride?'

Mun could no more ignore that challenge than he could demand the King's General of Horse have his men return to the folk of Hucknall Torkard all that they had stuffed into their bulging sacks. And so he stood taller, gritting his teeth against the many pains.

'With Your Highness's leave,' he said, bowing neatly.

Prince Rupert smiled and nodded and Captain Nehemiah Boone curled his lip in disgust. Released by a royal nod, Emmanuel winced and rubbed the back of his head and watched. MacCarthy cursed and moaned and drank to numb the pain whilst the other soldiers continued procuring assistance from the traders and merchants and good townsfolk against the Earl of Essex's rebels. The minister protested boldly, if carefully, but was ignored by all except the Prince's white poodle, Boy, who yapped at him tirelessly.

And Mun Rivers whispered in Hector's ear, mounted with practised ease, and prepared to ride.

CHAPTER THIRTEEN

'THEY SAY HE IS IMPOTENT,' MATTHEW PENN SAID, 'AS likely to get it up as Trencher here is to be made the next Marquis of Argyll.' Will Trencher's mother was Scottish, which accounted for Trencher's self-professed ability to put any man down with just one punch, for the Scots were proper fighters, born warriors, or so he was fond of reminding them. Penn took one hand off the reins and turned it palm up as though weighing something invisible in it. 'Must have balls the size of crab apples and twice as sour,' he went on, grinning devilishly.

'Which explains why the bastard always looks so bloody miserable,' Trencher said from the saddle of a heavy, plodding mare, chosen, he claimed, for her big heart and great strength, but really, Tom suspected, because she'd come cheap. But Trencher had a point about Essex. Now that Tom thought about it, he had never seen the general smile. He had heard the story of how the earl's marriage to the flighty Frances Howard, daughter of the Earl of Sussex, had been annulled on the grounds of non-consumption. Essex's second wife,

Frances Powlett, had turned out to be no more faithful and some whispered that she'd ridden further than her soldier husband, though not on any horse. But whilst his women had been cavorting, Robert Devereux Earl of Essex had been fighting, in the Netherlands and at Cadiz, and John Pym's Parliament valued his military experience, needed his vast personal fortune even more, perhaps. Which was why the earl had marched out of London at the head of an army called into existence by Parliament's Committee for Defence, and why Tom Rivers found himself riding north with men such as Penn and Trencher and, some said, ten thousand others.

No, Tom had never seen Essex smile, but it was entirely possible, Tom thought, that the men he now rode with said the same thing about him. Penn had taken to calling him Black Tom on account, he had said, of the ill-humoured scowl he believed must have been carved into Tom's face as an infant. 'You call yourself a Scotsman, Will,' Penn had said, 'but young Tom here could out-misery you six days out of seven.'

Not that Tom cared what men thought of him. Essex's sergeants had ploughed through the inns and alehouses, the churches, guilds and offices of Southwark, recruiting men to fight for the safety of the King's person and the defence of both Houses of Parliament. Together they would defeat His Majesty's feckless advisors, his Cavaliers and the papist forces that sought to subvert him. They would free the people from tyranny. As for these things Tom cared little and yet he had joined up with Penn and Trencher and their friends and they had asked but few questions of him other than could he ride and shoot and preferably do both together, to which Tom had answered that he doubted any man could do so better, though he had thought of his brother at that moment.

For what Tom needed was vengeance. Vengeance for Martha. For himself. He craved and thirsted and only the blood of his enemies would satiate him.

And now he found himself in a rag-tag army marching north. To give battle.

'We are a rabble, I'll not deny it. But by God, we are a frightening sight!' Penn said, twisting round in the saddle to take in the massive column of horse and foot regiments, the artillery and baggage trains hauled ever northwards by oxen, horse and mule. A smart troop of horse had joined them in Northampton. Good riders all and well kitted-out with firelocks, breastplates and helmets, they had been raised in Cambridge, Tom had heard, by an officer called Cromwell. There were hundreds of soldiers of fortune too, men who had taken Parliament's shilling and whose knowledge of war would be invaluable and inspiring, so said Penn, when the shooting started. But as yet they were a loose collection of regiments whose parts were more impressive than the whole. In Tom's mind Essex's army was like a stallion that would need to be broken before you could be certain it would jump the ditch and not halt on the edge and throw you off.

Trencher, it seemed, agreed. 'Too many pressed men,' he said in his gruff voice, dragging his shirt's sleeve across the sweat-soaked slab that was his face. 'I'd wager we'll lose fifty or more every night,' he added, then raised a thick finger. '*If* I was given to the sin of gambling. Which I ain't. They'll bugger off at the first opportunity.' His hat hung from his saddle and sweat was running in rivulets down his bald head, wetting his stained collar. 'But we have God on our side, boys, and God is a Scotsman. Which is why we shall scatter our enemies like chaff in the wind.'

'Well said, William,' Penn announced cheerily, raking a hand through his shorn hair and raising it into spiky tufts so that what little breeze there was might cool his scalp. 'Let those with the stomach for the fight march on with faith in their hearts. Let those with pale livers go back to their meaningless lives for we need them not. Besides,' he added, winking at Trencher but nodding towards Tom, 'we have Black Tom and his fine, fearsome pistols.' But Tom did not take the bait. He swayed gently in the saddle, hardly touching the reins, letting Achilles choose his own way along the well-worn road that was pitted with dips and holes. The loose fit of his shirt and doublet was a constant reminder that he had become thin and drawn, but he had not let Achilles starve and the beast was as strong as ever, his black coat lustrous, his mane thick and healthy. Tom had seen men look enviously at Achilles. Knew they wondered how an ill-dressed wretch could own such a horse. He cared not what they thought.

After a few moments of silence Penn sighed. 'Truly I cannot see what Ruth Gell saw in you, Tom. A cheery wench like that. There are rocks with more mirth than you. I've laughed more at Shakespeare's tragedy of King Lear than I do in your company.'

'Leave the lad alone, Matthew,' Trencher said, taking a long draught from an ale skin before leaning out of his saddle and passing the skin to Tom. 'So long as he fights, he need not be a bloody jester too. We've all got our reasons for taking the shilling, the lad here just like the rest of us.'

'Quite so, Will,' Penn said, 'only, Tom has never so much as told us his father's name, let alone how it is that he rides the finest horse in Essex's damned army, owns expensive pistols and a pretty sword and yet became a guest of the Leaping Lord. Not to mention a conscientious student of hard drinking.'

Trencher frowned and a tributary of sweat was channelled to run off the end of his bulbous nose. September was just a few days away but it was hot enough that the air above the fields either side of the road seemed to shimmer like water. 'Aye, Penn's got a point there, lad. I've never seen you praying, neither, not that I'd take you for a God-fearing man even if I had.' He hawked up a gobbet of phlegm and spat it onto the dry ground. 'Why have you come?'

But Tom gave no answer. He glanced down at the polished, flared handles of his father's firelock pistols holstered either side of his saddle. And he hungered for the killing to start.

Mun looked up at the grey sky, felt a fat raindrop splash on his cheek and cursed. He wished he was wearing a buff-coat like some of the others in Boone's troop, for the tough leather would keep the rain off much better than the steel back- and breastplate he now wore over his tunic. Little brown spots of rust were already beginning to appear even though he had cleaned and oiled the plates just three days earlier. But the harquebus armour had belonged to MacCarthy, in whose place Mun now rode, and he had been obliged to purchase it along with the man's three-barred pot helmet as recompense for breaking his leg – and, moreover, 'for denying the man the honour of serving his king', as the

Prince himself had put it, forcing a sombre look onto his face in front of Nehemiah Boone and the rest of the troop. And so Mun had bought the man's gear, paying over the odds at five pounds but hoping the generous price might go some way to lessening the hostility he still felt from the other men, despite having trained and ridden with them for several weeks now. But that had been a foolish hope, he realized, and he wished he'd only paid MacCarthy four.

That day in the market place at Hucknall Torkard Mun knew he had made an enemy in Nehemiah Boone. Like most of the highborn, wealthy men in Boone's troop, the captain was used to getting his own way and if it had been up to Boone, Mun knew, MacCarthy's broken leg would have been redressed with a rare beating. Maybe even with Mun's death. Instead, Prince Rupert had rewarded Mun. At least, that was how Boone saw it. For Mun had been granted the privilege of riding with the Prince's own chosen men, thus the pride of the Royalist army.

And yet Mun had had no choice but to show his skill, to do his best in spite of the beating he had taken which had made the ride through the square agonizing to the point of being almost unbearable. He smiled now at the memory. Boone's men had jeered as Mun had mounted Hector and those jeers had smeared a grin onto the captain's face that Mun had wished he could wipe off with a well-placed fist. Instead, he had ignored the insults and he had whispered to Hector, telling his friend that he needed him now. Together they would show these pompous bastards. God damn Nehemiah Boone. And damn Prince Rupert, too, if he was playing some sort of game with him, expecting to see Sir Francis

Rivers's son fall from his horse because of some hurt, because he had been fool enough to stand up to them. Because he had lain a horse down and the animal had broken a man's leg.

He had done one circuit of the square at the trot, just to test that none of his bones was broken and to give Hector a taste of the course. Then he had pricked the stallion to a canter and together they had moved as one creature, weaving in and out of the stalls and the debris, as neat as the seam on a silk purse. But on the third circuit Mun raised the stakes. To the men watching it would have looked as though he would pass to the left of a trestle and board upon which were laid some felts which Boone's men had not wanted. But at the last moment Mun had spoken with his knees and a flick of the reins and Hector had turned and leapt the stall, Mun low against his back, and landed six feet clear and then jumped the next obstacle too before threading between a butcher's bloody board and the leatherworker's stall and breaking into a gallop across the hard ground back to the church.

A couple of Boone's men, the Irishman O'Brien for one, had cheered. Most, including Boone, had stayed silent. But Prince Rupert had laughed and his dog, Boy, had yapped, which had sounded like laughter. The Prince had laughed so hard that he had placed a hand on his belly and raised a palm in surrender. And it was then that Mun knew he wanted to ride for this man, the King's nephew. Damn Boone and all the others too, but he would ride for Rupert.

And now, at last, summer had slipped away and the sky was grey and heavy. And Mun's armour was rusting because he wore steel instead of buff-leather. And most of the other sixty-nine men in the troop hated him. And he was riding to war.

From Nottingham they had ridden at the head of the Royalist army south-west to Stafford and then on to Shrewsbury, their number swelling as the unseasonably gloomy sky swelled with cloud. At last, money was coming in too as the King's cause began to gather momentum and his wealthier supporters gave generously through loyalty or duty, or even as bargaining counters for future rewards.

Sir Francis and Emmanuel had been sorry to see Mun leave them to join Prince Rupert's men, but they also knew such an honour could not be spurned, so the three had vowed to meet regularly, at least whenever the army made proper camp.

'And we three shall soon ride home victorious and full of tales,' Mun had said, sensing disappointment in his father, who, though he might not show it, feared losing Mun as he had lost Tom. 'It will be a celebration to shake Shear House to its very foundations.'

'I trust we shall have the victory, Edmund,' his father had replied with a curt nod, 'and be home before Christmas and grow fat on venison sent from His Majesty for our service.' He had frowned then. 'But that will not happen unless we can bring this rebellion to an end . . .' he thrust a fist into an open palm, 'with one great blow. A troop of horse requires one-and-a-half tons of bread each month. The horses alone need thirteen-and-a-half tons of hay. War is the very worst kind of business to be in,' he had said gloomily, and Mun had felt disappointed in his father. He wanted Sir Francis to show a hunger for the fight. Had he not been a fine soldier in his day? Could he not ride and shoot better than most men half his age? For the first time in Mun's life he'd looked at his father and seen frailties, more perhaps in spirit than body.

And yet there were, Mun was beginning to see, more selfish motives at work too. There was more to it than simply wanting Sir Francis to share the thrill of the chase. After all, he had Emmanuel for that. No, he needed his father to be a hawk to ease his own conscience, to blunt the point of that spur that gouged his soul at the prospect of fighting against – killing – fellow Englishmen. *Father just needs to catch the fox's scent on the wind,* Mun thought. *And then we shall hunt.*

A horse whinnied, wrenching Mun from his thoughts as they rode along a ridge skirting a yardland of wheat stubble a mile south of Worcester. The King had sent his nephew to secure the city, for, among other reasons, Sir John Byron was heading there with a large amount of plate from Oxford, which would be smelted into coin to finance Charles's cause. However, on examination the Prince had concluded that Worcester could not be defended and the Royalists were withdrawing even as Essex's vanguard was scouting the approaches to the city.

Now Mun found himself two miles south of the city near a village called Powick. A musket-shot to his east flowed the Severn River. Ahead of them the Teme, a tributary of the Severn, snaked from the north-west. They rode in column, two abreast, with a great hedge of hawthorn, blackthorn, field maple and hazel on their left along which they now and then passed folk, girls and boys mostly, out gathering fruits and nuts. Within this ancient boundary hedge sheep, goats, fowl and some draught horses scavenged amongst the stubble, but these creatures were safe enough from Boone's men this day. The Prince himself rode at the head of the column, his orders to secure Powick Bridge and thus cover the Royalist rear. Behind Mun's column followed another nine hundred troopers, some three hundred of which were dragoons, mounted men who fought on foot as infantry, their job to break up enemy formations with musketry before the cavalry charged. In all it was a sizeable force of men armed with shot, steel and speed. His father's own troop was with the main army and the King, but Mun was glad to be where he was. Near the enemy. His eyes scoured the landscape for signs of Essex's rebels, in case any had been foolish enough to try to overtake them. And there was nowhere in all of England that Mun Rivers would rather be.

Damn this rain though.

'Ground's getting too bloody soft for cavalry,' the trooper riding next to Mun said. A raw-boned, grey-bearded man in his forties, Daniel Bard was one of the oldest men in Boone's troop. He had fought with the Prince on the continent, had ridden at the head of Rupert's rash – most said mad – cavalry charge at Vlemgo on the Weser four years before and, even more impressive, had survived it.

'It's those poor wretches in the artillery train I pity,' said the big, red-bearded man named O'Brien, riding just ahead, raising his voice above the hissing rain. O'Brien was the man who, when they were battering Mun at Hucknall Torkard, had warned him not to go down. The giant's advice had spared Mun a rare beating, though Mun had never thanked him for it. 'Those bastards have it the hardest,' the Irishman went on. 'I just hope they get the chance to rip the rebels to

212

wet shreds with their guns after dragging the buggers across half of England.'

The talk round the cookfire was that O'Brien's enormous buff-coat had been specially made for him at the equally enormous cost of fourteen pounds, but Mun thought it probably a fair price, for the thing looked tough enough to stop a ball from a cannon royal! More importantly right now, it was keeping the Irishman dry.

'You just keep your powder dry, O'Brien,' Boone called over his shoulder, 'and don't let that big Irish heart of yours bleed for those daft bastard gunners. They make a deal of noise and smoke and doubtless some of the rebels will piss down their legs at the sight of 'em, but those muddy whoresons don't win battles. We do.'

'Listen to Captain Boone, men,' the Prince, who was riding beside him, added, and Mun did not have to see the Prince's face to know that that infectious smile was on it. 'Done properly and with unswerving courage, a cavalry charge is a beautiful thing to behold, better still to be a part of it and see the fear in your enemies' eyes.'

Mun wondered if Hector was ready for battle, for the noise and the chaos. For the cannon. During the previous weeks he had done his best to get the stallion used to the smell of gunpowder by firing small trains of it in Hector's manger, at first a little distance from the horse, but repeating the process closer by degrees. He had done the same thing with firing his pistol and banging a blade against his breastplate, and he had even paid a drummer to beat out a rhythm in the stable to get Hector accustomed to the noise until eventually the horse would eat his oats from the drum head. Nehemiah Boone had said that it was an achievement for any raw trooper not to cut off his horse's ears when training to fight mounted, and Mun, who had his father to thank for his advanced skill in this regard, knew his commanding officer had not spoken in jest. Now Boone had them galloping up to an ancient set of harquebus armour hung on a pole and for the first fifty charges Hector would veer off at the last, Boone screaming that Mun would never ride in his troop until he could bend his mount to his will. But in the end and partly to Mun's horror, though he did not admit it, Hector would overthrow the obstacle and trample it viciously. But still Mun did not know how the horse would behave in a real fight; did not know how he himself would react, either, and feared shaming himself or proving a coward in front of the other men.

Something down amongst the nettles and brambles caught Mun's eye. A weasel stood tall on its back legs, a half-eaten blackberry in its paws as it watched the men and horses for a few moments before bounding off into the undergrowth. Run to your hole and hide, little one, he thought. Do not linger here, for war is coming.

'We will rest in yonder meadow!' the Prince called, pointing back the way they had come, beyond the hedged enclosures to the open meadow on the other side. To his front, three hundred paces further along the narrow road, stood Powick Bridge, its five stone arches spanning the River Teme, carrying the road southwards. 'Dragoons will take up positions behind these hedgerows either side of the road. Captain Boone, bring your troop across the river so that we may appreciate the terrain beyond.' Boy, the Prince's white poodle, echoed his master's orders with a salvo of shrill yaps as two officers peeled off and rode back down the column repeating Rupert's commands. Then the Prince led seventy men up onto the road and across the bridge, the horses' hooves scuffing and clopping on the stone.

Mun leant over his saddle to look down onto the slow-moving river and as he did so he saw the last dimples across its surface fade and vanish as the rain stopped. At that same moment a pale gold light broke from the heavens, washing over the bridge and the fields and the glistening hedgerows lining the road, so that Mun almost believed God had stopped the downpour because it was midday and the Prince wanted to take his ease.

After a brief reconnoitre of the open fields south of the Teme the Prince seemed satisfied and wheeled his horse round, leading them back across the bridge, from which a foggy vapour was rising in the warm sunlight. Yet Mun felt a slight shiver run up his spine as they funnelled back along the road between the two tall hedgerows, because he knew that beyond them now, hidden from his sight, were some three hundred dragoons armed with firelocks, wheellocks and carbines.

A little further and they left the road and joined the six hundred men who had dismounted and were removing their armour and their buff-coats, watering their mounts, smoking pipes and enjoying the feel of the sun on their faces.

And three miles away on the other side of the Teme, a force of one thousand horse under Colonel John Brown rode up the Severn River's western bank. Heading for Worcester.

CHAPTER FOURTEEN

MUN WAS WOKEN BY A FIERCE CRACKLING WHICH IN THE dream of a heartbeat ago had been a fire blazing in the grate of the parlour at Shear House. But as he pushed himself up from the breastplate and blanket he had been using as a pillow he knew the ragged barrage of cracks for what it was.

'On your feet, Rivers!' Captain Boone roared in his ear as Mun looked round, for a brief moment taking in the scene of men waking from a haze like himself, others frantically fumbling at the straps on breastplates, helmets and saddles, and still others who were mounted and wheeling their excited horses, trying to keep them under control.

He glanced up at the sun. Late afternoon.

'Bloody rebels are on top of us!' O'Brien said through a grin, his pale blue eyes wide with the thrill of it as his thick thumbs thrust the hooks through the eyes sewn down the inside of his great buff-coat.

'God bless the dragoons for giving them a proper welcome,' Vincent Rowe exclaimed, a smile on his handsome face as he hauled himself up into his saddle. 'Hope they leave some for us.'

Prince Rupert was mounted and yelling orders, the butt of his two-foot-long Dutch wheellock carbine resting on his thigh, his other hand loosely gripping the reins. His white mare seemed perfectly composed. *This is it*, Mun thought. *It is happening.*

Mun had just got his backplate in place when Daniel Bard walked his horse up. 'No time for that, lad,' the veteran said, leaning over to take hold of Hector's bridle. 'Up you get.' So Mun dropped the backplate and slung his baldrick over his right shoulder, the sword scabbard falling between his legs and almost tripping him as he snatched up his helmet with its woollen skullcap nestled inside. Then he thrust the pot down, fumbled at the thong beneath his chin, placed his left foot in the stirrup and pulled himself up whilst Daniel Bard held the stallion steady.

'Pistols loaded?' the veteran asked, nodding down at the two firelocks hanging either side of the front of Mun's saddle.

Mun tried to speak but his mouth was too dry so he nodded. Then Bard wheeled off and Mun gave Hector his heels and followed, trotting to join the loose mass of cavalry that eddied and swirled round Prince Rupert like fierce white water around a rock. Horses were moving their bowels with nerves and excitement, and Mun felt a sudden desperate urge to empty his own bladder. To their south towards the bridge, firearms cracked sporadically, the faint noise of battle, of horses whinnying and men shouting, growing louder with each passing moment.

'Do not fire until you are upon them!' Rupert yelled, his usual easy nature replaced by a savageness, teeth bared like a wolf's.

Or . . . a child of war. That was what Sir Francis had said of the Prince and only now did Mun truly understand what he'd meant by that. 'For King Charles and for God!' Rupert yelled, thrusting his carbine into the air, and with that he gave the mare his spurs and she screamed and surged forward, and a great roar went up as his men followed.

Mun filled with the mad, terrifying joy of the chase as he gripped with his knees to show Hector he was still in command, yet allowed the beast's herd instinct to drive them on through the press of horseflesh, riders, leather and steel. Somewhere in his mind something screamed, *Pull back! Let other men be the first. More experienced men.*

Instead he found his voice. 'Heya! Come on, Hector! Come on, boy!'

The hooves of six hundred galloping horses beat out a frantic, furious rhythm on the soft earth. Tack jangled and armour clanked and men dug their spurs in, yelling wildly, willing the battle frenzy to seize them in its maw where there is no terror, only madness.

Then suddenly, up ahead, the rebels broke through a gap in the hedgerow, flooding the meadow towards them, desperate to escape the narrow road and the murderous fire of the Royalist dragoons behind the hedges.

'Kill the traitors!' a man yelled.

'King Charles!' roared another.

Clods of mud and turf were flying past Mun and then he could see his enemies' faces, see them raising their pistols. Instinctively he drew inwards, dipped his head, teeth clenched hard enough to crack his jaw bones, as a ragged volley of flame, smoke and flying lead thundered maliciously. And he rode into that storm.

Smoke wreathed the rebels but Mun could see that they were panicking, some drawing blades, others desperately fumbling with spanners at their wheellocks, having yet to fire.

'King Charles!' Mun roared into the wind, filled with a feral elation because he had not been hit; no lead ball had ripped into his flesh and smashed his bones.

'For England!' someone beside him screamed. Then the men around Mun gave fire and so he drew and cocked one of his own pistols, pointed it at the enemy mass, the long barrel jolting, his aim wild, and pulled the trigger. Men on both sides fell back in their saddles or slumped sidewards, dropping their swords. Then before Mun could draw another weapon the two forces collided in a great crash like a wave thrown onto the shore, and men and horses screamed. Pistols spat flame and steel blades clattered off breastplates and helmets and chaos reigned. Something struck Mun's helmet and he tried to haul Hector back around but there was no room and so he snatched his righthand pistol from its saddle holster and shoved its barrel into the side of a rebel who twisted and glared with terrified eyes as Mun pulled the trigger and a ball plunged into the man's innards, erupting from his other side leaving a hole the size of a dining platter, and spraying shards of rib and gobbets of gore over the buff-coat of the man beside him.

Suddenly it was not a battle of hundreds against hundreds but of man against man, the wider conflict shrunken to personal fights, to brutal murder.

Mun shoved his pistol home and pulled his sword free, raising the blade to his face like a shield as he twisted this way and that, more desperate to avoid death than kill.

O'Brien swung his wicked poll-axe backhanded into a man's face, chopping it in half so that the chin, gaping mouth and nose hung on a hinge of bloody meat for several heartbeats before the man fell from his horse.

The Prince slashed left and right with his sword, his white mare gnashing her big teeth at other horses, biting and tearing ears and muzzles. A sudden spray of blood blinded Mun, burning his eyes and getting into his mouth. He panicked, dragging his left arm across his face and blinking through the gore. Then a blade swung at him and he only just got his rapier in the way. *Kill him!* his mind screamed. *A dead man cannot kill you!*

But his enemy was strong and fierce, his pockmarked face a snarl of hatred, and Mun suddenly knew this man was going to kill him. The rebel struck again, this time locking swords and driving Mun's down, and then Mun saw the pistol in the man's other hand. The barrel came up and the rebel grinned triumphantly. Just as Nehemiah Boone put his own pistol to the man's head and blew his brains out through a hole in his helmet. Then Boone twisted in the saddle and plunged his sword into a horse's neck and pulled it free and the beast screamed and tried to rear but there was no room in the press and its master could only cling on as blood pumped out in great gouts, spattering others.

'Easy, girl!' the man yelled, but the beast lurched and his three-bar pot helmet fell off, vanishing beneath thrashing hooves, and Mun saw the man properly. Grey-haired and kindly-looking. His father's age. 'Easy!' Grey Hair yelled. But the mare was screeching and her eyes were rolling and the man was helpless as Boone hacked into his exposed neck. And then again, all but severing his head so that the rebel slumped forward, the glistening gristle of his neck flooding gore across his mare's brown coat as man and beast died together.

Mun dug in his heels, willing Hector to surge deeper into the enemy mass, and the stallion responded, using his great strength to plough forward. Something struck Mun's helmet and he threw himself flat against Hector's neck but realized the sword blow had been the backswing of one of his own side. Then, above the clash of battle he heard galloping hooves.

'They are running!' someone roared. 'Bastard scum are running!'

Gaps were suddenly appearing amongst the maelstrom. The rebels were wheeling away, spurring back across the meadow south towards Powick Bridge.

'Kill them!' Boone screamed, his eyes wild and his face a warped grimace of hatred. Then he whipped his horse with the flat of his sword and chased after the retreating enemy. So Mun howled at the heavens, kicked with his heels and followed.

Bess Rivers placed both hands on her belly and closed her eyes, dismissing all senses but touch. The baby inside her had not kicked for three days now and she could see it in her maids' eyes that they thought her unborn child was dead. None of them had said as much, of course, but that was what they thought, and perhaps some of them were curious to know what Bess had done to cause the miscarriage. She knew all the stories, just

221

as everyone did. If you looked at an image of John the Baptist at the moment of conception your child would be born covered in thick hair. Gazing at a hare could give the child a hare lip. Bess had heard these stories, knew her imagination could act on the unborn child and cause terrible deformities, and she had been afraid of that because her imagination had always had wings, so that she could never know where it might fly. Still, she was sure she had not harmed the baby growing inside her. She had been so careful.

And yet the child had not stirred for days.

Move, little one, she silently pleaded. Please move. Kick for your mama. Just once and together we shall thank the Lord God with all our heart. How we shall thank Him.

Perhaps it was God that was punishing her, for she and Emmanuel should not have lain together out of wedlock. They should have waited. But he had been going off to war and that truth had cast a grim shadow which had eclipsed all else, including certain sins of the flesh.

She opened her eyes and they fixed on the spot on the parlour floor where Tom had laid poor Martha Green after he and Mun had found her hanged. Bess could see again Martha's bluish face and that swollen tongue. The unnatural twist of Martha's broken neck. She closed her eyes again, desperate to dispel the image for surely nothing good could come of such black thoughts. Please move, my child, she willed.

The parlour door opened and she snatched up the embroidery she had been working on, a sudden sense of guilt flooding her cheeks with heat.

'They are coming, Elizabeth,' Lady Mary said, her

green eyes locking with Bess's own, that gaze never falling to the swell of her belly. 'I will not bring them into the house but will walk them through the gardens. Will you take the air with us? It is warm out.'

'I should like that,' Bess said, smiling as her mother nodded curtly and left to receive their visitors.

Captain Miles Downing had written to Lady Mary expressing his wish to visit her at Shear House. Bess had since seen the letter herself, the hand confident yet neat. Restrained mostly, yet with little flourishes here and there, especially the signature. There were, Downing had written, pressing matters to be discussed in relation to Sir Francis and his siding against the legitimate Parliament and the God-fearing men and women of the kingdom.

'The rebels want Shear House,' Lady Mary had said, pressing the letter into her lap, her face stern and her teeth worrying her bottom lip. 'They want our money for their unlawful war.'

Bess had conjured an image of the King's enemies plundering and looting Shear House to buy more guns to use against Emmanuel and her brother. Against her father.

'Tell him you will not see him!' she had said, horrified. But Lady Mary had shaken her head.

'No, Bess. We will receive Captain Downing. Let him come here and declaim his treason. And let us prepare ourselves.' And with that Lady Mary had sat down at her husband's dark oak writing desk, picked up his quill and dipped it into his small, green-glazed inkwell, and had begun to write.

Now the rebels were here. An officer and his escort of ten mounted soldiers had come, though it appeared only the officer had been allowed through the gate into the grounds. The first thing that struck Bess when she saw Captain Downing talking with her mother in the rose garden was how handsome he was. For some reason, she realized now as she walked towards them, she had expected him to look somehow more . . . rebellious. His eyes would be full of malice. His whole posture would be one of belligerence and defiance, his lips gripped in sneering disapproval. Certainly he would not smile the way he was smiling now, this young man who swept his hat from his head and bowed neatly as she came up to them. He wore tall boots and a buff-coat criss-crossed with wide leather belts, one for his sword and the other for his firelock carbine which hung behind him, its butt above his right hip. His waist was bound by a sash of rich green silk.

'My daughter Elizabeth,' Lady Mary said, her own mouth taut as a knot.

'I am honoured, mistress,' Downing said, his dark eyes flicking down to her stomach then creasing slightly at the corners in empathy. 'May I ask when the baby is due?'

Bess did not want to answer him, did not want to share pleasantries with such as him, but those eyes told her that this man was recently a father. Or else his wife is also with child, she thought.

'I have several weeks yet,' Bess said, smiling in spite of herself.

The captain nodded appreciatively. 'May our Lord in heaven see you safely delivered of a healthy son. Or daughter,' he added with a charming smile.

Bess nodded in thanks.

'Now we may consider the formalities over, Captain,'

Lady Mary said sternly, 'and if it please you we shall know why you have come to Shear House.'

The soldier's face betrayed that Lady Mary's frankness had thrown him, but he recovered in a heartbeat.

'Very well, my lady,' he said, dipping his head, his hat clutched against his chest. 'Parliament regrets very sorely that your husband has joined His Majesty's army.'

'He does his duty to his king!' Lady Mary riposted, the unspoken *as should you* left hanging in the air like musket smoke.

Again the young man nodded but this time Bess saw a flash of flint in those brown eyes. 'Sir Francis and your son Edmund have taken up arms and declared war on the rightful authority that is this nation's Parliament. They do you and your daughter a disservice.'

'They do what is right, Captain Downing, and I would not have them do differently,' Lady Mary countered.

'They are traitors, madam!' Downing exclaimed, sweeping his hat through the air. 'And stand against the laws of God, nature and reason!' There was a silence then as Lady Mary examined the man before them. The captain glanced up at Shear House, then let his eyes range over the smooth green lawns, gravel paths and statues beyond the low circular wall of the rose garden.

He is taking an inventory, Bess thought. He is appraising all that they may steal from us.

'Perhaps you may yet take some small comfort, madam,' he said, eyes narrowed now, probing, 'that you have one son at least who serves his country. Master Thomas rides in Lord Feilding's Regiment of Horse in the Earl of Essex's Militia Ordinance. It is not common knowledge, certainly amonst his fellow troopers, but I have it on good authority, madam.' Downing glanced up at the rear of the house again, letting his news sink in, as though instinct had told him it *was* indeed news. Then he looked back to Lady Mary. 'I am confident that Thomas is a brave soldier and that he will impress his commander by his zeal for our righteous cause.'

Bess felt as though she had been struck. Her mother's face turned ashen behind the trembling hand pressed against her lips, and the young captain pushed his advantage. 'My lady, by order of Colonel Egerton of Parliament's army you must relinquish this house. You and your family and retainers will be given safe passage to wherever you choose, but you will not take your plate or any of your husband's possessions, though you may pack your personal effects and such victuals as you necessarily require.'

Bess looked to her mother, but Lady Mary's unblinking eyes were riveted to the captain as though daring him to repeat the news about Tom, to tell her again that her son had joined the rebels.

'You may leave now, Captain Downing,' Bess said, her fingernails digging into her palms, 'and you will not be welcome at Shear House again.'

'Mistress Elizabeth,' Downing said, turning square on to her, 'I must warn you that if you disobey Parliament's behest and shut your door against us we will return with men and arms. With cannon.'

Now Bess could find no words, had no riposte to such a fearful cut.

'Captain,' Lady Mary said, lifting her head, straightening her spine and drawing a deep breath. 'You must do what your conscience demands and we shall do the same.' The young officer opened his mouth to speak again but Lady Mary raised a long finger warning him to hold his tongue. 'Now go,' she rasped, 'before I have my men set the hounds on you. They have not been fed yet today,' she lied.

And with that Captain Downing's face drained of colour and he glanced at Bess and then back to Lady Mary. Then he bowed again, turned and marched away.

When he was out of sight, Lady Mary took Bess into her arms, and though Bess could not see her mother's face, she could feel the sharp, uneven rise and fall of her chest. She could sense the rebel captain's words eating into the reserves of her mother's strength and spirit, like weevils blighting the crop.

And inside herself she felt her baby kick.

CHAPTER FIFTEEN

RAIN STRUCK MUN'S TENT IN INTERMITTENT VOLLEYS, LIKE handfuls of gravel thrown against the canvas. The day had dawned bright and warm but as the sun rolled into the west the clouds had gathered, turning from white to the iron grey-brown of a breastplate, and with that had come rain. Again.

Mun·could not sleep, not for the sound of the rain or the usual hubbub of a camp at night, nor even because O'Brien, with whom he shared the tent along with Vincent Rowe, snored like a hog. Mun could not sleep because he felt sick in the pit of his stomach.

Behind him someone stirred. He lifted the candle from the letter towards the two prostrate figures shrouded in their blankets and, once assured they were still asleep, he turned his back on them and read the letter again.

A groom named Coppe, looking exhausted and half drowned, had appeared outside the tent an hour previously and handed Mun the letter that bore his father's seal, though Coppe's presence itself told Mun the letter was not from his father. Having sealed it with the ring Sir Francis had left her, Lady Mary had given the groom a blunderbuss for his own protection on the road and sent him to find her son with strict instructions not to return to Shear House until he had put the letter in Mun's hands. He had ridden one hundred miles to bring the letter here, to Prince Rupert's regiment camped in the Severn Valley ten miles south of Shrewsbury. Mun had asked Coppe how he had found him when it seemed even the Earl of Essex did not know their whereabouts. Coppe had shrugged his solid shoulders, pinched rainwater and snot from the end of his nose and replied that a deaf and blind man could have found the Prince's army. And it was for Coppe's simple honesty, Mun knew, that his mother had sent him, for the groom could be trusted implicitly not to read the letter's contents but to discharge his duty scrupulously and with discretion. And now, as the rain lashed the tents within which the men of Prince Rupert's Horse slept, Coppe was already riding back up the valley in the seething dark, north to Parbold and Shear House.

It breaks my heart, Edmund, to have to bring you this news, though you may know it already, that your brother has taken up with the rebels against His Majesty the King.

He heard his mother's voice in his head as he read her words. Her hand was, as ever, legible and elegant, but Mun imagined her sitting alone at Sir Francis's desk, her curls still red, though threaded here and there with white now, damp from tears shed for her younger son and for his betrayal.

Elizabeth and I pray every day that your brother will come to his senses and remember his duty to his King and to his father whom I believe Tom blames for poor Martha's death. We pray for you also, Mun, and for Emmanuel and Francis, that you may all come home to us in time for Christmas.

Please tell Emmanuel that Bess is in good health and prays most ardently that he will return in time to see his child come into the world.

As for your brother, I leave it to you to tell your father discreetly and when you think it best, of this most sad event, for I would not have such news distract him from his duties to His Royal Majesty the King.

Be careful, my son.

Your loving mother, Mary.

Mun folded the letter and put it into a pouch tied to his belt, then draped his cloak over his shoulders and picked up his broad hat before stepping out into the rain. He turned to face south, looking down the Severn Valley in the direction of Worcester where Essex's army was camped, the slanting rain striking his right cheek and running down his neck. All around him tents loomed in what dim starlight seeped through the clouds, some, not many, glowing softly from the lamps that burned within.

'How could you turn against us?' he whispered into the dark, wondering if Tom was even now standing in the rain looking north. 'How could you betray us?'

His thoughts turned to Lord Denton and his son Henry and what they had done to Tom. What Lord Denton had done to Martha. He did not blame his brother for seeking vengeance against the Dentons. But to turn against his own family? His king? Perhaps their father could have done more to save George Green from the hangman's noose. Perhaps not. Yet, whatever might have been, Tom's siding with the traitors was unforgivable. He had turned his back on them all. He had sullied their name.

'Can't sleep, Rivers?' Mun turned to see Daniel Bard's gaunt, rain-soaked face emerge from the shadows, coming from the direction of the latrine pit. The veteran was threading his belt through its buckle, a pipe hanging from the corner of his mouth and water dripping from his hat, which had recently been weatherproofed with lanolin by the looks.

'Have you ever shared a tent with O'Brien?' Mun asked through a grimace.

'Aye, he's an Irish savage and no mistake,' Bard said, grinning. 'Which is why Captain Boone billeted you with the son of a sow.'

Mun did not doubt it and said so, at which the veteran chuckled. 'Well, now that you're up you might as well check on the horses,' Bard said, pointing his pipe towards where their troop's mounts were huddled in the dark, nickering softly. 'They don't like this weather any more'n we do.' The damp air was still sweet from the smoke of the earlier cookfires dotted through the camp that were now nothing but smouldering piles of grey ash. It was a smell Mun had come to love.

He nodded. 'And I'll tell the captain's mare that her master is a bloody bastard,' he said.

'I'll wager she knows that already, lad,' Bard said, then took the pipe between finger and thumb and pointed the stem at Mun accusingly. 'Though, Captain

Boone saved your neck at Powick Bridge, if my memory has the right of it.'

That was true enough, thought Mun, remembering that savage day and the shame he had felt, the shame he still felt at having killed other men. And yet he himself would have been one of the dead, part of the bloody butcher's bill, if not for Boone.

Somewhere out in the dark, beyond the camp's perimeter, a vixen screeched and it was a murderous, bone-chilling sound.

'He's a good soldier,' Mun admitted. 'But he is still a bastard.' Bard grinned again as though to say Mun would get no more argument from him on that score. Then the veteran nodded farewell, turned and stalked off, disappearing into the dark. Leaving Mun defenceless against memories that would not be turned aside. His mind conjured dead men's faces. Severed limbs. Images more horrible than any nightmare clawed at his soul, fraying its edges no matter how hard he tried to summon kinder thoughts. Somewhere in his head he heard the faint voices of the dead, soldiers scarce more than boys crying for their mothers as the blood left their bodies.

Come then, he thought. *And be done with it.*

He let his mind fill with it, like a cauldron brimming with rancid stew, as he walked through the sucking mud past the tents with their snoring, farting occupants, towards the horses. When a new thought struck him like a pistol ball. What if Tom had been with Colonel John Brown's rebel horse that day at Powick Bridge? He tripped on a guy rope and fell, plunging his hands into the soft earth. Someone inside the tent growled a sleep-stifled curse. 'God help us,' Mun murmured. But what if Tom had been part of that bloody madness?

My brother. He picked himself up and wiped his hands down his breeches, his mind reeling with pictures from that wild charge and the savagery of the mêlée.

After the brief bloody clash in Brickfield Meadow the rebels had fled from the field back along the lane towards the bridge, back through another hail of lead from Rupert's dismounted dragoons. Mun had seen men shot from their horses, seen the horses themselves fall and break their legs in the cramped chaos of the narrow bridge. He had seen men bleed to death in the mud of the riverbank and he had even seen a man drown in his armour. Though most of the rebels had escaped, it had been a mauling, a brief, horrifying episode of butchery. And he had killed his share. He had seen them piss and foul themselves as they died. He had known terror and elation and feral desperation all bound up in a few mad moments and now he turned it over in his mind like a plough blade turning the earth, seeing again things he would rather leave buried. Because he needed to know if he had seen Tom's face amongst it all.

Only a handful of men from the Royalist side had been killed, though many, including Prince Maurice, Rupert's brother, had taken bullet or sword wounds. As for the rebels, more than one hundred lay dead that late September afternoon. And the flies came to feed on the filth, and jackdaws and crows hopped across the bloodstained meadow between the fallen or watched from the oaks and elms, croaking of the murder they had witnessed.

Mun had not been a part of the troop charged with collecting arms and armour, stripping the dead for kit and piling the bodies up into grim mounds; that grisly task had fallen to the dragoons as most unsavoury jobs did. So for all he knew, Tom could have been amongst those corpses. But then Mun had not recognized Achilles amongst the captured animals and that was something at least. A flicker of hope in the rain-flayed night.

He squelched up to the horse picket and some of the animals snorted and nickered, curious or wary of someone approaching from the drenched dark. One of them, a big stallion whose coat glistened, pushed forward to the end of his tether.

'Hey, boy. Good boy, Hector,' he murmured, taking the stallion's head in his hands and putting his own cheek against Hector's muzzle. The stallion blew gently, comforted by his master's scent. 'You're my brave boy,' Mun said softly, water running down his face having soaked through his hat. And together they stood in the pelting rain, Mun dreading what he would have to tell his father. That Tom was now their enemy.

A great echoing cheer went up as the stained glass shattered and the dark shards rained down, chinking on the cathedral's stone floor. But part of the florid scene, of the Christ and a lamb, still held intact and so some of the men went back to hacking a pew to splintered lumps to get more ammunition to hurl up at the window. Others were on their knees trying to dig up brass inscriptions with knives and still others of Essex's army were tearing up prayer books and tossing the pages into the air. Most of the silver or brass candlesticks that Worcester Cathedral had to offer were now stuffed inside soldiers' knapsacks or wedged in the belts at their waists, but Tom had a better use for the heavy brass stick he had snatched from the stone altar just as a young Puritan with a grinning face full of pustules had clambered up, dropped his breeches and begun to piss on the silk cloth and the Bible lying on it. And now Tom pulled back his arm and hurled the stick and it struck the figure of Jesus Christ on his cheek, knocking the crucifix from its fittings so that it too crashed to the floor and snapped across the tortured Christ's emaciated stomach.

Will Trencher spat on the broken crucifix. 'Superstitious bloody idols!' he growled, then threw a round stone at another stained glass window. The stone went straight through without shattering the rest of the glass and he swore and picked up the crucifix and began smashing what was left of it against the floor.

Another cheer went up and Tom turned to see two troopers emerge from the chapter house draped in the bishop's vestments, voluminous white silks over back- and breastplates, black satin and lace caps on their heads in place of steel helmets.

'Papist piss lickers!' a soldier yelled.

'Damn the bishops and damn the Pope!' another called as the two men playing the bishop affected to cower and tremble and wring their hands in fear.

Another man was climbing a stepladder set against the organ in the transept, an axe in his hands as his fellows cheered him on, their voices swirling up to the enormous vaulted roof like a parody of the songs of worship that normally filled the cathedral. Once at the top, the man turned and gave them a grin, hefted the axe and struck one of the metal pipes, but in doing so lost his balance and fell and most of the men laughed until they realized their friend's neck was broken and he was dead.

But if any of the men took his death as an ill omen they did not show it as the frenzy of destruction gripped them still, and Tom took a long pull on the wine bottle he clutched by the neck and then poured some of the red liquid onto a discarded prayer cushion that another man had kicked towards him.

'Don't go wasting good wine, Tom,' Matthew Penn slurred, holding up his own bottle as a trophy, both having been plundered from the cathedral's chapter house.

'This is not good wine,' Tom growled, then hurled the bottle against a smooth marble pillar, exploding it in a spray of claret and glass.

'In the name of Christ, stay your hands!' someone roared and Tom turned as a small man strode up the aisle towards him, having entered through the north-side porch. 'This is God's House, you rogues! Not Bedlam or Bridewell! Get out, you devils! Out, villains!'

'Leave, old man,' Tom said, nodding back the way the man had come. 'Get out while you can. God will not protect you here.' The man was in his forties with deep-set, soul-scouring eyes and he did not break stride but marched up to Tom so that Tom was half taken aback by his audacity.

'You defiler!' the man roared. 'You filth!' Tom felt the man's spit on his face, felt his own anger flare like black powder in the priming pan. Then the man thrust a finger into Tom's chest. 'You dare deface God's House? You maggot pie!'

'Away from me, damn you!' Tom yelled, swinging his fist against the man's head, so that he staggered backwards and fell on his behind, eyes bulging with fury.

'You are a devil!' the little man screamed up at him, then from inside his tunic fished a string of beads on the end of which was a small wooden cross, brandishing the thing at Tom as though it had the power to turn him into a pillar of salt like Lot's wife. But Tom knew that God had no power, that the Devil held dominion over this world, which was why his beautiful Martha was in the cold grave.

'He's a papist!' Matthew Penn exclaimed, pointing accusingly with one hand, still gripping the wine bottle with the other.

'A papist in an Anglican church?' Tom said, but no one seemed to hear.

'We've got a damn papist here, lads!' another soldier yelled, pulling up his breeches.

'You're a fool,' Tom hissed at the little man, snatching Penn's bottle and taking a long draught, the dark liquid spilling down his beard and tunic. And then he leant back against the choir wall and slid to the cold floor and from there he watched five men, Will Trencher amongst them, throw a rope around the little man's neck and drag him kicking and choking back down the aisle towards the north door. The remaining soldiers continued looting and smashing whatever could be smashed.

'We should fetch an officer,' Matthew Penn said, gesturing after the gang and their prisoner, swaying as though he stood on a ship's deck. 'They'll hang that man if we don't.'

Tom closed his eyes and let his mind conjure an image of his love swinging gently on a rope beneath the old stone bridge above the Tawd. It was a soul-torturing image. But he held on to it.

'Let the fool hang,' he snarled, raising the bottle to his lips.

Some time later he woke cold and stiff, his skull hammering and his mouth dry as old bones. He'd been awakened by the scuff and clop of hooves against stone, the sound amplified in that huge space, and had opened his eyes to the strange sight of men leading their horses down the nave. Sunlight flooded through the ten pointed arches of the great east window, filtering through the jagged coloured glass that clung stubbornly along their edges and illuminating the human faeces that someone had left on the high altar. Autumn morning light surged down the nave, engulfing the strange congregation and throwing spear-straight shafts through smoke that rose lazily from the grey embers of an old fire. Vaguely Tom recalled some of the men smashing pews to kindling some time in the night and setting a fire against the chill. Churches are always cold, he thought.

He pushed himself upright and looked across the way, where Matthew Penn lay snoring on a bedroll, cradling an ale jug. Here and there other men were waking, rubbing their eyes, holding their heads, farting. They were glancing around at the carnage, the broken glass, hacked-up pews and misericords, splintered altar rails and ripped-up prayer books. At the broken crucifix, Christ snapped into pieces as though to pile misery onto misery. Dry-mouthed, yet needing to empty his bladder, Tom climbed to his feet and stood almost still for a moment. Wondering if he would vomit.

'Look after my gear, Matthew,' he said, swallowing the lump that was rising up his throat. Penn stirred and grunted something which Tom took to be his assurance, then he crossed the south aisle towards another door, through which more men were leading their mounts.

'You lot had a good night then?' one young trooper said to him, smiling mischievously.

Tom ignored him and stepped out into the new day, turning his face from the harsh light and holding his eyes closed for a few moments. To his right a hundred or more horses were picketed in the southside cloisters and more weary-looking troopers were coming in, which was why they needed to use the vast space inside the cathedral, too. Somewhere amongst those horses was Achilles and he would be hungry, but several boys were moving amongst them with sacks of hay and Tom knew that the stallion would be sure to demand his portion. Around the cloister's edges men were huddled around cookfires, talking in low voices whilst their fellows yet slept in the tents set against the wall behind them. Bacon, onions and garlic sizzled on skillets, the sweet aroma drifting on the breeze and making Tom's mouth water. Spitted joints of mutton turned beside fires, glistening and dripping fat and promising a much better start to the day than the usual stale bread and cheese.

'Compliments of the good folk of Worcester!' a soldier announced to his fellows, brandishing a knife on the end of which was skewered a chunk of roasted meat.

Essex's men had looted the city and were now enjoying the spoils. Tom supposed the earl could have done more to stop the abuses, but perhaps he was not wholly averse to his men showing the people of Worcester the error of their judgement in siding with the King.

He left the cloisters through the west gate and began down the gentle grassy slope towards the river.

'Want some breakfast, Tom?' He looked to his left where Will Trencher and a group of soldiers lay around

239

a pile of embers, some tending iron pots half buried in the coals. The big man beckoned Tom over, smiling to reveal the few teeth he still had.

'Have you got ale?' Tom asked, squinting against the light and walking, half stumbling, over to join them.

'The best in Worcester for Black Tom!' Trencher exclaimed, grabbing a pitcher by the handle and lifting it as proof. Some of the liquid sploshed over the side and one of the men swore at Trencher for wasting it, but the big man took no notice.

A trooper named Hewson, whom the men called Weasel on account of his narrow face and close-set eyes, handed Tom a mug into which Trencher poured a generous measure of ale. Then they all watched as Tom raised the mug in mock salute and drank, draining it before dragging a hand across his mouth and stifling a great belch.

'It tastes like piss, Will,' he growled, shuddering and wondering again if he would vomit.

The men round the fire were laughing and Will Trencher shrugged his broad shoulders and winked at Weasel. 'I didn't say it was any good,' he said through a grin, 'just that it was the best in Worcester.'

At which Tom grimaced but anyway offered his cup to be refilled. Trencher happily obliged and when Tom raised the cup to his lips again he saw something in the grass behind the men that he had not noticed before. But then, he was half blinded by that vengeful sun that was driving nails into his brain. Doubtless there were lots of things he had not noticed this morning.

'It's that bloody papist from last night,' a short, red-faced man named Nayler said, thumbing over his shoulder.

'Penn said you'd hang him,' Tom replied. The little dead man lay on his back, those outraged eyes still staring but cloudy now. His limbs had stiffened overnight and one arm was bent at the elbow so that the pale hand pointed accusingly at the sky.

'We didn't hang him,' Nayler said.

'It wasn't worth the bloody effort,' another man added. 'Bastard pope-lover was slippery as an eel. Gave me this.' He tilted his head and yanked his bloodied collar down to reveal a livid gouge on his neck. 'Nails sharp as bloody cats, papists.'

'So we made him swallow those beads of his, cross and all,' Weasel announced, grinning at his friends. 'He choked for a good hour but it did for him in the end.'

'Aye, he won't bother you with baubles and spells again, Tom, you needn't worry about that,' Trencher said, leaning over to stir the steaming contents of his pot with a long knife.

Tom let his eyes linger on the stiff corpse for a few moments and some part of his mind asked another part what he felt, looking at that little man whose death was on his hands as much as on those of the men before him. The answer came and Tom put the cup of ale to his lips and drank. Then he continued down to the riverbank to relieve himself.

Because he felt nothing.

CHAPTER SIXTEEN

'THE MORE I SEE YOU RIDE, WILL,' MATTHEW PENN SAID, buckling the girth strap of his dun mare's saddle, 'the more convinced I am that you should have joined that lot.' He nodded towards the great lumbering mass of the Parliamentary artillery train now passing them. 'If ever there was a man born to heave terrible encumbrances from here to there and back again it is you.'

'You'll be glad I didn't when Prince Rupert charges and you wet yourself,' Will replied, feeding his own horse a lump of old cheese. 'You'll just be glad Uncle Will's there to look after you.'

'If that devil Rupert charges at us, the only reason you'll linger, Will, is because you'll have fallen from that fat mare of yours in the panic to flee,' Nayler said, a half grin on his red face. There were some murmurs of agreement and some curses at this, for they had all heard about the Royalist assault at Powick Bridge. How the Prince had charged with devastating effect, fighting at the front like a demon, and how their own troopers had fled and kept going until they met the Earl of Essex's Lifeguard regiment near Pershore some ten miles away. It had been a rout and, worse, an embarrassment.

'I'd still rather fight that devil than be with those poor sods,' Trencher said, gesturing at a gun team of about thirty men and eight horses that was struggling with a brass demi-culverin in the cloying mud.

Tom did not have saddle holsters for his firelocks, so shoved them into his tall boots, then watched the gunners flounder in the mud, the horse team neighing in protest at the corpulent conductor who was endeavouring to enliven them with a stinging hazel switch.

'It's an expensive bucket that can never be filled, is what it is,' Captain Preston said, adjusting his mount's bridle. 'A bloody quern stone hanging round our necks. On this ground at least,' he added, gesturing at the earth that had been churned to a mire by so many men, horses and beasts of burden. 'How we are meant to outmanoeuvre the enemy with those guns holding us back I do not know.'

Despite the captain's boyish features, his clear complexion, snub nose and short tufty fair hair, Tom put him at about twenty-five. He suspected the man knew his business, too; must do or else Essex's generals would not have raised him from a lieutenant in the London Trained Bands to a Captain of Horse in Lord Feilding's Regiment. But whether or not Preston was up for the fight only time would tell.

They had struck camp an hour before sunrise and now Parliament's army was marching out of Worcester in the drizzling rain because Essex had received word that the King was making for London. No one knew precisely where the Royalists were, but they had to be stopped from reaching the capital. Tom's nerves had begun to thrum with anticipation of a fight and a big fight too. Everyone knew they were winding up to a confrontation which both sides hoped would finish this war before it really got started. But Tom thought Captain Preston was right about the cannon. How could they overtake the enemy and force the issue with that forty-six-piece artillery train plodding through the mire, holding them back?

And yet it was not just for their cannon that they needed this shambling convoy. The artillery train supplied small arms ammunition to the whole army, cavalry included, as well as muskets, pikes, lances and swine-feathers, which made cavalrymen shudder because they knew what those metal-tipped stakes could do to a charging horse. The column also brought pistols, armour, swords and sword belts and the tools that an army on the move required to function, such as spades, mattocks, duckboards, axes, horseshoes, nails, rope, hides, tar and countless other necessities. As for itself the artillery train needed hundreds of horses and oxen that all had to be fed. It needed carpenters, wheelwrights and blacksmiths just to keep it moving at all.

'Still, not our problem today, boys!' Captain Preston announced, mounting with fluid ease.

'Why's that, Captain?' Matthew Penn asked, fastening the short buff-coat that had been a gift from his father, a lawyer in a Southwark firm. The coat was poorly made and could not have cost more than five pounds but it was better than nothing and Tom had it in his mind to kill a wealthy Royalist officer and get such a coat for himself.

'Because, Penn, today we get the chance to stretch our legs. Give the horses a good run.'

'Bloody hell. Sorry, old girl,' Trencher muttered under his breath, patting his big mare in consolation.

'We are to ride south-east ahead of the army to find billets near Warwick. The King's target is London. It must be. And so we shall overhaul His Majesty and all his Cavalier devils, but first we must accompany the quartermasters and find billets.'

'Sounds like dragoons' work,' Trencher moaned, sweeping rain from his bald head and putting on a rusty pot.

'Chin up, Trencher,' Captain Preston said, 'it cannot be more than fifty miles and it's barely raining. Besides, it is an honour, that we might ride ahead of the rest. If anyone's going to run into the King's men it'll be us. Think of us as the vanguard, boys.'

The other fifty-two men in the troop mounted up behind their captain and prepared to ride east, their horses well fed, courtesy of Worcester, firelocks cleaned and oiled and blades wickedly sharp. *If anyone's going to run into the King's men it'll be us.* That's what Captain Preston had said. Which to Tom meant two things: that Preston was not afraid of a fight, and that Tom might soon taste battle. Which was what he wanted more than anything in the world.

They rode fast for the first ten miles, the three-beat gait of the canter thumping its rhythm on the soft ground as the men and their horses revelled in the chase. After a week of being cooped up in Worcester the horses needed a good run and Captain Preston was happy to give them one. But after their initial ebullience was spent, they slowed to a brisk trot, passing the villages of Rous Lench, Abbot's Salford and Bidford and asking of folk if they had news of the King's army.

'If you seek the King's army then what army are you?' one ruddy-faced farmer had asked, scratching his cheek in perturbed confusion.

'We, sir, are Parliament's army!' Captain Preston had announced to a chorus of oinks and snorts from the man's pigs.

'Parliament's army?' the man said, his face screwed up in utter perplexity. 'What on this earth would Parliament be doing with an army?'

'We are at war, sirrah!' Captain Preston had said, his own cheeks flushing red. 'Your king has declared war against his people. You did not know this?'

The farmer seemed to consider this for a moment, then hawked and spat a gobbet of phlegm into the mud and proceeded to scour his bristled chin with his filthy nails.

'So long as His Majesty is not at war with my pigs,' he said, 'for they do not like their habits disturbed.' He shook his head. 'They can be obstinate buggers if their habits are disturbed.'

With that Captain Preston had cursed, apologized to God for cursing, flicked his reins and led the column off, leaving the farmer and his beloved pigs staring beady-eyed after them.

They followed the Avon upriver towards Stratford, crossing there and continuing east, crossing the spear-straight Fosse Way and riding on north of Kineton, then across the rolling, rugged ironstone hills of Burton Dassett amongst which countless sheep grazed, happily unaware that war was coming.

By late afternoon they had crossed a squat stone bridge over the River Itchen and arrived damp and hungry at the outskirts of the village of Wormleighton some fifteen miles south-east of Warwick.

'What is your appreciation of this place, Captain?' one of the two quartermasters asked, swaying lazily in his saddle and removing his hat to run plump fingers through his lank white hair. His name was Tromp and Tom had heard that the man had gone to Lord Feilding himself and asked to be allowed to conduct this undertaking of searching for billets from the relative comfort of a horse-drawn cart. Tom had understood the request that morning when he had laid eyes on Tromp, for the quartermaster was enormously fat. Too fat to sit a horse, one would have thought, and yet surprisingly he rode fairly well. It was Captain Preston who had thwarted Tromp's request, claiming that they might as well haul a cannon as keep pace with a cart, and Tromp had steeped in his own juices ever since. Now he had emerged from his gloomy silence and was testing the captain in front of his men.

'Good open ground and rising up towards the village,' Preston answered, playing along, glancing round from his saddle and taking in what he could of the undulating terrain in the dim dusk light. 'Only a few small spinneys by the looks. Enough for firewood but nothing for our enemies to hide in.'

'Plenty of fresh water too,' Lieutenant Hyde put in eagerly. 'Yonder brook runs back to the river and there's likely to be more like it.'

'I agree, Lieutenant,' Captain Preston said. 'In the morning we should have a good view of the surrounding land from the manor and the church tower.'

'The ancient boundaries of the village were set out in the charter of King Eadwy in the year of Our Lord nine hundred and fifty-six,' Tromp announced, 'by which he gave the village to an Earl Æfhere.' It was a riposte to which Captain Preston seemingly had no answer.

But Matthew Penn did. 'You see, nothing has changed, not in all these years,' he said. 'The King makes rich men richer, gives his fool-born foot-licking friends and retainers the pie while the rest of us make do with the crumbs.'

This got some ayes and a few curses by way of agreement and the fat quartermaster went to great efforts to twist round in his saddle to get a look at the man who had spoken the much-welcomed sedition.

'That was neatly put, young man,' Tromp said, staring at Tom, the whites of his eyes glowing dully by the light of the half moon that had appeared through a tear in the clouds.

'Wasn't me that said it,' Tom muttered, wondering how Tromp's horse was still walking beneath the fat man's enormous bulk. 'I could not care if the King gave all of England to the King of Spain.'

Tromp's eyes bulged. From the corner of his own, Tom saw a flash of Penn's teeth as he shook his head with incredulity.

'Now now, Thomas, you'll upset folk with talk like that,' Captain Preston warned. 'Mister Tromp might take you seriously.'

'If it was in jest it was in poor taste,' Tromp said, scowling as he turned back to face his front. They were making their way up the muddy road and had almost reached the messuages on Wormleighton's western edge: some low thatched dwellings each with a garden, service buildings and animal pens. 'He has an ill-favoured look, that one,' Tromp added. 'I would be wary of him, Captain.'

Tom ignored the indirect insult, but Penn did not. 'I have a pretty friend who would disagree with you on that, Mister Tromp,' he said, 'isn't that right, Tom?' Tom thought of Ruth Gell, of the nights they had shared. 'Poor girl,' Penn went on, 'but I believe she was in love with Tom in her way. Broke her ample heart to see her young warrior ride off to war, even if he does make a desolate Puritan like Trencher here seem a mirthful fellow.' Trencher grunted something nasty. 'Come to think of it, Mister Tromp, you are quite right, for I swear on my life it never rained so much before I met Black Tom.'

'Quiet, Penn,' Captain Preston said, raising his left hand. They were passing the first houses now, continuing up the gentle slope. A breeze was blowing up from the south, bringing with it a damp fog from the fields, that drifted in amongst the buildings and willow hurdles. This mist was thickened by spice-smelling wood smoke wafting up from one or more unseen dwellings beyond the southern slope.

An owl hooted and suddenly Tom was aware that his senses had pricked awake. The sweet, damp aroma of fallen leaves filled his nose and his ears sifted every sound: the horses' snorts, the clink of equipment and the creak of saddles and leather buff-coats. Even the thump of his own heart. He felt a chill crawl up his spine, bristling the hairs on his neck. It was the same sense, he guessed, that had caused the captain to hush the column.

There was no sign of anyone moving in the autumn dusk, but that in itself was not so unusual. Most folk with any sense would make themselves scarce at the appearance of fifty armed and mounted troopers. No, it was something else that had whetted his instinct. But what?

He was aware of the pistols in his boots pressing against his outer calves. Of the rapier's hilt at his left hip.

'Who are you?' a voice called from the murk. 'State your business here.'

Captain Preston raised his hand again and stopped his horse, halting the entire column. He glanced at Lieutenant Hyde, then nodded, affirming his decision.

'I am Captain Preston of Lord Feilding's Regiment of Horse, serving the Earl of Essex and His Majesty's Parliament,' Preston called, straight-backed, peering ahead, searching for the body to which the voice belonged.

No reply came out of the gloom.

'I don't like this,' Will Trencher murmured, drawing the great blunderbuss from its saddle holster.

'On the left, Captain,' Tom said.

'What is it, Rivers?' Preston asked, the strain of keeping his voice calm palpable in just those four words. But Tom had no answer, did not know what he had heard. Not heard. Felt.

'Show yourselves!' Captain Preston yelled.

Gouts of flame flashed, followed in an eye blink by a ragged salvo of cracks, and Lieutenant Hyde grunted and slumped forward and the horses whinnied and Tom gripped Achilles hard with his knees, trying to control the startled stallion as he drew both his pistols.

'Behind us! They're behind us!' someone clamoured from the column's rear, as more tongues of fire spat from the murk, illuminating men for an instant before the darkness reclaimed them. Men around Tom fired their own carbines and pistols but he could see no one to kill and so he held his fire.

'Forward!' Captain Preston roared, but then, suddenly, there was the enemy, charging out of the dark and screaming as they came. Captain Preston fired his carbine and Tom saw a man fall from his horse and then liquid slapped his face and he looked at the man beside him, at the gory, bone-flecked hole that had been Trooper Edwards's face.

'Heya!' He spurred forward with his captain and there were more gouts of flame as the enemy cavalry emerged in a hateful wave and the two sides struck, horses and men screaming and blades flashing in the moonlight. A sword slashed at Tom, just missing his face, and he leant out quick as a lightning strike and thrust a pistol into a man's face, pulling the trigger. The man's head vanished, spraying Tom's pistol and hand with hot fluid. Captain Preston hacked and slashed, his blade ringing against his opponent's. Instinctively Tom ducked and flame spewed towards him and he heard the savage hiss as the ball whipped past and saw in the flash the whites of a horse's wild eyes. Then he pointed his other pistol and fired and heard it pierce a breastplate and then the horse was riderless and he shoved his firelocks into his boots and hauled his sword rasping from its scabbard.

Quartermaster Tromp had drawn his own sword and was slashing about himself wildly, but then Tom saw at least two men drag the quartermaster screaming from his horse and Tom cursed because the enemy had infantry amongst them now too.

'Heya, Achilles!' he yelled, digging his heels in and driving the stallion forward towards Captain Preston, who was fending off two attackers with desperate sword work. One of the enemy riders sensed the danger and pulled his mount round just as Tom slashed at him, striking his breastplate. Then Will Trencher was there too, his blade flashing, and the Cavalier hauled on his reins and his horse stepped neatly backwards, disengaging them from the fray. Just as something hammered into Tom's ribs, knocking the wind from him so that he gasped for breath. The musket butt came again, thumping into his left thigh, and Tom heard himself roar with pain even as he twisted and brought his rapier hissing out of the dark from his right and down across the musketeer's face, cleaving it apart with a wet chop.

'Quarter!' someone yelled. 'We surrender, damn you!' Captain Preston was yet hacking a man to death even as he yelled for the killing to end. And with good reason, Tom knew. For now the enemy had broken from cover Tom could see a score or more musket matches glowing malevolently in the dark around them. If they were not cut from their horses they would be shot from them and now Captain Preston wanted to save his men's lives. Those who still lived.

'We surrender! It's over, men!' he bellowed. 'Quarter, damn your eyes!' he screamed at a musketeer who was raising his matchlock, its muzzle a mere two feet from Preston's side.

Some more cracks split the night and Tom wheeled Achilles round in circles, his sword raised and yet hungry for blood, then he saw a musketeer and kicked Achilles forward, eager to cut the man down.

'Hold, Tom! It's over! Hold, man!' It was Matthew Penn and he had bravely grabbed Achilles's bridle to stop the beast; Achilles snapped his teeth but Penn held on, shouting for Tom to stop. Then Tom recognized his friend and hauled on his reins.

'Whoa, boy, steady, Achilles,' he growled, the words raspy as a raven's call because his mouth was so dry. He glanced around at the carnage dimly illuminated in the cold moonlight. Bodies lay everywhere in a gloom curdled by the anguished screams of men and horses. Other bodies lay still. Riderless horses stamped or shied, their eyes rolling, and as Tom held his sword out before him he realized that he was trembling madly. Not fear. Just the battle thrill, he hoped. You have killed men, his conscience whispered, frayed as a banner whipped by a musket ball.

'Put down your swords,' Captain Preston ordered, handing his own weapon to an enemy officer while two musketeers trained their matchlocks on him. 'All of you, weapons down.'

'Down!' a musketeer barked at Tom, his weapon aimed at Tom's torso. The match clamped in the serpent glowed and Tom had the notion that if it had still been raining they might have escaped, because many of the enemy's muskets would not fire in the wet. But the drizzle had stopped some time before they had entered the village and now all the man in front of him need do was pull the trigger. The serpent lock would lower the lit match into the priming pan, igniting the small charge there which would in turn ignite the main charge in the barrel through the touch-hole. There would be a flash and Tom would hear a crack but by then the lead ball would have already torn a hole through him.

'We're beaten, Tom,' Penn said. 'Do what the bastard says.' And so as if in a dream Tom threw his sword point-first into the soft ground, then dismounted and stood amongst the dead and dying, his breath loud in his steel helmet.

'Some must have got clear,' Penn said, looking around. Twenty feet away Quartermaster Tromp lay bludgeoned to death, the whites of his bulging, terror-filled eyes striking against his gore-dark face.

'Bloody ran and left us,' Nayler said, holding his hands up as a Cavalier relieved him of his wheel-lock pistol and sword. Penn was right, Tom realized, for though there were plenty of dead there were not enough, and he guessed that at least twenty had broken clear and galloped west.

'We might have won. Beaten these whoresons if they'd stayed,' Will Trencher growled. His big mare lay bleeding out in the mud and he stood watching her die, blood dripping from a gash in his bald head.

A broad-shouldered, halberd-wielding corporal strode up to Tom and used his weapon's butt to knock Tom's helmet off into the mud. Then he spun the shortened halberd around and ran its slender wicked point along Tom's neck until its crescent-shaped axe blade pressed into the flesh beneath his jaw. The corporal's pot had a rim all the way round from whose shadow his eyes glared hatefully.

'You rebel scum,' he sneered into Tom's face, gripping the halberd's shaft with white-knuckled hands, 'I'm going to slice your rancid head off.' He spat, the phlegmy string catching in his beard where it glistened in the moonlight. 'That man down there was my friend,' he snarled, jerking his head towards the musketeer whose face Tom had sliced open. Tom glanced down at the blood-spattered ruin, his nostrils full of the stench of the musketeer's open bowels. The corporal smelt it too, if the grimace on his face was anything to go by.

'He stinks,' Tom gnarred. 'Or is it you who have fouled yourself?'

The axe blade at Tom's throat twitched and Tom threw his right forearm up, knocking the blade clear, then stepped in and hammered a fist into the corporal's mouth. The big man staggered and then Tom was on him, but the corporal tripped over his friend's corpse and grabbed Tom's tunic in one strong hand, pulling him down after him. The man had let go of his halberd and slammed a fist into Tom's temple, exploding white light in Tom's skull, but Tom's hatred was stronger than pain and his fists were flying, slamming into the corporal's face again and again, and he was vaguely aware that men were standing around them yelling, like a crowd round the bear pit. Somehow the corporal squirmed out and managed to twist his torso, throwing out his right hand and gripping Tom's neck. The pressure was enormous and blackness began to flood Tom's vision. He drove a fist into the corporal's elbow joint and the arm collapsed and in the same instant Tom slammed his forehead into the big man's face, breaking the corporal's nose with a splintering crack. He wrenched his neck back and smashed his head down again. And again into the hot, blood-drenched mess.

'That'll do, rebel,' someone said, swinging a leg over Tom's back and wrapping two strong arms around his neck, all but suffocating him. 'That'll do or I'll gut you, lad,' the man threatened in his ear, slowly standing back up so that Tom must either stand with him or have his throat crushed.

'Do what the man says, Tom,' Captain Preston said.

'They'll murder you otherwise.' But Tom had no choice in the matter and his vision began to blur as he struggled to drag breath into his lungs.

'Don't kill the lad, Bard,' a Cavalier said, 'the captain will want to question him.'

'Easy, Tom,' Matthew Penn said, 'easy, lad.'

Tom could not breathe. He glared at the faces around him and they glared back, as though he were some wild animal caught in a snare. And then their faces blurred and he felt his limbs go slack. His knees buckled and the trooper called Bard lowered him onto the muddy ground. It was over.

And they had lost.

CHAPTER SEVENTEEN

————————

'WHAT WERE THIS LOT DOING HERE?' O'BRIEN ASKED, squatting to wipe his bloody sword on a dead man's breeches.

'Same as us, I'd wager,' Mun said, putting his firelock to a big mare's head. 'Looking for billets.' The horse was whining with each breath, its belly inflating and collapsing unnaturally as its organs clung to life even as its blood pumped from the cut artery in its neck. Mun pulled the trigger and the horse went still as the concussion roared in the dark. Cheers issued from the gloom further along the track towards the village and Mun guessed that one of the prisoners was enjoying a rare beating, probably at the hands of Corporal Scrope, if Mun had to wager.

'Don't waste your powder, Rivers, you fool,' Boone said, 'that horse would have died soon enough.' Then the captain turned to Daniel Bard who was ferreting through a dead rebel's clothes with nimble, well-practised ease. 'Go and sort them out, Dan,' he said, gesturing up the track, 'I need the bastards able to talk.'

'Sir,' Bard said, stalking off, shoving some coins inside his tunic.

'What shall I do with this one, Captain?' Vincent Rowe asked, kneeling by a rebel who was choking on his own blood. A musket ball had pierced his breastplate and he lay there looking up at the stars, his beard and moustaches frothy with dark liquid.

'You just heard what I said to Rivers, lad,' Boone replied, ramming his sword back into its scabbard, having cleaned the gore from it. 'Don't waste your ammunition.' With that Rowe stood and stared at the dying man for a few more moments, then raised his slender sword and hacked down into the rebel's neck. But the man writhed madly and so Rowe hacked down again and a third time before the body went still, the head all but severed. Then Rowe dragged a sleeve across his sweat-slick brow and stared at Mun with round eyes.

'You see, Rivers,' Boone said, nodding towards Rowe whose handsome, fine-boned face was spattered with blood, 'that's how it is done.' Then the captain turned to his lieutenant, Samuel Begg, who was guarding a narrow-faced rebel who reminded Mun of a rat. Or a weasel, maybe.

'Tie them well and get them mounted,' Boone said. 'We ride for Meriden.'

'Yes, sir!' Begg replied, slamming the hilt of his sword between the man's shoulder blades to get him moving.

Mun walked amongst the dead, turning bodies over to look at their white, moon-washed faces, now and then putting his ear to a mouth to check there was no breath.

'He's a fine beast if I'm any judge of horseflesh,'

O'Brien said, walking over and patting a horse's neck, and when Mun looked up, his chest tightened and his breath snagged in his throat. It was a great black stallion, its glossy coat shining in the dark.

'Achilles,' he said under his breath and the stallion tossed his head, his black mane flying. Then Mun spun round and looked to where the rebel prisoners were gathered and though he could not see their faces he knew one of them by his silhouette, by the line of his shoulders and by his stance. It was his brother. It was Tom.

He stopped himself calling out, fought every instinct which clamoured at him to shout his brother's name. He did not even approach, instead hanging back in the shadows because he feared Tom would see him, and whatever sense was overpowering his natural instinct to greet his brother told him also that no good could come of doing so. Yet there he was. Tom! His mind reeled at the sight of his brother standing amongst the rebels. His brother with the enemy, one of Parliament's traitors. And yet alive, his inner self screamed. My brother!

And there were plenty of men that weren't alive after the brief fight. More than twenty of his brother's confederates lay dead, gashed and shot and never to see another dawn. Never again to embrace a loved one.

'Mount up!' Captain Boone yelled. Somewhere a dog was barking but the villagers of Wormleighton stayed in their houses, though Mun had seen some faces at windows.

'That tall lad gave you a battering, Corporal,' Richard Downes remarked, shaking out his lavish but flattened curls before pushing his bar pot down, the single nasal-bar bisecting his grin.

'Whoreson tripped me,' Corporal Scrope replied, his voice muffled by the massive hand cupped over his smashed nose. Blood was seeping between his fingers. 'I'll pay the bugger back though, I promise you that.'

'Maybe,' Downes said, putting his foot in the stirrup and hauling himself into the saddle, 'if Captain Boone doesn't do for him first. They're to be questioned and if I know the captain he'll be the one asking the questions. Can't see the Prince getting his hands dirty. Doesn't look good . . .' he pushed a wheellock into its holster, 'a foreigner beating confessions out of Englishmen. Even if they *are* rebel scum. Better to let another Englishman do that.'

'So long as the cur is alive when I get my hands on him,' Scrope said, mounting his own horse, wiping his bloody hand on the mare's mane.

Their hands bound behind their backs, the surviving rebels were mounted on spare horses and placed in the middle of the column, as Captain Boone's troop rode out of Wormleighton across the ploughed, night-shrouded fields north-east towards Meriden. Mun rode behind the prisoners, his jaw clamped shut, his head low, and whenever the clouds broke, allowing pale moonlight to illuminate the column, he watched the young prisoner who sat a brown mare, smouldering like match. And he whispered thanks to God that he and his brother were still alive after that night's killing. He whispered thanks to MacCarthy, too, whose leg he had broken and whose armour he now wore, because that rusty steel had stopped a sword slash that would have carved him open.

It was the middle of the night when they arrived at the camp, a mass of tents, horse pickets, provender, ordnance and other stores sprawled over eight square miles of open fields. The prisoners were taken to Prince Rupert's quarters which comprised a two-storeyed timber-framed red brick farmhouse and outbuildings all of which were surrounded by a moat which stank because the soldiers used it as a latrine pit. An old plough shed next to the barn became a gaol and Captain Boone ordered two men armed with firelocks to guard its only door, giving them orders to kill any rebel who tried to escape.

The smell of blood and death still in his nose, Mun gave Hector to one of the grooms, who led the stallion off to be rubbed down, fed and watered, then he found his tent and ducked inside. It was empty. O'Brien and Vincent Rowe were off with the rest of the troop, likely celebrating their victory by drinking themselves into a stupor. They had lost five men in the fight but that was a small price to pay for the deaths of nearly five times the number of rebels and the information they would prise from the captives. He undid the straps of his back- and breastplate, noticing that his hands still trembled from the fight, then he left the armour at the foot of his bedroll along with his helmet. He lifted the jug off the stool and filled his cup with ale, drinking deeply, then stepped back out into the night and looked north across the camp. Somewhere amidst those countless small fires which palled the night sky orange, were the tents of the King's Lifeguard of Horse. And amongst them his father's tent.

'I've killed men this night, Father,' he whispered. Now, with the violence and the chaos passed, the thought that he had butchered other men made him nauseous. Made him feel ashamed, too. But no good could come from dragging one's feet through that foul mire, he knew, when he ought instead to thank God or the fates or blind luck that he had survived. And now all he had to do was cross the camp and tell his father that Tom was here. For perhaps Sir Francis could have him freed. He had the ear of the King, after all.

Yet it would not be as easy as that.

'What should I do?' Mun whispered, looking up at the heavy, moon-silvered cloud. 'What should I do, Bess?' he asked, wishing his sister were there. Then he shivered, as though the ale in his stomach had frozen suddenly, and turned his back on the far field in which his father slept unknowing that his sons had done murder that night and that his lost boy was found. Not yet, something warned. Now is not the time to bring Father that news.

So Mun swallowed the sour taste that filled his mouth, left the dead to the dead, and, fixing his thoughts on his brother who yet lived though he was in great danger, he walked towards the sound of drunken men.

'What happened to you?' O'Brien asked, beckoning Mun over with a wave of his wineskin. If there was another benefit of riding in Prince Rupert's Horse, Mun knew, it was that there always seemed to be plenty to drink. And wine helped a man forget the shame of being terrified, of feeling no better than a beast when the blood was flying. When men were butchering and being butchered.

'I had to see to Hector,' Mun lied, forcing a smile. 'He took a head cut. A lot of blood. But I washed it and it's not bad.'

'Head cuts bleed like a stuck pig,' O'Brien said, 'but it's usually all show.' He grinned, digging an elbow into

Vincent Rowe's ribs. 'Like this dainty bit,' he said.

'Bugger off, you Irish sheep-fucker,' Rowe growled.

'Begging your pardon, missy,' O'Brien said, winking at Richard Downes. 'Pretty girls make me twitchy.'

'Tosspot,' Rowe snarled, snatching the wineskin from his friend. The troop was split around three fires and it looked to Mun as though many had resigned themselves to sleeping where they now lay. For Mun was coming to understand that there was comfort in company, in the clamour of companions and even in mockery. Anything was preferable to silence. He shared a jibe with O'Brien, this time at Downes's expense, then walked up to Corporal Scrope and squatted behind him, tapping one solid shoulder.

'Corporal, a word if I may?'

'What do you want, Rivers?' Scrope growled. 'You can see I'm busy.' He lifted his mug and did not turn round. Mun knew that Scrope disliked him, had done since the very beginning at Hucknall Torkard, when Mun had stood up to Captain Boone and spilled MacCarthy from his saddle.

'It's about that rebel. The one that improved your looks,' Mun dared.

'Watch your mouth, Rivers,' Scrope rumbled, but he twisted round this time and Mun knew he had the big man nibbling the bait.

'He's the same wretch that cut Hector in the fight,' Mun said.

Scrope's eyebrows arched. 'You love that horse, don't you, lad?' The grin was insinuating. The nose was a mass of crusting blood, and the swollen, blackening skin beneath both eyes beaded with tiny drops of sweat.

'Better than I love most people,' Mun admitted,

thinking it was not entirely untrue. 'I want to teach that scum a lesson he'll remember us by.'

The corporal's lip curled and he flapped a hammy hand. 'There'll be plenty of time for that,' he said, turning back round. 'Piss off.'

'Not if he's moved,' Mun pressed, 'which he will be. They all will. I've heard that the King himself wants to see them. His Majesty has it in his mind to know what a traitor looks like up close. Then they'll be hanged likely as not.'

The corporal turned back to face him, then shook his head. 'The captain wants to talk to the toad's arse. Wants to question all of 'em. The King'll have to wait his turn.'

'If there are questions to be asked, the King's own men will be doing the asking,' Mun said, 'my father for one. You think they'd let Captain Boone beat the villains to death before they've been . . .' he put his fists side by side and rotated them in opposite directions, 'wrung out for information?' Mun felt other men's eyes on them but kept his own riveted on Scrope's.

'What's going on, Corporal?' someone called from the other side of the fire. Mun glanced up. Short and belligerent-looking, Purefoy was the kind of man who smelt scheming on the air, which was surprising, Mun thought, what with one nostril currently stuffed with finger.

'Never you mind, Purefoy,' Scrope gnarred, scratching his bushy, blood-encrusted beard. Purefoy shrugged as though he cared not, then turned to the man beside him, snatching a taper off him to light his pipe. One eye though at least, Mun felt, remained fixed on them.

Scrope pitched to one side and let out a long rumbling

fart, earning some complaints from the men either side, then leant back, so that Mun could smell the sour wine on his breath. 'What have you got in mind, Rivers?' he asked in a low voice.

Sweat rose on the skin between his shoulder blades and in his scalp, making it itch as they walked towards the Prince's quarters and the plough-shed gaol. Convincing Corporal Scrope that they should pay the tall, fair-haired rebel a visit that very night while it was yet dark had been the easy part. Now Mun's heart was hammering in his chest and his mind was in disarray – because he had not thought this plan through, knew he had failed to discern the road's end before giving spur to the idea. But there was no going back now.

There had been no talk of killing – just of repaying the rebel prisoner in kind – violence for violence, a drop of blood perhaps. And yet now, as they made their way through the flame-licked gloom, he saw that Scrope's hand rested on the two-lobed guard of the ancient ballock dagger thrust in his belt. What if Scrope simply walked up to Tom and gutted him where he stood? Cold-blooded murder was not, Mun suspected, beyond Corporal Scrope. Which meant that Mun might now be making things even worse for Tom than they already stood. From the pan to the fire.

He had doubted there would be opportunity to free his brother, not once he'd roped in Scrope, which he must to get access to the prisoners. But he had thought that maybe he could hand Tom a knife, possibly even a pistol, to keep secreted away until the opportunity arose. At the very least his presence might give Tom hope, show him that he was not alone and that something might be done. Now, though, Mun feared he was bringing his brother a rare beating at best, a cold blade in the dark at worst. And yet perhaps, deep down, in that part of Mun which thrummed in the chaos of battle, like a ship's rigging in a storm – in that part of him which had awakened to savagery, even revelled in it – he had never intended letting Scrope, or anyone else, prevent him from securing his brother's freedom. No matter what needed to be done to win it.

'I always knew you were a hateful bastard, Rivers,' Scrope said and Mun noted a tone verging on admiration in his voice. 'But I get the first dance with him, do you hear me? You don't touch a hair on the whoreson's head until I say you can.'

'Whatever you say, Corporal,' Mun replied, forcing a wicked grin.

They crossed the duckboard bridge over the moat and passed between two livestock pens, then came to the old shed that stood in the shadow of a barn which was now used to stable the horses of the princes, Rupert and Maurice, and their immediate retinue. The two guards greeted their corporal but then one of them, a young lad with a mop of greasy black hair and a hare lip, frowned and shuffled his feet.

'No one is to see the rebels, sir,' he said, coughing nervously, 'orders of Captain Boone.'

'Shut your mouth, trooper Burke. I'm your bloody corporal!' Scrope said, thumbing for the lad to step aside. 'If you don't get out of my way I'll have you shovelling horse shit till Christmas!' He glared at the other man who was already moving away from the door. 'You 'n' all, Massie.'

That was threat enough for Burke to fumble at his

belt, turn round and thrust the key into the makeshift lock across the old shed door. He hauled the chain free and stood back.

'Can I borrow that, Burke?' Mun asked. The young trooper shrugged and handed the chain to Mun, and Corporal Scrope looked at the chain in Mun's hand, his lips twitching with malice.

'You two keep your mouths shut about this,' Scrope warned the guards, pulling the creaking door open. They nodded and Massie shot Mun a conspiratorial grin which said *give them one from me while you're at it.* 'And no one comes in, understand?' Scrope added. 'Not unless it's the Prince himself.' Then he stepped inside and Mun followed, his heart pounding, a maelstrom of doubt threatening to burst his skull.

'Get where I can see you, you traitorous dogs,' Scrope growled into the dark space that smelt of lanolin, sweat and damp wool. Other than the six men the place was empty. 'All of you over there,' he said, pointing to the far corner. There was just enough moonlight spilling through the cracks between the split timber walls for Mun to make out the prisoners' faces, and five of them were glaring at the big corporal, the whites of their eyes shining in the gloom. The other shadowy face was turned towards him. Tom.

Sensing his brother's nearness in that makeshift gaol both fed Mun's courage and yet leeched it away because of what it meant he must do. If he *could* do it.

'Not you, scum, you get back,' Scrope growled at Tom, gesturing to the opposite corner, 'over there. It is you I've come to see, you lucky lad.' He hawked and spat a great globule of blood that splatted onto the shed wall and began a slow descent.

'If you are looking for your nose, you ugly sow, it's on your cheek. Just there,' Tom said, nodding because his hands were tied behind his back.

Some of the prisoners grinned but one, a short-haired, keen-eyed soldier, hissed at Tom to hold his tongue and Mun guessed that this rebel knew full well what the corporal had come for. Mun could almost smell the violence coming off Scrope.

'You should listen to your friend,' Scrope said, glowering at Tom, 'not that it will do you any good now.' He moved forward, a massive shape in that small place.

'Let him alone, you pig-faced son of a whore,' a solid, bald-headed rebel growled. 'If it's a fight you've come for, I'll happily oblige. I'll turn you inside out, you fen-sucked hag-rider.'

'Shut your mouth, rebel,' Mun said, glaring at this man whose glistening pate was crusted with blood. Mun's pulse was like a drum in his ears. The three-foot-long length of chain felt cold in his hands. Felt heavy too. Then Scrope backhanded Tom across his face and he thumped against the wall, fury blazing in his eyes.

'I'll admit I envy you that snout of yours, rebel,' Scrope said in that nasal voice, gingerly touching his shattered nose whose nostrils were sealed with dark scabs. 'You see, mine's full of snot and blood while yours is neat as the Queen's petticoats.' He grimaced. '"Wrath is cruel, and anger is outrageous. But who is able to stand before envy?"' His eyes were on Tom but he half turned his face towards Mun. 'That's from the book of Proverbs,' he said, arching one bushy brow. 'I'll wager your wet-nurse never whispered that drop of wisdom into your shells while you hung from her tit.'

He drew his dagger, the slender blade glinting wickedly in the murk. 'Well, scum, I'm going to cut your sniffer clean off,' he said, flicking the blade from left to right. 'Then I'm going to cut you a nice smile. Right here, under your chin.' With the index finger of his other hand he traced a U across his own throat. Tom's teeth flashed in the darkness.

'You're not the ugliest bastard I've ever seen,' the bald-headed rebel snarled at Scrope, 'but you look just like him. Fight me, you ill-favoured turd.'

Scrope ignored the insult and the challenge, instead stepping forward, slow and deliberate, the ballock dagger coming up.

'I don't think you should cut him, Corporal,' Mun said, wrapping each end of the length of chain round a fist. *Do it now!* his mind screamed. *Now!* But his limbs were frozen, muscles clenched like fists. 'Boone won't like it. If the lad's cut up.'

'Shut your mouth, Rivers, or I'll bloody cut you 'n' all.'

The world around Mun seemed to shrink, crushing him, veiling past and future and leaving only the moment.

'Don't be shy, lad,' Scrope said, beckoning Tom with the dagger. 'Come to old Scropey.'

With two strides Mun threw his arms and the chain over Scrope's head, yanking it around his neck, then hurled himself backwards with all his strength and Scrope came too, so that Mun's back slammed onto the ground and the corporal's huge bulk knocked the wind out of him, crushing him. But Mun arched his back, stuck out his chest and wrenched the chain, hauled on it with every fibre of his arms, his muscles screaming.

His nose was full of the stink of Scrope's greasy hair and part of him wanted to stop it all now before it was too late, but it was already too late and so he gritted his teeth and heaved on the chain and Scrope's booted feet hammered and scuffed against the earthen floor and his big hands clawed at the chain round his neck, seeking a finger's breadth between iron and flesh. A wet gurgling sound was escaping from Scrope's throat and Mun was vaguely aware that the guards outside might hear it, or else hear the corporal's boots striking the floor. Or, if they could not hear these things their suspicions might be aroused by the silence now that no one was talking. So he pulled that chain.

But the corporal's neck was like a young oak and the big man refused to die.

Then there was a boot heel on Scrope's throat and Mun was staring into Tom's grimacing face as the younger man crushed the big corporal's windpipe. And still Scrope would not die. His hands clawed at Tom's boot and Mun could see Tom's surprise at the man's enormous strength. So Tom leant into his work, fighting to keep his balance because his hands were bound behind his back, and Scrope would not keep still. Then another prisoner was there, the bald, solid-looking rebel, and he stood so that Tom could lean against him and with this leverage Tom was able to increase the pressure.

Three sharp raps shivered the gaol's door. 'Everything all right in there, Corporal?' Massie hissed.

Die, you damned stubborn ox! Mun's mind clamoured. *Before they come!* He heard a crack. Felt something give, just a little. But he kept pulling. He was aware of Scrope's right hand flapping against the earthen floor like a caught fish, but he knew it was done. Finished. This part of it, anyway. At last, the body on top of him was just so much dead meat and Mun rolled and bucked until he was able to squirm out from underneath and climb to his unsteady legs, sweat sheeting down his face, his arms trembling from their incredible efforts. And from the fear of what he had done.

'Brother.' The word was a hoarse whisper and Mun stepped forward so that the body on the ground was not in his line of sight. He felt sick.

'I wondered when you would come,' Tom replied. 'I saw you in Wormleighton.'

During the fight? Or afterwards? Mun wondered but did not ask. Questions could wait.

'We haven't much time,' he said, looking back at the door beyond which the two guards, or perhaps the whole of the King's army, waited, blades and firelocks ready. Suddenly, and with a dread that cut him to the marrow, he knew that Tom had no chance of escaping. Probably he never had. And now Mun's fool's enterprise had likely killed them both. 'Father will get you out of here,' he said, clutching at hope that was as substantial as musket smoke.

Tom shook his head, smiling grimly. 'If you believed that, you would not have just killed your corporal,' he said, nodding down at the corpse. Mun thought he would vomit, but held his brother's eye.

'Corporal, shall we open the door?' Massie called softly, his face pressed to the wood by the sound of it. Mun heard an edge of fear in his voice.

'There must be a way,' Mun hissed, still gasping for breath.

Tom shook his head. 'Say nothing to Father. The son of Sir Francis Rivers caught killing Cavaliers?' Tom let that idea hang in the fusty air. 'He rides with the King's Lifeguard, I presume.' Mun felt himself nod, sensed the other men's shock at the revelation of who their father was. 'They would hang me, brother, as an example. And Father would be ruined.'

Mun knew the truth when he heard it, and it choked him as surely as a chain around his own neck.

'Corporal Scrope!' Massie hissed, knocking again.

'Will you get us out before we see the end of a rope?' one of the other prisoners asked. Mun recognized him as the rebel captain whose surrender had saved the others' lives at Wormleighton. 'Give me your word and I'll see that you don't hang for this,' he said, nodding down at the dead bulk of Corporal Scrope.

'I will not leave without them, Mun,' Tom said in a low voice, steel glinting in his eyes.

Mun could not breathe. His mind was reeling.

'Your word, damn you!' the captain snarled.

Mun nodded.

'Untie me,' the captain said. 'Quickly, man. We have but moments.'

Before he knew what he was doing, Mun was working at the knot which bound the captain's hands behind his back. When he was free the man rubbed his wrists and nodded resolutely.

'Stand still,' he murmured.

'Boone's coming,' Massie growled against the gaol door.

'Ready?' the captain asked, and before Mun had time to reply a fist slammed into his mouth, knocking him to the ground.

He tasted blood and spat a shard of tooth. 'More,' he said, standing up, and Preston cracked his knuckles against Mun's temple and Mun staggered, putting a hand to the gash that was spilling blood down his cheek. Preston clenched his fist again, showing him the finger ring that had done the damage.

'Untie me,' Tom said, glaring at Mun. 'You need another man untied.'

Mun shook his head. 'I want to get you out not get you hanged.'

'Tom's right,' Captain Preston said, working at the knot behind Tom's back, 'it will be more believable with two of us.'

'Aye, he was a big bastard,' Will Trencher put in, kicking Scrope's body. Mun's head was ringing like a bell.

'Untie the rest of us,' Weasel hissed, 'we'll make a run for it.'

'We're in the middle of the King's bloody camp, you turnip brain,' Nayler said, rolling his eyes.

'Do you want to strangle your brother, Tom, or shall I do it?' Captain Preston asked.

'You do it,' Mun said to the captain, so Preston nodded and took up his position behind Mun, clamped his forearms round Mun's neck and began to squeeze.

He is going to kill me, Mun thought, then the man strangling him relaxed his vice-like grip for a moment. 'Call for help,' he said. So Mun called. Or at least tried to. He yelled Burke's name and then was cut off and could no longer breathe.

The door burst open and there was Burke and the other guard and more men besides. And Captain Nehemiah Boone was there too, Purefoy standing beside him with an expression like a dog that has brought its master a grouse.

'Let him go or you'll all hang before dawn!' Boone yelled, pointing two pistols at Mun's attacker. There were at least a dozen more firelocks pointing into that dark shed, the faces of the men holding them shocked and angry at seeing their corporal face down in the dirt.

'I won't tell you again, rebel,' Boone said, the pistols steady, fingers on the triggers.

The rebel captain released Mun and stepped back, hands raised, and Mun fell forward, choking. Really choking.

'What in God's name happened here, Rivers?' Boone clamoured. But Mun could barely breathe let alone speak and he crawled forward on his hands and knees as though desperate to escape his tormentors.

Burke was kneeling by Corporal Scrope, his ear down by the man's mouth.

'He's dead, sir,' he said, twisting back to Captain Boone. 'Dead as a damned doornail.'

'Bard, Downes, bring that treasonist rebel cur to me,' Boone said, turning and striding back out into the night.

'Lucky we stopped by, eh, Mun!' O'Brien said. The Irishman was checking the knots on the prisoners' bindings to make sure none of the others could wriggle free. 'You should have said you were coming to pay your respects to these lads.' He grinned. 'I'd have joined you.'

'Bastard cut Hector,' Mun grumbled, rubbing the back of his neck and nodding towards Tom.

'Looks like 'im or 'is mate finished the job on Corporal Scrope, too,' O'Brien said, then leant in to

Tom. 'For which I thank you,' he said under his breath with a wicked grin. 'You've made our lives easier and no mistake.' Tom glared straight ahead at the night beyond the open door and said nothing.

Two soldiers got hold of Scrope's feet and dragged him outside and Mun followed, avoiding his brother's eye as he left him in that death-smelling dark space and stepped out into the moon-washed night.

'Step away from the prisoner,' Captain Boone said, and Bard and Downes did as they were told, leaving the rebel captain standing tall on his own in the midst of two dozen of Boone's harquebusiers. 'Did you happen to be amongst Colonel John Brown's Parliamentarian Horse at Powick Bridge?' Boone asked the man. 'For they were a pitiful mob. Pissed themselves to a man as they died.' But the captain had nothing to say to Nehemiah Boone, who shrugged as though it did not matter. 'You, sir, are a traitor to your king and a murderer,' he said, 'but more importantly, you are an example to your men.' And with that Boone lifted both pistols and pulled the triggers, their charges exploding simultaneously, and for two heartbeats Captain Preston looked down at the raw, gaping hole in what had been his chest, then his legs buckled and he collapsed as the rotten egg smell of burnt black powder wafted over Mun.

'Lock the door, Burke,' Captain Boone said, a haze of smoke still lingering around his fine pistols as some of his men called out to others in the camp that all was well and there was no alarm. He turned to Mun, cocking his head to one side. 'If you ever go behind my back again, Rivers, I will put you on a charge and I do not care who your father is.'

'Yes, sir,' Mun heard himself say, as he stared at the dead captain. The expression on his boyish face was a mix of confusion and disappointment, a look Mun was coming to recognize on the recently killed. His thoughts raced in his aching skull, trying to catch up with all that had just happened. But one truth had broken from the pack and rode a full length ahead of everything else. It was the only thing that really mattered on that night, beneath that heavy sky and the half moon now and then breaking through the clouds.

Tom was alive.

CHAPTER EIGHTEEN

'WE HA GRAIN, MY LADY, AND LIVESTOCK. ELEVEN HEIFERS and thirteen beeves, all in fahne fettle,' the man said, glancing up at one of the two stone lions on their plinths either side of the gate in the boundary wall that stretched around Shear House and its grounds. 'Some pigs and sheep too,' he added, 'and a few daft hens and a cock who thinks he's lord o' the manor.' He flushed at that, forcing a nervous grin. 'If my ninny li'le lass has ney let 'em scarper,' he said, thumbing over his shoulder. 'Margery's a li'le wibbet.' Clearly hoping the animals would secure his family's entrance to Shear House, the man, who had introduced himself as Mister Cawley, now launched the second stage of his offensive and stood aside to give Lady Mary and Bess a better view of his family. They were all, it seemed to Bess, trying their hardest to keep the livestock from wandering off, though not entirely succeeding. 'We've come fro' Heskin,' Cawley said, 'and it's ta'en us all day to get here what with the cattle, but I thank God we came across no rebels abeawt for we should ha lost our animals if we had.' He scratched his neck, making it red.

'The traitors are devils. Them'll tek what they want,' he said, eyeing the six men armed with an assortment of matchlock muskets, swords and clubs who stood behind Bess and her mother just inside the gate.

'Well you and your family are safe now,' Lady Mary replied, trying to put the man at ease for he was clearly nervous, judging by the tremble of his hand and the sweat sheening his weathered brow.

The monotonous thump of hammers on wood and chisels on stone underpinned barked commands and the occasional crackle of musket fire, composing a melody that was to Bess's ears at odds with the still autumn afternoon as she considered the new arrivals, the third family to come in that day. She could see Cawley's wife, two boys aged around ten, a girl a little younger and another girl no older than five, who saw Bess and curtsied, flashing a smile that was more gaps than teeth.

'You are welcome here, Mister Cawley,' Lady Mary went on, 'though I will tell you the same as I have told the others. In return for our protection you will be required to share the work and what victuals you have.' She cocked her head, examining the stout, unkempt-looking fellow before her and making no pretence otherwise. 'You can shoot, I presume?'

'I have tried it once or twy, my lady, but I doesn'd own a piece,' Cawley said.

Lady Mary nodded. 'Up at the house Isaac will show you to your quarters and then you, Cawley, will report to the Major of the House. Your wife will be given her instructions in due course.'

With that Cawley dipped his head respectfully and Bess and her mother stepped aside to allow him, his family and their livestock train through the gate.

They had come from all across the West Lancashire plain, whole families flocking to Shear House and other estates whose protection they sought against the armed rebels who rode across the country preaching their sedition, decrying their king, beating some who would not waver in their loyalty to His Majesty, and even, sometimes, stringing up those they suspected of papism.

At first it had just been the tenant farmers, the copyholders and leaseholders, who had come through those lion-guarded gates: those whose livelihoods were tied to a lesser or greater extent to the fortunes of the Rivers family and their estate. But then others had come because word had spread that Lady Mary Rivers would turn none away who asked her protection. Now, Bess reckoned there were upwards of three hundred and fifty men, women and children living at Shear House, and of those some ninety-four men had been formed into a garrison of sorts by an ex-soldier and friend of her father named Edward Radcliffe. Radcliffe had fought on the continent and though his best days were clearly behind him, Lady Mary believed his experience would prove invaluable in the coming days and had employed him as Major of the House, tasking him with the procurement of arms and other necessaries.

Another salvo of musketry battered the damp air, making Bess start and her unborn baby kick. She looked up the drive and saw a thin skein of musket smoke waft up from behind the spinney of birch and sweet chestnut. The men were being drilled, as they were every day, and yet still Bess had not grown used to the horrendous noise. Even when she had watched them load and present their matchlocks, knowing the thin, thunderous cacophony was coming, she could not help but flinch.

Another musket cracked belatedly. Then another. But the fusillade had been neater than usual.

'They're getting better,' Bess said to her mother as she watched Cawley's train progress up the drive, his cattle lowing and his sheep bleating at the noise. Cawley's youngest daughter was clinging to her mother's skirts as they approached the woods beyond which the paltry assemblage of matchlocks had roared their defiance.

'They will need to if your father does not return before the rebels come,' Lady Mary said, gesturing for Bess to follow as she walked towards the first of several wooden platforms being erected against the eight-foot-high boundary wall over an earth rampart. Each was a simple construction fifteen foot in length upon which a handful of men could stand head, shoulders, chest and, most importantly, muskets above the wall. 'There is not enough wood in West Lancashire, nor time or labour to make a proper rampart all the way round,' Lady Mary said, 'but Mister Radcliffe assures me that these will give the rebels cause to think. They will buy us some time.'

Looking up at the structure before her Bess doubted these platforms would count for much, doubted the farmers and servants of Radcliffe's garrison would stand up there for long once the rebels came. But she said nothing, smiling at one of the labourers, who blushed crimson and renewed his hammering with gusto.

'Do you know what he actually said? Radcliffe, I mean,' her mother went on, giving that smile of hers that was so controlled, as well schooled as one of Sir

280

Francis's best mares. '"We shall preach to the rebels from these pulpits, m'lady,"' she said in her best imitation of the one-eyed veteran, '"and they shall repent of their pernicious perfidy under fire, brimstone, and musket balls."'

Bess smiled again, knowing the smile had not lit her eyes. 'I feel much safer for having Mister Radcliffe here,' she said, which was almost true. Either side of the wooden platform men were hammering chisels into the boundary wall, cutting loopholes through the red bricks, which was no easy task for the wall was over a yard thick. Bess's hands instinctively cupped the swell of her belly.

'He will be back soon,' Lady Mary said, and Bess knew they were no longer talking about Edward Radcliffe. Her mother had meant her Emmanuel. Her love.

'And in the meantime your father will keep a close eye on him. He is very fond of Emmanuel. In spite of certain . . . difficult circumstances.' Bess felt the baby kick again, as though in mockery of her mother's subtle reproach. 'I'm certain His Majesty's Lifeguard will not see any serious fighting. I believe they are held in reserve,' Lady Mary went on, turning her back on Bess and peering through one of the new loopholes. 'The King is many things, my dear, but he is not a warrior. I cannot imagine that Emmanuel will get anywhere near the rebels for all his desire to play the soldier.'

'I pray you are right, Mother,' Bess said, sickened by the thought of Emmanuel bravely riding into battle, riding to do his duty to his country and king. To her and their unborn child. And yet Bess had found cold comfort in her mother's words, most of which she had spoken into a hole dug out for matchlocks, unable to meet Bess's eye.

For in her heart Bess knew that her mother was afraid and that those words were weightless, of no more substance than musket smoke drifting on the breeze.

Osmyn Hooker was a dangerous-looking man. He reminded Mun of other veterans he knew, friends of his father who had fought in the Low Countries, for Hooker had all of their swagger and the self-assured poise of those used to giving commands and having them obeyed. But there was something else about him too, something that made Mun's flesh crawl and his jaws clamp together so that he realized the muscles in his cheeks ached now as they sat in the shadow-played dark of Emmanuel's tent. Perhaps it was the livid scar engraved across Hooker's forehead, the vestige of an old slash wound that could so easily have taken those narrow, malevolent eyes. Or perhaps it was the five musket-ball dents Mun had counted in the man's forge-black breastplate, only one of which was likely to be the maker's test shot, for they spoke of Hooker being a man many had tried to kill. Maybe it was the man's strange accent, which made it impossible to tell where he was from, deepening the enigma and suggesting that this tall, lean soldier was a man without roots. A man without familial ties.

And yet it was none of those things. Mun's unease at being in Osmyn Hooker's company was, he knew, down to the fact that Hooker's only loyalty was to money. For the man standing before him there was no King or Parliament, no religious ideal or appetite for social revolution; there was just crowns, shillings and pennies.

Which was exactly why they had sought him out.

'The risks are great,' Hooker said, 'for all of us.' The man's stare was biting. It took all of Mun's composure just to hold his eye.

'We are prepared for the risks,' Emmanuel put in, squatting beside them as the breeze played against the canvas. Mun glanced at him and Emmanuel nodded, confirming that he was willing to play his part in the plan that could see them all shot or swinging on the end of a rope if it went awry.

'Just play your part, Hooker,' Mun said, 'and we shall all get what we want.'

Hooker leant forward, so that Mun caught the scent of tobacco smoke that clung to the mercenary's curled moustaches. 'As to what *I* want,' Hooker said, 'I shall expect the balance of what we agreed at sundown the following day. I will send someone to collect it from you. Make sure he leaves with it.'

'We are good for it, sir,' Emmanuel said, bridling.

Hooker's teeth gleamed in the dull yellow bloom of a single candle. 'Oh, I know you will pay,' Hooker said, turning his piercing stare on Emmanuel, 'for you fine gentlemen know that I will cut your throats if you don't.'

Mun felt Emmanuel tense at this, but to his relief his friend did not bite back.

'I will have the money ready,' Mun said. We are supping with the Devil here, he thought.

Osmyn Hooker leant back on his stool and pulled his beard through a scarred fist.

'Who is this man to you,' he asked Mun, 'that you

risk so much, not least your father's reputation?'

Mun was taken aback but tried not to show it. He had not revealed his name to the mercenary and yet Hooker knew he was Sir Francis Rivers's son. 'He is my brother,' he said.

Those eyes weevilled into Mun's soul. He got the strange feeling that the mercenary was somehow divining the pain in his heart, the torment of a family betrayed by a son, the sorrow of a brother set against his brother.

'"He who brings trouble on his family will inherit only wind,"' Hooker said, one eyebrow arched, and Mun was surprised for the second time for he had not expected such a man as this to quote from the Bible. He wondered too whether the quote was aimed at Tom or at Mun himself, for if their plan failed it would be questionable which of them had dragged the family name into the deeper mire.

Hooker stood, opened the tent's flap and peered out at the camp. Two men engaged in hushed conversation passed close by and the mercenary waited at the threshold until they had gone, then he turned and locked eyes with Mun one last time.

'Tomorrow night, then. Be ready.' Mun's eyes flicked to Emmanuel, then he nodded. But Hooker had gone.

'I can see why Colonel Lunsford tried to recruit the man,' Mun said. 'I get the impression it would be better to have Osmyn Hooker in your pay than in your enemy's.' He worked a crick out of his neck, surprised how relieved he was that the mercenary was gone. 'Where on earth did you find the fellow?'

Emmanuel grinned. 'It was Hooker and his men that brought the silver out of Oxford. Officially it was Sir

284

John Byron's task, of course. Doesn't look good His Majesty turning to the likes of Hooker to get jobs done. It's too easy for folk to imagine the King will do the same thing to win this war . . . pay mercenaries from Ireland or the continent. But it was Hooker that delivered all that plate . . .' Emmanuel smiled again, 'while you were giving the rebels a good hiding at Powick Bridge. Gods, I wish I had been there.'

'I would not wish for such a thing if I were you,' Mun said, a shiver running through him as a fusillade of bloody, chaotic images exploded in his mind's eye.

Emmanuel shrugged. 'When Colonel Lunsford said he wanted to find Hooker before the rebels did, I volunteered to go recruiting.'

'So Hooker *is* working for Lunsford? For the King?' That thought was horrifying, considering what they had just planned with the mercenary.

Emmanuel grinned. 'Not tomorrow night, he's not,' he said.

The wind had been building and by sunset next day it was whipping through the Royalist camp, causing tent canvas to snap loudly and unsettling the horses. The camp was spread across mostly open ground and the best the King's men could do was lash down their tents, soothe their horses, and hunker down. It was too windy even for fires other than those set in pits dug out of the earth, and this was good, Mun knew, because it meant the camp was even darker than usual.

Grumbling of loose bowels, he had left Rowe and O'Brien drinking beer in their tent and, snatching up a hand axe from a wood block, had walked east through the camp to where one of the many powder magazines had been set up in open ground away from camp fires and soldiers with their tobacco pipes. It loomed as a great silhouette now against the inky horizon as he and Emmanuel crouched in a ditch beside a boundary hedge. They were near enough to thousands of men and horses to hear them settling down for the night, talking and laughing, and close enough to catch their stink now and then on the wind. But they were removed enough, Mun hoped, not to be noticed as they skulked in the dark like foxes by a hen coop. Two tents had been erected, one inside the other, to ensure the neatly stacked barrels inside, or rather the precious black powder within them, stayed dry. Two guards, musketeers with lit match between their fingers, walked in opposite circles around the magazine, the flax cords burning fast and angry in the gusts. Inside would be one, maybe two more men, though these would be armed only with blades to avoid any unwanted accidents with sparks igniting the cache.

Still, they will have blades, Mun thought, and blades can kill as well as matchlocks. A blade can keep coming.

The plan was simple. One that relied on men's natural fears, on their base instincts to survive. But Mun had already seen enough of battle, of the confusion that descends when hooves pound the earth and flame licks black powder to know that even the simplest plan can go to hell in the time it takes to whisper the Lord's Prayer. Besides which, some men, sometimes, could be stupidly brave. Or just plain stupid. And Mun could not still the nerves that writhed and twisted like serpents in his guts, making him nauseous. Emmanuel, on the other hand, seemed more excited than afraid. Eager, even. As though he thirsted for the danger. Which made Mun fear for the man's safety even more. He offered up a silent prayer to God to keep Emmanuel from harm, but a sudden wash of doubt and guilt flooded him. Was he mad? Coercing Emmanuel, the man whom Bess would marry, into playing a leading role in this reckless act. As for himself, Mun was already a traitor. He had all but killed a man on his own side, his corporal no less, to save his brother's life. And the rebel captain, a good man it seemed to Mun, had died too. But now he was making Emmanuel a traitor also.

Emmanuel put a hand on Mun's shoulder. 'I chose freely,' he said as though he had read Mun's thoughts. Mun could only nod. Then Emmanuel tipped the slip-ware cup he held so that Mun could look inside. The length of match curled within was smouldering, one end glowing menacingly. Mun nodded again. Hidden inside the cup the lit match would not give them away in the dark. In his other hand Emmanuel held a stick, around one end of which he'd wrapped a swath of pitch-soaked linen, its tarry scent whipped this way and that by the wind. Attached to his belt was a powder flask with a thin spout. The man was up to his neck in it now come what may.

'Thank you,' Mun said, those two words seeming short measure though he hoped his friend felt the weight in them. Somewhere out in the dark, amongst the wind's howl, an owl screeched. Mun glanced around to make sure they were alone. There was almost no moon, just a nail-paring and even that obscured more often than not by clouds that raced across the sky as though fleeing from some celestial terror.

'We are family,' Emmanuel said in a low voice that would not be carried off in the wind. 'At least, we will be soon enough.'

'Soon enough,' Mun agreed, smiling. 'Can we trust him?' he added, letting the axe's short haft fall through his hand until he gripped it by the neck. He had not brought his sword because it might rattle in the scabbard or trip him and he needed stealth more than steel. He had brought his two pistols, though, had loaded them and shoved them into his belt just in case.

'We have no choice,' Emmanuel said.

Mun knew that was the truth of it. 'I saw men building gallows today. Bard said they're for the prisoners. They're going to hang them, Emmanuel. As an example.'

'They'll not hang Tom,' Emmanuel replied with a half grin.

Mun had not told Emmanuel about the events of four nights past, and the admission that he had been the one who all but killed Corporal Scrope rose in his throat. But he swallowed it back down. Breaking his brother out of a Royalist gaol was one thing. Murdering the corporal of his own troop was quite another and he could not risk his friend abandoning him at this stage. He hated himself for exposing Emmanuel to this risk, but he needed him, too.

'It's time,' Mun said, glancing around. It had been properly dark for an hour now and Hooker and his men would be in position. Waiting for his signal. 'If something goes wrong,' he began, locking eyes with his friend, 'run. Understand? Do whatever it takes to get away.'

Emmanuel's brows arched, though he said nothing, didn't need to. Mun knew full well that the chances of them, two troopers from Prince Rupert's Horse, getting to their mounts and breaking clear of the Royalist camp if something went wrong, were slim. Even if they escaped, then what? Their and their families' reputations would be ruined.

What would become of Bess? his mind questioned. *What of her fatherless child?* 'Are you ready?' he asked, pushing such thoughts away. Emmanuel nodded, checking the match in the slipware cup again, then setting it on the ground to free up his hands. Then he dug his fingers into the soil and scraped up clumps of damp earth and Mun did the same, smearing the muck across his own face and beard, the rich smell of wet soil filling his nose.

'How do I look?' Emmanuel asked, his teeth and eyes glowing against his pitch-black face.

'Much improved,' Mun replied through a strained smile, and almost said that at last he could see what Bess saw in him, but thought better of it. Better to leave Bess out of it for now.

Some creature, of a fair size by the sound of it, rustled in the hawthorn hedge, breaking twigs as it scurried away from them.

'Let us hope those men don't want to die today,' Mun said, gesturing with the short axe towards the gunpowder store. And with that he crawled out of the ditch, keeping low like a predator, the wet ground soaking his breeches, his sleeves wicking water. He suddenly wanted to speak to his friend again, to run through the plan one last time, but the time for talking had passed and now God would see them either triumphant or destroyed.

He fell flat, his face down in the grass, and sensed Emmanuel do the same as one of the guards stopped on his round some thirty-five paces away. Mun did not even look up. He feared the whites of his eyes might

289

betray him or else the musketeer might sense that he was being watched the way men sometimes could. He held his breath. The wind moaned above him and somewhere to the east beyond the powder magazine a dog was howling and Mun's ears were straining to detect any movement from the guard that might suggest they had been seen. Then he heard the intermittent splatter of liquid and exhaled slowly because the musketeer had only stopped to relieve himself. The clatter of the wooden powder flasks hanging from the man's bandolier told Mun he had pulled up his breeches and recommenced his round and so Mun dared lift his face from the grass. Emmanuel was already moving again.

Damn you, Tom, a voice seethed somewhere in his mind.

It was achingly slow going, using their forearms to drag themselves forward inch by inch. Then there must have been a tear in the cloud because suddenly Mun could see a guard's face as he came round the right-hand end of the tent; could see that his breeches were grey and his tunic was blue, could count each of the twelve powder boxes hanging on its pair of strings from the bandolier across his left shoulder. Mun's mind screamed a curse as he let go of the axe's haft, his hands squirming down to the pistols tucked in his belt. Surely they would be seen. He braced for Hell to break loose, for the musketeer to yell and raise his matchlock and fire. But the guard kept walking and Mun whispered thanks to God, though he knew they were by no means in the clear yet.

Rein in your fear, he commanded himself silently. They know there are thirteen thousand loyal men around them. They are complacent. They will not see us.

They will not see us.

He froze again, relieved to sense that Emmanuel had too. They could go no closer without being seen. He felt the cold sweat on his back, his heart pounding against his breastbone. Now, no more than twenty paces away, it was time to wait. Every few minutes there came a point when one guard had passed their position so his back was to them and the other was still on the tent's far side, yet to round the corner. Mun's muscles bunched. With ghost movements, slight contractions of sinew and tendon, he told each of his limbs what was expected of it.

Then it happened. He was up. Running in a half crouch, the wind gushing past his ears. Then down. The smell of damp canvas and lanolin filling his world. And Emmanuel was on his back beside him. Mun lifted the hem just enough and Emmanuel slithered beneath it and was gone. Then the hem lifted again and Mun sensed that the guard was only feet away but he did not look up, just crawled under and there was no explosive percussion from a matchlock. They crouched in the narrow dark space between the two tents, their eyes adjusting to the deeper gloom and Mun's lungs burning as he fought to keep his breathing quiet and measured. Slowly, he lifted the flap of the inner tent and peered in, eyes searching. Barrels. Lots of barrels, filling the tent with the sweet scent of oak. Slow, slower than he had ever done anything in his life Mun crept towards the nearest of them, then eased himself up until he could peer over it, and there, near the tent's entrance, sitting on a stool, his back to Mun and a shortened halberd lying across his knees, was the last guard. Beyond the rippling canvas the wind howled and Mun had the notion that God was on his side because that storm was drowning out the sound of Emmanuel crawling, powder flask in hand, backwards from the barrels, pouring a zigzag trail of gunpowder as he went.

Mun saw in the inky dark a hand extend towards him and so he gave Emmanuel the short axe. Then he drew both pistols. He cocked one and spun the other over so that he gripped it by the barrel, then edged closer to the guard, willing the man not to turn.

The man turned.

'One word and I'll shoot,' Mun rasped.

The guard leapt up, bringing his halberd scything through the darkness so that Mun felt the air as it passed a finger's length from his face. He launched himself forward and clubbed the man across his face with the pistol's butt and the guard fell backwards against the canvas.

The sound of splintering wood filled the tent as Emmanuel hacked into a barrel like a man possessed.

'Bloody fool!' Mun hissed at the guard, relieved to see that he was still moving, flailing, trying to stand.

'Help! Guards!' the man yelled.

'Hurry!' Mun growled into the dark behind him.

'Guards!'

Then the entrance flap was yanked aside and two silhouettes loomed against the dark grey of the night beyond, lit match between their fingers.

'Rebels!' one of them yelled, as the tent bloomed with light and filled with the blustery roar of flame because Emmanuel had touched the burning match to his torch.

'Get out!' he screamed. 'Get out now!' and all three

guards turned and ran because fire was the Devil and black powder was his servant.

'Do it!' Mun snarled, so Emmanuel touched the torch to the end of his gunpowder trail and it flared into furious, hellish life and raced, and Mun and Emmanuel scrambled beneath the first tent and the second and then they were back in the open, running for their lives.

The first explosion lit the sky but the second filled the world like God's wrath. Then there were more but Mun and Emmanuel did not stop. They ran north to the brook and threw themselves down, scooping up water and sloughing the mud from their faces even as the camp burst into life and men yelled and horses screamed. And somewhere to the north-west, if Osmyn Hooker could be trusted, and if God was on Mun's side, the rebels were breaking out.

CHAPTER NINETEEN

'GOD ALMIGHTY!' MATTHEW PENN EXCLAIMED AT THE FIRST explosion. Then a series of even louder booms ripped through the night, their thunder lingering after the initial blasts, rolling across the plain as Tom pushed back against the gaol wall to lever himself up onto his feet – no easy thing after the beatings he'd received.

'Not God, Matthew, more like all bloody Hell breaking loose,' Nayler said. Hands bound behind his back, the short man was on his tiptoes, one cheek pressed against a crack in the wall as he tried to spy on the wind-scoured world beyond.

'Our boys are attacking!' Weasel announced, his eyes showing bright and hopeful in the gloom, so that Tom was amazed how well his own sight had adjusted to the dark.

'Sounds more like an accident,' Will Trencher said, 'like some stupid bastard lit his weed in the powder magazine.'

'Could be our lot, though,' Weasel protested, an edge of disappointment in his voice. 'Right, Will?'

'If it is, the numbskulls have forgotten their bloody

muskets,' Trencher replied, and Tom saw Weasel's narrow shoulders slump at that because Trencher was right and there was no crackle of gunfire to accompany the initial massive salvo. But that barrage, accident or not, had unleashed chaos into the night beyond those rotting walls. Officers yelled orders, horses galloped past, flaming torches flew, their red-yellow light flaring through the cracks in the gaol's walls, illuminating the men around Tom fleetingly before the darkness reclaimed them.

'Whatever it is it's got this lot jumping,' Penn said.

Then a fusillade of musketry tore through the howling wind and Weasel turned to Trencher. 'See! I told you!'

Trencher shrugged big shoulders.

'That's close!' Nayler said.

'Very bloody close,' Penn agreed.

Then something thumped against the gaol's door and Tom and the others instinctively backed away. Another thump, shaking the whole decrepit structure. Then one more and the door fell off its hinge and a giant with a breastplate and an ancient pot helmet on his huge head stood where the door used to be, a grimace splitting his bird's nest beard.

'Here they are,' he growled over his shoulder, then stepped aside as another man strode in. By the wan light Tom saw a face that was battle-scarred and murderous. The man's three-bar pot and breastplate were black and he gripped two long wheellock pistols which he pointed into the shadows as though he had come to execute them.

'Which one of you is Thomas Rivers?' he asked, scouring each of them with cold eyes.

Tom stepped forward. 'I am,' he said. 'And who are you?'

The scarred man grinned savagely. 'Unless you want to swing from those gallows out there tomorrow, you're all coming with me.'

A horse whinnied in the gloom behind the scarred man and Tom felt the others' eyes on him as the giant and two others came in clutching wicked-looking knives. The giant came up behind Tom, grabbed his bound wrists in one hand and began to saw through the rope. The others were being cut loose too.

The wind moaned and whistled past the open door and to the east muskets cracked intermittently.

'The only way you're going to live through this is if you keep your heads down and do what I say,' the scarred man said, gesturing with a pistol for Tom and the other four men to follow him out into the night.

Freedom and the fresh night air flooded Tom's blood as he glanced this way and that, trying to make some sense of what was happening. Torches streaked through the darkness. The wind flailed all sound like chaff sifted from grain, so that some carried across the moat to them but most did not. It was disorientating, but Tom guessed that men were being formed into companies. Somewhere close by, the King of England must be wondering if the battle was at last beginning, he thought, as the giant thrust the reins of a grey mare into his hands.

'I want *my* horse,' Tom said, the wind whipping his long hair across his face. The mare looked frightened, one foreleg was stamping the ground and her ears were twitching madly, trying to sift the dissonant sounds of the night around them.

'You'll take what you're bloody given,' the giant rumbled, his massive beard bristling in the gusts. Penn, Trencher, Weasel and Nayler were already mounted, necks craning, tense and alert, so Tom hauled himself into the saddle.

The scarred man's handful of troopers positioned themselves around them, their eyes searching the dark paths between the barn and other smaller outbuildings and the shadowy plain beyond. Then Tom saw the two guards who had been stationed outside the plough shed. They were twenty paces away, lying in the long grass where the ground sloped down to the moat. The young man with the hare lip – his name was Burke, Tom remembered – was almost certainly dead, his pale face mutilated by a dark, savage gash. As for the other man Tom could not say, for all he could see of him was his boots.

'Steady now, keep your damned heads,' the scarred man said over his shoulder, his big horse tossing its own head spiritedly. 'Rivers, you stay by me or I'll slice off your balls and feed them to Bartholomew here.' The giant gave a feral grin that Tom wanted to smash through the back of his massive skull. Instead, he gripped the reins and kicked his heels and rode between the two livestock pens in which the beeves shuffled in the shadows, lowing at the wind and the night's tumult. Then they walked their mounts across the duckboard bridge over the moat and into the main camp, where a burly sergeant was swinging his halberd, bellowing at the soldiers that were forming into battalia as best they could amongst the tents and paraphernalia of the camp.

'Who are you?' the sergeant challenged them, then he got a better look at the scarred, arrogant-looking man leading them and he recoiled slightly, ramming the halberd's butt onto the ground. 'The watchword, sir, if you please!'

'Rubicon,' the scarred man replied haughtily, barely deigning to look down at the sergeant, who dipped his head and stood back to let the riders pass. Tom felt eyes on them in the dark, sensed the Royalist soldiers watching them, wondering who and what they were, for they must have made a strange sight. Then, as they turned their mounts north away from the main camp and rode towards the outlying pickets, a shout carried to them on the wind from the direction of their island gaol.

'They've found the lads we clobbered,' Bartholomew said matter-of-factly. 'Should've sunk 'em in the moat with the rest of the shit.'

'Where are we going?' Penn hissed to the man leading them.

'Shut your mouth,' Bartholomew growled.

Then a musket ball fizzed past Tom's right ear, accompanied by a distant crack, and all of a sudden men were running after them and more matchlocks spat angrily, gouts of flame rending the night's thick veil.

'Move! Rivers, with me!' the scarred man yelled, spurring his horse so that it lurched forward, and Tom's own mare followed, breaking into a gallop as the small troop tore away. Hooves hammered the soft earth and the wind dragged tears across Tom's cheeks and muskets spat lead balls at them.

The scarred man fired a wheellock to their right and Tom saw a flash of red tunic as a sentry spun away in the dark.

'Heads down!' the scarred man yelled, because there were men up ahead too, more Royalist pickets, their

298

match-cords glowing malevolently as they blew on them and put muskets to shoulders.

Tom threw himself forward as a ragged volley roared, and Weasel's horse screamed and fell but the rest galloped on. One of the scarred man's troopers whooped madly and another fired his wheellock and the pickets yelled their challenges.

Tom hauled on the reins and his grey mare squealed in protest, but she had no choice but to turn with the savagely wrenched bit in her mouth and Tom kicked with his heels and together they galloped back the way they had come. He saw Weasel's horse thrashing on the ground and rode up to it, leaping from his own mare before she had come to a stop. A musket ball had ripped into the horse's neck and blood bubbled from the wound, but there was no sign of Weasel.

'Weasel!'

'Here!'

Tom spun and saw him crouching in the dark, cradling one arm, his face a knot of pain. Then his eyes widened. 'Look out!'

Tom turned, recoiling as a musket's butt flew past, missing his face by a finger's length, the sentry roaring and bringing the matchlock round again as though it were a club. Tom threw up his arms and twisted away out of reach of a blow that would have snapped his ribs, then threw his right leg forward and swung his arm in a wide arc, crashing the fist against the man's cheek with the distinct crack of breaking bones. The man dropped but another musketeer appeared from the gloom, slashing at Tom with a crude sword, his powder boxes dancing noisily across his chest. 'Mount up, Weasel!' Tom yelled, desperately avoiding the sweeping blade.

'Rebel scum,' the musketeer growled, his sword's point striking out like a snake as Tom leapt backwards. Hooves thundered and a great horse galloped by and the musketeer's head exploded in a spray of brains and gore that stung Tom's face as they spattered him. The rider who had hacked the man's head apart had wheeled his mount around almost before the musketeer's body hit the ground. It was superb horsemanship.

'Told you to stay with me, Rivers!' the scarred man bawled, extending an arm down. 'Get on!' Tom glanced behind him. Weasel was mounted and ready, so Tom grabbed the man's arm and pulled himself onto the horse's rump as musket balls ripped shreds in the air all around them. The scarred man raked his heels and the horse snorted and obeyed, breaking off into a gallop, its hooves drumming their four-beat rhythm against the soft ground. 'He never said you were a damned fool!' the man yelled, as priming pans flashed and muzzles spat tongues of flame towards them.

'Who?' Tom yelled in the man's ear, arms around the armour, hands clenched against the breastplate.

'Your goddamned brother!' the scarred man roared, then bawled at his horse to run faster.

Because death was all around.

After a little over a mile the horses had begun to blow and so they had slowed to a trot, riding north for another three miles, Tom guessed, then cutting west through newly ploughed fields whose muddy furrows glistened wetly in the dim half light. It was heavy going for the horses until the scarred man led them down into a hollow way whose high earthen banks were lined with brambles, hawthorn and blackthorn and which was just wide enough for them to ride three abreast. In that sunken lane they were out of the wind and it felt like a sanctuary of calm amidst the wild night.

'The King's curs will never find us now,' Trencher said, breathing hard after the ride. For a while some Royalist cavalry had chased them across the rolling land and Tom had even heard a dog yapping after them. But the wind whipped all sound in different directions and with no moon to help them the King's men had given up the chase. Tom knew Trencher was right. To the Royalists it would seem as if they had simply vanished on the wind.

Bats flitted above them, catching Tom's eye now and then, their squeaks piercing the drone of the wind beyond the sheltered track. 'She's a fine horse,' he said, his breeches wet from the mare's sweat, for she had carried the two of them and had never faltered.

'If she's lame after this you'll owe me ten pounds,' the scarred man said over his shoulder and Tom clenched his teeth within a bitter smile. He did not even have ten pennies. His two most treasured possessions – his father's pistols and Achilles – were somewhere back in the enemy's camp and all he had left were the clothes on his back and the ring on his finger.

'Where are you taking us?' Penn asked. The leader of this group of mercenaries – for surely that's what they were, Tom had decided – gave no reply, as though he deemed the men he had freed unworthy of an explanation. But they got their answer a little while later, when they rode up the hollow way's western bank towards a copse of oak and beech. There on the fringes, the trees' skeletal, wind-stirred limbs clawing at it in the dark, was an old dwelling whose thatch roof had fallen. Besieged by tall nettles and climbing brambles the place was clearly abandoned. Until now.

'You'll stay here until your brother comes,' the scarred man said when they had dismounted. 'There's food in there to last you until then.' Trencher was examining Weasel's arm, carefully squeezing here and there to check for broken bones while Weasel flinched and cursed and watched the big man's face intently, as though he suspected Trencher was enjoying himself.

'What about the rest of us?' Penn asked, glancing at Tom. 'Are we free to return to our regiment?' The giant Bartholomew and the other eight mercenaries were busying themselves lighting pipes, retrieving wineskins from the dilapidated house where they had stashed them earlier, wrapping themselves in bad-weather cloaks and sheltering from the wind.

'I just told you, you'll stay here. What happens to you is up to Edmund Rivers,' the scarred man said. He was leading his horse back and forth, his hawk's eyes scrutinizing the way it walked for any tell-tale signs of injury. Tom could see that the horse was fine. 'My job was to get you out,' the mercenary said without looking up, 'and here you are.'

The wind was moaning and so Weasel and Trencher drew closer, Weasel scratching the wispy beard that was sprouting in patches from his cheeks and chin. His other arm was in a sling improvised from a swath of dirty linen. 'Makes sense your brother would try to get you out before they put a rope round your neck,' he said, beady eyes flicking from Tom to the scarred man and back again, 'but why did this lot put themselves in harm's way for the rest of us? We are your brother's enemies.'

'Weasel's on to something there.' Nayler joined them, rubbing his backside which was sore from the ride. 'Your father is Sir Francis bloody Rivers.'

Tom felt his lip curl. 'My father doesn't know I fight for Parliament,' he said, arranging the pieces of the puzzle in his own mind. 'If these men had broken only me out, the rest of you would be questioned. You saw what my brother did to his own corporal. You would know he was behind all this, and you'd spill it to save yourselves a beating. Why wouldn't you?'

'Aye,' Trencher agreed, 'one way or another the trail would lead back to Tom's brother.'

Weasel still looked confused.

'Breaking us all out looks like the rebels' work,' Penn told him, still grinning at the word *rebels* as he turned back to Tom. 'Still, your brother has taken an appalling risk.'

'He's a bloody fool,' Tom said.

'That's as might be,' Will Trencher put in, 'but Cavalier or not I owe the man a drink.'

Mun came two days later. The storm had passed and the night was crisp and dry, so that the scarred man and his troopers had known someone was coming long before they had seen him. Mun came on Achilles, armed as though riding into battle and stiff with tension.

'He's an evil bastard,' Mun said, nodding towards Achilles and patting the stallion's neck as Tom took the bridle and put his face against Achilles's muzzle, whispering in greeting. The others were a little distance away, sharing a fire whose crack and pop echoed off the trees in the still night.

'You blew up a powder magazine?' Tom asked, still looking at Achilles, stroking his poll.

'Hooker needed a distraction,' Mun said with a shrug, taking a thong-tied leather bundle from under the cantle of Achilles's saddle. Tom glanced over at the mercenary, putting the name to the man.

'They'll hang you, brother,' Tom said.

'They'll hang you first, Thomas. Unless you come to your senses and come over to us.' Mun's jaw firmed and he gave a slight shake of his head. 'How can you ride with these men? They are rebels and traitors.'

Tom looked into his brother's face upon which the fire's light fought with shadow, revealing then concealing his eyes. 'You should get back before you are missed,' he said.

Mun's eyes flared in the orange glow.

'I did not do all this so that you could continue down this road to ruin. It's madness, Tom. You are a Rivers! We are the King's men.'

'I am not,' Tom said. Mun shook his head and glanced over to the other rebels who were sitting rubbing their hands near the flames and coughing as the smoke wreathed each of them in turn. 'It is not they who have bewitched me, brother,' Tom said, reading Mun's face, 'but it is through their cause that I will find what I seek. It is through such as they that I will make it right.'

When Mun's gaze swung back to Tom his eyes were heavy with sadness. 'You cannot bring her back, Thomas,' he said, reaching out and gripping Tom's shoulder, making him flinch.

'I loved her,' he said, his throat constricting.

Mun nodded slowly. 'I know you did, brother.' For a moment Tom held Mun's eye, but then he looked down at the muddy ground. 'But vengeance is not the way,' Mun said. 'In vengeance there is only pain. More pain, even, than you feel now. Listen to me, Tom.' The grip on Tom's shoulder tightened. 'Father was trying to protect you. He was trying to protect us all. Minister Green was a secret Catholic.' Tom shrugged off Mun's hand, stepping back. 'I am almost certain of it,' Mun said. 'They found certain effects. Things in the minister's house that proved it.'

'And you believe them?' Tom challenged. 'That whoreson Denton staged that whole play. I'd wager Achilles on it.'

'Why would he?' Mun asked, turning his palms up.

'Because the people were baying for blood and Denton thought if he gave them George they would be appeased. They would go back to their work and his rents would keep coming in.' Tom swept an arm through the air. 'Or because he knew war was coming and he thought that throwing his weight around would remind folk that he was Lord Denton. They'd see what happened to anyone not in his favour. Anyone not on his side when the shooting started. Or because he is an evil-minded, poisonous bastard.' Tom felt his hands ball into tight knots by his sides. 'He raped her, Mun,' he said, the pain welling in his chest, so that he felt each beat of his heart and feared it would burst.

'I am sorry,' Mun said, the muscle in his cheek bouncing, his eyes brimming with tears. 'But you are wrong to blame Father. Think of Bess. Think of Mother. You will ruin us all.'

'Think of Martha!' Tom spat, the empty pain of longing flaring into anger, like black powder in the priming pan when the serpent snaps down. 'Martha lies in the grave!' His mind summoned a picture of his love, of her chalk-skinned face being eaten by maggots, the larvae writhing and twisting in the jelly of her green eyes. 'Father could have stopped it all,' he said. 'He could have tried.'

'And so you betray him?'

'He betrayed me!' Tom said.

'And your king?' Mun challenged. 'Is he to blame for your troubles, too?'

'Go, brother,' Tom heard himself say. 'Go back and hope they do not discover what you have done.'

But Mun shook his head and stood still, his eyes driving on, though he knew his words had fallen short.

'Come back with me, Tom. We'll deny whatever they accuse us of. They never discovered your name, did they?'

Tom shook his head and hope flared in his brother's eyes.

'You can enlist with Prince Rupert's Horse,' Mun said. 'We'll ride together.'

'I will not go with you,' Tom said. 'I cannot.'

'The rebels cannot win this war,' Mun said. 'They cannot hope to defeat His Majesty's army.'

'Then I will die in battle and I will be with Martha,' Tom said. He felt a tear spill down into his beard. 'Tell your king he will find us at Kineton.'

Mun stood there for a little longer, brother looking at brother.

'Then God be with you, Thomas,' Mun said, his jaw clenching as soon as the words were out. He looked down at the leather bundle in his hand, hesitated for a heartbeat, then handed it over. Then he turned and went to Achilles, fetching a bag of coin which he took over to Osmyn Hooker.

Tom did not need to unroll the leather parcel to know what was inside. He knew by its weight that it held his father's long firelock pistols and he wondered what risks his brother had taken to get them back.

'You do not need to count it, Hooker,' Mun said, 'you have my word it is all there.'

'Am I to trust the word of a man who kills his own comrades?' Hooker asked theatrically, cocking his head like a bird of prey, examining Mun.

'For my brother I would kill you where you stand,' Mun said, glaring at him.

Hooker grinned. 'What shall I do with the others?'

'Let them go,' Mun said. Hooker shrugged as though it mattered to him not at all. Then Mun mounted one of the horses which had carried the rebels to freedom, turned it round and walked it away from the old house in the trees and he did not look back.

And Tom watched him go.

CHAPTER TWENTY

THE BOOM WAS LOW AND GUTTURAL, LIKE GOD'S WRATH AS it pummelled the still October dawn, and the iron ball slammed into the brick wall, spraying shards across the muddied ground. Bess knew that if not for the earth that had been hastily dug and thrown up against the wall – Edward Radcliffe's idea – that ball would likely have punched straight through and continued in its flight. But the piled earth absorbed some of the blow, albeit this rampart did not reach the top of the wall or even extend the full length of it.

'And so the guns begin to play,' Radcliffe said with a nod that was almost approving. The other men of Shear House's garrison glanced around nervously but the Major of the House barked at them to keep their eyes on the rebels. Those rebels were strung out in a thin cordon three hundred yards beyond the boundary wall and were still busy throwing up earthworks and sorting themselves into troops, though the gunners had announced that they at least were ready.

'A demi-cannon, milady,' Radcliffe said, knuckles sweeping some dried mud off the lace-trimmed falling band lying over his ancient and oft-mended buff-coat. 'Fires a twenty-seven-pound ball a distance of sixteen hundred feet. With the right charge,' he added, extending the nub that was all that remained of the index finger on his right hand. War had exacted a heavy price from the veteran and yet he was unbowed, for which Bess admired him.

'A formidable weapon then,' she said, trying to keep her voice measured and even despite the gun's furious roar which she would have sworn yet rolled across the Lancashire hills like a decaying thunderclap.

'Bess, go to the house,' Lady Mary said, then turned back to Radcliffe who had assumed that stance of a man long used to the music of war, feet planted shoulder width, hands clasped behind his back.

'Formidable indeed, Miss Elizabeth,' Radcliffe said, rewarding her observation with a nod and half smile that made Bess feel entirely justified in ignoring her mother's command. 'In the right hands such a gun can spit ten balls every hour.'

'And *is* it in the right hands, Major?' Lady Mary asked, shooting a disapproving glance at Bess, which Bess affected not to notice. Lady Mary was dressed in her riding gear: felt tunic and breeches tucked inside tall boots, and had strapped on the ornate back- and breastplate that had been made for Mun when he had turned fifteen. Her hair, red threaded with white, was tied back from her regal face and, looking at her mother, Bess imagined Lady Mary to resemble Boudicca, warrior queen of the ancient Britons.

'Ask me again in one hour, milady,' Radcliffe answered in all seriousness. 'What I can tell you is that the rebels are amassing quite a horde out there. The demi-cannon alone requires a team of at least ten horses or sixty men to move it from here to there. Nine men to fire it.'

One of the men up on the makeshift rampart against the boundary wall called for the major's permission to fire his musket as his match was almost burnt out. But Radcliffe shook his head.

'No point wasting powder and shot!' he called. 'At that range you'd only tickle the traitorous curs.' Men laughed at that and Bess gave silent thanks that they had Radcliffe on their side, for the defenders on the platforms and those peering through the loopholes cut in the boundary wall took confidence from the old veteran and Bess had the idea that confidence was worth a lot in war, perhaps as much as a demi-cannon that spat iron balls.

Lady Mary stepped up to the wall and a young farm hand dipped his head and stepped aside to allow her the vantage of his spy hole upon the enemy. Bess shivered at the sight of the young man's weapon – a bill with its long cutting edge and rear and top spikes – because it seemed barbarous that such a crude agricultural tool might now be turned against other men. Might now hack at flesh rather than lopping the limbs from trees.

'I wish we had such a gun,' Lady Mary said, peering through the loophole.

'Il fait plus de peur que du mal,' Radcliffe said.

'It frightens more than it hurts?' Bess said, working out the major's poorly accented French.

'Like raising children, eh, milady?' Radcliffe said, turning his one eye on her. Lady Mary turned her head and raised an eyebrow and Radcliffe winked at Bess and gave that half smile of his that somehow changed his whole face, taking twenty years off him, and hard years too. Bess blushed in spite of herself because she had the sense that the old veteran was flirting with her. Then, suddenly aware of her greatly increased size, her cheeks burned all the more fiercely because she knew her father's old friend was merely being kind.

'I appreciate your wanting to comfort us, Major,' Lady Mary said, turning to face him properly now, 'but I am not a child to be spared the cold realities of war. I will have the truth if you please.'

Radcliffe seemed taken aback and Bess felt embarrassed for him, but he recovered almost instantly.

'Yes, of course, milady,' he said with a curt nod.

'Look abeawt!' someone yelled and Bess turned, hunching, her arms across the great swell of her belly as another boom kicked dawn's guts, followed by a crash and more flying shards of brick. She turned back to see the last tremble of the boundary wall and dust blooming in the crisp morning air.

The only one who had not flinched or cowered was Radcliffe. Instead he seemed to be judging the distance along the brick wall between the first strike and this last.

'They are reasonably fast,' he said with grudging admiration, 'but their aim is poor and they only have the one gun.'

'So we are safe for now?' Bess asked, wondering if the terrible roar of the demi-cannon frightened the child inside her.

Radcliffe glanced at Lady Mary and then back to Bess, weighing his response carefully. 'I would feel much happier if you would return to the house, Miss Elizabeth,' he said sternly. 'This wall cannot be defended.' He looked at Lady Mary, who nodded as though she appreciated the truth of it, no matter how disagreeable it was. 'Without that gun they would sit out there until Christmastide. With it they need never come in range of our muskets. Providing they have enough shot, they will batter us, milady. Sooner or later this wall will come down and there is nothing we can do about that.' Bess saw despair darken her mother's face like a sudden storm cloud across the sun.

'Yet the curs will not have it as easy as all that,' Radcliffe went on, sweeping an arm back towards the house. He saw the look on Mother's face, too, Bess thought. 'We still have the inner defences, milady, and they are more easily defensible,' he reassured, 'for we can concentrate our fire, you see.' He pointed to the section of wall from which the mortar had been blasted, leaving the structure hopelessly vulnerable. 'They will have to move that gun, all six thousand pounds of it,' he said, 'and when they do they will be vulnerable.' Lady Mary studied her husband's friend for a moment, then seemed satisfied that he was telling her the truth of it for she nodded curtly and came over to Bess, taking her hand and turning her away from the failing defensive wall.

'I will take my disobedient daughter back to the house and when I come back we will discuss how we can make life unpleasant for our unwelcome guests.' With that she led Bess up the gentle slope towards the long drive that disappeared into the birch and sweet chestnut wood on its way to Shear House.

'And I will buy us time, Lady Mary!' Radcliffe called after them. 'I will bleed those rebel dogs and I will buy us time. You may rest assured about that.' Then the old

312

veteran strode up to the wall and, hands clasped in the small of his back, thumbs circling each other, he peered through a hole at the enemy.

Because the rebels were at the gates of his lady's house and it was up to him to stop them.

Bess had made a crescent of several bed pillows and it was in this nest that she lay night after night, craving sleep that never came. The nest relieved some of the discomfort caused by her distended stomach and the weight of the child growing in it, but not all of it, and even when her eyes grew heavy and sleep lured her into its forgetful embrace it was fleeting, vanquished by a little fist or kicking foot inside her. For if the baby had once frightened her with its stillness, these days, it seemed, it rarely if ever stopped wriggling. But at least she had a bed, and Bess knew she ought to be thankful for that. Shear House was full. It had become a refuge and a garrison. It was a bastion loyal to His Majesty King Charles; a rock around which chaos in the form of rebellion flowed. Families bedded down wherever they could, many lying on fine old tapestries which Lady Mary had given them against the autumn chill, for much of the seasoned wood was stacked in piles reserved for cookfires and not to be wasted as fuel for warmth.

Her own breath pluming in the cold of her bed-chamber, Bess shifted position and, lying on her side, pulled a bolster deeper beneath the weight of her unborn child. She scrunched her toes and rubbed her legs which had gone numb, though that, she was sure, had more to do with being with child than it did with these unseasonably cold October nights.

She placed a palm on her belly, above a probing hand or foot. Be glad you are cosy and warm, little one, she thought. For many are not.

Most of the men were out there in the dark defending the perimeter wall. Bess pictured them talking in low voices, shivering in their cloaks a mere five hundred paces from other men, their enemies, who were doing just the same.

A sense of guilt coupled with the need to feel her legs again made her throw off her blankets and she waddled to the window, leaning back to counterbalance her precious burden. Damn the rebels for starting this war. They would see the world turned upside down.

She focused her hatred on the one face she could summon without even trying. Captain Downing had called again on Lady Mary but this time she had not let him set foot inside the grounds and Bess no longer thought he was in the least bit handsome. The young Parliamentarian officer had stood beneath the imperious gaze of the gatepost lions and matched their pride with a new arrogance of his own: a haughtiness which he wore thick as his buff-coat, a defence against her mother, Bess guessed, who the upstart had learned was a formidable opponent.

'You must yield up Shear House and all the persons, goods, and arms within it, into my hands, to receive the mercy of Parliament,' he had said, this time not even deigning to look at Bess, much less ask after her health. 'And I shall have your final answer by two o'clock tomorrow.'

'You shall have it in the morning, at eight, Captain Downing,' Lady Mary had replied. 'Good day to you.' And with that she had ordered the gates shut, and the captain had mounted and turned his horse around before the great beam was dropped into its stanchions.

'Why did you not give him our answer now, Mother?' Bess had asked, for she had wanted to see this man's conceit pierced by a woman's pride, had burned to see the grey flint flash in those brown eyes.

'I have my reasons, Bess. Be patient,' Lady Mary had said.

Now Bess stood alone in the gloom of her bed-chamber, looking out across the grounds, her breath turning to cold water on the window glass. By the bone-light of the moon she could see men stationed behind barricades, gabions which Major Radcliffe had had them construct in strategic positions on the lawns in front of the house. These, along with the rose garden wall at the rear, would act as a secondary redoubt should the boundary wall be breached. *When* it was breached. The last defence, if it ever came to it, would be the house itself, but the thought of the rebels turning that hateful, thundering gun on Shear House's walls did not bear thinking about.

A shiver of apprehension scuttled up Bess's spine as she returned to her bed, because today was the day that Captain Downing would receive his answer from the mistress of the house.

Daylight woke her, and Bess realized she had slept for two hours, perhaps even longer, for which she was grateful. She would need all of her strength to support her mother and play her part. With Sir Francis, her brothers and Emmanuel gone, it fell to them, the Rivers women, to uphold the family's honour and do their duty to their king. Come what may.

Now, she eased down onto her knees, resting her

elbows on her bed, palms clasped against her chin. 'Please, Lord, give me the courage to do what must be done,' she said in a voice barely above a whisper. 'Make me brave like my mother, that I may fear no evil. Make me strong, Lord.' The prayer was softly spoken and yet sent Heavenward with the force of a ball from a musket. For she would not let her condition weaken her in the face of the challenge. The child would not diminish her by its vulnerability. Rather it would lend its burgeoning strength to her own. The unborn's vitality, its naturalness, would flow through Bess's veins and steel her sinews against the enemy, against these unnatural traitors who would make war upon their own king.

She climbed to her feet and went over to the window. 'You are my father's enemies and so you are my enemies,' she said, looking out across the dew-soaked lawns, beyond the defenders smoking their pipes behind their barricades and gabions, their muskets and pole-arms leant against the bulwarks. 'God have mercy on you.'

There was a knock on the chamber door and at her word it opened wide enough for a shock of unruly copper hair to push into the room.

'Lady Mary is expecting you, Miss Elizabeth,' young Jacob said, his eyes fixed on the floor. Crab was there too, the wolfhound's big brown eyes looking up expectantly at Bess.

'I've told you you must call me Bess, Jacob,' she said, gathering up the fur-lined wool cloak she had taken to sleeping beneath, and throwing it round her shoulders.

'Yes, Miss Eliz—' He gave a chastised nod. 'Bess.'

'That's better,' she said, smiling at him and rubbing Crab's head. The boy had become a quiet, serious young man in the months he had been living at Shear House and Bess's heart bled for him. For all that he had lost. 'That vain young Captain Downing is here for his answer then,' she said, following Jacob and Crab down the stairs, 'and so he shall have it.'

'I heard some of the men talking . . . Bess,' the boy said, glancing at her from beneath fair lashes. 'They were laying a wager on whether Lady Mary would surrender the house.'

'They still have money to waste?' Bess exclaimed, as Isaac limped to the front door ahead of her and opened it. 'Then we shall be able to buy more powder and shot.'

'Ah, there you are, Elizabeth,' her mother said. With her was Major Radcliffe and six of his best men, all armed with matchlocks and assorted blades. The men dipped their heads at Bess and she nodded and smiled back, hoping to give them a portrait of calm resolve. 'Are you feeling up to a little walk, dear?' her mother asked, a wry smile tugging her lips. 'The young captain is waiting for us.'

'The air will be good for me, Mother,' Bess said, and with that the small party set off along the drive and the men at their positions in trenches and behind gabions filled with earth doffed their caps and stood tall as they passed.

When they arrived at the main gate Lady Mary ordered it opened and this time she invited Captain Downing to step inside the walls his demi-cannon had been pounding on and off for the last four days. The captain seemed surprised at the invitation and Bess saw an expression flash across his face that looked for all the world like relief, and she knew that he thought they had seen the sense of giving in to him. He believed they would yield up the house, and suddenly Bess feared that they would.

Two belligerent-looking men in buff-coats came with the captain and they eyed Radcliffe like farmers sizing up a bull at the market and wondering how much it would cost them. The Major of the House paid these men no heed at all and Bess saw how this riled them, though they uttered not a word, leaving all the talking to their young captain.

'The time for civilities has passed, my lady,' he was saying, 'and this issue will be resolved.' He held his three-bar pot under his arm and his other hand rested on the pommel of the sword at his hip, a subtle reminder perhaps of what the defenders of Shear House could expect if they resisted further. 'You have done your duty and your husband could not expect more. You have put up an admirable show of defiance,' he went on with a smile that was so many crumbs strewn across the ground for the hungry. 'You have received the attentions of our big guns—'

'You have only the one gun,' Radcliffe interrupted, 'a demi-cannon for which you've insufficient powder else you'd fire it more. Though you could have a cannon royal aimed at my arse and I would not break a sweat,' he said, his one-eyed glare threatening to burn a hole through Radcliffe, 'for your gunners could not hit a barn wall from the inside with the doors shut.'

'I can assure you – Mister Radcliffe, is it? – that our powder cache is more than sufficient,' the captain replied. 'As for my gunners, do not mistake clemency for incompetence.' To Downing's credit he returned a glare of equal contempt to the old veteran's. But there were other eyes lending their weight to this exchange too, Bess knew. Radcliffe's men stared down from the makeshift ramparts or turned their faces from the loopholes in the boundary wall. She knew also that back at the house women and children would be pressed to the upper windows, eager to catch a glimpse of Lady Mary, their protector, talking with the rebels.

'Now, my lady, I must insist on having your answer,' Captain Downing said, clearly buoyed by his riposte to Radcliffe.

'Very well, Captain Downing,' Lady Mary replied, her voice considerably louder than it had been thus far. 'You have persisted with this outrage, with this most grave offence, and as due reward I would have you hanged from this very post,' she said, nodding up at one of the stone lions. 'But, Captain, you are nothing more than the foolish instrument of a traitor's pride.' Bess saw the young captain flush, but he held his tongue. 'Take this answer back to . . .' she paused for effect, 'Colonel Egerton, is it? That he, insolent rebel that he is, shall have neither persons, goods, nor house. If the providence of God prevent it not, my goods and house shall burn in his sight; and myself, my daughter, and my soldiers too, rather than fall into the rebels' hands, will seal our religion and loyalty in the same flame.' At this the men of Shear House's garrison cheered and the three rebels looked around them warily. Major Radcliffe was grinning, the corners of his remaining eye creased like a crow's foot.

'God save the King!' Lady Mary exclaimed.

'God save the King!' came the reply from those nearby and was echoed as it travelled across the lawns by other men at other stockades.

'God save the King!' Bess heard herself yell. And God save us, she thought, because death is coming.

CHAPTER TWENTY-ONE

Friday, 21 October 1642

TELL YOUR KING HE WILL FIND US AT KINETON. TOM'S WORDS
rolled over in Mun's mind like pebbles tumbling in the
never-ending surf, as rain seethed in the darkness.
Twenty-four men rode hunched in their saddles, bad-
weather cloaks cinched tight at their necks to keep the
water off firelocks, wheellocks and powder flasks. At
the head of the short scouting column rode Captain
Nehemiah Boone, his mood as black and foul as the
night because he did not trust Mun's information and
thought they were drowning in their own skins for
no good reason. For Mun had claimed that one of the
prisoners had betrayed Essex's position to Corporal
Scrope with the big man's hand round his throat and
his knife at his eye – before they had attacked Scrope,
killing him and almost killing Mun, too.

'They never mentioned Kineton to me, Rivers,' Boone
had said, smoothing his moustaches between finger
and thumb, his eyes searching Mun's as though he

suspected him of some deceit. 'I'll wager the traitorous scum are still in Worcester.'

'Corporal Scrope was persuasive, sir,' Mun had said with a shrug of his shoulders, glancing at Prince Rupert. 'The rebel thought we were going to kill him if he did not tell us what we would hear.'

The Prince had scowled at that, for he had already expressed his disappointment in Mun for going along with Corporal Scrope's vengeful plan that night, saying it was not behaviour becoming a gentleman in Mun's position let alone the son of a knight. But other matters had overshadowed the events of that night and now the Prince was still fuming at the prisoners' escape. He almost refused to believe that the rebels had dared infiltrate his camp, blow up a powder magazine and break a handful of men out from under his regal nose.

'He *was* a rough fellow, your corporal,' Prince Rupert had said to Boone, not looking up as he filled a pipe with tobacco, thumbing the leaves into the bowl.

'I was somewhat persuasive myself, Your Highness,' Boone had replied, clearly put out by the unspoken suggestion that Corporal Scrope would have inspired more fear in the captured Parliamentarians.

'I am sure you were, Captain,' the Prince said, raising a placating hand. 'But perhaps the rebels decided to hold their tongues when they heard the hammers on the gallows you were building a spit away from their gaol. Not much point in talking if you're for the rope anyway,' he said, hoisting a dark eyebrow.

Boone had conceded the point with a purse of his lips as he took his own pipe from inside his tunic.

Then the Prince had looked up at Boone, fixing him

with those intelligent eyes. 'Take a small party and ride to Kineton. It's a market town, is it not?' Boone nodded. 'Sniff it out, Captain. If Rivers believes the rebel was telling the truth then it is surely worth a short ride.'

'But Rivers and Scrope were going to throttle the bastard,' Boone had protested. 'The runt would have said anything.' He took a wax taper from the table and held it to a candle flame until it lit.

'And you were going to hang them, Captain,' the Prince had said, drawing deeply on his pipe and exhaling so that the smoke wreathed his handsome face and coiffured curls. Mun had felt Boone bristle beside him at that. 'Besides, my uncle has already sent Lord Digby and four hundred Horse out west looking for the rebel curs,' the Prince said almost plaintively. 'Rather we find the enemy than Digby, heh?'

'Digby couldn't find his arse with both hands,' Boone said, at which the Prince had almost smiled.

'Ride to Kineton,' Prince Rupert went on, 'and then we shall know one way or the other.'

Boone had raised the taper to his pipe, the stem of which was clasped between his lips, then stopped and took the pipe out, a frown contracting his brow in the molten copper play of firelight.

'Now?' he'd asked, his top lip curled to reveal a flash of tooth.

'The dogs of war heed not the rain,' Prince Rupert had replied, one hand pulling the candle across the table to illuminate some crude maps, the other gesturing to the door, flapping languidly.

Now, the King's army was on the march again, heading for Banbury to attack Parliament's outpost there, thus opening the road to Oxford and undermining Essex's stronghold at Warwick with its well-garrisoned castle. And Mun was soaked to his marrow and stretched on the rack of his own guilt. He had murdered Corporal Scrope albeit with his brother's help. He had blown up a Royalist powder magazine and orchestrated an attack which had seen men on his own side killed. He had freed enemy prisoners, rebels who would conceivably kill King's men in the next days. Even if none ever discovered the truth of it, if he managed to keep it buried until the end of his days, he would have to bear it. The betrayal would yoke him. And yet, he questioned what sort of man he would be if he had stood aside and watched them hang his brother. Family is family.

'Blood is blood,' he muttered to himself, earning a sideways glance from O'Brien. But the Irishman did not probe and Mun was thankful for that as the recent events turned over in his mind and his conscience scavenged like crows in a ploughed field, finding nothing of sustenance. *If Tom had seen reason and turned from his path of vengeance, I would not shoulder this shame*, a voice in his mind dared suggest. *We should be in this storm together, brother, fighting with father. Rivers men doing our duty to our king.* But the voice was drowned out by louder truths. I failed to turn Tom from his course, he thought. I failed us all.

'You want war, brother,' he murmured. 'Well, it is coming.'

The brooding, rain-lashed Wormington Hills were no fit place for a God-fearing man to be on such a devilish night, so the red-haired Irishman O'Brien was saying when Daniel Bard came galloping out of the dark, his raw-boned face glistening beneath his pot helmet as he pulled up and walked his horse to Captain

Boone. He had ridden to the top of a scrub-lined crest while the rest of the small troop had gathered beneath the dripping branches of a gnarly ancient oak, moaning about having to be out when others were keeping warm and dry.

'They're here, Captain,' Bard said. His long grey hair was plastered against his hollow cheeks and Mun thought he looked like a living skeleton. A look the savage grin on his face did nothing to contradict.

'How many, Corporal?' Boone asked and Bard's grin twitched at the use of his rank because he had not wanted the promotion. Boone and Prince Rupert had forced it on him. With Scrope dead the troop needed an experienced man and Bard was as experienced as they came.

'All of them,' Bard said. 'Every mother's whoreson. Every last bloody one of them by the looks of it.'

As Bard turned his horse back around Boone looked at Mun and for a heartbeat Mun almost thought the captain was about to acknowledge that Mun had been right and he had been wrong. But there was more chance of the sun suddenly appearing in the sky and drying their bones, he knew, as Boone kicked his heels and followed his corporal up the rise to take a look for himself. Mun and the others followed.

There, on the plain below, their myriad fires struggling against the deluge, was Parliament's rebel army. It was vast and the sight of it made Mun's breath catch in his throat. Well, little brother, his mind whispered, here we are. Just like you wanted.

But Mun wanted it too, he realized now, looking down upon the enemy camp. At last the game of cat and mouse could end and the real fight begin. The

King's righteous army would crash into these rebels like an avenging wave, sweeping them from the plain and drowning their sedition once and for all.

'Now that's a sight to freeze a man's balls,' O'Brien said, shaking his head in wonder.

'Then it's just as well you don't have any, you Irish troll,' Richard Downes said, spitting rain.

Vincent Rowe sniggered at that, earning a growl from O'Brien. 'Another snort out of you, young Vincent, and I'll ride back to camp with yer own balls 'neath my saddle,' the Irishman threatened.

'So Lord Digby is still chasing shadows and we have found the rats' nest,' Captain Boone remarked, as much in awe of the sight before them as the rest of them, or so it seemed to Mun. 'Corporal, what would His Highness the Prince do were he here now?'

Leaning forward over his saddle's pommel, Bard looked across at his captain, the whites of his eyes glowing dully. 'The Prince would charge down this hill and put the whoresons to flight,' he said, 'the whole bloody lot of 'em.' Mun got the impression he was only half jesting.

'And I'd wager they would fly, too, like starlings, the damn cowards,' Boone agreed. 'But I fear His Majesty the King would resent not being invited to the ball. For it shall be quite the dance,' he said, hauling his big mare round, his lips pulled back from his teeth.

Mun turned Hector and gave him the heel and in a heartbeat he was flying through the sheeting rain with the others, his nerves thrumming because they had found the enemy and now there would be a battle. There had to be. But as he flew, his world shrunken to himself and Hector and the mad rhythm of many hooves drumming the drenched earth, an iced rope snared his guts. It drew tight as a noose. Because he knew the time had come to tell his father about Tom.

Mun wished he had been there to see the Prince receive the news, but he could imagine well enough his reaction. It would be sheer feral joy, for the Prince was a child of war. Battle was what he lived for, it was the yardstick against which he measured himself and others. Mun had seen him shortly after Captain Boone had delivered his report. The Prince had walked through the camp like a common soldier, appearing suddenly in the feeble glow of the fire by which Mun and the others crouched and stood, trying to dry their clothes, for the rain had seemingly abated.

'Rivers!' Prince Rupert said. Beside him his white poodle, Boy, barked his own greeting and Mun crouched to rub the tight wet curls on the dog's head. It gave a rolling growl and snapped its teeth and Mun pulled his hand away to the sound of the Prince laughing. 'He's eager for the fight like the rest of us,' the Prince said. 'Would you believe it but the rebels have written songs about him! They say Boy is the Devil in disguise come to help me. That he is invulnerable to attack and can catch bullets fired at me in his mouth! Now that's a faithful hound, hey?'

'They also say he can find hidden treasure, Your Highness,' O'Brien said, grinning. 'Now that's what I call a dog!' They all laughed at that, for the big Irishman, standing there drying his stockings above the fire, looked like a man who could use a few pieces of buried treasure.

Mun had also heard it said that the dog was the

Prince's familiar. He suspected others were thinking the same though none chose to mention it.

'It would seem Corporal Scrope did not die for nothing, would it not?' Prince Rupert asked him. 'And we can be glad he squeezed that rebel like an arse sponge. Though it is a pity Scrope gave his life for the information.'

Mun smiled. 'He was a good soldier,' he said, which was no lie. There was something about the Prince that made Mun loath to lie to him.

'Tomorrow at last we shall have our battle. If the rebels stand,' the Prince added. 'Is Hector ready for the tumult? There will be more guns than you have ever heard.' He grinned. 'It will sound like the gates of Hell opening.'

Mun was surprised and flattered that the Prince had remembered Hector's name. 'He is ready, Your Highness. As am I.'

'We're all keen to whip the rebel curs,' a portly, red-nosed trooper named Lawrence said, stifling a great belch that threatened to explode his face. 'We shall squash them. Like lice between your finger and thumb.'

'Well said, that man,' the Prince said, looking from him to the other men in the troop who were standing tall in his presence. He surveyed the big Irishman O'Brien and young Vincent Rowe, Corporal Bard, Richard Downes and the others, and he appeared to like what he saw.

'I have come to tell you all that you will have the place of honour in the field, I shall see to that.' Some of the men cheered and some raised their cups and pitchers towards the Prince, who received their gestures gracefully. Then with a swirl of his scarlet cloak he moved on to the next fire and the men around it, reminding Mun of a boy who is too excited to stand still for any length of time.

'If Bard asks after me, I'll be back before dawn,' Mun said to O'Brien, taking up his helmet and rubbing it on a dry part of his tunic.

'Where are you off to?' the Irishman asked.

'To see my father,' Mun said.

'Ah, well, give His Majesty the King my best when you see him, won't you,' O'Brien said, a grin splitting his red beard. 'Tell him to be kind to Ireland, too, there's a good lad.'

'Anything for you, Clancy,' Mun said, leaving a wake of bawdy laughter and a scowling Irishman.

'Who told you?' the Irishman called after him.

'Your ma has sewn it into your tunic!' Mun called behind him, and the laughter boomed in the night.

The regiments of the King's army had been scattered across one hundred square miles of countryside between Kineton and Banbury, but Mun knew he would find his father near the King himself, who was at the home of Sir William Chancie at Edgecote. When, after an hour's unhurried ride, he got there, he found the King's camp a maelstrom of soldiers and horses and the many chaotic components of the artillery train. Mun had the sense that the air itself was trembling, like a great banner in a stiff wind, such was the excitement for the coming battle. Soldiers of the King's Lifeguard, the Prince of Wales's Regiment and Sir Richard Byron's Brigade of Foot were striking camp and preparing to march, for this was the beating heart of the Royalist cause and the news of Essex's proximity – and thus of a fight to be had – was spreading from this point, like trails of black powder whooshing in all directions.

It took a while, given the chaos, but eventually Mun found Sir Francis talking with Sir Edmund Verney, Knight Marshal to King Charles. The two men had come from a war council with the King himself and Mun knew that Prince Rupert would be furious to know that there had been such a meeting to which he had evidently not been invited. But then Mun knew that the upper echelons of the King's officers had begun to form factions for and against the Prince. Mostly against if the rumours were to be believed.

His father smiled broadly at the sight of Mun. 'My son Edmund,' he announced proudly, 'who serves with the Prince's Horse.'

Sir Edmund Verney eyed Mun and nodded appreciatively, as though in Mun he saw what a son should be, and Mun cursed inwardly at his timing for he remembered that Verney's eldest son, Sir Ralph Verney, had also turned his back on his father and sided with Parliament.

'Your prince must be busy teaching his officers the Swedish tactics he has so faithfully studied,' Verney said with evident sarcasm, snatching the broad-brimmed hat from his head and running a hand through his long hair, 'for we had not the pleasure of His Highness's company just now.'

Mun felt his hackles rise at the suggestion that the Prince had deliberately slighted the other generals. But then, perhaps he had.

'Sir Edmund will have the honour of bearing the Royal Standard as we sweep the rebels from the field,' Sir Francis said, reading Mun's face and changing the subject.

'Then you will not be left wanting for excitement, Sir Edmund,' Mun said, trying to smile. 'The rebels will be thick as flies around your party. May God be with you, sir,' he said and meant it. For it took a brave man to wave the King's standard at fifteen thousand enemies.

'And with you, Edmund,' Verney replied. 'Now if you'll excuse me, gentlemen. Sir Francis, I'm sure your boy did not trudge through the mire to wish me luck.' One-handed, he placed the hat back on his head. 'For God and King Charles,' he said.

'For God and King Charles,' Mun and Sir Francis repeated in unison, then Verney headed off into the whirling chaos of the King's army.

'Some wine?' Sir Francis said when they were as alone as they could be among hundreds of armed and arming men. 'My quarters are nearby.'

Mun shook his head. 'I cannot stay.' Sir Francis nodded, understanding. As always, Mun was struck by how much bigger, broader his father looked in his buff-coat. But Mun knew the ageing body beneath it: the pale skin, the frail legs from which the muscle had melted over the years. The shoulder that ached in damp weather and which must therefore be aching now, though none would know, and the knuckles that were swollen with pain.

He is too old for battle. The thought struck Mun like a hammer blow.

'Are you up to it, my son?' his father asked, his brows knitted with concern.

And yet he worries for me? 'Yes, Father,' he replied, 'we will beat this rabble and march on to London where we'll pull the rest of the rats out by their tails.'

Sir Francis nodded, but his smile was a ghost. 'Then what is troubling you, Edmund?'

Mun considered swallowing what he had come to say. He could tell his father that everything was fine. They could share some wine and then he could head back to join his troop, leaving unsaid what needed saying.

'It is Tom, isn't it?' Sir Francis said and even by the erratic light of camp fires Mun saw his father's face turn ashen.

Mun nodded. 'He is alive, Father.' Sir Francis's eyes flared but he held his tongue. Waiting.

Mun took a breath. 'He fights with the rebels.'

His father flinched as though he'd been struck, his knees buckling, and Mun threw out an arm but his father refused it, somehow keeping his feet.

'No, Mun. It is a lie. I will not hear lies! No lies.'

'It is the truth, Father.'

'How do you know this? Who told you?'

'I have seen him. We have spoken.'

Sir Francis shook his head, as though to dislodge those terrible words from his ears and stamp them underfoot. He looked mired in disbelief and fury, unable to pull free, and Mun sensed that his father resented him then for keeping this secret. He will blame the son standing before him, he thought, for that is all he can do. So be it.

'Tom was one of the rebels we captured at Wormleighton village. One of the men who broke out four nights ago.'

Sir Francis flinched again, glancing around to see who might be in earshot. Then he stepped in and clutched Mun's arms, glowering. 'Did you break him out?' he hissed.

Mun said nothing.

His father was glaring at him, then he scrubbed his face as though waking from a nightmare. 'Who else knows about this?' he rasped. 'Does Emmanuel know?'

'Yes,' Mun said, and his father drew back, aghast.

'What could you have done, Father?' Mun asked, shrugging. 'You eat the King's bread. Drink his wine. What about your reputation? Our name?'

'Damn my reputation! He's my son!'

Mun swept his helmet through the air between them in place of words he could not find. There were tears in his father's eyes and so he looked away, watching a tall sergeant wielding his halberd threateningly at a knot of pikemen who were lingering by a freshly fed fire, passing round a pitcher of wine instead of being where they ought to have been.

When he looked back, his father's eyes were still boring into him, bristling with questions.

'Is he at Kineton with . . . the rest of them?' Sir Francis's voice suggested he had saddled his temper and was thinking now.

'I am almost certain of it,' Mun said. 'He wants this fight, Father. He has changed. He is not the Tom we knew.'

Sir Francis nodded, pulling his short grey beard through his fist.

'Death . . . war changes all men,' he said.

'He is full of rage. He craves revenge.'

'Revenge against me?' Sir Francis asked, nodding as though prepared for the answer. Yet Mun could not say it.

'Not you, Father. Lord Denton and his son, Henry.

He blames them for Martha's death. Denton raped her. And there was more you don't know.'

Sir Francis shook his head. 'It seems there is much I do not know,' he said.

A rampart of silence was thrown up between them and each seemed to be waiting for the other to breach it. Around them men yelled, horses whinnied and beasts of burden moaned.

'And now for something which *you* do not know. Something I should have told you,' his father said.

Mun's blood froze in his veins. His mother and Bess broke the surface of his mind like the dead he had seen floating in the river at Powick Bridge.

'Shear House is under siege,' Sir Francis said. 'Or at least it may be by now. The rebels have risen in Lancashire. Your mother wrote some weeks back informing me she had received an ultimatum from a captain serving under a Colonel Egerton.' Now fury bloomed in Mun but he held it in check. 'I wrote back telling her to yield the house. That there was nothing else to be done in our absence.' Sir Francis shook his head. 'But I do not know if the letter got through for I have received no reply.'

'You kept this from me,' Mun said. It was half question, half statement.

'You could not ride back and break a siege, Edmund,' his father said, the weight of so much on his shoulders. 'Not even you could do that.'

Mun's chest was a furnace of hate for the enemy. 'Tomorrow, Father, we will beat the rebels,' he snarled. 'Then together we will ride home. The King will give us men. And if this Colonel Egerton is within a hundred yards of Shear House I swear I will kill him.'

Sir Francis visibly shuddered. He looked unwell. 'But tomorrow . . .' he said, 'tomorrow we face Tom. And he is our enemy.'

'There is still a chance he will come to his senses,' Mun said, as though reaching for a ball that had already left the pistol's barrel. 'A chance that he will decide not to fight.'

Sir Francis seemed to consider this for a few moments. Then he smiled and it was a smile of such sadness that Mun felt his heart might rupture. 'God be with you, my son,' he said.

'And with you, Father,' Mun replied. He thrust out his hand and Sir Francis gripped it with both of his.

'Be strong, Edmund,' he said. Mun nodded, then turned and left his father standing there motionless. As the King's men prepared for battle.

CHAPTER TWENTY-TWO

Sunday, 23rd October 1642, Edgehill

IT SEEMED TO BE TAKING AN AGE FOR PARLIAMENT'S ARMY to set itself into battalia. Tom muttered a behest to God to let the killing start soon, for he knew God for what He truly was: a vengeful, spiteful Lord who revelled in mankind's misery. At least the wait had given him time to appraise the terrain upon which the blood would be spilled. The Vale of the Red Horse, that was the name of the place, though Tom had caught no sight of the hill figure the ancients had cut into the earth, for which the place was named.

'That's some omen if you ask me,' Weasel had said, digging something foul from his nose and smearing it on his breeches. 'A red horse. A horse slathered in blood.'

'Shut that superstitious mouth, Weasel!' Will Trencher had growled, the Puritan in him offended by such talk. But Tom agreed with Weasel. A bloody horse had some strong augury about it on a day when thousands had gathered under their respective standards to kill each other.

He sat Achilles in the pale October sun, which had been rising behind the King's men when they had first appeared on the long ridge known as Edgehill, their colours snapping in the morning breeze and the relentless beat of their drums descending to the plain. But then the Royalists had begun to move, a great tide spilling down to the vale, and it had taken them all morning, proving no easy task, especially for the Horse, due to the hill's steepness. Now that enemy waited in bristling pike-divisions, bodies of musketeers and troops of wheeling cavalry, and Tom cast his eyes over them all, searching for a standard of a rampant gold griffin in a black field, for he knew that to be Lord Denton's colour and if the spiteful God let Tom live through the slaughter, he would kill that black-hearted bastard and spit on his corpse.

But the enemy was still too far away for eyes to read standards and so Tom contented himself with studying the ground that separated the armies of King and Parliament. The plain was open, for the most part featureless, part hay meadow but mostly arable land which had been ploughed ready for the sowing of winter wheat. To his right and behind him, on the west of the field, was a swath of poor quality land, mostly gorse and brambles, which no doubt the folk of the parishes of Kineton, Oxhill and Radway used as rough grazing, though there were no animals there this day. Still, such ground would disrupt formations of men and horse as efficiently as cannon if the fighting crept westward. Far to the east, close to the Kineton–Banbury road,

Tom had earlier made out some small, hedged fields which again could hamper movement, so it would be best for both sides if they came straight on and met on the open plain which, being almost featureless, offered advantage to neither army.

And yet that hill may serve them well, Tom thought. Like a tree climbed to escape a savage dog.

'Not again!' Will Trencher exclaimed, watching Nayler dismount. The man only just got his breeches down in time, squatting between the press of horses to empty his bowels in a foul gush of liquid.

'I can't bloody help it!' the red-faced trooper exclaimed, dabbing his face with the orange scarf round his neck.

'Well you could have buggered off and done it on their side of the field,' Trencher said, rubbing the ears of a mare that was to Tom's eyes even sorrier-looking than the one the Royalists had shot at Wormleighton village.

'You're forgetting, Will, that their side of the field will soon be *our* side of the field,' Matthew Penn put in, gesturing towards the Royalist lines, 'and I'd rather Nayler crapped where I can see it than I step in it later.'

'A fair point I suppose,' Trencher admitted grudgingly, removing his pot to scratch his bald head. 'Could do with a piss myself.'

The air was clogged with the stench of dung and urine, sweat and damp wool. Tom twisted in his saddle and saw that everywhere men and horses were emptying their bowels. Some of the men were throwing up last night's dinner or holding their bellies as though they were about to. Others were checking matchlocks and straps, disentangling powder flasks on bandoliers,

338

kissing charms or the swords and guns they would soon kill with, and still others were standing or sitting their mounts with eyes closed, their mouths moving, as though communing with God or perhaps their loved ones far away. Ministers were threading through the ranks leading prayers, assuring men they were about to do God's work, encouraging them that even if they died this day they would be granted eternal life hereafter. One, a big, broad-faced minister with a neat grey beard and fire in his eyes, strode boldly through the press of Sir William Balfour's Regiment of Horse, spittle flying from his mouth and hanging in his beard as he proclaimed the righteousness of Parliament's cause.

'Is the King not accountable to God?' he roared. 'Is his duty not to protect and reward virtue? To honour true religion and punish wrongdoers?'

There were shouts of 'Aye!' and 'Down with the King!' But even more railed against the King's damned advisers, Laud's bishops and papists, rather than lay blame at His Majesty's own feet.

'Our enemies are possessed of demons!' the minister bellowed. 'They practise witchcraft! They talk of the Divine Right of Kings! Such talk is heresy!' He caught Tom's eye; Tom looked away but it was too late and next thing the big man was pushing between Achilles and Trencher's horse like a thirsty man to a cup of ale. He grabbed Tom's leg with meaty hands, craning his neck and turning those soul-raking eyes on Tom.

'Young man, do you exist for the glory of God?' Tom said nothing and the minister's brow darkened like the sky before thunder. He tugged the orange sash that Tom had wrapped over his right shoulder and knotted at his left hip. 'Boy! Is your first concern, above all else, to do God's will?'

Tom thrust his foot forward, striking the minister's chest, so that he staggered backwards, eyes bulging.

'Get away from me,' Tom snarled.

'You devil!' the minister roared. 'How dare you!'

'Touch me again and I'll cut off your ears,' Tom said, and some of the troopers around him growled and tongue-lashed him for his disrespect.

'He means nothing by it, minister,' Trencher said, 'he's just afraid, that's all. *I'll* have your blessing if I may?'

The big man glared at Tom and Tom glared back.

'Do you exist for the glory of God?' the minister asked Trencher, his face red as garnet as he tore his eyes from Tom and riveted them on the slab-faced man on the horse beside him.

'I live and breathe for no other reason,' Trencher replied dutifully, one eye glaring at Tom. But Tom was staring ahead, watching, waiting for a glimpse of a rampant griffin clawing against a black field. Looking for the man he hungered to kill.

'You don't like making friends, do you, Tom?' Matthew Penn said, shaking his head which was encased in steel, the three bars of the face guard lifted so that it jutted into the air. His horse whinnied and it sounded like laughter.

'I don't need friends like him,' Tom replied, as the minister moved on to harangue other men. 'I've got you, Matthew, and Will and Weasel. And that's too many.' Tom was only half joking. It was clear that the others were drawn to him for some reason he could not fathom, not that he put much thought into it. But ever since they had broken out of the Royalists' gaol they had barely left him alone. It was as though they looked to him for leadership. 'I cannot seem to shake you off,' Tom said.

'If not for you, Black Tom, we'd be swinging from a gibbet,' Penn said, eyebrows arched. 'You're a useful man to know.'

'But you don't know me, Matthew,' Tom countered.

'That's true enough, I suppose,' Penn admitted, 'but I always knew there was *some* story to you, though I didn't have a crown on you being the son of a knight. Wish I had. If today goes badly for us you can persuade His Majesty to grant me, Nayler and Weasel a royal pardon.' He grinned. 'Fuck Trencher. That tosspot wouldn't accept one if it was offered on a silver dish.'

'I think I've burned that bridge, Matt, don't you?' Tom said, feeling something like a smile twitch on his own lips.

'Aye,' Trencher put in, 'you've done to your inheritance what Weasel's done to some poor farmer's field.' He nodded at Weasel who was pulling up his breeches.

'Fathers can be forgiving, Trencher,' Penn said. 'Mine's dragged me out of more whores' beds than I can remember—'

'And jumped into them soon as your back was turned,' Trencher finished for him.

Penn pursed his lips, suggesting that this stone might not have landed too far from the bucket, then swept a hand out before him. 'Well, Essex has set us up defensively here,' he said, as though the chosen battlefield were a chess board, 'which makes me think he can't be too confident that we'll win.'

'I heard we're still waiting for half the bloody army

to catch up,' Weasel offered, mounting again gingerly, a grimace slitting his pinched face.

'That's not why we're lined up here like skittles at the arse end of the alley,' Trencher said, 'it's because the earl does not want to be held responsible for attacking the King of England. Otherwise we'd have torn into the swaggering bastards when they were tumbling down that hill like a flock of drunk bloody sheep this morning.'

Some of the men agreed with that and Tom thought there was probably some truth in it. From what Tom understood of Essex's strategy, Parliament's twelve infantry regiments were grouped into three brigades of between three and four thousand men, making up the van, the middle, and the rear. Rather than forming a mass of pikemen twenty deep and flanked by musketeers that could roll across the field sweeping an enemy aside, each regiment would be able to act independently, lending help where it was needed. As for the cavalry, almost all of it was drawn up under Sir James Ramsey's command to the north, on their left, twenty-four troops according to Captain Clement, for that was where the Royalist devils had concentrated the weight of their own cavalry. Clement had been given command of a new troop of harquebusiers cobbled together from one which had been mauled at Powick Bridge and the men of Tom's own troop who had escaped the ambush at Wormleighton village, so that Tom now found himself in Balfour's Horse. A dour Puritan with a long face and a livid birthmark smeared across his cheek that gave him cause to be angry with the world, Clement was not popular with his men as Captain Preston had been, but he was a professional soldier who had served in the

Dutch army. He had the men's respect, which, along with their obedience, was all he asked of them.

'Look around yourselves, men!' Captain Clement had called as they were walking their mounts to the field on the right wing of Essex's army. 'We on the right are three regiments only. And three will be enough so long as you discharge your duty to God and to Parliament.'

Tom and the others had glanced around perturbed, for sixteen troops of horse did not seem enough, not when facing Royalist cavalry.

'Least we've got that lot,' Trencher had muttered, thumbing at several troops of dragoons that had come to support them on the right. The thought of those men with their firelocks pouring bullets into the enemy from the flanks was a comforting one.

But Weasel was not impressed. 'They'll scarper soon enough when the King's hounds are loosed,' he had said with a sneer. 'Bastards won't stand against cavalry, not without pikemen holding their hands, or an advantage of terrain.'

Clement, though, was optimistic. 'And I have been informed that that devil the King's nephew is on the other side of the field,' the captain had added, pointing over to the Royalist right. 'So we won't have the pleasure of humbling him today.'

'Thank Christ,' Penn had muttered at that, and Tom had felt a shudder of relief for that meant the chances were that he would not face his father, Mun and Emmanuel when the butchery began.

Now it was afternoon and perhaps a half hour had passed since someone had announced it was two o'clock. Men were still pissing away their nerves, checking their gear, babbling about women and drink and their favourite inns. They talked of the weather and of what they would eat if they could have any meal brought to them there and then – anything to steer their thoughts from what was coming.

And then the big guns began to sing.

Crows and rooks that had been scavenging the ploughed soil took to the sky, crying angrily. Horses neighed and whinnied and snorted and some kicked or pawed the ground. Achilles's ears were mobile, his neck carriage high and his eyes bright and alert.

'It's all right, boy,' Tom soothed him, rubbing his poll and patting his thick, muscular neck. 'It's just the guns, boy. Nothing to worry us.' The cannon thumped the air like a drum skin, ragged salvos of thunderous noise accompanied by clouds of dirty white smoke that hung above the regiments, obscuring the great banners.

'This is it, boys!' an infantry sergeant yelled, raising his halberd into the grey day. 'This is what we came for!'

Tom had never heard noise like it, would not have imagined thunder could sound so loud if you were riding forked lightning. Each new iron-spitting fusillade pounded his head and thumped his guts and he could feel Achilles flinching beneath him so he steadied his own breathing because the stallion would take comfort from it. 'Easy, Achilles. It will soon be time to run.'

But the guns roared for an hour and the armies faced each other, some regiments wheeling this way or that but most standing still as boulders, and some died on both sides, torn apart by cannon shot, but not many.

And then, after what seemed an age, the squall of

the big guns began to ebb and Tom began to shake and some men began to puke again.

'Now,' he whispered. Now came the real killing.

The enemy had drawn up in two lines in a chequerboard formation which would enable the brigades in the second line to plug the gaps in the first if necessary. But now, with the fury of the big guns spent, the King's army began to march and it was a sight that raised the hairs on Tom's neck and arms as he sat Achilles in the front line. Musketeers and pikemen came on, a great brawl of colour spreading across the ploughed field to the beat of their drums. The two lines merged into one rolling wave that sought to wash away Parliament's challenge before it was properly begun.

A man in buff-coat, back- and breastplate, with a blue feathered plume jutting from his helmet and a matching blue sash round his waist, rode out in front of the regiment and turned his horse to face his men. It was their commander himself, Sir William Balfour. Men said Sir William was a great soldier, that he had distinguished himself fighting the Spanish in the Netherlands. Looking at the Scot now Tom had no reason to doubt it.

'We are not needed here!' Balfour yelled, his short, pointed beard jutting belligerently from his chin. 'This will be a scrap between their dragoons and ours. Lord Feilding will hold this flank, should their cavalry grow bold.' He kept his sentences short and clear, hand loose with the reins, letting his mount turn this way and that. 'So we shall find employment elsewhere on the field.' With that he wheeled off to the right and Captain Clement yelled at his troop to follow Sir William wherever he might lead.

'Heya!' Tom called, hauling on his reins and riding after them. He glanced up to see two rooks beating their black wings, heard their hoarse *craa* above the thump of countless hooves, and in that moment he was reminded of his childhood, when he and Mun had thrown stones at a pair that were eating the eyes of a drowned woman. They had watched a farmer pull her out of the Tawd, her hand still clasping the herbs she had been gathering, and the farmer had told the boys to stay with her whilst he rode to tell her kin. But then the rooks had come and Mun had said they must defend her even though she was dead.

'Keep it tight! Stay together!' Captain Clement yelled, as they threaded between Essex's brigades, Tom noting the pale, fear-filled faces of a hedge of young pikemen awaiting commands. Then they came to a tract of foot-churned ground between the van and the central brigade and here they stopped, Sir William roaring commands at his officers. The rest, men and horses, waiting. As four regiments of enemy infantry marched towards them.

'We're to be used in the hottest part of the fire,' Penn said, counting the carbine balls in the leather bag tied to his saddle. Tom had seen him do it three times already but knew that it was instinct that made a man busy his hands before a fight.

'I would be in no other part,' Tom said through his teeth, taking in the gut-churning sight before him.

'I'd wager that's what the last man said who wore that buff-coat,' Penn muttered with more grimace than grin, and Tom glanced down at the ominous dark stain which bloomed from the coat's collar to halfway down the lacings. Seeing that Tom owned no other armour, dour Captain Clement had given him the coat, claiming the former grocer's widow would take little comfort from the bloody thing were they to give it to her, and so long as Tom didn't mind a bit of hard scrubbing the tough leather coat was his. But Tom knew a stain like that would never get out and so had not even tried. As for the poor quality pot on his head, Sir William himself had provided that, saying that his men would be no good to him or God with the porridge of their brains leaking from their skulls. Bloodstained leather and thin steel. But it would keep him alive until he had done what he must.

He felt the reassuring discomfort of his father's pistols in his boots, their long barrels pressing against his lower legs. He had lost his sword at Wormleighton village but he had a wicked-looking poll-axe now instead, its haft thrust into a crude holster against his saddle. *I have all I need*, gnarred a voice in his head.

Sir William Balfour's Horse formed up again, Tom's troop drawn up seven across and nine deep – sixty-three men ready to unleash shot and sword upon the enemy. Tom sat Achilles three from the right in the first line, a faint trembling announcing itself in his limbs as the infantry brigade to their left began to move forward to the drum's beat. Muskets were crackling now on both flanks of the field and smoke was drifting across from east to west, so Tom knew that without the talk of the drums both armies would be deaf and blind.

Officers bellowed commands, trumpeters passed on orders, men yelled to give themselves and each other courage, and horses screamed. Drums beat, muskets cracked, tack jangled, buckles rattled against armour and the big guns roared sporadically. The air was clogged with the stink of smoke, of men and horses and dirty clothes, and what could be seen of the October sky was now endless grey and threatened rain as Sir William rode once more along his line and Royalist musketeers took potshots at him though he took no notice.

'We're going to blood the enemy, boys!' he called, hoisting his carbine above his head, his blue helmet plume dancing. 'Are you with me?' Some yelled that they were, but not enough to satisfy Balfour. 'I said, are you with me?' This time a great wave of noise crashed over him and he grinned savagely. 'Give them steel and Hell!' the Scotsman roared.

'God be with you, Tom,' Penn called through the clamour.

'Just kill the bastards, Matt!' Tom shouted back. Then Sir William wheeled his grey stallion round, his words lost in the tumult, and gave the beast his spurs. And Tom dug his own heels into Achilles's flank and charged.

Hooves flung up clods of mud and manes and tails flew and men shrieked. Achilles tore up the ground and Tom loved him as he pulled his righthand pistol from his boot. The enemy, which ten breaths ago had been only a sea of indistinct faces, now became individuals whose features were twisted with terror and hatred.

'Go on, boy!' Tom yelled, a musket ball plucking at the shoulder of his buff-coat on its way past. He squeezed the trigger and the firelock roared and a Royalist musketeer fell back in a spray of blood. Then Tom hauled the poll-axe from its sheath as he ploughed into the green-coated ranks alongside Sir William who was screaming and part of Tom was aware that he was screaming too. The musketeers were thrown back into the men behind and the press was such that they could not even raise their arms as Tom's poll-axe swung down, chopping into a man's shoulder so that he shrieked like a vixen. Tom ripped the blade from the meat as Achilles plunged deeper into the crush. A musket flared and Tom felt the ferocious heat of it against his face as he leant out and brought the poll-axe down, hacking off the hand that thrust the musket up in defence. On his right, Penn was slashing wildly, his sword flinging out gloops of blood, and on his left Weasel was fighting like a devil, wielding his hanger about him in a desperate, animal fury.

'Kill the pigfuckers!' Weasel was screaming.

'With me!' Balfour roared, and Tom yelled at Achilles to push on, and into the press they drove, a wedge of perhaps fifty, hacking and slashing, carving into the Greencoats who were terror-stricken and trying to fly but could not for the weight of men behind them. A sergeant jabbed his halberd at Tom's face and Tom snapped his head back, but then the sergeant yanked the halberd back and its axe head caught the right bar of Tom's pot's face guard and he felt his head being wrenched off, the rusty axe blade half a finger's length from his right eye. He was being hauled from the saddle so he pulled his left foot from its stirrup and snatched the other pistol from his boot, bringing it across himself, then fired blind and the snagged axe blade jerked so he threw up his arm and knocked it away, pushing into his right stirrup to seat himself back in the saddle.

He pressed himself down against Achilles's neck, pushing the pistol back into his boot and glancing around to see that there was suddenly space around him, for the Greencoats had broken. They were running, though their one-eyed commander was screaming at them to stand, hauling men back by the scruffs of their necks, and Tom recognized him as Colonel Lunsford, the man he had seen slashing apprentices at Westminster.

'With me, boys!' Balfour cried, wheeling right, desperate to use their momentum and spread the terror their charge had planted in the Greencoats' bellies amongst other men. Bluecoats these, and as fine-looking a regiment as Tom had ever seen. Achilles surged amongst them and Tom swung the poll-axe underarm, cleaving a man's head in an explosion of gore that spattered those fine blue coats with crimson.

A hanger struck Tom's back but his buff-coat stopped the blade, then Achilles screamed but Tom did not see who or what had hurt him. All around him Balfour's troopers were sowing death and terror, their blades plunging into the mass, carbines roaring, but then Captain Clement was yelling for them to withdraw. A musket butt jabbed up at Tom and he beat it aside with the poll-axe and Achilles slammed his head down onto the musketeer and he dropped.

'Withdraw! Withdraw!' Clement was yelling and then Tom saw why. A blue-coated pike-division was coming for them, six ranks of men each hefting sixteen feet of ash tipped with a steel blade. For a moment Tom held his ground and Achilles stamped the churned earth furiously.

'We've done our work! Time to go,' an experienced trooper called Horton shouted, fighting to control his own mount, when his head burst in a spray of blood, skull and brain. Tom stared at Horton. One of the man's legs was shaking violently, the foot still in the stirrup, but surely he had to be dead, for half his face and head was gone.

'Withdraw, Rivers!' Clement yelled, bringing his horse alongside. 'Get back, damn you!' he roared, spittle flying. 'That's an order!' But for Tom everything had slowed and he felt as though he were mired in a deep dream; one of those he sometimes had which he could control. Or thought he could.

Troopers were riding back past him in their panic to escape those wicked pikes and one of them cut across another, so that the second man's horse pulled up and then the horse screamed and the trooper's face contorted, eyes bulging, nostrils flaring as a pike blade erupted from his shoulder and another ripped open his neck.

Tom glanced round. Clement was gone. But Trencher was there, screaming at him. All Tom could hear was a roar like that of the sea hurling itself against rocks, and musket balls cracking the air around him or thunking into armour. Or slapping into flesh.

Then some part of him reacted. He wrenched on the reins and Achilles shrieked and turned and dug in and tore away with the others. As the blue-coated pikemen came on.

CHAPTER TWENTY-THREE

'THE KING AND THE CAUSE!' PRINCE RUPERT YELLED, raising his sword to the grey heavens.

'The King and the cause!' men roared. They had begun at a walk, then a rising trot, harnesses and gear jangling, leather creaking. But now the Prince dug his spurs into his horse's flanks and it lurched forward, headlong towards the enemy waiting in battalia at the crest of a small hill. The rebels had placed musketeers in the hedges and enclosures on the flank to rake the Royalist right, but the Prince's dragoons had chased them off.

'Heya, boy!' Mun yelled, raking his heels back and snapping the reins as all around him the Royalist right wing broke into a full-blooded charge.

A stuttering volley of pistol and carbine fire spat at them and Mun felt the thrum of lead ripping through the air but nothing hit him and he raced on, Hector matching the Prince's mare for speed, his hooves adding to the rolling thunder, flinging mud.

And the enemy were breaking! Some of the orange-scarved riders were hauling their mounts round and giving them their spurs. Others, appalled by the failure of their volley to slow the Prince's charge, wheeled left and right in panic, yelling at their fellows to stand.

'Death to traitors!' someone yelled.

'Kill the scum!'

Then they hit. Mun saw the Prince hack off a man's arm and blast a hole in another's chest with his carbine, but Mun knew he could match any man's horsemanship and grabbed his own carbine, controlling Hector with his knees as the stallion bit an enemy trooper's leg and the man screamed. From his right a sword slashed down but Mun caught the blade on his own and sent it wide, bringing the carbine across and pulling the trigger. The gun snarled fire, hammering the rider from his saddle, though his left foot was caught in the stirrup and he was wrenched horribly as his horse galloped off, his steel-sheathed head turning the mud like a ploughshare.

With one savage swing of his poll-axe O'Brien scythed off a man's head, the neck stump spouting crimson gouts into the air as the head struck the ground and was kicked by a hoof, so that it rolled ten feet through the filth.

'Sweet Jesus Christ!' Vincent Rowe shouted, wide-eyed and spattered in blood. He wheeled his horse round and round. 'Sweet Jesus! Did you see that?'

The rebels were breaking, men whipping their mounts with the flats of their swords, desperate to escape from the ruin of their left wing.

'Ride on! Ride on!' an officer roared, hoisting his carbine and thrusting it towards the north-west. But Mun was already moving, plunging on towards the Parliamentarian rear, Hector eating up the muddied ground, black mane flying.

'Cannon!' someone yelled as they came over a slight ridge and Mun's breath snagged in his chest for there, waiting for them, were three cannon, their crews making ready to unleash the big guns' fury.

A ragged salute of booms pounded Mun's world and he cringed, dipping his head, but the gunners' aim was all wrong and the cannon coughed their iron balls too high and Mun did not know where they landed as he galloped on. Towards several knots of musketeers, many of whom had their matchlock butts in the mud, desperately reloading, plunging scouring sticks into barrels. Others were blowing on match-cords to make sure their tips were burning, then fumbling them into the serpents' jaws and hoisting the heavy muskets to their shoulders. Those muskets spat fire, their lead balls fizzing past Mun's ears, and a trooper in front of him was struck but the horse galloped on, its master slumped over, jolting horribly in the saddle, so that if the ball had not killed him the broken neck would. But most of the musketeers hit nothing and then Mun was upon them, slashing an enemy's face open as he raced past, his fellow troopers' yells and screams like those of wild animals. For they were full of the mad thrill of battle. A frenzied blood-lust gripped them, gripped Mun, like a hawk's talons, because musketeers had no chance against cavalry. All the rebels could do was die on Royalist blades, and then Mun was through, past the last real resistance on Essex's left wing and plunging onwards across the waterlogged fields with hundreds of other gore-spattered men.

Fleeing before them were the remnants of Sir James Ramsey's rebel Horse, riding as though the Devil himself were on their heels. And perhaps he was, for Prince

Rupert hungered to kill and his men craved vengeance on these treacherous curs who had thought to defy their king and plunge the world into chaos.

Onwards, across ditches and ploughed fields, hooves thundering. All around Mun groups were peeling off after their own prey, like hounds catching the scent of another fox and breaking from the main chase, but he followed the Prince through a field of gorse and through a gap in a thick hedgerow and there, sitting amongst rough grazing and ripe for picking, was the Parliamentarian baggage train. Ox-drivers, women and children and the handful of men who had been left to guard the train recognized the horsemen galloping past them, saw the devils they were fleeing from, and took to their heels, running north for their lives. But a knot of twenty or so rebel troopers, perhaps realizing that they had led the Royalists to such an important prize, pulled up, their horses whinnying, eyes rolling, and turned to make a fight of it. Yelling encouragement to each other they dragged swords from scabbards and hoisted poll-axes and bravely charged.

'Go on, Hector!' Mun roared, extending his right arm forward so that his rapier pointed at a trooper in a bloodied buff-coat who was wielding a curve-bladed hanger and screaming as he came. 'Go on, boy!' Thirty paces away. 'Yah!' In a matter of heartbeats the two lines would clash with steel and fire. Fifteen paces. Then his opponent veered left and Mun brought his sword back and scythed it at his head, but the man got his hanger up and it cut Mun's blade in half, the ring of steel loud and Mun's arm screaming with the pain of the impact.

'Whoa, Hector!' Mun leant back, left hand hauling

the reins, and Hector obeyed, turning. All around, blades clashed and men and horses gave vent to fury and the desperate will to survive. The rebel was a fine horseman and had turned his mount and now spurred forward, grinning savagely. Mun let go the reins and drew a pistol and the other's eyes widened as he realized his mistake and the pistol roared, its ball punching a fist-sized hole through the man's chest, spraying fleshy bone shards out of his back.

Mun saw the Prince wheeling his horse in a death dance with an enemy trooper, the combatants slashing and parrying. But the Prince had the longer reach and managed to slash his adversary's left arm and, unable to control his horse, the trooper screamed for mercy, blood spraying from his forearm, which was all but severed.

'You have betrayed your king!' Prince Rupert bellowed, then his horse lurched forward and Rupert plunged his blade into the rebel's neck and hauled it out quick as lightning, wheeling his mount, hungry for more prey.

Nehemiah Boone came up on a foe's blind side and hacked into his grey mare's quarters and the animal screeched, making a wild traverse, bending her haunches away from the savage blade. The man fought to bring the mare round but Boone slashed him twice about the face and neck and he toppled from the saddle with a crunch of iron and bone.

The enemy's brave stand crumbled and those that could broke off and spurred away, flying for their lives. The Prince wheeled his horse round, pointing his sword towards those of his men who were already sacking the Parliamentarian baggage train or else trotting over to it. 'Captain, get those men back to the King!' he yelled, eyes blazing in a crimson-spattered face.

Mun looked west and saw in the distance a great host of the Prince's Horse galloping up and over a small rise after the main body of the enemy cavalry. Then the Prince dragged his spurs back and galloped after them accompanied by twenty of his closest and best.

Dragging breath into his lungs, Mun took in the scene: dead men lying all around or sitting slumped in saddles, their horses standing placidly as though awaiting their masters' commands. Several horses were bleeding out where they stood. Two writhed on the ground, trying in vain to rise, eyes rolling, the foam-slathered bits clinking in their mouths.

'Well, Corporal . . .' Captain Boone said, chest heaving, scabbarding his sword and nodding to the carts and oxen and the men that were scavenging that train like hounds on a dead fox, 'shall we?'

The lantern-faced veteran grinned and spat and together they walked their mounts across the field. Mun followed, patting Hector's sweat-lathered neck and glancing about him, looking for his friends. He caught O'Brien's eye and the big Irishman nodded grimly, a greeting infused with the horror of what they had just been through and relief at having survived. And there was Vincent Rowe, reloading his carbine with trembling hands, and Mun was glad to see that the young man was unharmed.

'Good boy,' he said, feeling the stallion's hot sweat even through his leather glove, 'you're fine, boy. Nothing can hurt you.'

'Anything worth anything?' Captain Boone asked a grizzled trooper who was standing up on a cart pulling clothes from a chest and flinging them aside. The trooper was just about to reply, when he grinned triumphantly and produced a fat purse, weighing it in his hand appreciatively.

'That's a start,' Boone said, fluttering a gloved hand, which was as good as a command, and the trooper tossed him the purse before bending back to his task. All along the train men were doing the same. Some were laying hands on letters and pipes, leather jacks, pottery jugs full of wine, cloaks, shirts, tunics and breeches, whilst others were crowing at the sight of silver plate that glowed dully in the grey day.

'Good fishing,' Richard Downes said at Mun's shoulder, for clearly these were the personal possessions of senior Parliamentarians.

'Aye,' agreed O'Brien, 'but it isn't a trout until it's on the bank. As my da used to say. We haven't won the battle yet.'

In the distance, to the south-east, the big guns still thundered. Now and then Mun caught the crackle of musket fire on the breeze and he thought of his father and Emmanuel, his chest tightening. His whole body, muscle and bone, thrummed madly. 'Captain, we must get back to the fight,' he called. There were at least fifty men ransacking the rebels' baggage train, men who, having routed Essex's cavalry, should have been back on the field harrying his musketeers.

'All in good time, Rivers,' Boone said. The captain had dismounted and was striding along the train, his magpie's eyes searching for shiny things amongst men's everyday belongings. Some of the other men were looking back towards the sounds of battle, but most were preoccupied with plundering.

'The King needs us, Captain!' Mun called.

'We've played our part, Rivers,' said Humphrey Walton, a trooper with a sharp blade of a beard, as he flourished two cups of ale towards another man, who raised his eyebrows and pursed his lips admiringly. 'Let them dance without us, lad. Just for a while. By Christ we've earned it.'

Mun felt the anger rise in his chest, hot bile brimming up his throat. He looked at Downes but the man shrugged.

'He has a point, Mun,' he said, dismounting stiffly to join the looting. 'Come on, O'Brien, you're an Irishman aren't you? The only thing you do better than stealing is drinking.'

O'Brien nodded and made to dismount.

'Stay where you are!' Mun barked and the red-haired giant frowned, shrugged and remained mounted. 'Captain, I insist we rejoin the fight,' Mun said. 'As the Prince commanded.'

Boone turned and glared. In his hand he held a gilt dress spur with a silver rowel. 'The Prince meant for us to await his return,' he said, pointing the spur at Mun. 'We are too few and must wait for His Highness to round up the rest.'

'That is not what he said,' Mun said, as Hector made a side pass, sensing his master's anger.

'Are you calling me a liar, Rivers?' Captain Boone asked.

'Careful, lad,' Corporal Bard growled from a waggon bed.

'I'm saying you would rather fill your own purse than do your duty to the King,' Mun said, sensing eyes on him as men stopped ferreting to watch the exchange.

Boone's sword rasped from its scabbard as he strode towards Mun, hatred flaring in his face like black powder in the priming pan.

'Dismount, Rivers,' Boone snarled, fury trembling his pointed beard.

Mun hauled his foot from the stirrup and swung down to meet the challenge, but had barely got both boots onto the ground when Boone struck him across the face with the dress spur and Mun staggered backwards, blood dripping through the fingers pressed to his cheek.

'You bastard coward!' he rasped, drawing what was left of his sword.

'No, Mun!' O'Brien cautioned.

Boone was grinning, beckoning him on.

'Put that blade away, Rivers,' Corporal Bard said, and Mun looked up to see Bard's carbine pointed at him, the grey-haired soldier shaking his head slowly. 'Don't be a fool, lad. You didn't get through that tussle back there to end up shot by your own bloody corporal.'

If you only knew what I did to my last corporal, Mun thought. 'Your carbine isn't loaded, Corporal,' he said, his fist bone-white on his ruined rapier's hilt. In truth he did not know whether or not Bard's carbine had a ball snug in its barrel, but had guessed that the man had not yet reloaded.

'Even if that were true, lad, what are you going to do with that?' Bard asked, nodding at Mun's broken blade.

'My father is fighting for the King,' Mun said, loud enough for others to hear. 'I am not the only one with kin back on that field. You expect me to play the guttersnipe, pilfering men's Sunday clothes whilst the rebels still hold the ground?'

'I expect you to follow orders, you damned cur!' Boone yelled.

Mun glared at his captain, wanting more than anything – almost anything – to thrust that broken length of cold steel into Boone's rancid heart. But what he wanted even more than that was to rejoin the battle whose distant murmur sounded like the ocean, and if he acted on his hatred he would be killed in his turn by Bard or someone else.

He tossed the broken sword aside and turned, mounting Hector with fluid ease.

'What do you think you're doing?' Boone rasped. But Mun gave no reply as he cuffed blood from his face, wheeled the stallion round and rode towards the roar of the cannon.

'Wait for me, you damned hot-headed fool!'

Mun twisted and saw O'Brien riding after him. There were others too, including Rowe and Downes, the latter stuffing some shiny loot into his knapsack even as he spurred forward. Mun waited, then nodded to the big Irishman when he had caught up.

'They can't shoot me for doing my duty now, can they?' O'Brien said, a grin splitting his red beard.

'I wouldn't put money on it, O'Brien,' Mun said, smiling back. Then they gave their mounts their heels and rode.

They cantered south-east, following the line of the Kineton to Banbury road with hedges on their right beyond which was the rebel left flank, then on past knots of their own dragoons and musketeers in the ditches and boundaries, and when they came back to the open plain and its deafening, smoke-shrouded chaos, Mun's guts turned to ice. The rebel foot regiments

361

were pushing forward, pikes bristling, their musketeers firing and loading, firing and loading, enveloping their own ranks in reeking fog.

'What do we do now?' Rowe asked, standing in his stirrups, peering through the smoke-charged air, trying to discern what was happening.

'We ride to the centre, to Sir Nicholas Byron's brigade. We form a troop with the men we have and we hope the Prince or Captain Boone brings back the rest.'

'Isn't *that* Byron's lot?' O'Brien said, lips pulled back from his teeth. A musket-shot away, two components of Essex's foot had passed his stationary van and were assaulting a large Royalist battalia in the flank, their massed firepower overwhelming the Royalist line.

'They've still got bloody horse!' Downes remarked, pointing to a force of rebel harquebusiers and armoured cuirassiers who were cleaving their way into Byron's disrupted ranks.

'Whilst ours are halfway to St Albans by now,' O'Brien said, 'because the highborn bastards think they're out for a day's hunt.'

Mun twisted in the saddle and counted his companions, now fishing in pouches for balls, jabbing scouring sticks into pistol and carbine barrels and winding wheellocks with spanners. Eleven men. Not enough. Not nearly enough.

One of his own pistols was still loaded but he set about loading the other and then his carbine, as around him horses tossed their heads and snorted, tack, arms and armour jangling.

The small group tried to make sense of the battle. In the near distance men were dying, their screams drowned by the savage salvos of muskets, cannon and the great murmur of battle. The air was thick with the stench of it. 'God give me strength,' Mun growled. He knew the others were looking to him, waiting for him, though he did not know why, and felt the trembling grow more fierce in his hands as he holstered his pistol against the saddle and whispered soothing words to Hector, all the while hoping that more of the King's Horse would appear and some or other officer could tell them what to do.

'Are you all ready?' Mun heard himself ask, which was strange, he thought, for he did not feel ready in the slightest to plunge back into that seething cauldron, still less so with only a handful of companions. 'Don't waste your shot,' he warned.

'And keep away from those damned pikes unless you're wanting a second arsehole,' O'Brien added, clutching his poll-axe whose blade's heart-shaped holes, Mun saw, were blocked with dark congealed gore.

Then they were trotting across the foot-churned field and past a mass of musketeers, some of whom called out asking whose men they were; but not knowing who the musketeers were, neither Mun nor any of his companions gave them an answer. Then on past the Royalist right wing which had fragmented from the centre to make a stand in a good defensive position behind a ditch supported by some cannon and a troop of dragoons.

'Christ's wounds, where's the rest of you? Where is the Prince?' a buff-coated captain yelled. Assuming only King's Horse would come so close in such a small number, the ashen-faced man had come forward from his company and raised a hand to halt Mun's troop. 'Essex still has cavalry on the field. Where's ours?'

'His Highness is regrouping,' Mun said, hoping it was true. 'What of our left wing? Wilmot's Horse?'

The captain waved an arm to the west. 'I heard he swept their cavalry from the field but no one has seen him since.'

'We have no Horse left in the fight?' Mun felt sick at the thought, for without cavalry the King's Foot was horribly vulnerable to Essex's superior numbers, not least to the mixed cavalry they had seen ploughing into Sir Nicholas Byron's brigade.

'There are some of the King's Lifeguard hereabouts,' the captain said. 'We passed them on our way across here. But only twice your number.' He shook his head. 'Maybe a few more.' Seeing he could expect no help from the remnants before him the captain cursed and turned his back on them and marched back to his position, his men eager to hear what news he had.

'They won't stand without cavalry,' Downes said.

'They'll stand,' O'Brien replied. 'They'll stand or they'll lose.'

They went on at a sitting trot and Mun ducked instinctively as a musket ball whipped past.

'We're King's men, you fool-born villain!' a man behind him named Rowland Temple roared at a young dragoon who, perhaps thinking they were Essex's men slipped through the lines, had taken a potshot at them. 'Son of a rancid goat!' Temple exclaimed, shaking his head as they rode on and a big sergeant cuffed the young dragoon about his head, knocking off his felt cap. 'Our own side are trying to kill us now. That's all we bloody need.'

Then Mun gave Hector the pressure of his right leg and the stallion broke into a canter along the rear of Byron's battalia and Mun hoped he was not alone but had no time to find out. Because the Royalist centre was collapsing. Rebel horse were surging into the gaps, breaking up Byron's formation, and there, wavering at the heart of Byron's foot soldiers like a challenge that no man of Parliament could ignore, was the Royal Standard.

Then Mun looked up ahead and saw a small troop of the King's Lifeguard of Horse, no more than a score of them, charging from the south into the fray, trying to get to the Royal Standard before the rebels could. And he knew there was a chance, however small, that his father was one of those men, encased in his fine cuirassier's armour and closed helmet which had captivated his sons since they were old enough to walk.

And he and Hector plunged into the chaos.

'Yah! Heya!' Mun was yelling, slowed now by the press of Byron's retreating men but forcing a rough way through, O'Brien at his right shoulder and Downes to his left. If they could just link up with the Lifeguard they might form a wedge and drive into the rebels. Force them back.

Royalist musketeers were sheltering amongst shattering pike-divisions, unable to load their guns in that hedge of staves.

'Protect the colours!' Mun roared, thrusting onwards, suddenly wishing he had a sword. 'The colours!'

A musketeer put his gun to his shoulder and Mun ducked as it roared, cursing as the ball fizzed past, for musketeers were supposed to wait for orders to fire volleys at massed ranks rather than trying to pick off individual horsemen. But now Mun had other concerns as the rebel horse wheeled left, hitting Byron's beleaguered line in the rear.

'We'll never get through!' Downes said, his face a grimace through the smoke as the King's panic-stricken men flooded past, seeking the relative safety of the Edgehill escarpment.

'We'll get through!' Mun snarled back at him, spurring Hector on, desperate to link up with those brave men of the King's Lifeguard of Horse who had fought their way to the Standard and were now trapped. For a block of rebel pikemen had moved to cut off what remained of Byron's line from the Royalist rear and now they levelled their wicked blades at Mun's small troop.

'Well, we can't go that way,' O'Brien said, thrusting his poll-axe to their right, where a formation of musketeers waited, ready to pour a fusillade of flesh-ripping lead into any Royalists who came too close.

'Give them a volley!' Mun yelled, and pulling his carbine round on its strap pointed it at the pikemen and pulled the trigger. Several rebels fell to the ragged volley but the rest held their ground, their faces all teeth and hatred as they screamed curses and dared the whoreson Cavaliers to come closer.

'We can't stay here!' Downes yelled.

Mun cursed again because he knew his friend was right. There was no way through to the men who now desperately fought to defend the King's standard. He roared in fury and frustration and Hector squealed, then Mun stood in his stirrups and through the drifting, acrid, throat-drying clouds watched Essex's foot and that audacious troop of Horse overcome the Royal Colour party.

And he knew his father's friend, Sir Edmund Verney, was as good as dead.

CHAPTER TWENTY-FOUR

'BLOODY BALFOUR'S LOOKING TO WIN THIS WAR ALL BY himself,' Nayler said through a grimace. With the back of his hand he was gingerly sweeping wet grey gobbets from his buff-coat's shoulder. 'You could have told me I had some bastard's brains all over me, Weasel,' he moaned.

But Weasel ignored him, too busy leaning forward in his saddle, straining to hear what Captain Clement was yelling above the battle-din as his troop, fresh from the fight, prepared to re-enter the fray.

'When you say by himself, you mean himself and us,' Trencher announced, taking up Nayler's first point as he cranked his wheellock, winding the internal serrated wheel that would release when the trigger was pulled and spin against the piece of iron pyrite on the cock, creating sparks that would ignite the barrel's charge.

'Not just us. The Foot are bleeding too,' Tom said, thrusting his loaded pistol back into his boot.

'Aye and they'll need to,' Trencher said, 'for we're up against men of quality, highborn bastards who wear their honour like damned cuirassier's armour.' He spat.

'It'll take everything Essex has got to get them to quit the field with their king's beady eyes on them.'

'Not all of them are honourable men,' Tom said, his own eyes scouring the seething masses as he leant, rubbing Achilles's muscled neck. 'Are you ready to fight again, old friend?' he asked the horse. The proud stallion tossed his head and there was a great clatter of staves and a chorus of furious yells as, two hundred paces away, two pike-divisions locked in a dance of death. Ranks of musketeers poured thunderous volleys into each other. Sergeants roared commands. Drums beat out the language of battle. Horses whinnied and hooves rumbled across the earth and the whole terrible tumult was cut with the anguished, animalistic shrieks of the wounded and soon to be dead.

'No quarter!' Captain Clement yelled. 'If we lose they'll hang us all!'

'There ain't enough rope in all England,' Nayler said.

'No quarter!' Clement bellowed again, then turned his mount and joined Sir William Balfour, who raised a gloved hand and with that the troop began to move.

Essex had sent two regiments of foot against the enemy's centre, within which the King's standard now and then swept through the grey day as a dogged display of royal authority. Those regiments were driving on at push of pike, thinning the King's ranks, but as he rode at a rising trot at the head of the only cavalry Essex had left on the field, Tom knew Balfour was about to tip the balance.

'Good boy, Achilles. This time we'll break them.'

They picked up the pace, cantering now around the enemy's flank which was already beset by Essex's own regiment of foot.

'Soon now, my friend,' Tom said, though surely the horse couldn't hear him above the mad din, and now he could see the horrified faces of pikemen in the rear of the King's battalia who saw the enemy behind them but could do nothing about it. Balfour's troop swept up to their rear and along with more than a hundred others Tom pulled his pistol and gave fire, a ragged ear-splitting fusillade that tore into the pikemen, and for a heartbeat Tom saw thin clouds of red mist rise as men fell in the press.

'Kill them!' Balfour yelled, drawing his sword and plunging into the screaming mayhem, hacking like a frenzied butcher, and then Tom was there too, swinging his poll-axe at men whose only defence were the blades on the end of their pikes sixteen feet away in the opposite direction from the death now amongst them.

'For Parliament!' Matthew Penn roared.

'For God!' Trencher hollered louder. Tom hammered the poll-axe down, the blade splitting a helmet and wedging in the skull beneath, and suddenly he had a dead weight on the end of his arm, until the man's helmet strap snapped and the axe came away with the helmet attached. He did not hesitate, swinging the axe and smashing the snagged helmet into another man's face, crushing it in a spray of dark gore.

Some of the pikemen were bringing their staves up and over to meet this new threat but little good it would do them for the horsemen were too close, safe beyond the killing zone of most of those wicked points; and so others of the King's men were abandoning their pikes now, hauling crude swords into the death-gorged day.

'Stinking cack handlers! Whoreson devils! Piss-licking, gore-bellied scoundrels!' Nayler was screaming, battering men down with his sword, driving his horse deeper into the crumbling mass.

Tom brought his poll-axe up and yanked the blood-slick helmet off the blade, then swung for a man who had swiped at Achilles. Without pikes they're dead, he thought savagely.

'Give this to your king!' Trencher spat at two men who were trying to haul him from the saddle, then thrust his blunderbuss into a face. It roared and the man's whole head vanished in a spray of bloody gristle.

'Your right! On your right!' came a yell from behind Tom and he glanced over to see that a small troop of Royalist harquebusiers were trying to intercept them, though there was no way through. A greater threat was the larger group of horsemen thrusting into the mass ahead of them from the other side. Richly dressed, some in cuirassier armour, they looked like remnants of the King's Lifeguard of Horse.

'Do not let them save the colours!' Balfour roared, for he had seen this troop too and savagely spurred his mount on, parting the pikemen like a wedge splitting an oak. Above the heads of the disintegrating mass, Captain Clement aimed his pistol at the King's men and fired and a man in a full suit of cuirassier armour was thrown back in his saddle. But he recovered straight away, the armour having stopped the ball, and pushed on towards the Royal Standard.

All but a brave few of the King's infantry and that small knot of horse were fleeing back to the Edgehill escarpment upon which officers were trying to staunch the flow and form battalia amidst waving colours and the incessant beat of the drums.

And then Tom saw it. To his right, and like a boulder

around which anarchy seethed, leapt a rampant gold griffin in a black field, the standard bearer tirelessly sweeping it left and right as a rallying call. A fireball bloomed in Tom's gut. He pressed with his left leg and hauled the reins across, urging Achilles on, and spurred towards his enemy, knowing that some of his fellow troopers had broken from Balfour's charge to follow him.

But Lord Denton had musketeers and those men were blowing on their match-cords and bringing their muskets to their right shoulders or steadying them in stands.

'Heya! Go on, Achilles!' The stallion was bowling men over who were too slow getting out of his way and then those muskets roared and Tom half saw the rider on his left flung backwards, and Achilles screamed and seemed to shudder but galloped on. 'Go on, boy!' Swords and pike blades flashed in his peripheral vision and muskets and firelocks cracked but all he could see was that golden griffin leaping above the fray. A voice in his head screamed at him to keep going. To push on!

He knew Achilles was hit, could feel the beast's anguish, but he gave him the spur and whipped the reins, and then he saw Lord Denton beside that standard, yelling orders, screaming at his men who were priming their pans, shaking black powder down their muzzles and ramming down bullets and wadding.

Another devils' chorus and this time he felt the impact of the ball against Achilles's chest. The beast galloped on and then stumbled and suddenly time seemed to slow, Tom vaguely aware that the stallion was falling and he with it.

Then time caught up in a whirring blur and he found

himself foundering in the mud, not knowing if he was shot or if any bones were broken, and horses thundered by. He could hear someone screaming Denton's name, demanding the bastard cur come and fight, and after a moment realized the voice was his own. His fingers closed around the haft of the poll-axe and he pulled it from the mud as he hauled himself up on unsteady legs, half aware that Achilles lay bleeding and panting fifteen feet away.

'Get on!' someone yelled and he looked up and saw Nayler up on his mare, bloody sword in one hand, reins in the other. 'Get on, lad, we can't hang about here!' Then Nayler's throat ripped open and his eyes bulged as he slumped dead.

A blade scythed down and Tom staggered, slewing sidewards out of reach, then roared and flew at the musketeer, knocking the sword wide and bringing the poll-axe underarm in a two-handed swing, cleaving the head apart from chin to forehead. He lifted his left leg and plunged the booted foot into the dying man's belly, yanking the axe free.

'Denton!'

Then another man rammed his musket's butt against his head and he felt the world inside his barred helmet explode in white heat, but he kept his feet, blindly swinging the poll-axe about him as his vision flooded back and he screamed in rage and hateful fury.

'I've come for you! Denton!'

A musket ball plucked his shoulder. He felt his axe blade bite flesh again and he snarled, swinging madly, consumed by frenzied blood-lust. Then another musket butt slammed into his back, knocking him down, and another hammer blow to his helmet's tail drove his face into the mud, so that filth filled his mouth and nose and he could not breathe.

Then there was nothing.

The breeze had all but died and the battle's smoke hung in the stinking air thick as London fog. It was dusk now and getting cold. Men coughed and hawked and spat black phlegm. Some lay bleeding and moaning, dying where they had fallen. Other wounded soldiers dragged themselves across the muddy, blood-churned ground, feeble and pathetic as infants as they sought the protection of their own lines. For the cauldron of battle had boiled over and the raging flames were doused, each side pulling back from the butchery to draw breath, exhausted, appalled but alive.

Bone-weary, his head pounding, Mun sat Hector on Edgehill's lower escarpment, his eyes trying to untangle the snarl of war's debris littering the plain below. The pale sun hung before him, a white disc in the grey western sky. Below it the mass of Essex's Parliamentarian army drew back like a scalded hand, brigades coalescing in an attempt to give the impression of a cohesive whole but failing to convince.

Nevertheless, looking around him now Mun knew the King's army was in no shape to test Essex further. Because the Royalists were retreating up the slope, musketeers and pikemen ascending in loose clusters, the hum of their voices and clatter of their equipment cut with the occasional ragged fusillade of musketry from those few troops still holding their position on the field below. To the north-east, beyond the King's cannon which had been overrun earlier in the day, Mun could make out several hundred mounted men.

Prince Rupert perhaps, returned with the troopers he had managed to recall from that crazed, extended fox chase that had ranged so many miles off. But those men did not seem to be drawing up into battalia, which suggested they were in no mood to charge the enemy again. As for the remnants of his own troop, they were withdrawing up Edgehill with the rest. O'Brien and Downes, blood-fouled and weary, had tried to persuade Mun to go with them, that there was nothing more to be done but regroup and revive, but Mun had refused to follow, instead remaining on the lower slope as battered refugees streamed past him. And yet, amazingly, some pike-divisions and musketeer regiments looked relatively fresh, unblooded, as though they had not yet tasted battle. And perhaps they hadn't, for it had been chaos.

'Where are you, Father,' he whispered, suddenly fighting the urge to vomit. He wished he had some water to slake his terrible thirst but wished even more that he could water Hector, who had shown such valour that Mun felt the stallion was the most noble and loyal creature on God's tumultuous earth.

'What's your name, trooper?'

Mun twisted to see a young captain trotting towards him, his buff-coat, breastplate and dark, handsome face blood-spattered.

'Rivers, sir,' Mun replied. His muscles thrummed, trembling like a banner in the wind.

'Sir Francis's son?' the captain asked, halting his spirited horse beside Mun and calming her with a firm hand. Mun nodded. 'My name is Smith,' the captain said. 'Are you and that black beast of yours still fit?' There was fire in the man's dark eyes and Mun got the impression that the captain was angry that they were withdrawing.

'Hector could chase the wind itself, from now until Judgement Day,' Mun said.

The captain frowned. 'This is Judgement Day,' he said, and maybe it was, thought Mun, for some men believed God's eternal judgement was already upon them, manifest in this great and terrible conflict for their nation's soul.

'Are we mounting a charge, Captain?' Mun went on. 'With what men?'

Captain Smith grinned savagely and pulled two orange scarves from inside his breastplate, handing one of them to Mun. 'I'd wait till we get down there before you put it on,' he said, 'but you see there?' Mun followed the line of his outstretched arm until he saw the object of the young captain's attention. There, beyond a well-ordered rebel pike-division and walking their horses slowly back across the field towards Essex's own bloodied but victorious Regiment of Foot, were six men – three cuirassiers and three harquebusiers – guarding a seventh on foot, all adorned somewhere about their person with Essex's orange. And through the hanging smoke Mun saw that the footman carried what looked to be regimental colours rolled up around the shaft.

'Whose colours are they?' Mun asked.

'Why, they are the King's, Rivers!' Captain Smith said through a twist of lips. 'Those treasonous scoundrels make off with the Royal Standard.'

Mun felt as though he had been horse-kicked. When his small party of Horse had been forced to withdraw from the fray he had feared the worst for those making a desperate defence of the Standard. To see it now in enemy hands was as if he heard those brave men's death-knell.

'Loaded?' Smith asked, nodding at the carbine hanging at Mun's side and at the pistols holstered on his saddle. Mun nodded. 'Shall we?' the captain asked, and Mun clamped his teeth, rubbed Hector's poll and gave the stallion a little pressure with his thighs, following Smith back down the hill at the trot.

The pungent powder smoke stung his eyes and he blinked it away, his breathing loud inside his helmet now as he broke clear of the fractured masses ascending Edgehill.

Smith was tying the orange scarf around his waist and so Mun took his own around his carbine belt, knotting it at his chest over the rusting breastplate, his bowels feeling as though they had turned to water as he hit level ground and rode south-west, back straight, hands loose on the reins. A stone's throw away a massive hedgehog of bristling pikes wavered menacingly and he could only wonder at the strength of the men who hefted those long staves for hours on end.

'We'll try guile first,' Captain Smith said, looking forward as he spoke. 'If that doesn't work we'll kick the cur and run.' In that moment Mun wondered if the captain might be mad, but then what did that make Mun for following him?

They were closing fast now and one of the cuirassiers turned, on instinct perhaps; but appraising the two riders' unhurried approach and their orange sashes he turned back to his front, unconcerned.

'You men! Stop there!' Captain Smith called as they drew alongside the small but viciously armed party.

The riders pulled up, grim-faced, their horses tossing their heads and snorting, and then the man carrying the colours looked up and Mun saw an unarmed man in his forties with flinty pride in his eyes.

'What is this?' Captain Smith demanded, glaring at a cuirassier with elaborate moustaches whose armour was the finest and who had the most arrogant air about him. 'You would have a damned penman bear the King's standard back to the earl? Have you been struck about the head, sir?' The cuirassier stared, somewhere between shock, fury and confusion, but Smith held his nerve. 'This man is not worthy of the charge!'

'We can hardly carry the damned thing!' the cuirassier barked, indicating his fellow soldiers, who any fool could see were on horseback too and thus not ideally placed to carry a ten-foot pole wrapped in a huge swath of silk.

'Don't be a damned fool! It's just a question of balance,' Smith insisted. 'Here, man, let me show you.' He pushed his mount between another cuirassier and a harquebusier, extending his hand to receive the Standard. But the man holding it hesitated, looking to his comrade in the fine burnished armour, his face revealing his dilemma.

'And who are you?' a big harquebusier asked Smith, glancing at Mun too, thick brows knitted.

Mun noticed that his own hands were trembling. He desperately wanted to feel his pistols' flared butts snug in his fists, for that would stop them shaking, but he kept his hands on his reins and his teeth clenched.

'Captain Smith of Sir Philip Stapleton's troop,' the young Royalist replied waspishly, heavy on the *captain*, and this seemed enough for the penman, who passed the Standard up to him, mumbling that he had only been doing what he had been told.

'Forgive me, but I've ridden with Sir Philip since London and do not know you by face or reputation,' the big harquebusier said, his hand reaching for his wheellock.

Smith drew first and fired and the harquebusier fell back in a spray of blood, then a cuirassier kicked his mount forward and slashed at Smith, catching the neck of his buff-coat, but Mun grabbed his carbine and fired and the ball punched through the cuirassier's armour, bursting from his backplate, and he toppled from his horse.

'Yah!' Smith yelled, turning his mount and giving it his heels, and Mun hauled Hector round and whipped the reins as wheellocks roared, and he felt a pistol ball deflect off his backplate's shoulder but kept his head down and rode.

Seeing what had happened, some of the pikemen up ahead broke from their block and tried to intercept them, but they easily skirted those cumbersome staves and galloped on, snatching off their orange sashes and casting them away as they neared a troop of Prince Rupert's dragoons that had moved to the plain to cover the Royalist withdrawal. Captain Smith pulled up and Mun slowly let the reins slip through his hands, straightening his legs and back, so that Hector responded to the release of pressure in his mouth and slowed, huffing.

'The lily-livered urchins didn't even give chase!' Smith said as Mun caught up. The captain looked genuinely disappointed but then his lips spread into a smile as Mun shook his head at the audacity of what they had just done. 'Did you fight in Flanders, Rivers?' Smith asked, the Royal Standard couched like a lance, so that even in Mun's stunned stupor at what they had just achieved, he could not help but admire the man's superb horsemanship.

'This is my first battle,' Mun said, glancing at some dragoons who were trotting over to them. There was a biting edge to the dusk air now and their mounts' hot breath rose in clouds. 'I hope it is my last,' he added, his empty stomach clenching, threatening to have him retching any moment.

'I can assure you it will not be your last,' Captain Smith said, 'but neither should it, man! You're a born soldier, like me. Saint Michael the Archangel lends us courage and puts swords of fire in our hands that we may smite God's enemies.'

'You should have told that to those rebels; they'd have chased us then,' Mun said, trying to smile.

One of the dragoons introduced himself and asked who they were, to which Captain Smith replied, grinning, that he and Mun were two of St Michael's men, and the dragoon lieutenant frowned because the introduction had more than a little popery to it, but then he recognized the standard Captain Smith held and his eyes widened.

'Your eyes do not deceive you. We have recovered the King's colours,' Smith confirmed, 'and shall deliver them to His Majesty without delay.'

'Then allow us to escort you, Captain,' the young dragoon said, nodding gravely, for colours recovered were colours formerly lost and there was shame in that. The troop turned towards the escarpment but Smith noticed that Mun had not.

'Are you coming, Rivers?' he asked.

Mun shook his head. 'I have something to do.'

'Something more important than returning His Majesty's standard? Are you shot, lad? Have your senses leaked out?' His eyes were wide. 'I dare say His Majesty will be grateful for its return. I suspect we have more than earned our twelve shillings today.' Then that grin again, that got men to do what they did not want to do. But not this time.

'Please pay the King my respects,' Mun said, then turned and walked Hector back into the freezing, smoky gloom, onto the field from which the living had retreated, leaving it to the dead.

CHAPTER TWENTY-FIVE

BESS SHIVERED AND PULLED THE FUR-TRIMMED CLOAK tighter, the frozen knot of her hand clutching it at her throat as she stepped out into the night.

'Miss Elizabeth.' The young man guarding the entrance porch straightened, lifting the blunderbuss he gripped in white hands a little higher. Try as he might he could not hide his trembling with cold.

'Don't tell my mother, Joseph, but I must have some air.'

The young man shifted uncomfortably. 'But Miss Elizabeth, it int safe outside the house.' He gestured with the blunderbuss out across the grounds where groups of shadowy figures froze behind gabions, the earth-filled wicker baskets looming in the waning moon's dull glow. 'Your mother said—'

'Tomorrow the rebels will have the house and we all shall be dead or captured,' Bess snapped, 'and so tonight, Joseph, I will do as I please.' The young man recoiled as though struck, and Bess saw fear flare in his eyes, so that she wished she could take those words back. 'I will be just here,' she said, pointing down to the forecourt, 'and feel perfectly safe with you watching over me, Joseph.' The young man nodded resolutely, the fear in him tempered with pride now as Bess descended the steps and stood in Shear House's cold, black shadow, her breath fogging and her eyes watering. She looked up at the stars, as ever awed by the night sky's immeasurable vastness, appalled by the stars' indifference to the trials and tribulations of Man.

The air was bitterly cold but she sucked it in, letting it cleanse her throat and chest, inviting the raw night to scour her of the moans of the wounded and dying that clung to her very soul like cat's claws in a threadbare blanket. She revelled in the numbing, biting night because it purged her of the foul stink of rotting flesh that tainted every room in the house and was almost unbearable in the dining parlour upon whose floor those luckless, wounded men lay.

She had known one of them, Robert Birch, almost all her life, since he had taken employment as a labourer on the estate, and it was strange, she thought, that the man should only see the inside of Shear House now that he was dying. He had taken a musket ball in the thigh the day the rebels had breached the boundary wall and though they had got the ball out, the wound had turned gangrenous. Bess had watched Prudence their cook cut the putrid flesh away by degrees, even down to the bone, but it was no use and the stench was now intolerable and Bess was certain Robert Birch would die.

And more would die tomorrow. Because the rebels' demi-cannon had eventually punched a hole in the boundary wall and when this had happened Edward Radcliffe had pulled his garrison back to their secondary defensive positions behind ditches and gabions, the spinney and the rose garden wall.

'We can still hold the wall,' Lady Mary had insisted, even as a great cheer went up from the rebels beyond and the last bricks and rampart timbers settled amidst a cloud of dust. But Radcliffe had shaken his head in a way that said he doubted his men's ability if not their nerve.

'If that young cur knows his business, m'lady,' Radcliffe said, and Bess knew he was referring to Captain Downing, 'he'll storm that breach and we won't have the concentrated firepower to stop him. They'll get behind our lads and once that happens we'll have lost half the damned garrison.' He coughed into a fist, almost blushing at his profanity. 'M'lady.' But Lady Mary showed no sign of being offended.

'Then I fear we must put our faith in the inner breastworks, Major. At least we shall know where to aim our muskets,' she said, nodding resolutely towards the breach in the wall one hundred paces away. 'I'd rather that than the traitorous devils come over the wall in a dozen places.'

'Quite so, m'lady,' he had said, forcing a smile. 'Now, if you don't mind.'

'Of course. Carry on, Major,' she said, and with that had turned, linked arms with Bess and walked unhurriedly back towards the house, the veteran's barked commands cutting the crisp afternoon air, defying the last of the enemy's cheers.

Now, Shear House's makeshift garrison of servants, labourers, stablehands, farmers and merchants waited out there in the dark, praying that a Royalist force would march to their rescue and sweep away the rabble at their door, but knowing they would not.

A sound startled her and she turned, recognizing the approaching figure as Mister Cawley, the farmer from Heskin who had come in with his wife, four children and an assortment of livestock through which the defenders had been eating their way.

'Mister Cawley,' she greeted him, regaining her composure and huffing into her hands.

'Miss Elizabeth,' Cawley said, touching his hat's brim and resting his musket's butt on the ground, the end of the match between his fingers glowing hotly. The farmer seemed comfortable with the firearm and Bess could not but think Radcliffe had done well to turn men such as Cawley into soldiers.

'At least your match and powder will be dry,' she said, nodding at the musket and forcing a smile. 'So long as your fingers are not too numb to load and fire it.'

Cawley grinned. 'No fear o' that, Miss Elizabeth, but I'd wager those clerks and apprentices int used to being abeawt in this sort o' cold.' He grinned. 'If you listen carefully you can hear 'em shivering.' She smiled and he thrust a meaty hand inside his tunic and pulled something out which he offered her, seeming glad to be rid of it.

'A letter for my mother?' Bess asked, not recognizing the seal on it.

Cawley shook his head. 'I were told to give it to you, Miss Elizabeth, and to no other. One of their fifers slipped over t'wall wi' it. Nearly got izel shot full o' holes, but yer own Mister MacColla saw he were just a pup and let the lad say 'is piece.' His eyebrows arched. 'Brave little bugger,' he said, then nodded at the letter in Bess's hands. 'That letter is what he risked 'is neck for. It's from that rebel captain. Downer.'

'Downing. Captain Downing,' Bess corrected him, the name tasting foul on her tongue. 'And Mister MacColla did not think a letter from our enemy should be given directly to my mother?' she asked, at which Cawley shrugged and raised a palm.

'Just doing what I were told, Miss Elizabeth,' he said. Then he glanced left and right and took a step closer to Bess, so that she could smell his sweat and the tang of stale pipe smoke on his tunic. 'I get the feeling Mister MacColla is more comfortable i' t'master's wine cellar than he is sleeping in t'ditch.' Bess eyed him keenly, nodding for him to go on, which, after an internal debate, he did. 'Some of the lads think you might persuade Lady Mary to seek terms,' he murmured.

'And that's what this is about?' she asked, looking at the sealed letter and placing her other hand on the swell of her belly.

Cawley shrugged again. 'Just doing what I're told,' he said again, picking up his musket. 'Now I'd best be gettin' back. We all know what's coming in t'morning.' He held Bess's eye, his last words dangling like a baited hook, as though he sought confirmation of what lay in store. But Bess did not bite.

'Thank you, Mister Cawley,' she said, walking forward beyond the pool of shadow. 'But I'd have you stay a little longer if you please.'

'As thee wish, Miss Elizabeth,' the farmer said, turning his eyes out towards Shear House's defences as Bess broke the wax and began to read by the cold light of the stars.

When she had finished she folded the letter neatly

and slipped it down the front of her bodice.

'Will you escort me to the gate, Cawley?'

'Should I fetch the major?' he asked. Bess shook her head.

'Just walk with me to the wall,' she said, 'for I must speak with Captain Downing.'

'Very good,' he replied, fixing the glowing match in the serpent's jaws. He raised the musket and pulled the trigger, checking that the match's glowing end would strike the priming pan, whose cover was closed. 'But may I ask that thee stay behind me?'

'Thank you, Cawley,' she said, and with that they set off down the long driveway. Towards the enemy.

Her heartbeat was suddenly loud inside her head and her breathing quickened, each exhaled breath fogging past her cheeks like the bow wave before a ship as her booted feet crunched the frost-stiffened grass. Her unborn child was kicking furiously and Bess wondered if this was a sign that she should turn round and go back, that no good could come of meeting with the arrogant young captain who had brought his war to their home. But her mind was made up and she did not turn round and anyway, perhaps the child's stirring was an affirmation of her decision, a call to action. Besides, what was fear, she silently asked herself, if not something to be overcome?

'The garrison looks somewhat sparse,' she said, observing the great gabions and the men standing behind them, some of whom were looking their way, faces shadowed by helmets, broad-brimmed hats and cloak hoods. Bess felt her muscles begin to tremble with the cold and she clenched her hands together, squeezing them as she walked.

'The major has whittled us deawn, that's for sure,' Cawley replied, hoisting a hand to a friend who had rasped a greeting from where he stood in a nearby trench that was wreathed in pipe smoke. But there were fewer men than Bess remembered. 'A bunch of 'em went up to t'house at sundown. God knows what for.'

'Ah, yes,' Bess said. She recalled seeing men gathering at the rear of the house by the dairy and had assumed Major Radcliffe anticipated an attack from the north, despite earlier saying that such an event was unlikely due to the rocky, rising ground behind Shear House. 'Though surely we will need every man here,' she said, 'for the rebels will come through the breach. Captain Downing may be a traitor but I doubt he is a fool. He will not leave his big gun without adequate protection.' She had said this last as a question, but Cawley sniffed and, lifting his musket, dragged his coat's sleeve beneath his nose.

'Ask me to neuter a hog or plough a yardland and I could do it wi' mi eyes shut, Miss Elizabeth, but matters of war I'd rather leave to the likes o' Major Radcliffe.' She sensed Cawley's implication that she ought to do likewise.

But Major Radcliffe was not here now, was he? And there was no one else who would dare tell Bess not to climb through the ragged gap in the boundary wall looming before them and talk to the enemy.

'You had better not go further,' she said, for they were thirty paces from the wall and the great gate which was now more in the rebels' hands than theirs. Bess could see musket muzzles poking through the loopholes Radcliffe had had his men cut into the wall, and whatever eyes were on her now, clearly the rebels had been ordered to hold their fire.

'God be wi' thee, Miss Elizabeth,' Cawley said.

'And with you, Cawley,' she replied, glancing across at the great gate and noting that it was still intact and barred, though surely not for long. Then, taking a deep, icy breath, she began to cross the last bit of ground that could still be said to be hers rather than theirs, towards the breach in the wall through which the enemy would come on the morrow. And her heart was hammering like hooves at the gallop.

'Miss Rivers.' Captain Downing was standing on the mound of rubble, a gloved hand extended down to her, his lips spread in a tight smile. His lace-trimmed falling band glowed white in the dark. 'Please. Allow me to help you.' Bess did not want his help but she did not want to fall amongst the rubble either and so she nodded and reached for the offered hand, allowing the captain to guide her up onto the displaced bricks that shifted underfoot. 'Thank you for coming,' he said as she stepped down onto the frosty grass. 'It cannot have been an easy decision given what you must think of me.'

'Yet you judged that you had more hope of my coming than if you had written to my mother,' Bess said.

She saw a flash of his teeth as he bent to pick up his three-bar pot. 'Lady Mary's resolve would be admirable,' he said, straightening, 'if it were not—'

'Foolish? Futile?' She spat the words like a challenge, daring him to agree.

But the captain shook his head, placing the helmet under his arm. 'If it were not going to cost the lives of your garrison. And likely some of my own men too,' he said.

This took Bess aback and she was not sure how to respond. Instead she looked around her. There were a handful of rebels at the wall, muskets pointing through the loopholes, but the bulk of Downing's force was still fifty paces from the breach. She could see heads and shoulders sticking out from the trenches, faces moon-washed white, and other soldiers milling around gabions, the great wicker baskets filled with earth excavated from the trenches. A fire burned in the distance, crackling now and then, several shadowy figures huddled about it. Laughter and pipe smoke carried to her on the breeze. Somewhere, someone was singing a sad song of love found and lost and in that heartbeat she thought of Emmanuel.

'You *must* know what will happen tomorrow, Miss Rivers,' Captain Downing said, one hand resting on his sword's hilt. Bess thought he looked different. Tired. Perhaps he was not made for sleeping under canvas night after freezing night. She looked past him again and this time could just make out the shape of the great demi-cannon sitting there, a fire-spitting beast in the darkness. Sleeping. For now.

'I am not a soldier, Captain.' She felt the cold trying to worm into her jaw bones and start them trembling.

He regarded her for a moment as though he suspected her of mocking him. 'At first light we will bring our gun forward,' he said, nodding back towards the hole in the wall, 'and from there it will batter Shear House itself. Given time there will be nothing left but rubble. And that is the best you can hope for, if your . . . garrison . . .' he said the word contemptuously, 'should by some miracle hold.' His eyes bored into hers, a little of the stars' cold glow reflected in them. 'What is more likely is that my men will sweep across your lawns in a rolling wave of steel and musketry, and your aged misguided Major of the House, Mister Radcliffe, will drown in a river of blood.' He shook his head. 'Blood that need not be spilled.'

Bess wanted to sneer at the man's hyperbole, but there was something in those dark eyes that made her hold her tongue. Remorse? Pity? Whatever it was sent a shiver scuttling up her spine. Somewhere over to her right, near a copse of birch whose skeletal branches were silhouetted against night's jewelled veil, a small herd of oxen lowed and snorted.

'You are with child, Miss Rivers. A woman's instinct must be to protect the life she is nurturing.'

'And what would you know of a woman's instinct, Captain?' she asked, the fog of her breath rising between them.

'My own child will be born any day now,' he said, those words and his half smile disarming Bess and bringing to her mind an image of a pregnant woman somewhere, wishing her husband were with her instead of fighting in some God-awful war. 'The King's army is one hundred and forty miles away,' he went on. 'It is likely that they are already beaten and His Majesty's cause lost. That Charles and his retinue are prisoners. Or else His Majesty has fled and is already halfway to France.' The young man dipped his head respectfully. 'I do not know your father, Miss Rivers, but I do not think Sir Francis would want his womenfolk fighting for him. Or his house destroyed. Does he even know what is happening here?'

'My mother has written,' Bess said, as though that were answer enough. In truth they had received no reply from Sir Francis, but she would not admit that to this recreant devil. 'I am not a naive child, Captain. If the King were beaten we would know of it. And as for a mother's duty, that is surely to bring up her child in the true faith and obedience to its sovereign lord. I will not have an act of cowardice his first example.'

His. Yes, it is a boy, she thought. I know it.

With this sudden assuredness that she carried a boy, the fog in her mind cleared and she knew beyond certainty what her answer to Captain Downing must be. There had been doubt. If not, why had she come to meet him? But now that doubt had dissipated like breath in the numbing air and she saw in her mind's eye Emmanuel, Mun and Sir Francis on some far-away field, fighting for their king, doing their duty no matter the cost.

Captain Downing shook his head in a gesture that suggested this was a fight he was resigning himself to losing.

'I beg you to reconsider,' he implored, his helmet held like an offering, 'to convince your mother to yield. For the sake of good men, yours and mine.'

Bess pulled her cloak even tighter, hoping he could not see her bones rattling with cold. And fear.

'I am ashamed that you thought me less than my mother,' she said. 'That my courage and steadfastness were not equal to hers. But let me make this clear, Captain Downing. I shall put a musket to my own shoulder tomorrow. I shall fight you with a mother's heart. A mother's strength. And you will learn what duty is.'

He cocked his head, as though seeing her properly for the first time, then put on his helmet, pushing it down savagely in a gesture of intent that made Bess clench her teeth and want to step back out of his reach.

'Get that gun moving!' he bellowed into the dark, inhuman again with his head ensconced in cold steel.

And then the night exploded. Hooves thundered and pistols and carbines roared, tongues of fire licking the darkness, and suddenly Captain Downing flew at her, putting himself between her and the attackers, his arms thrust out behind him, corralling Bess so that she could not move.

Horses shrieked and men yelled and more firearms flared and now came the screams.

'What in God's name?' Downing growled, though he did not step away from her as the riders slashed about them and some fired into the huddle of oxen who bellowed in pain and impotent fury. And then Bess saw her mother in back- and breastplate, red hair flying wildly in the half moon's light, her white face all bone and shadow and fury. A rebel musketeer thrust his matchlock's muzzle up at the rider next to Lady Mary and pulled the trigger, launching him from the saddle. Lady Mary hauled on the reins and her grey mare, Hecuba, reared at the musketeer, her hooves smashing his head open in a flood of black gore. Hecuba's forelegs slammed down to the iron-hard earth and for a heartbeat Lady Mary looked over at them, the whites of her eyes glowing, then she howled and turned the mare and with a dozen others spurred off towards the big gun.

Captain Downing strode forward now, drawing his sword and yelling back to his men at the boundary wall to hold their positions in case of a full-scale sally from Shear House's defenders. Horrified, Bess watched as soldiers clambered out of their trenches and formed into ranks, walls of musketeers facing different directions, blowing on their match-cords, muzzles pointing into the dark. But the attackers were already gone, the thunder of their hooves fading in the distance, and Captain Downing knew the attack was over before it had really begun. He turned and strode back towards her, eyes raging.

'You knew about this?' he yelled, his sword accusing her.

'No,' she said, hands pressed against her belly. 'I swear.'

'Damn it!' he roared, scything his sword through the air and turning back round to assess the damage. From what Bess could make out, seven men and four of the six oxen lay dead. Several more of Downing's troopers lay moaning and bleeding, their fellows gathered around them doing what they could. It looked as though only two of the attackers had been killed, men she could not identify, and her mother had got away safely. Her mother!

'Keep the bitch as a hostage, Captain!' a gaunt-faced soldier sneered, grabbing Bess's arm with savage fingers, his stink filling her nose.

Captain Downing stepped up and backhanded the man across his face, sending him staggering, but he stood glaring at Bess still, yellow rat's teeth bared.

'Touch her again, Dix, and I'll kill you,' Downing spat and Bess felt herself recoiling from his fury as he turned back to her. 'Get back to your people, Miss Rivers,' he said, struggling to throw a bridle over his wrath. 'Get out of my sight!'

Bess was already moving, clambering up the rubble

of the breach, no offer of help now, numb fingers scrabbling for a hold on the sharp shards and bricks, the weight of her unborn child trying to pull her down.

'And tell Lady Mary that she can expect no quarter! Do you hear me? Tell her men to get on their knees and make their peace with God!'

She did not reply, stumbling and almost falling but keeping her feet which were now on Shear House's lawns. Then she heard a whistle and glanced left to find Cawley waiting in the shadows, beckoning her on with a flurry of hand. And she was relieved to feel the weight of his big arm on her shoulder as he threw his own cloak around her and led her up the slope towards the defences and the house. And she hoped beyond hope that their menfolk would return, that her father would ride to their defence.

Because a river of blood was coming.

CHAPTER TWENTY-SIX

HE COULD NOT BREATHE. SOMETHING WAS CLOGGING HIS *mouth and throat and so he clawed at his own face and found the end of something and pulled. It kept coming and coming, spooling up from his gullet as though it would never end and then he realized what it was. Hair. Raven black, thick as a horse's tail and twined in loose curls. He was choking on it. It was killing him. Then he saw her, tramping through snow away from him. She turned and looked, her face white as lace, and he tried to wave but could not move his arms. Were the bones broken? He yelled. No sound. She did not see him and then she turned and traipsed on and his heart ripped open because he knew he would never see her again. Martha.*

Then terror struck him. He was being pulled and wrenched this way and that.

Dogs?

A pack of dogs had found him. Big mastiffs, whose coarse hair and fetid breath stank like death. They were tearing at his clothes, trying to get to his flesh, but he could not move to fight them off. They must have come

*all the way from Lathom green. From the bear post.
Why him? They tugged and tore and he knew with
dread certainty that they would, any moment, find his
bare flesh and rip into it and begin to eat. He tried to
summon her face again. If only he could make their
eyes meet the dogs would leave him be. Somehow. But
he could not conjure her, could not remember what she
looked like. And then he realized it was not hair that
was choking him. It was rope. Thick and coarse and
suffocating him.*

Darkness. The smell of blood and faeces. And earth.
A shrill, broken laugh. Wraiths moving through the
frozen gloom, flapping and croaking like carrion crows.
Bending and crouching amongst the—

Corpses?

Seeking. Stealing. Cutting.

A man five feet away cried out for his mother. One
of the wraiths twisted suddenly and sidled over. Tom
saw a flash of blade, heard a wet gurgle and splutter
and smelt fresh shit as the dying man's bowels opened.

If they see I am alive they will kill me. If I am alive.

He was half aware of a deep sense of repugnance at
having been stripped naked. He knew his feet were bare
even, though he could not feel them. Like crows they had
pecked him clean and moved on. They were all around,
plundering the dead and the nearly dead, yanking rings
from fingers or hacking the fingers off and stuffing
them into knapsacks. They cawed and squabbled over
purses and helmets, back- and breastplates and swords.
They hauled buff-coats, boots, doublets and jerkins off
stiffening men, leaving pale pathetic corpses in the mud
that was hardening and hoary with frost. There was
no pity, just greed, and Tom looked up at the stars,

indifferent and eternal and infinite, and he had a sense that this was not how he was meant to die. But God was hateful.

I was shot. My shoulder?

He felt no pain. The freezing night had eaten into his very marrow. Numbing him.

He tried to move but could not. A corpse's leg lay across his own, heavy as iron. Slowly, as though his own blood was thickening, clotting with ice in his veins, he turned his head. There, beneath a shock of silver hair, was a dead face, the expression frozen in eternal surprise.

'Did you check that one?' A woman's voice, cold as frostbite.

'I can't remember. You do it,' a man replied.

'Lord preserve us, but it's another gold one,' the woman hissed. 'Give me the knife. Quick before someone else sees it!'

Tom kept his eyes shut and wondered if he was still breathing. He tried to think of Martha but could not remember her face, so he recalled a scene from his childhood. Mun and his friends had not let Tom play with them, saying he was too small, and he had cried. But Bess had taken her savings, sixpence in all, and walked to Lathom market, there paying a carpenter to make a pair of stilts specially for Tom. Together they had gone up to Gerard's Wood to find the other boys and when Mun saw Tom tottering along, his face a mask of concentration, he had laughed until his stomach ached.

I love you, Bess.

He wished she were with him now. She would fight for him.

He kept his mind's eye fixed on her face as his arm

jerked and twitched. And he begged for death's embrace.

As they sawed off his finger.

'Away, villain!' Mun growled, pointing a pistol at a toothless crone who cursed him and shuffled off to find easier pickings. The looters were everywhere, shadows moving amongst the dead, and the sight of them would have made Mun sick if he were not already numbed to the horror of it all. Dead and dying littered the field, piled up three deep in places, and Hector would have been hard-pressed to find footing amongst them. So Mun had left the stallion tethered at the foot of the escarpment, telling him to go with no other until he returned, and Hector had nickered softly that he understood.

Some of the ruined men still clung stubbornly to life, their moans cloying the stench-thickened air in a hopeless lament. The night was bitterly cold and clear and by the stars' light Mun searched, as he had done for the last two hours. He had seen hundreds of dead faces, not knowing for the most part which side they had belonged to in life. All were now united in death. A great army of the dead. He wandered aimlessly, stumbling over stiff limbs, all but oblivious to the plaintive cries of those who were not ready to die though they surely would.

But he had not found his father or Emmanuel. He had a vague idea where on the field he had seen Sir Edmund Verney and a small knot of foot and horse make their final, desperate stand beneath the Royal Standard, and what he found at that place was a scene of unimaginable awe: sixty or more corpses fallen thick as wheat before the scythe. Many were naked, already stripped and plundered by local folk who had, like carrion-feeders, flocked to the field of the slain. White flesh glowed in the cold, waning moon's light and some of the dead stared at Mun accusingly or pointed at him with stiff arms and clawed hands. And if his father had fallen near this place, his fine cuirassier's armour would have drawn looters like beggars to a bishop's train.

'Be gone or you'll join the dead!' he barked at another scavenger, this one a mere boy with pale hair and arms straining beneath a bundle of swords.

He had never felt so tired. Empty. Exhausted to his very soul, so that he suspected that if he were to sit down now amongst the dead he would simply become one of them.

Of course, there was a chance his father and Emmanuel were even now reunited with the rest of the King's Horse, or else walking their tired mounts back south-east after their relentless pursuit of the enemy. But he did not think either of these was true. He knew his father well enough to be almost certain that Sir Francis would not have left the field to chase after a broken force, like an over-eager young blood caught up in the mad thrill of it all. Neither would Sir Francis have been unable to curb his horse, simply letting it run itself out rather than remain in the fray, as some men had surely done. No, his father had not sought this war, but with its coming would not place anything above the execution of his duty and the preservation of his honour. And though Mun had not seen him amongst those men he had watched trying to force a way through to defend the King's standard, he yet knew that Sir Francis had been there. And Emmanuel, whose fire outblazed his sense at times, would have been there too, staying by his lover's father, loyal to the end.

Only when he was challenged by a small troop of rebel Horse did Mun give up the search. With nightfall a considerable portion of Essex's army had remained on the field and now their fires blazed and crackled in a ragged line along the north-west, and in his stupor Mun had wandered too close.

'Who are you?' a trooper had called and Mun had heard swords rasp up scabbard throats and the clicks of pistols being cocked.

'I am looking for my father,' he had replied, barely looking up at the dark mass of mounted men. 'And for my friend.'

'You are the King's man?' the horseman asked.

'As should you be,' Mun said, knowing he still gripped his pistols though he could not feel them for his hands were useless, little more than numb, rigid claws.

'Insolent bastard,' one of the troopers growled.

'Away with you, man,' the first rebel said. 'There has been enough killing today. Go back to the living and leave the dead to God.' And with that Mun had turned back towards the Edgehill escarpment and the fires of his own side winking here and there on its heights, and tramped through the slain once more.

His heart stopped when he thought he saw Tom torn and bloody amongst mounds of horseflesh, some of the beasts still breathing and lifting their heads now and then. But the dead man was not Tom, and so he moved on, his whole body shuddering with cold.

The bitter night was at its deepest when he found some of his own troop huddled in cloaks against the cold. They sat beside a meagre fire they had made from broken pike staves, musket rests and whatever else they could find that would burn, and of his friends Mun saw O'Brien first. The big man was cradling a cup of ale to his chest as though there was heat in the thing, not cold liquid, and absent was the good-natured raillery that was the usual accompaniment to the fire's crack and spit. Rowe and Downes were there too and Mun was glad to see that those three at least had survived the day.

'I was beginning to think we'd lost you,' O'Brien said, looking up at Mun with glazed eyes and offering him the cup. Mun drank of it deeply, handed it back and shuddered, dragging a frozen hand across his mouth and beard.

'Captain Boone was looking for you,' Vincent Rowe told him, the feeble flamelight making sharp angles of the young man's face.

'With a face like a bulldog licking piss off a thistle,' O'Brien added, cocking an eyebrow but not taking his eyes off the flames.

'And there was me thinking that bastard would be too busy enjoying his spoils to care,' Mun said, holding his hands near the flames and wincing as the hot aches began to fill them.

'Want some?' Downes asked, ripping a hunk of bread off a loaf and offering it to him. He took it with a nod of thanks. 'Found it in the rebels' train,' Downes said through a mouthful. But when Mun tried to eat the bread he found that his mouth would not work properly. The jaw bones themselves were numb, so that he could not chew, and he stuffed the bread between his sash and his breastplate instead, saving it for later.

'I heard we got the King's colours back,' Rowe said in an obvious attempt to lift the mood. One man muttered that they should not have lost them in the first place, and another questioned what was an ensign against the lives given for it. Mun sat by O'Brien, looking into the flames and half listening to the talk but not wanting any part in it. Some managed to get a little sleep. Others, many still in armour for want of anything warmer, walked back and forth between the resting men, for it was the only way they could find to keep some vestige of heat in their flesh and bones. Mun gave himself over to this strange semi-conscious state, too weary to be properly one of the living but too repelled by the day's events to sleep. And before the first hint of the new day announced itself as a cold, white glow beyond the hill upon which the King's army hunched, Captain Nehemiah Boone returned, his tired eyes flaring when they recognized Mun amongst those still huddled by the smouldering embers.

'Rivers,' he spat, beard and moustaches unkempt, his cloak pulled tight at his neck. In his other hand he clutched a wine pitcher that moved as though empty or nearly so.

'Captain,' Mun acknowledged him, blinking exhaustion from his own eyes, trying to sharpen them. With Boone were Corporal Bard, Humphrey Walton and several of the others in the troop who had lingered amongst the rebel baggage train rather than rejoining the battle, but from their looks they did not seem eager for the confrontation.

'You care to finish what you started earlier in the day, you brazen cur?' Boone snarled, handing the wine jug to Bard and stepping in amongst the ring of slumberous soldiers. Bard put the jug to his lips and drained the last of the liquid, never taking his eyes off Mun.

'And get myself hanged for fighting an officer?' Mun said.

'Let's put the whole thing behind us, eh?' O'Brien suggested with a smile.

'Shut your damned Irish mouth,' Boone warned, pushing his long, lank hair back from his face and glaring at Mun. 'You won't live long enough to hang, you base bloody villain.'

'So be it,' Mun said, climbing to his feet, every muscle complaining, every sinew taut as a bowstring.

Then a shiver ran through the assemblage thronging the hillside and with it came a murmur like that of the sea and all turned east towards the spreading glow of dawn.

'What is it now?' Rowe said, craning to spy what was causing the fuss, huffing into cold hands as, all around, men were getting to their feet.

'Holy Christ, it's the King himself,' O'Brien said, standing with the rest as the King of England, Ireland and Scotland descended the slope with a retinue of knights and musketeers. He wore a broad-brimmed hat and a black cloak and was conspicuous as much for not being apparently armed as for being the King.

'He's smaller than I imagined him,' Downes murmured as men began to fall to their knees and bow their heads, though all, Mun noticed, watched their king from beneath their brows as he passed.

'And he has a face like thunder, too,' O'Brien added, wincing through aches as he went down to one knee, and Humphrey Walton replied that that was hardly surprising seeing as His Majesty had today learned that his own subjects were prepared and willing to turn their muskets and cannon on him.

'Make way for His Royal Majesty, Charles, by the grace of God King of England, France and Ireland, King of Scots and defender of the faith!' a courtier yelled in a sergeant's voice, and Mun saw another man beside the King, in a buff-coat and three-barred pot, point in their direction.

'Smarten up, boys, they're coming this way,' Corporal Bard said through a grimace, sweeping a filthy hand through his filthy grey hair, and suddenly the men in Mun's troop looked as terrified as they had before the day's first charge, turning their eyes to the ground as though they wished it would swallow them. And then he was there, amongst them. Charles Stuart, King anointed by God.

'You are our nephew's fellows, are you not?' the King accused, his Scots accent taking some by surprise, Mun saw from their furtive glances. 'You swept Ramsey's Horse from the f-f-field but having done so it was a p-p-pity you did not see f-fit to return to us. In your beating of them you near beat us,' he said.

Mun kept his eyes on the ground, wondering if any would dare reply. Then someone coughed into the awkward silence.

'Your Majesty, many of our men are young. Inexperienced.' It was Captain Boone. 'Their enthusiasm for the fight ran away with them.'

'Devious God-damned worm,' Mun whispered to himself.

'But if it please Your Majesty, we will do much better next time,' Boone went on. 'If the traitors dare face

Your Majesty in the field again, for surely we have today given them a rare thrashing.'

'And you are?'

'Captain Nehemiah Boone, Your Majesty,' he said, seizing the moment. 'I served with the Prince in Germany. It was I who seized the enemy's baggage train today after a fierce fight of it.'

'Indeed?' The King turned one eye on him. 'And we had been led to understand the rebels flew like sparrows from the cat.'

'I can assure Your Majesty—'

A royal hand silenced Boone. 'Is this the man, Captain Smith?' the King asked. Mun lowered his head again and could see the King's bucket-top boots now, the brown French calfskin leather stained at the toe, and it struck him how small the feet must be inside those boots.

'Yes, Your Majesty, this is the lad.'

'Edmund Rivers.' The King spoke as though he had long sought the face to the name, and Mun raised his head though did not look his king directly in the eye.

'At your service, Your Majesty,' he said.

'Indeed,' said the King again. 'Captain Smith – Sir John – tells us that you and he alone were responsible for retrieving our colours from the miscreant devils.'

Sir John? thought Mun, glancing at Smith, and nodded. 'I rode with Captain Smith, Your Majesty,' he said.

'And Sir John tells us that the two of you defeated ten of the base fellows?'

Mun's eyes flicked to Captain Smith who gave an almost imperceptible shrug and the ghost of a grin.

'It all happened so quickly, Your Majesty,' Mun

said, 'that I cannot say how many we faced. I merely followed the captain's bold example.' His eyes were drawn upwards until they were looking into the King's. 'By God's grace we wrested the prize from them and they had not the heart to make a chase of it.'

The King glanced at Smith then as though what Mun had just said did not entirely match the captain's story.

'Well, we are g-g-grateful to you, Edmund, and are pleased to have men of courage and virtue in our army.'

'Your Majesty,' Mun said, lost for words.

'Neither do we forget the service of your loyal father, Sir F-francis Rivers, who we f-fear did not survive the day.' The words struck like a musket ball and Mun's soul shuddered under the impact. 'Indeed, there is a certain tragic irony that the son should recover what the father died trying to protect. But take comfort, Edmund, that your loyal father is now with G-god, f-f-full of glory and never again to know sin or sorrow. His king shall not f-forget him. Neither shall your courageous act go unrewarded.'

'I seek no reward other than to serve Your Majesty and put the rebels back in their place,' Mun said, at which the King cocked his head, pulling his thin beard through bone-white knuckles.

'Nevertheless, I have come all this way,' the King said. 'And have had my fill this day of what my subjects would or would not have. Sir John, will you stand as Edmund's sponsor?'

'I will, Your Majesty.'

The King nodded. 'My spurs,' he said, at which Captain Smith, now Sir John Smith, for the first time that day, it seemed to Mun, appeared ruffled; yet he went to one knee and began to fumble at the buckles of the King's spurs.

'Do you swear to never traffic with traitors?' the King asked.

'I swear it,' Mun said, hardly believing what was happening.

'Do you swear to never give evil counsel to a lady, but to treat her with respect and defend her against all?'

'I swear it,' Mun heard himself reply.

'And do you swear to serve God and your king f- faithfully so long as you live?'

'I swear it.'

In the distance men were yelling and oxen lowing as gun teams yet hauled cannon up the Edgehill escarpment, but for a hundred paces in all directions around the King the only sounds were of crackling flames, the snorts and whinnies of horses and the occasional bark of a dog.

'Sword,' the King said. There was a rasp and the next thing Mun felt was the flat of a blade on his left shoulder. 'I dub thee Sir Knight,' King Charles said, then struck Mun's other shoulder. 'Arise, Sir Edmund Rivers, loyal Knight and defender of the realm.'

Mun climbed to his feet and glanced about him at those still on their knees. O'Brien winked at him through matted strings of thick red hair. Downes and Rowe were grinning. He could not see Captain Boone's face but could guess well enough the expression on it.

The King circled a finger in a *get on with it* gesture at which Captain Smith fell to one knee again, this time behind Mun, and took off Mun's spurs, replacing them with the King's own, whose highly polished silver yoke and rowels glowed in the ebbing gloom.

And with that Charles Stuart turned and swept away, his well-armed entourage, including Captain Smith, rattling in his wake as they made their way back up the hill through the press of battle-stunned men.

'Sir Edmund bloody Rivers,' O'Brien said, half looking at Captain Boone which was the same as rubbing salt into a cut. 'Who would have thought it?'

Boone glared at Mun and there was murder in his eyes, but then he turned and strode off, leaving Mun trying to make sense of all that had just happened. 'Is there any more where that came from, Clancy?' he asked, nodding at the cup on the ground beside the big Irishman.

O'Brien frowned at the use of his Christian name, but then teeth split his red beard and he held up a thick index finger. 'It just happens I might know where the last of it is stashed, Your Grace,' he mocked, bowing his head deferentially. 'And as my da used to say, it's the first drop that destroys you; there's no harm at all in the last. So we might as well drink ourselves silly.'

There were more than a few murmurs of agreement at this, from men who wanted nothing more than to forget all that they had seen that day. All that they had done.

Mun turned and looked down onto the field where the slain lay in heaps yet swathed in night's shroud. It would be several hours before the breaking dawn spilled its light over the escarpment, flooding the plain and illuminating the extent of the carnage.

'Dear God.' He felt the whisper escape his lips. 'What have we done?' He shivered. Down there somewhere, amongst tortured flesh, amidst the ruins of countless families, lay his own father. Alone in the cold. Defiled by looters.

Emmanuel was down there too and Mun's heart bled for Bess who would never see him again, and for the unborn child in her belly who would never know its father.

'Try not to think about it, lad. At least not tonight.' He felt the arm on his shoulder and recognized the voice of Corporal Bard, smelt the tobacco on the man's breath. But he did not turn round. Because there were tears in his eyes.

CHAPTER TWENTY-SEVEN

AM I DEAD? HE IS COMING FOR ME. I HEAR HIM. HIS BREATH.
Hell.

His next conscious thought – some considerable time after the last, he somehow knew – was that he was not dead. Satan was not coming for him. The faint, rhythmic sound in his ears was his own breath, shallow as a puddle of blood.

I am blind! Panic flooded in, crushing him, and then the stench hit him and he screamed but the sound was blunt and stifled and he tried to thrash his limbs but he could not. He was being crushed. He screamed again, the terror rending his soul, and suddenly he could feel his heart pounding in his chest and he thought it must burst.

Then a flare: burning white light that ripped into his eye sockets. Instinct turned his face away. He was going to be sick.

'Mother of God!' A man's voice. Not his own. 'Margaret! Margaret!'

The searing blaze shrank away and Tom blinked again and again and the brilliant white light became blue.

Sky. I am alive.

'It is a miracle!' A woman's voice. 'Dear Lord! The poor boy is alive!'

'A Lazarus before our very eyes!' the man said.

Then Tom was shivering wildly, teeth rattling, limbs jigging like a hanged man.

'Here, lad, take my hand. You're safe now.'

There were arms and legs and pale faces. Blood. And that atrocious stench. He flailed and thrashed amongst the dead, horror clutching his being, and then strong hands gripped him, living hands, and pulled him from the cart, from the pain-filled, questioning faces of the naked, stiff corpses who had accepted Tom as one of their own. Who would not have him leave.

He bent, then fell to his knees and retched, but his stomach was empty and all that came up was bitter strings of bile that burned his throat and mouth.

'Get him some beer, Margaret! It's all right, lad. It's all right. You're safe now. Here, put this on.' The man took off his cloak and a moment later Tom knew the cloak was wrapped around his shuddering body but he could not feel it. He was naked. All the corpses were. Three feet away was a pit and in it were more of them, arms and legs entangled in a macabre intimacy that only the dead would countenance.

'Where am I?'

'What's that, lad? What are you saying?'

He swallowed. It felt as if he had a length of burning match stuck in his throat. 'Where am I?'

'Kineton village, lad.'

Tom glanced around expecting to see soldiers and colours, horses and tents. But there was just open land, brambles and hedges and rough grazing. A

412

stone's throw away were the ruins of an old church. Two crows squabbled on the overgrown remains of the nave wall.

'The ground is still consecrated, so they say,' the man explained guiltily, brows arching outwards, eyes glancing away.

'Makes no difference to me for I'm not going in it,' Tom said through chattering teeth. He looked at his right hand and retched again. The third finger was gone, in its place a gory stub of congealed blood and white bone, and the wraith of a memory skimmed through his mind, of a shadow man stooping over him with a knife.

Then the woman was back and she gave a leather jack to her husband, who carefully gave it to Tom, wrapping Tom's hands around it and keeping his own over the top of them to help guide the jack to his lips.

He drank it all, feeling the liquid splash in his empty belly, then handed back the empty vessel and the man nodded brusquely. 'We had better get you inside,' he said. 'Don't want you dying on us after coming back from the dead like that. That'd be a pity, eh? Think you can walk?'

Tom nodded, accepting the arm offered him, and climbed to his feet, his head spinning and his brain hammering. And then he felt the agony in his left shoulder. It felt like a red-hot knife twisting in his flesh.

'Aye, you were shot from the looks of it,' the man said. 'I'd say the ball went through yer flesh. Don't think it's still in there. Probably did for the fellow behind you instead. But we'll give it a good wash and have a proper look. Now now, lad, no more looking at them. That won't do you any good. You're with the living again now.' With that the man turned him round, away from the open grave and the cart still laden with bluish corpses, and his wife, Margaret, who before had seemed afraid to come too close, took his other arm and put it across her shoulder.

'My boots,' Tom said, looking at his bare feet, numb as stones and white against the mud and grass.

'I found you as you are,' the man said.

'Achilles!'

'Peace, lad. Save yer strength.'

'My horse,' Tom said, as the memory of Achilles falling and of him being thrown came crashing in on him like a wave on shingle.

'As I said, lad, there was nothing else. Just dead folk and dead horses. And bloody crows.'

Worse than the pain of his ravaged shoulder and the loss of his finger – the stump of which was still numb, thankfully – and the loss of his pistols and everything he owned, worse even than the horror of spending a night among the dead, was the hard cold truth that Achilles, his loyal friend, was dead.

The Dunnes' house was a small, timber-framed affair in a modest row of dwellings on Warwick Road across from St Peter's church. Two rooms above two rooms, its ancient wattle-and-daub walls were crumbling and its thatch looked hard-pressed to prove a challenge to anything more than a spit of rain. And yet inside it was warm, dry and safe, and what little Edward, Margaret and their daughter Anne had they seemed happy to share with Tom. He had the sense they would have taken him in even if he had fought for the King, with whom they had 'differences', as Edward had put it, though he could not be sure because the Dunnes did not seem inclined to discuss their allegiances. Which was fine by Tom. Edward had set a fire in the dark, modest parlour and sat Tom beside it to thaw his bones. Then Margaret had washed Tom from head to foot and he had let her do it, being too exhausted for a show of modesty now after all he had been through. Besides which, the Dunnes had two sons of about Tom's age, who were off fighting for Parliament.

'Take my word for it,' Margaret had said, gently wiping dried blood from his cheek, 'there is nothing you've got that I haven't seen before.'

With the wound clean they had seen that Edward had been right and there was no ball stuck in the meat. It had gouged a piece of flesh and a sliver of bone from Tom's shoulder and gone on its way.

'So long as we keep it clean, you ought to recover well enough,' Edward had said, satisfied they had washed all the filth and any fibres from Tom's clothes from the wound. Margaret had made a poultice of honey and oats and because Anne had the steadiest hand and the best eyes, so said her father, the task was given to her of smearing the salve into the raw furrow. Now that he was warm the pain had been appalling, but Tom had clamped his jaw shut on the curses that clamoured to be loosed upon the agony, and only afterwards had it occurred to him the real reason why Edward had given the job to Anne. The girl was a beauty. No older than seventeen by Tom's guessing, she was golden-haired, blue-eyed and clear-skinned, but the most potent weapon in her arsenal was the slight upward curl of her lips that hinted at a mischief at odds with the rest of her. If anything could bolster a man's courage against pain and stop him filling a godly house with ungodly curses, Tom mused after the job was done, it was the nearness of a beautiful woman. As for the third finger on his right hand, that stub smarted like the devil, too, and he was glad when Margaret had bound it so that he no longer had to look at it.

'You were lucky the night was clear and cold,' Edward had said, noting the grimace that Tom realized had been on his face for some while, 'for it was the cold that saved you, I'd wager a half sovereign on it.' Tom doubted Edward Dunne had a half sovereign to his name but thought the man was probably right about why he was alive. 'The cold stopped the bleeding or else you'd have bled out like a hog.'

'Perhaps I *was* dead,' Tom had said, staring into the flames. 'Perhaps I was dead but not even Hell wanted me.'

'Hush your mouth, young Thomas,' Margaret had chided from the kitchen, 'I'll not have that sort of talk in my house!' And then she had bustled in with a steaming bowl of pork stew and half a loaf of cheat bread and Edward had gone back out to continue his work of burying the dead, for which one of the Earl of Essex's captains had promised to pay him and several other men a shilling each.

Tom had wolfed the meal, helping it down with a great wash of weak ale; and afterwards he slept as he had never slept before: a dreamless slumber half as deep as death.

And the next day the King's men came to Kineton.

It was midday and Tom had not been long awake when Margaret threw open the parlour door, a frozen, wild-eyed stare announcing her terror before she opened her mouth. Then he heard the commotion outside: two voices, boys', cawing that the Cavaliers were coming. Their voices faded away as they ran on along Warwick Road and Tom gingerly stood and began to dress in worn breeches and an old shirt that belonged to one of the Dunne boys, as Margaret gathered up his bedding and hurried away with it.

The front door banged and he froze, then exhaled as Anne came into the room. 'You must hide,' she said, her cheeks flushing because she had caught him half dressed.

Tom shook his head. 'I won't put your family at risk,' he said, tucking the shirt in, cursing under his breath because he did not have his tall boots and his father's pistols. 'I'll go north. I can walk well enough,' he lied. In truth he did not think he would get far, for his body was pain-racked and bone-weary.

'They will be mounted,' Anne said, 'and if they find you trying to flee they will know what you are.'

'As they will if they find me here, cowering in the house of a man in Parliament's employ.'

Then Margaret swept back into the room. 'You've got a lot to say for a man just back from the dead, young Thomas,' she said, grabbing his hand, hauling him to the stairs at the back of the parlour. 'Up you go. I won't tell you again. You know as well as I that the King's men will have sent riders north and west to trap any Parliament men bolting from the village.'

Tom knew she was right and furthermore admired the clear thinking that seemed so contrary to her obvious fear. So gingerly he climbed the stairs, his heart thumping now because he could hear horses and men outside. There were three beds in Anne's room:

hers and her brothers', upon which piles of blankets sat neatly folded. But there was nowhere obvious for him to hide and he said as much.

'If *you* don't know it's there then let us hope *they* do not, either,' Margaret said, falling to her knees by the fireplace and pulling the heavy grate out onto the boards. 'Now up you go. Quick as you can.'

Tom crouched and peered up the shaft, amazed to see iron rungs fixed into the stone, ascending into the dark. There was no sign of light or sky.

'It is not a flue,' he said, his head spinning, legs trembling from climbing just those few stairs.

Margaret arched a brow. 'A Catholic lived here before,' she replied, as though that explained everything, and Tom imagined a frightened family hiding their priest up there in the cramped dark whilst pursuivants searched the house. 'Go all the way up and you'll see.'

'But be as still as you can,' Anne warned, going over to the window and looking down. 'I have heard mice scurrying about up there, so we shall hear you like thunder if you fidget.'

'No fidgeting,' Tom acceded with a half smile.

Anne turned back suddenly. 'Quick now, they're coming!'

Tom locked eyes with Margaret. 'If they find me—'

But she cut him off with a wave of her hand. 'Stay still and stay quiet. And don't come down until we say it's safe.'

He turned and squeezed up into the narrow space, able to bend only his right leg, just enough to step up the rungs, both feet onto each before moving to the next, his shoulders scraping the wall, knocking bits of mortar from it that rattled down onto the grate which Margaret had put back.

At the top he clambered over a lip into the roof space, his eyes adjusting to the gloom until he could make out a clutter of ancient beams and the roof's sloping eaves. He could feel sweat bursting from his skin, soaking his clothes and making his scalp itch. A wave of nausea threatened to swamp him but he sharpened his mind and fought it off, knowing it was some effect of the blows his head had taken.

Taking a deep breath he tried to slow his racing heart. The smell of dry wood and bird droppings was cut with the almost sweet tang of mouse urine. He shuffled up against a roof beam and stilled his breath so that he might become one with that dark place.

A mouse scurried across the boards. Something rustled above his head, a creature nesting in the thatch perhaps. And then he could hear the King's soldiers, shouting to each other, thumping on doors. Demanding to know if the folk of Kineton harboured any rebels and if they did to give them up or face their king's punishment for they were vile traitors. So he put his head back against an old timber, the wound in his shoulder a savage bloom of pain, and waited in the dark.

'We've got one, Captain!' a big trooper yelled, appearing at the door of a modest house and dragging a man out into the street where more Royalist soldiers waited with the horses. 'Found the cack handler hiding under a bed like a whipped bloody cur.' He swung his victim round, sending him sprawling across the muddy horse tracks where he lay helpless, begging for mercy.

'Poor bastard looks half dead,' Rowe said to Mun as they watched the scene, their swords drawn. O'Brien was pounding a big fist against the door of another house on Warwick Road. It would be only the fourth house the three of them had searched but O'Brien was already tired of the task. Mun was, too, if he was honest. It was dragoons' work. Besides which, he was exhausted. Soul-weary. And his mind kept conjuring images of his father and Emmanuel, two corpses in the cold mud.

'I hope they hang him,' he said as two soldiers hauled the rebel from the filth and bound his hands behind his back. 'Damned traitor.'

'Here we go,' O'Brien gnarred as the door opened and a small, nearly toothless man stood trembling at the threshold, hooded eyes flickering over the soldiers and blades before him. To replace his broken rapier Mun had chosen an Irish hilt from the munitions captured after the battle. A real bone-breaker and heavy too, its broad blade was balanced by the basket hilt of wide bars and large spherical pommel, and though not a fine weapon it was a fearful one.

'We must search your house, old man,' O'Brien said, 'in case any rebels sneaked in while you were dozing by the fire.'

'There are no rebels here,' the man lisped, waving O'Brien away with a skeletal, liver-spotted hand. 'I am old not blind.'

'I wouldn't trust those rusty peepers to see your piss hit the pot,' O'Brien replied, pushing past him, and Mun and Rowe followed into the small kitchen, their blades held before them in case of ambush. A cat hissed at Mun, its back arched, and Mun stamped near it but it held its ground as he moved through to the small parlour and Rowe stomped up the stairs.

'Have you seen any Parliament men since Kineton Fight?' Mun asked, eyeing the old man for signs that he was lying to them. He shook his head and Mun looked around him. A small iron pot hung above the fire, its bubbling contents filling the humble house with the smell of onions and parsnips. Food for one.

It seemed the man had little else, nor a wife by the looks.

'I want no part in the quarrel, sir,' the old man said, wringing his hands, his head wobbling on his scrawny neck. 'I just want to live out my days in peace. Don't want trouble.'

'Nothing up here!' Rowe called, clomping back down to join the others. O'Brien had found a spoon and was busy dipping, blowing and slurping, bushy brows bridging slitted eyes.

'Yet the quarrel has found you, old man,' Mun said, 'as it has found us all. It is left to you to choose the side. For your king or against him.'

'Remember, though, if you lie down with dogs, you rise up with fleas,' O'Brien put in, then cocked his head. 'Spearmint,' he said. 'Just a sprig or two, mind, but it would improve it. And perhaps some parsley?'

'Leave the old man's food alone,' Rowe said, grinning. 'He doesn't want your Irish drool tainting it.'

O'Brien shrugged and turned his palms innocently. 'A good word never broke a tooth, young Vincent,' he said, 'I'm simply imparting my wisdom, for I know food. God bless her but my ma could have fed the King's army with five fishes and two loaves, so she could.'

There was another commotion outside and Mun

nodded to the others that it was time to go. O'Brien sighed, handing the spoon to the old man as he followed Mun and Rowe back outside. 'O'Brien, you barnacle-brained numbskull!' the Irishman berated himself, halting at the threshold and turning back, startling the old man, who had followed them to the door. 'Crushed coriander seeds,' he announced, pressing finger to thumb as he stepped out onto the road, 'just a pinch. But then it'll be worth eating.'

'I want no trouble,' the old man mumbled, shaking his head, then shut the door and was gone.

'You see if I'm wrong!' O'Brien clamoured at the closed door.

'You should have seen her, Mun!' Mun looked across to see Richard Downes standing in the road, staring up at the first-floor window of the house next door. 'She's a beauty, a real beauty,' Downes said. 'Hair like spun gold.' He put on his three-bar pot, leaving the chin strap hanging, and cupped his hands against his chest. 'Tits you could hang your helmet on! And those lips . . .' He grinned. 'I told Walton I'd let him have the mother, and we'd keep the whole thing to ourselves, but the old fart wouldn't hear of it so we had to make do with relieving them of their dinner.' He kicked the sack by his feet. 'Smelt good, too.'

Humphrey Walton shook his head at Mun as though cursing his luck for having been partnered with Downes, but Mun ignored them both, his gaze drawn across the road and the men leaving the church hefting an iron-bound chest between them. Corporal Bard was with them, barking orders at a trooper named Ellis to deliver a message to Captain Boone.

'What have they got there, then?' O'Brien said,

following Mun's lead and tucking his powder flask inside his thick buff-coat for it had started to rain: thin veils of drizzle that did not feel like much but would soak a man and his powder in no time, making the one miserable and the other useless. 'A bit small for the Earl of Essex's coffin,' the Irishman added through a grin.

'And not heavy enough to be coin, by the looks,' Mun said, crossing the road so he could see better.

'Dead men's effects,' Bard explained in answer to the questioning glances from the men gathering around, drawn like Mun to the chest for the glorious possibilities of what it might contain. 'The men of Kineton have been burying the dead yonder.' The sergeant threw a hand eastward. 'By an older church that's nought but ruins now. The things they find with the corpses, the things they don't have a use for,' he added, cocking an eyebrow knowingly, 'letters and the like, they give to the minister for safekeeping.'

'Because the hedgeborn apple Johns can't read,' Downes mumbled in Mun's ear.

At Bard's signal the two men set the chest down and the corporal opened the lid, stirring a groan of disappointment from the men. 'I told you, you suspicious bastards,' he said, 'there's nought here that should keep you from your work. Anything of worth will be hidden under boards, in dank cellars and stuffed up skirts,' he said, nodding back towards the long row of thatched houses that continued on Southam Street, 'so get back to it, you tosspots.'

Men murmured grumblingly and when Mun turned back towards the task in hand he caught a glimpse of a pale face and golden hair at a first-floor window.

A heartbeat later it was gone, but he recalled what Downes had said and was surprised to consider that the man had perhaps not exaggerated how beautiful the girl was who lived in that house.

Then he drew his sword again and followed O'Brien back across the road. To search for rebels.

CHAPTER TWENTY-EIGHT

THE MAN JERKED LIKE A FISH ON A HOOK AND THE ON-lookers jeered. His legs wrenched this way and that, the sheer violence of it at odds with his slight frame and genteel looks. Not that he looked particularly genteel at this moment with his eyes swelling furiously and his tongue bulging grotesquely, forcing his lips apart. Then a dark stain bloomed at his crotch and within half a choke the piss was dribbling from his right foot and the crowd gave a great cheer at the sight of it.

'I'd still rather hang than be crucified,' O'Brien said thoughtfully, through the clamour, eyes fixed on the dying man and holding out his wrists. 'It's the nails I can't bear the thought of. Do you think you still piss yourself hung up on a cross?'

'I think I'd rather not think about it, Clancy,' Mun said as another cheer went up, this one accompanied by wafting hands and fingers pinching noses. The man's bowels had opened and the liquid streaming from his breeches' leg now was brown, foul and stinking.

'Death to traitors!' someone yelled.

A seething, gurgling sound was escaping the man's strangled throat.

'I think Mister Blake is trying to tell us something,' a soldier yelled.

'That he's sorry and he won't do it again,' his friend hollered back, rousing a chorus of laughter that made Mun think of the rooks back home in Parbold.

They had found more than rebel soldiers at Kineton. On the village outskirts, at the foot of Pittern Hill by the remains of the ancient earthworks known to local folk as King John's Castle, they had found several carts loaded with muskets and pikes, and all sorts of ammunition. Guarded by a small troop of dragoons, some of whom were wounded, this train would have followed Essex's army on its march towards Warwick. If it had got away in time. But it had not, and now it belonged to the King.

But they had also found letters. Most of them were from family members to their loved ones: men who were now the plundered dead and food for worms. But some of those letters were for the living, for the Earl of Essex himself no less, from the pen of a man called Blake, who was Prince Rupert's personal secretary. And in them Blake had given details of Royalist manoeuvres, had even requested richer rewards for his betrayal. Which was why he was now dancing a jig at the end of a rope.

'The bastard's taking his sweet time about dying,' Downes said, his handsome face made a twist of grimace by the stink of faeces.

Mun's memory conjured Martha Green hanging from the old bridge across the Tawd, her face, beautiful in life, abhorrent in death. And that soul-wound flowed

426

back to Shear House, to his mother and Bess who had lost everything and yet did not know it. He tried to picture their faces, tried to imagine their grief when they eventually learned what had become of Sir Francis and Emmanuel, for if he could envisage their desolation and sorrow perhaps he could somehow steel himself for the act of breaking the news.

I should have told them already, he thought, the heavy, choking truth of it flooding in on him. I should be with them now. But he could not tell them because the King still needed his army. They had marched south to threaten Banbury, but the cannon they had trained on that town had not needed to roar for the Earl of Peterborough and the six hundred of his regiment to come out, lay down their arms and ask His Majesty's pardon. And now, two days later, they were in Oxford watching a traitor hang.

'And to think the dog almost slipped his lead,' O'Brien yawped in Mun's ear, hauling him from his mire of dark thoughts. 'They found him packed up and about to make for Warwick to lie on the earl's lap and get a rub behind the ears.'

'I heard he was so afraid of what the Prince would do to him that his legs seized up and he couldn't walk,' Downes put in. 'Hooker had to put the bastard over his shoulder and carry him to Rupert.'

'Nothing wrong with his legs now,' O'Brien remarked, for Blake was still thrashing.

'Hooker?' Mun said, surprised to hear that name.

'Aye, that ugly bastard over there,' Downes said, nodding to the press of men on their right. 'The one with the scar where someone's tried to open his head like a boiled egg.'

Osmyn Hooker must have sensed he was the object of scrutiny for he suddenly looked up, locking eyes with Mun and nodding in greeting, a half smile playing beneath his elaborately curled moustaches.

'You know him?' Downes asked.

'No,' Mun lied. 'Might have seen him around camp.' He felt his cheeks flush at the lie and his pulse quicken at the thought that his past association with Hooker might be discovered.

'He's a mercenary.' O'Brien all but spat the word. 'He'd run the King through for a fistful of silver.'

'And you'd step over ten pretty whores to get to a pint of ale,' Downes said with a grin. 'We all have our faults.'

But O'Brien wasn't amused. 'Still,' he said, 'better fifty enemies outside the house than one inside it, if you ask me. You can't trust a man like that.'

'Then let us hope His Majesty's friends in Oxford come up with the silver they've promised him,' Mun said, 'so that he can ever afford to buy the loyalty of such men. For we have missed our chance to take London and I fear this war is just beginning.'

O'Brien nodded soberly at that and even Downes had no quip on the end of his tongue, as Blake gave his last pathetic salvo of kicks and died. For the Prince had urged his uncle to agree to a bold plan which would see Rupert lead a flying column of cavalry, dragoons and mounted musketeers to London, there to seize the members of the Lords and Commons in Westminster and hold them at Whitehall until the King arrived with the rest of the army. Taking the capital could, Prince Rupert argued, win them the war. But the King's advisers had no faith that the scheme could work, claiming the city's ancient defences, the London Trained Bands, and a force raised by the Earl of Warwick would combine to thwart any such bold endeavour. Now the moment was lost and winter was here and the King was making himself comfortable at Oxford.

'Rivers.' Mun looked round and found Corporal Bard standing behind him as the crowd fragmented and men streamed past, the evening's first entertainment over.

'Corporal,' Mun acknowledged with a nod, clapping gloved hands to get some warmth into them for it was turning bitter. The winter sun was setting in the west, splashing bloody streaks above the city's silhouetted towers and spires, fading to orange and then grey in the dusk sky.

'Make yourselves scarce, you two,' Bard said to O'Brien and Downes, who nodded and slapped Mun's shoulder in solidarity as they headed back to their billets.

'Let me guess, the captain demands satisfaction?' Mun said, half hoping it was true for he was in a bloody mood.

The veteran smiled. 'I think Captain Boone would rather leave your disagreements in the past,' he said, 'what with you being Sir bloody Edmund Rivers nowadays. Chances are at this rate you'll be given a commission and end up outranking us all, so we ought to be bloody nice to you, God save our black souls.' Mun almost smiled at that. 'No, Rivers, I've come about something else.' Bard's raw-boned face turned grim; grimmer than normal. 'Has the captain given you anything of late?' Mun felt the frown darken his own brow. 'Since that day we found those rebels in Kineton village?'

'What is this about, Corporal?' he asked. 'Why would Boone have something for me?'

Bard tilted his head to one side, avoiding Mun's eyes and scratching his bristled cheek.

'What does the captain have that's to do with me?' Mun said, left hand resting on the pommel of his Irish hilt.

Bard looked him in the eye now, his brown teeth worrying at his bottom lip as though trying to keep words in that wanted to be out. 'Look, Rivers, you're a brave lad. A good soldier. That day in Kineton we found all sorts, ten types of horse shit. Including letters. Lots of 'em.'

'I know, Corporal, and so does he,' Mun said, thumbing back to the dead man hanging from the creaking jib. Bard nodded, then looked around to make sure he was not overheard.

'Amongst that lot we found in the church was a letter addressed to your father. A letter Sir Francis never laid eyes on.' The mention of his father's name was like a blow to the gut. 'Now, lad, I'm not good with my letters, never had cause to learn 'em properly. But Captain Boone can read like a lawyer. Maybe you should ask him what was in that letter.'

Mun felt the sullen embers in his stomach suddenly spark. What was that bastard Boone keeping from him?

'Why are you telling me this, Corporal?'

Bard shrugged. 'As I said, you're Sir Edmund Rivers,' he replied, leaving Mun to draw the inference that a favour given is a favour owed. 'Just leave me out of it,' he warned, pointing a filth-stained finger. 'However you found out about that letter it wasn't from me. Understand?'

430

Mun nodded. 'Where is Captain Boone?' he asked, eyes ranging across the crowds leaving the hanging. Music fought to be heard amongst the murmur of drinking men and the lowing of cattle being herded into the great quadrangle of Christ Church college.

'I'd wait till morning if I were you, lad,' Bard said, 'he's with the Prince. We're to push on down the valley to Windsor. Some fat city merchant has earned His Majesty's wrath and holed up with fifteen hundred rebels in the castle. We're to prise them from their shell.' Somewhere, a lute was making merry and a viol was trying to keep up. A woman laughed wickedly and a knot of soldiers gave a bawdy cheer.

'Where is he, Corporal?' Mun asked again, eyes riveted to the older veteran's.

Corporal Bard considered his answer for a moment, then nodded as if to say *I've come this far . . .*

'They're at the New College. Saint Mary on Holywell Street. Grand as grand, like this,' he said, nodding at the impressive square tower beside them, 'you can't miss it. It's now the main magazine.' He gave a wry grin. 'The clever young sods must be doing their learning in the alehouses these days,' he said.

But Mun was already walking, his boots scuffing the cobbles of St Aldate's, then on, pushing through the crowds on High Street, through the whores and hawkers, the food-sellers and the drunks and all the folk of Oxford who had flocked like gulls to sell the King's army whatever they could. With each step his anger wound itself tighter, like the spring of a wheellock, and those men and women who saw his face gave him clear passage even if they had to offend another to do it. Turning onto Queen's Lane he saw the grand buildings ahead of him, their arched, glass-filled windows blurry with warm yellow light.

He ploughed through his own billowing breath but was no longer aware of the cold by the time he came to St Mary, built beside the looming four-hundred-year-old city wall. Then through a dark passage in which a woman was on her knees and the soldier she was servicing grinned at Mun but he did not grin back, and finally into the cloistered courtyard, where he stopped to get his bearings, his breathing loud inside his helmet. It made for an impressive sight, a perfect and ordered quadrangle of stone buildings. Across from him in line along the north range was an enormous timber-roofed chapel, its stained glass glowing dimly, promising respite from the sin and revelries of the bustling night. Above the huge windows gargoyles leered in the gloom, ignored by all who passed below. Flowing on from the chapel, sharing roof and façade though its windows were smaller, was a great hall. In the far corner of the east range stood a four-storeyed square tower above whose gateway three niches held statues of Virgin, Angel, and another figure who Mun supposed might be the college founder. Officers paced along the torch-lit colonnades, laughing and carrying on as though the war was as good as won, and Mun wondered how many of them had fought in the blood-drenched havoc at Kineton.

Then a dog barked and he looked to his left. At the western end of the quadrangle, by the gaping arch of a passage below the imposing apartments, stood a knot of men. Mun could not see their faces, but the dog, which was dashing between light and shadow, having clearly caught the scent of a cat or some other creature, gave the party away. Far from the usual mangy, flea-ridden mongrels that accompanied the army this was a noble, lustrous-haired creature that Mun guessed ate better than most musketeers. It was the Prince's white hunting poodle, Boy.

'Ah!' exclaimed the Prince, looking up as Mun approached. 'Sir Edmund! The very man who wrested my uncle's ensign from the enemy and spared us some considerable embarrassment.'

Mun grimaced at the introduction, but the others, except one, seemed impressed enough, shaking his hand and nodding and murmuring their appreciation. Boone made no efforts to hide his enmity, lip curled as though Mun had trodden in something of Boy's.

'I simply followed Captain Smith . . . Sir John,' Mun explained, 'and had little idea what he was getting me into.'

'Now now, young man, there's no need to be so modest here,' a portly officer with a tuft of beard and a wisp of moustache said. 'Save the coyness for the ladies.' He laughed at his own wit. The other men smiled generously and Mun recognized one of them, a clean-shaven man with sloping shoulders, shrewd eyes and a hooked nose. But he could not place the man and so looked back to the Prince.

'By your leave, Your Highness, I would speak with Captain Boone.'

The Prince frowned, indicating his associates. 'But we are busy, Sir Edmund,' he said. 'Tomorrow we prepare to strike out for Windsor. There is a fox who must be dug out of his den. Colonel John Venn is one of the eleven that will never have my uncle's pardon. But *we* shall have his head,' he said with a grin, then nodded to a squat, richly dressed man wearing a small cloth skullcap. 'That is, of course, if Mister Garland here can give the den a vigorous shake with his guns.'

The little artilleryman cocked an eyebrow and flicked his long hair, from whose dirt his expensive suit was protected by a heavily laced falling band. 'I wouldn't drag my guns forty miles if I did not have faith in them, Your Highness,' he said, adjusting his embroidered baldrick. 'I have more faith in my guns than I have in the Lord.' The familiar-looking man with the hooked nose grinned at that.

'You see, Sir Edmund,' the portly officer said, 'you won't find Mister Humble around here.'

Again Mun ignored him. 'Sir, I have reason to believe Captain Boone has in his possession something which is rightfully mine,' he said, glaring at Boone who was glaring back.

The Prince's brows arched as he regarded the two men. 'Well then, Sir Edmund, be quick about it. And if I should ever misplace one of my own colours I shall expect you to see to its safe return,' he said, waving a hand at Mun to get on with it.

'What the hell do you want?' Boone snarled.

'Where is the letter, Captain?' Mun asked.

'What letter?'

'You know very well the letter I refer to.'

Boone rolled his eyes. 'You will have to remind me, Rivers, I am a busy man.'

'Very well. Amongst the letters taken at Kineton village there was one addressed to my father. Sir Francis Rivers of His Majesty's Lifeguard,' he said, aware of the eyebrows around them hoisting at his father's name.

'Oh, yes,' Boone said, frowning. 'There *was* a letter.

434

It must have fallen into rebel hands before it could be delivered to your father, God rest his soul.' He twirled his moustaches around a ringed finger and gave Mun a flash of teeth. 'Now then, where did I put it?' Mun wanted nothing more than to punch those teeth through the back of his skull. 'Ah, of course . . . I think I might have it here,' Boone said, plunging a hand down the front of his buff-coat. 'Corporal Bard did suggest I ought to give it to you some time ago, but . . . it must have slipped my mind.' He pulled out the letter and handed it over to Mun. By now the Prince and the other men were engaged in conversation again. Mun turned his back on them all and began to read.

My dear and only love, I pray that this letter finds you and the boys well and in good spirits, your steadfastness ever bolstered by the certain knowledge that you perform honourable duty to your king and your God. And yet it is with a heavy heart and – I may say this to you alone, my love – not a little fear that I write this. For the rebels' gun – a demi-cannon, Edward tells me – has breached the wall and we are fallen back to our trenches and gabions before the house. Let me assure you that I would no less do my duty than you would do yours and that we shall steel ourselves to the task. The upstarts will suffer for their unnatural infidelity. But, my dear, we cannot hold. I am blessed to have Bess here for she is as brave as Mun and Emmanuel and of great comfort. I will try to write again. If you can come home – if I could grasp even the slim hope that you were riding north even now, I would dare to believe we might prevail. My heart is with you, my love, and

I know you believe it for my life is bound up with yours. Mary.

Mun turned, glimpsing the ghost of a smile on Boone's lips before he slammed his fist into the captain's face, hurling him against the wall from where he dropped to his knees, clutching his chin.

'What the devil!' exclaimed the fat man.

'Rivers!' Prince Rupert yelled. 'How dare you?'

'Your Highness,' Mun rasped, glowering at Boone, 'that rabid cur kept this from me because he's a spiteful, damned villain!' Boy was barking and snarling at Mun, big teeth flashing in the night.

'Give it to me!' the Prince demanded, extending a hand. Two amongst the party had drawn their swords as though to protect the Prince from this lunatic, their eyes flicking nervously from Mun to Rupert. Hook Nose simply took a step backwards into the shadows, but another man, a tall grey-haired officer, watched calmly as Mun handed Rupert the letter. Then Mun raised his palms to show he meant no harm to the Prince, who, though angry, did not seem in the least afraid for his safety.

'Well, Captain,' the Prince said when he had finished reading and was refolding the letter, 'if you'd kept such a thing from me I would have spilled your guts.' Boone was climbing to his feet, still holding his jaw, blinking as though he could not see properly. Other officers walking the grounds had stopped to watch.

'He must hang for that, Your Highness,' Boone slurred, the words deformed, then spat a wad of blood onto the ground. 'I demand it.'

'Hang a man whom the King has just knighted?'

the Prince asked, handing the letter to Garland, who began to read. 'Don't be absurd.' He gestured to Mun. 'Sir Edmund's house and family are besieged. From the sounds of it they're giving a good account of themselves. Or were,' he added, glancing at Mun.

'Your Highness, let me take some men north to break the siege,' Mun said. 'We shall rout them, send a message to the rebels in that part of the country that the King's reach is long.'

'Hold your tongue, Rivers!' Boone said.

The Prince shook his head. 'It's out of the question.' He frowned. 'This letter is weeks old. The chances are Shear House has already fallen.'

'If the rebels have a demi-cannon pointing at it,' Garland put in, 'then you can be assured it has, lad,' he said in an artilleryman's matter-of-fact way.

'A small troop won't be missed,' Mun said, ignoring the gunner. His family's peril eclipsed any regard for etiquette. 'I'll smash the rebels and ride straight for Windsor to join you there.' He took a step towards the Prince and saw Boone flinch. 'My mother and sister cannot be expected to do the King's fighting for him. Bess is with child!' His right arm trembled with the urge to haul his sword into the night and run Captain Boone through. 'I will not stay here while they are alone. I will not abandon them. Neither would my father had he known.'

'Let him go, Rupert,' the tall man who had not yet spoken said. He was Scottish and had at his waist an Irish hilt like Mun's only more elaborate. 'What man would no kick the Devil's bollocks to protect his mither? Let Sir Edmund loose on the rebel bastards. It'll do us more good than bad.'

Rupert seemed to consider this for a moment, then he nodded. 'You can go,' he said.

'This is absurd!' Captain Boone exclaimed, but was silenced by the Prince's hand.

'But I can spare no soldiers. Go to your family before the captain here persuades me to string you up with that whoreson Blake. Be sure to return to us with news of the rebels' movements in the north.' He flicked a gloved hand nonchalantly. 'Now leave us.'

Mun nodded, shot Boone a withering glare, then turned and strode into the freezing night, his blood simmering in his veins. But by the time he was back amongst the tents, makeshift shelters and fires strewn across Christ Church Meadow that made up the camp of Prince Rupert's Horse, his anger was tainted by something else. Fear. What had become of his mother and Bess? How had they even managed to mount a defence? Had not his father written to his mother, telling her that she must not resist the rebels?

'You should have given them the damned house, Mother,' he gnarred into the night.

And then there was Boone. Had the captain had any intention of giving him that letter? Probably eventually. The bastard would have picked his moment. Knowing how Mun would react, Boone would have orchestrated the affair so that he could deliver immediate retribution under the warrant of his rank. Mun knew he owed Bard, for if not for the veteran he would yet know nothing of his family's plight. I owe Boone too, he thought, feeling the hot serpent of violence writhing in his limbs, and that debt would be settled with blood.

But how had the letter fallen into rebel hands in the

first place? He guessed it had been the groom Coppe who had brought his mother's letter south, as he had done previously. Mun knew the man well enough to be sure that he would have protected that letter and his duty with his life. Which meant that Coppe was likely dead. And all Mun could do now was throw his saddle over brave Hector's back and ride north.

He would have liked to explain to his friends why he was leaving, for he would not put it past Captain Boone to tell them he had deserted. But there was no sign of O'Brien, Downes or Rowe either at their tent on the flame-lit bank of the River Cherwell or nearby and he had no time to go looking for them in Oxford's thronging alehouses or between whores' legs. So he packed two knapsacks with spare clothes and blankets, his leather bottle full of ale, extra musket balls and powder, his tinder box containing his fire-lighting kit, a wooden bowl and spoon, and eight shillings and eightpence – a paltry sum, he reflected, for a knight who had just inherited the family estates – then collected Hector from the picket.

'We're going home, boy,' he said, patting Hector's withers, inhaling the stallion's scent and taking comfort in it. Hector nickered as though he understood, and perhaps he did, Mun thought as he came round to the horse's head and slipped the bridle on. 'There's a good boy, Hector. We'll soon see Bess, hey. You'd like that, boy, wouldn't you? And she might have had the baby by now.' Hector snorted, his nostrils fogging the air between them, and Mun put his forehead against his muzzle, holding on to the familiarity like a shipwrecked man clinging to a floating timber. Home was almost one hundred and seventy miles away. If they set a good pace they could be there in four days. But God alone knew what he would find there.

'Rivers.' He turned, his hand falling to his sword grip, as a tall man stepped out of the flame-played shadows.

'Hooker,' Mun said, somehow not surprised to see the mercenary. 'What do you want?' Hooker's pet giant Corporal Bartholomew loomed like a rock behind him.

'It seems we are to be brothers of the blade once more, Rivers.' The mercenary grinned. 'Or should I call you Sir Edmund?'

'Call me Mun. And spare me the riddles, man. What do you want? Our business is concluded.'

'The Prince sent me. It seems you need my help. Again. And so here I am.' He swept off his broad hat and gave an elaborate bow. 'At your service.'

'Prince Rupert sent you to help me?'

'His Highness said my men and I are to help you break the siege of Shear House. If we arrive in time. If not . . .' he shrugged, 'we ride to Windsor.' He ran a hand through his curled hair. 'Will your brother be joining us?' The smile was all in his eyes.

Mun flew at him, grabbing fistfuls of the cloak at Hooker's neck, but then he was hauled off and held in a vice that would have crushed his ribs had he not been wearing his back- and breastplate.

'Put Sir Edmund down, Corporal,' Hooker said, brushing himself down with a sweep of a gloved hand, 'he is simply happy to see us.' As soon as the giant's arms relaxed Mun scrambled free and stumbled into space, the stink of the corporal's hedge of a beard filling his nose.

'You don't talk about him!' Mun said. 'Ever!'

Hooker raised his hands. 'That's your affair,' he

admitted. 'But my affair is breaking the siege of Shear House. For which, by the way, the Prince assures me you will pay handsomely.' This was said half as a question.

'Why would the Prince send you to help me?' Mun asked.

'Who can fathom the mind of that German devil?' Hooker said. 'But perhaps he sees the fire of the cause in you. Or maybe he simply wants me out of the way for a while. Some of the other officers in His Majesty the King's grand army hold a dim view of our prince and the company he keeps.' He smiled. 'Either way, I think we can safely assume he has no idea of our last . . . enterprise. Or else you would be . . .' he moved a hand languidly back and forth through the air, 'swinging.'

'And you beside me,' Mun said. 'Do not forget that.'

Hooker shook his head. 'I have a talent for smelling trouble on the air and would be gone at the first sniff.' He raised a brow. 'I suspect Parliament would have their uses for me. You, I fear, would not find it so easy to join the other side. Officially, anyway,' he added with a curl of his lip, then wafted the issue away. 'No matter, though, for we have work to do.'

'And the Prince does not need you at Windsor?' Mun said.

'Breaking a siege is one thing, but my talents would be wasted in prosecuting one. Besides which, they will never crack that shell, for all the stock that little prick Garland puts in his cannon. No, Sir Edmund, I don't do well watching stone walls. It wearies me. Eats up a soldier's soul. You know my talents, which is why you are already rifling your memory for those boards in Shear House under which your father stashed his *mishap* silver. You need me.'

Mun did not like Hooker. Knew that was written on his face, too. But the arrogant whoreson was right. Mun did need him. The mercenary was a proper soldier, a professional, as were his men. And Mun needed soldiers if he was going to save his family and his home.

'I'll pay you your worth when it's done, Hooker,' he said, mounting Hector and pulling him around.

'I know you will,' Hooker said, gesturing for Bartholomew to bring up their mounts.

And with that they set off into the night to meet with the rest of Hooker's troop. To break a siege.

CHAPTER TWENTY-NINE

THE SCREAM RIPPED FREE OF HER THROAT, FOR TWO HEART-beats flooding the dark chamber with the stark, raw energy of unbearable pain. And yet she *was* bearing it and she clamped her teeth together like a beast's, biting back the shrieks, refusing to yield.

'I can see yer chylt!' Joyce Cawley exclaimed, looking up with wide eyes, her hands glistening with blood. 'I can see yer li'le babby, Mistress Elizabeth, so keep pushing, d'year?'

Bess might have nodded as the face between her legs hardened and the two women gripping her sweat-slathered arms either side of the birthing stool exchanged a worried glance. 'D'year me, Elizabeth?' Joyce Cawley said sternly, 'push now, wi' the Lord's own strength!'

Bess growled a response, closed her eyes and pushed.

It had begun two evenings ago. Her womb had started to squeeze, the sudden pain doubling her as she walked among the wounded, filling their bowls with pottage. The first spasm had abated as quickly as it had begun and yet she knew her child was coming. Isaac, who was with her, had known it too, had in his time

443

seen enough women begin the labour pains to know it when he saw it, and so had helped her upstairs. And then, just as they opened the door to her bedchamber, Bess's waters had broken in a great gush and Isaac had hurried off to fetch Lady Mary.

Women came, curtains were drawn and caudles were drunk. The chamber door's keyhole was stopped up, straw was strewn across the floor and candles were lit. The stabbing, squeezing pains in her womb had repeated in bouts which, like waves nearest the shore, became more frequent: floods of pain that washed over her, then retreated, leaving her stunned and exhausted. But then these waves had slowed, almost stopping completely, and Bess had feared the worst. That her child had died.

'Trust i' God and i' nature,' Mistress Cawley had said, as much to Lady Mary who stood ashen-faced, mopping her daughter's brow, as to Bess. And they had been glad to have a midwife with Mistress Cawley's experience there. Lucky, too. 'By mi wark, yo'r strength, and God's mercy and providence theaw'll be delivered o' this li'le one,' the farmer's wife had stated like a challenge to the fates themselves and to the frightened aspects of the other women in the room. And sure enough the excruciating shortening of her womb, like the drawstring on a purse being yanked tight, began again, and if the pain truly was women's punishment for Eve's sins then God was vengeful indeed.

The world roared and the whole chamber shook and masonry crashed to the forecourt amidst terrified screams. For beyond the birthing chamber walls, another battle raged.

'God preserve us all!' Hester exclaimed, squeezing

Bess's arm so that Bess felt fingernails dig into her flesh. She guessed the girl was about her own age, though she had never met her before now.

'Ha' the devils nowe decency at all?' Winifred, a miller's wife with a kindly face, exclaimed, putting a cup of hot wine and egg yolk caudle to Bess's lips. But the smell of saffron and ginger turned Bess's stomach now and she averted her face from the syrupy gruel and Winifred took it away.

'Go, Mother,' she snarled through her teeth, bracing against the pain and suddenly overwhelmed by a desperate need to bear downwards into her pelvis. 'Go.'

Her mother's grip tightened on her shoulders. 'I'm not leaving you,' she said, leaning over and planting a kiss on Bess's sweat-sheened brow. 'Major Radcliffe is there. He will know what to do.'

Bess felt a surge of relief. She was afraid. Afraid that God would take her baby. Afraid that He would take her, for she was weakening now, had been for hours though she had not allowed herself to admit it. But the pain was too much. It had gone on too long and she was tired. So tired.

'I want some good, deep breaths, Mistress Elizabeth,' Joyce Cawley said. 'We dunno' ned this going on lunger than neds be,' and Bess glanced down to see the midwife's bloody hands enter her again.

Outside, beyond the dark confines of the birthing chamber, muskets cracked, their reports savage in the late autumn dusk. Men yelled and clamoured, their words mostly unintelligible amongst the chaos. But Bess did make out one soldier's chilling cry that the rebels were getting set to fire that devil of a gun again.

'Go, Mother!' she growled again. 'They need you.'

'Breathe loike I told thee!' Joyce Cawley snapped, not looking up this time.

Bess could not hold the next scream in. It burst savagely out of her as she pushed with every fibre of her being, willing . . . demanding the baby to help them both. To be out of her. Somewhere, at once far away and yet horribly close, in some dark place, life and death wrestled over her soul and she thought she must lose her mind.

And when she next came back to the candle-lit chamber, her sight sweat-glazed as she looked at the pale faces around her, her mother was gone.

When at last the baby came, Bess's screams had not been the only ones rending the night. The rebels' demi-cannon had roared four more times, slamming iron balls against Shear House and sending lethal shards of stone flying. Captain Downing had led a charge, too, but somehow Major Radcliffe and his garrison had beaten off the attack, sending Parliament's men back to the boundary wall to lick their wounds and regroup. But Radcliffe had lost eleven men in the desperate defence: seven dead and four too wounded to fight on, and now shrieks of pain flew along Shear House's dark corridors like vengeful demons seeking out new souls to torment.

'How long do we have?' Bess asked, the words little more than exhaled breaths across her dry, cracked lips. She felt dangerously weak, as though she were not fully there at all but rather that her soul was half out of her body. On its way somewhere else. But the baby at her breast was alive. Her baby! Her boy.

And so she would live too. No matter what, death

would not have her, and she forced some caudle down, hoping the warm drink would renew her strength.

'I don't know. Not long,' her mother replied, sitting on Bess's bed, staring at the swaddled babe suckling at his mother's breast. For Bess's instincts had been right and she had given birth to a healthy, chubby-limbed boy. He had squawked with impotent, red-faced rage while Joyce cut the cord and sponged the mess from him and Lady Mary stood in the flame-gilded dark with her hands over her mouth and tears in her eyes.

'He wants to get eawt there and feight the devils,' the midwife had said appreciatively, looking exhausted herself after the lengthy ordeal.

Bess put her nose against the baby's blood-crusted head and inhaled, breathing in his urgent, vigorous life. 'I'll be ready, Mother,' she said. 'I just need a moment's rest.'

'Don't talk, my love. Save your strength,' her mother replied, smiling weakly.

The sanctity of the birthing chamber had been defiled and Bess was vaguely aware of men standing at the windows, boots crunching broken glass, muskets on stands pointing down onto the lawns. Lady Mary was wearing back- and breastplate over a thick tunic of green felt, and a sword hung from a baldrick across her shoulder. A firelock pistol and pikeman's brimmed helmet sat beside the basin and pitcher on the dark oak chest of drawers, and Bess knew the end was near. Her mother's foolhardy but inspiring sortie four nights ago had hurt the Parliament force. They had killed seven, including Captain Downing's chief gunner, but more importantly they had killed four of the enemy's oxen and wounded another, so that Downing had had to harness his own men to the gun to drag it up to the wall and this had taken time. But to their credit they had done it and now the demi-cannon was thundering again, this time its shot hammering the walls of the house itself. They will come in the morning, her mind warned. At first light.

'I wish Father was here. I wish they were all here,' Bess said and suddenly felt tears streaming down her face. They fell onto the baby's skin but she did not wipe them off.

'I wish it too,' Lady Mary said. When Bess had watched her mother ride Hecuba into the rebels' camp, her red hair flying, teeth like a predator's, she had seemed invincible. She had been a warrior queen from classical legend, an Amazon bringing death to her enemies. Now, though, she looked tired and frail and her arms and armour struck Bess as faintly ridiculous.

'They would have come if they had known,' Bess said. It was more question than statement.

'Of course they would have come,' Lady Mary said. Which raised the question neither Bess nor her mother gave voice to. What had become of them?

'Something must have happened to Coppe,' her mother went on, 'so that your father never received the letter,' and to her shame Bess hoped that was so, for otherwise it might mean something had happened to Sir Francis.

Lady Mary took the little pink knot of the baby's left hand between her finger and thumb. Her eyes had sunk into dark pools and there was dirt across her forehead, oil from her helmet perhaps. 'What will you name him?'

Bess watched her baby suckle, willing it to gorge on

her, to be strong. 'I will wait for Emmanuel,' she said. 'We will decide together.'

Her mother nodded, then tucked a tress of Bess's hair back behind her left ear. 'Get some rest now,' she said, standing. 'Winifred will take the boy when he is full and you must try to sleep.'

Bess closed her eyes as her mother left the room, then she opened them again. And watched her baby boy.

And in the morning, the rebels came.

'Long live King Charles!' one of the men at her window yelled down into the cauldron of musketry and mayhem that had been lawns and flower beds but was now trenches, earthworks and gabions. Bess jolted, pushing herself up against the headboard, instinctively horrified that there were men in her bedchamber.

'My baby!' she yelled.

The other man turned, pulling the peaked *montero* cap from his bald head. 'Forgive the intrusion, mistress, and the smook, but Major Radcliffe haz men at mooest o' the second-floor windows. Sez he that howds the high ground howds the advantage. So 'ere we are.' His cheeks flushed red. 'My wife is seeing to yer li'le one.' He smiled. 'He's a bonny babby.'

'Winifred is your wife?' Bess asked, taking a cup off the bedside table. Her hand was trembling.

'Aye, she has a way with weans,' he said proudly, 'so dunno' thee worry. They'll be sum pleck safe.' Bess nodded and put the cup to her mouth. Cold beer sluiced down her dry throat. She felt it hit her stomach. It was almost inconceivable that there should be soldiers in the room where just hours previously she was giving birth. But this only showed how desperate their situation had become.

''Ere they coom again,' the other, younger man said whilst blowing on the end of his match.

''Scuse me, Miss Rivers,' the first man said, replacing his cap and turning back to the window. A volley of musket balls clattered against the bricks and the younger musketeer grunted, dropping his matchlock, and staggered back from the window, blood gushing through the fingers of the hand clutching his throat.

Bess struggled out of her bed, onto weak legs, getting to the young man as he dropped to his knees, his wide eyes begging her for help as his lifeblood soaked his tunic and spattered on the bare boards.

'Back in from the window, Mistress Elizabeth!' the other man said. 'There's nowt thi can do for the lad. He's kilt.'

She went to the chest of drawers and fetched a linen, folding it over her stomach. 'I can try to stop the bleeding,' she said, kneeling by the young man who was now lying on his back, his face deathly white against the bloody mess of his neck. Gingerly, Bess pulled his hands away and saw that his throat had been ripped out. The ball had shredded flesh and cartilage and torn through the back of his neck and even as she pressed the linen to the ruin, watching the white bloom red as it soaked up the gore, Bess knew the other man was right. Nothing could save the young man.

'Lord, please take this man into your embrace,' she whispered, as the stink of his open bowels hit her nose and she realized that he was dead.

She stood again, her head spinning, legs threatening to buckle, and she felt sick though she knew she would not be. Perhaps what she had been through had steeled her, prepared her for such horrors.

'What is your name?' she asked the soldier. He opened his priming pan and pulled the trigger and the musket roared.

'Ellis,' he said, wreathed in the smoke which was drifting back into the room. 'Alexander Ellis.'

'Well do not turn round, Alexander Ellis,' she said, pulling on woollen skirts and a simple bodice that laced up the front, the pain between her legs excruciating. But the musketry outside was constant now, which meant the rebels were closing in on the house. Bess sat on her bed to pull on her riding boots, pain-sweat greasing her brow, then fetched an open-fronted robe from a hook on the wall and flung it around her shoulders. Then she went and stood beside Ellis and looked out, trying not to cough as the acrid smoke caught in the back of her throat.

'My God,' she said.

Fifty or so rebel musketeers had formed a skirmish line which was creeping closer to the trenches and gabions behind which Radcliffe's men desperately loaded and fired with seemingly little effect. But what was even more terrifying was a company of the enemy who were concentrating their fire on one defensive position at a time. They were arranged in four ranks of eight, each rank firing in turn then reloading as the next line of men threaded through them to present and fire their own muskets.

'Aye, and it's warkin', too,' Ellis said grimly, filling the pan with black powder. 'We've got nowt to stand against tat.' He closed the pan and blew on it to do away with any loose powder, then put the butt on the floor and poured more powder down the muzzle.

Bess saw that the rebel musket block had already

swept the defenders from the trench at the south-east corner, leaving bodies in its wake. Now this killing wave threatened to overwhelm another defensive position in front of the forecourt consisting of two earth-filled gabions. The eight garrison men behind this bulwark dared not step out of cover to fire their own weapons and were relying on others to stop the rebel block. But the other defenders had the skirmishers to worry about.

Then two of the garrison men sprang from behind their gabion and fired wildly, but the rebel front rank fired a heartbeat later and the two defenders were ripped to bloody shreds.

'Just a li'le closer, yo bastards,' Ellis growled, ramming the ball and wadding down, then replacing the scouring stick beneath the barrel. 'When they're on their own I've got noawe chance of hitting 'em. Thaz moor chance o' gerrin' knighted.' He blew on the match-cord until the tip was burning, then pressed it into the serpent's jaws and slid open the priming pan. 'But when they're bunched up lik'n that . . .' He fired, the sound deafening inside the house, and Bess saw a rebel in the musket block fall. ''Tis babby-wark. Death to traitors!' Ellis roared down at the enemy, exulting in his kill. Then another hail of lead pelted the brickwork and Bess ducked instinctively, fear flooding her veins.

'Back fro' the window, Miss Elizabeth,' Ellis said, his eyes wild with the thrill of killing. 'Thi's got a li'le 'un to look after neaw.'

'While this is still my house, Mister Ellis, you will not tell me what to do.' She could see her mother at the western edge of the forecourt, spurning the relative safety of the house and, with Major Radcliffe, directing the defenders.

'Begging your pardon, madam,' Ellis said, 'but thi saw what 'appened to t'lad there.' Bess turned and looked at the dead man lying on her bedchamber floor, his blood pooled beneath the ruin of his throat. His eyes were still open, staring at the cracked ceiling. She went over and draped the blood-soaked linen over his face, then picked up his matchlock, making it seem lighter in her arms than it was.

'I have a right to defend my own house,' she said in answer to Ellis's frown.

'Dost know how to load and fire it?' he asked.

'I have two brothers, Mister Ellis,' she said, as though that were answer enough.

CHAPTER THIRTY

———

'I'M LOOKING FORWARD TO SOME HOME-COOKED FOOD, polite company, and a soft chair,' O'Brien said, wincing as he shifted in the saddle. 'I think my arse died forty miles back.'

'We're nearly there now, Clancy,' Mun replied, offering the Irishman his leather bottle, filled from a stream six miles back at Barrow Brook. The Irishman took it and drank, then tossed the bottle back.

'This reminds me of Ireland,' he said, glancing around at the rolling landscape of the south-west Lancashire plain and dragging a big hand across his red beard and moustaches. 'Cold and damp.'

Mun smiled. He was grateful to have O'Brien along. When he and Osmyn Hooker had met up with Hooker's forty men north of Christ Church Meadow he had been surprised to see that they had brought the Irishman with them, having found him in a makeshift alehouse off St Aldate's aptly named the Prince's Poodle. O'Brien had been drunk enough to agree to go with them, which meant almost too drunk to sit his horse, but he had sobered on the ride north and there was no one Mun would rather have at his side. Well, maybe there *was* someone, but . . .

'The Prince said you should have a man with you who earns the King's shilling honestly,' Hooker had said as two of his men helped the slurring O'Brien onto his big mare. The mercenary had grinned then. 'But what His Highness really meant was that another pair of eyes watching my merry band would not be a bad thing. You see, the Prince and his sort need me . . . but they don't trust me. Think I'm as likely to plunder honest men as I am to earn my silver honestly.'

'I dare say His Highness knows you well,' Mun had answered, to which Hooker had flashed his teeth and replied that if anyone *was* to keep an eye on him then it might as well be a drunken Irishman who couldn't see straight.

But Mun was glad to have O'Brien. The big man's familiar presence and for the most part cheerful disposition buoyed Mun's spirits against the weight of guilt and sorrow that threatened at times to pull him under. Guilt for the things he had done, the betrayals he had committed for a brother who had turned his back on them all. Sorrow at his family's loss. His own loss. He wondered if his father's death, Emmanuel's too, would have cut him less deeply had he seen them lifeless with his own eyes. As it was, there was a small, perhaps irrational part of him that could not admit that they were gone, that he would never see them again. And now he was nearly home and soon it would be time to share the burden he carried, though in truth he would rather bear it alone to the ends of the earth.

Dawn had begun as a pale blue line tight against the eastern horizon, like a sliver of fine steel. Then the strip had turned a dull orange, its glow beginning to shape the world out of darkness. Now, as Mun drew closer to his home amongst the sandstone hills, the new day was a blooming red stain spreading across the sky. It was cold enough for puddles to be skinned with ice and damp enough to make men fear for the powder in their flasks. Mun's feet were blocks of ice in his boots, which was the trouble with riding on a cold day, for you could not stamp your feet on the ground to warm them. But he knew the others would be cold too. They had ridden through the night, Hooker and Corporal Bartholomew leading the column, Mun and O'Brien behind them, and the rest of the troop following two abreast. Hooker's men made for a fearsome sight. Loyalty to money alone made a man rich by the looks of it, O'Brien had observed after the first day's ride. Or dead, Mun had replied. But he could not deny the mercenary life had served these men well enough, for they all rode big, fine horses of fifteen hands, not one of which would have fetched less than eight pounds at market. Each trooper wore buff-coat and back- and breastplate and was armed with a pair of wheellocks or firelocks as well as an assortment of swords, poll-axes and other edged weapons. Neither were they a ragged band of ill-disciplined villains, Mun knew, for almost to a man they had fought on the continent and knew their business better than most in either the King's or Parliament's army. They were hard men. Killers.

'A good scrap will see the chill gone from the bones, hey,' O'Brien said, pressing a finger against one nostril and blowing snot from the other.

'Whatever Parliament men are up here in the wilds,' Hooker said, emphasizing 'wilds' for Mun's benefit, he knew, 'I'd wager they are of poor quality. One look at you, O'Brien, and they will kneel in their own piss and pray to God to spare them.'

'That suits me,' O'Brien replied, not caring whether it was an insult or a compliment as he huffed into bare, cold-chapped hands. 'The bastards will be easier to kill if they keep nice and still.' A flock of jackdaws barrelled across the lightening sky, raining down amongst the bare branches of ash and elm and filling the dawn with a chorus of crisp noise that sounded like a thousand shards of flint being struck one against another. 'Even the bloody birds are laughing at us freezing our ballocks off,' the Irishman said.

'Quiet!' Mun hissed. He had heard something, a low guttural sound that was only made by one thing on God's earth. Hooker had heard it too, for he raised a hand to stop the column. 'Charge your firearms!' he called and was answered by the clicks of spanners on wheellocks and firelocks being half cocked. As the jackdaws' wild chatter died away Mun heard the lighter snap of distant musketry fading in and out on the breeze. His stomach clenched like a fist. Mother. Bess.

'It sounds as though your kin are making a fight of it,' Hooker said, grim-faced, tightening the strap of his three-bar pot. The mercenary leader checked his own firelocks, suddenly cloaked in the demeanour of a man about to risk his life in battle. His movements were slow, deliberate and well practised, ritualistic almost, as though each action was the spinning out of time and the saddling of fear.

But Mun itched to kick back his heels and fly. His very bones trembled and his heart was pounding like a regiment's drum. 'Let's ride, Hooker,' he said, despising himself for every moment spent not defending his loved ones and his home.

'I would be happier if you left this part to me,' Hooker said. 'You can't pay me if you're dead.' He arched a brow. 'Yet I suspect there is no convincing you to hang back and wait until it is over?'

'If I die, O'Brien will see that you're paid,' Mun said grimly, nodding at the Irishman.

'That I will,' O'Brien said, dipping his head. 'Now if we could go and kill the curs?' He glanced from Mun to Hooker. 'Turns out the stone rolling around in my boot is my God-damned toe. Jesus, it's colder than a whore's heart out here.' Hooker threw a hand forward and the column moved off again, thrumming now with the excitement and fear of imminent violence.

Mun had told Hooker that any siege would be concentrated on the front of the house, the ground at the rear being unsuitable for horses and artillery, so now the mercenary followed Mun's lead as they spurned roads and well-worn tracks in favour of an approach across grazing land that would bring them out to the west of Shear House.

'The ground rises to the west leading up Parbold Hill,' Mun had said, 'and from there we should have a good vantage of the rebel lines.'

Keeping the crackle of musketry on their right, beyond an ancient stone wall that followed the ridge north, they had ridden across rough, rocky ground that bristled with tall, frost-stiffened grass. Now, Mun led the troop to the flat-topped final summit of the ridge, then to its eastern edge from where they overlooked the approach to Shear House.

'That's not a house, Mun,' O'Brien said, eyes bulging. 'It's a bloody palace.'

Below them the fight was raging. Smoke suddenly bloomed around the demi-cannon at the main gate and a heartbeat later its boom kicked dawn's guts. They could see that the gun had already battered the house, gouging craters into the thick walls and smashing one of the pillars beside the great iron-studded front door. The whole façade was scarred, like the face of someone ravaged by the pox, and masonry lay in piles all about. Men were scattered across the grounds, many of them wreathed in musket smoke. But this was not a battle like Edgehill, of ranks of men firing great volleys into opposing masses. Rather this was, for the main part at least, a series of individual duels, which the rebels were winning, Mun saw by the stark reality of how close they were to the house itself. Most of the garrison's defences had been overrun and bodies lay everywhere.

'One day later and your house belongs to the Earl of Essex,' Hooker said, patting his horse's neck.

'One day sooner and some of those men would still be alive,' Mun replied through a grimace.

'Four ranks! Open order!' Hooker yelled, at which his men arrayed themselves with proficient ease. 'You see that squadron of musketeers, Corporal?' he asked, pointing at the thirty or so men who had fought their way to the forecourt and were now a stone's throw from Shear House's front door. 'What do I love about them?'

The bush-covered slab of Bartholomew's face threatened to crack. 'They don't have any pikemen,' he rumbled.

'Not a bloody gentleman amongst them,' Hooker agreed with a smile at odds with the terrible scar across his forehead. Then he half turned his face back to his men. 'Hold your fire until you can smell them!' he hollered. 'We shall tear the guts out of that squadron down there and the rest will bolt like rabbits.' There were some ayes and growls at this. 'Shall we introduce ourselves?' he called, and with that all forty of Hooker's men began to howl, a primitive, ululating cacophony that clawed at some innate sense inside Mun, making him almost feel like prey. 'Time for the pack to hunt,' Hooker shouted to Mun above the din, then led them forward down the ridge.

They began at the walk, which must have made the enemy wonder whose men they were, but Mun knew this was better than risking a horse falling and fouling the charge. Then, as the ground began to flatten out, they instinctively went into a sitting trot. More rebels had seen them now and some of them halted their attack on the house and took cover until they could be sure who the newcomers were. Then, as Hooker's wolves rose to a rising trot, some of the rebel musketeers turned their matchlocks towards them and gave fire and Mun heard a ball scream past his right ear.

'Hooker's lot know their business,' O'Brien called above the jangle of tack and arms, the drumming of hooves and the horses' excited neighs.

'God be with you, Clancy!' Mun said, his limbs thrumming with the fear-drenched thrill that was becoming a familiar prelude to a fight, then he gave Hector his heels, pricked him with spurs that had belonged to the King of England, and rose to the canter, his guts churning, the world around him shrinking as he eyed the musket block ahead of them. An officer stood beside those musketeers, sword in one hand, pistol in the other, bellowing orders, and the front rank began to wheel right while the men in the middle and rear ranks fumbled with bandoliers and scouring sticks, desperate to reload.

'Give them hell!' Hooker yelled, spurring his mount so that it lurched forward, breaking into a gallop, and Mun's soul flooded with fury and hatred for the men who had brought guns, blades and rebellion to his father's house. To my house, he thought.

'Heya, boy!' he yelled. 'Go on, Hector!' And they flew, hooves hammering the ground, the cold wind scouring his face between the three bars of his helmet that framed his world whichever way he looked. 'Kill them!' he screamed. 'Kill them all!' and he outstripped Corporal Bartholomew, drawing level with Hooker who had drawn his sword. Off his right shoulder O'Brien was bellowing Irish curses, hanks of wind-whipped red hair escaping his own helmet. Mun hauled his sword from its scabbard, holding it wide as the front rank of the musket squadron suddenly vanished in a cloud of white smoke and he heard a clank of ball against steel plate and then a scream somewhere behind. But he felt no fear now. Only rage.

The rebel musketeers knew they could not stand against cavalry and now they panicked, some running, others drawing their own swords, inspired by the officer who held his ground, arm extended, pistol steady. He fired and Mun heard the ball thunk against Hooker's breastplate and a heartbeat later the mercenary scythed off the man's head as neat as ninepence. Mun crashed into the disintegrating squadron, slashing his heavy sword down into a rebel's shoulder, Hector's momentum wrenching the blade from the meat as they plunged on. And Mun hacked down again, cleaving another man's arm off at the shoulder as he raised his matchlock as a shield. 'Go on, boy!' he roared, and Hector surged forward into the mayhem, trampling a man whose scream ripped through the battle's din. Blades plunged and blood flew, the rebels having no defence against mounted men, and those who tried to run Hooker's wolves chased down, slaughtering them with wild joy.

Turning Hector with his knees, Mun pulled his carbine round and fired at a man's back, the ball blasting a hole right through him, spraying gore and flecks of white bone over a black mare's hind quarters. His breath was like the sea, surging inside his helmet as he turned and saw O'Brien slam his poll-axe into a bearded rebel's temple, the man's legs buckling, so that his weight yanked the poll-axe from the Irishman's grasp. Hooker spurred after a fleeing man and rode him down, his horse trampling the rebel until all that was left was a mangle of flesh and jagged, glistening bones.

'That's it, Corporal, teach the dog some manners!' a mercenary cried to Bartholomew, who had dismounted and was throttling a musketeer to death with his enormous hands.

Then Mun saw his father's old friend Edward Radcliffe striding towards the rebels, his one eye glaring like fire beneath the rim of an ancient, much-dented pot, his pistol raised. 'Come on then, you idle bloody lot!' he yelled at the garrison men behind him and those in a nearby trench. 'Now is your chance!' Then he fired and a rebel spun away in a spray of blood. 'Kill the rabid curs! Send them to Hell!' he roared, drawing his sword. The Shear House men cheered and charged, reversing their muskets and brandishing blades and ten or more tore into the stunned remnants of the rebel squadron in an orgy of vengeance, staving skulls and spitting bellies.

'O'Brien!' Mun yelled, hauling Hector around. Hooker's men followed his lead and, leaving the murder to the garrison men, they galloped back across the grounds, hacking and slashing men who were running for their lives. Some of the rebels threw down their weapons and fell to their knees, baring their heads, hats or helmets held out before them, but their appeals for mercy fell on deaf ears and Hooker's wolves savaged them.

Mun galloped past a man who had thrown his musket away and made a run for it, then he pulled Hector up and turned him so that they faced the rebel, who realized there was no escape.

'Sir, I beg you!' the man whimpered, falling to his knees, wringing his hands like some Hell-bound penitent. 'Clemency, sir, I beseech you!' the lad, who Mun guessed was younger than he, wailed, tears rolling down dirty, powder-scorched cheeks. Everywhere, men were shrieking and dying in the gore-flying havoc.

O'Brien came up and, working the reins to steady his mount, drew a pistol from his saddle holster and trained it on the young man. 'This is my friend's home, you traitorous dog,' he growled, then pulled the trigger and the rebel's face exploded in a crimson burst, the body slumping to the mud.

'I was going to spare him,' Mun called.

'Bastard wouldn't have spared you,' O'Brien said, wheeling off to find more prey. What Parliament men still lived were running but they wouldn't get far. One of Hooker's men yelled that a small troop of rebel cavalry had turned tail and were riding off south.

'Let's run them down!' another trooper yelled, no doubt hungry for rich pickings.

'Let them go,' Hooker replied, wheeling his horse in a circle, taking a brief inventory as the killing ebbed and his men dismounted to wipe the blood from their blades and loot the dead.

'Edmund! My son! Is that you?' Mun turned Hector towards the house, leaving the all but headless boy to be scavenged by two of Hooker's men. 'God in Heaven, it is you!'

'Mother?' For a moment he watched her walking across the churned, blood-slick lawns towards him, wearing a pikeman's helmet and an old back- and breastplate that Mun recognized as his own. Then he dismounted, feeling as though a saddle girth had been looped round his chest and yanked tight. Hector whinnied and snorted his own greeting, recognizing Lady Mary despite the man's armour that obscured her femininity, as Mun strode towards her on legs still trembling with the mad flush of battle. They both took off their helmets, Lady Mary dropping hers on the ground and stopping to properly take in the sight of her son returned from war. But Mun denied her that luxury, sweeping her into his embrace with a rap of steel on steel.

'My son. My boy,' she said, then pulled away so she could look up into his face. 'You came.' She put a hand on his cheek, her green eyes flicking across his face as though they found it changed.

'I'm sorry, Mother, I did not know.'

'I wrote to your father,' she said, those eyes scouring

464

his own for answers as ardently as Hooker's men pilfered the dead.

'He never received the last letter. Did you send Coppe?'

She nodded. 'Then something must have happened to the poor man, for we have not seen him these last weeks.'

Mun nodded. 'The rebels had the letter,' he said. 'I came from Oxford the hour I read it.' His mouth filled with the foul bitterness of words yet to come.

'These are the King's men? The Prince's?' she asked dubiously, taking in the scene. Nearby, one of Hooker's troopers in a bloodstained buff-coat was on his knees plundering a dead rebel as vigorously as a dog trying to get the marrow from a bone.

'They are mercenaries,' Mun said. 'The Prince could not spare his own men.'

'Are they . . . safe?'

Mun wasn't sure he knew the answer to that. 'They have done their work and will be gone soon. When I have paid them,' he said, recognizing Peter Marten and Owen O'Neill in new armour and carrying matchlocks. 'If I can pay them,' he added, for it must have already cost a small fortune to arm Shear House's garrison.

'We are not ruined yet,' his mother said, staring at him as though he had been gone for not one year but ten. An icy gust blew across the field of the slain and Lady Mary's hair, more white in the red than Mun remembered, blew across her face. 'Come, Edmund, let us get inside. I have a surprise for you.'

Mun nodded and called to Clancy and when the big Irishman looked up, Lady Mary frowned. 'Don't worry, Mother, O'Brien's not one of them. He is my friend.'

'Then you must introduce us properly, Mun,' she said with a mother's chastening look as the Irishman walked over.

'It is an honour to make your acquaintance, Lady Rivers,' O'Brien said, removing his helmet and bowing, a great grin splitting his beard, his wild, sweat-soaked hair steaming in the freezing day.

Mun looked for Hooker but he was busy seeing to his men, three of whom had been shot, though from what Mun could see only one was dead. So far.

'My lady,' O'Brien said, offering her his forearm. She gave a sober nod and put her arm in his, the dignified scene incongruous amidst the dead and those looting them. And they walked towards the house across mud and grass wet with melted frost, towards the men and women who were coming out to witness the carnage and enjoy their freedom now that the siege was over.

And when Mun saw Bess standing by the ruins against the front door, a linen-swathed bundle in her arms, a lump rose in his throat to half choke him and hot tears rolled down his cheeks.

In the midst of death, Shear House burst into life. Lady Mary tasked Major Radcliffe with seeing to Hooker and his troopers, whilst the men of the garrison set about preparing to haul the rebels' demi-cannon up to the house. Though the greatest prize of all was the enemy's baggage train: four carts laden with weapons and, more importantly, food. There was cheese and cheat bread, salted and pickled meats and livestock too, as well as apples, pears and other candied fruits, and more than twenty barrels of small beer. The defenders had all but exhausted their own supply of meat and grain, and so had given a raucous rooks' chorus when Lady Mary declared that no one would go to sleep that night on an empty belly.

Of the carts themselves, two were immediately broken up for firewood and two put to use by men who were now free to forage for more fuel in the nearby woods, so that by late afternoon a great bonfire blazed on the lawn, casting Shear House in its copper glow and warming soldiers, old men, women and children alike, who celebrated the victory and mourned their dead in equal measure. Fires were set in the house too, in the parlours and the bedchambers, so that the chimneys spewed smoke that sweetened the crisp, cold air. The wounded were fed and made as comfortable as they could be and the dead were prepared for burial. They were washed, clad in clean shirts and wrapped with sprigs of rosemary in shrouds that for the most part had been household bed linens. Then each was laid out in the buttery so that friends and relatives could come to pay their respects and sit with the body if they wished to. A few days hence they would be taken to Parbold village and buried in the yard on the south side of Douglas Chapel. Those with no families to mourn them would be piled onto one of the carts and taken to Parbold or Lathom on the morrow. But the rebels who had driven the defenders from their own homes and then attacked Shear House were given no such respect, nor even consecrated ground.

'The dogs stood shoulder to shoulder in their treason,' Major Radcliffe had said, eyeing the Parliament men laid out by the trench those same men had dug some hundred paces from the boundary wall and gate, 'so let them now lie shoulder to shoulder in the same worm-filled hole.' And no one had spoken against the old veteran, so into the trench they went, some sixty men, including Captain Downing whose head had been found eight feet from his body. From her window, Bess had watched the tall, fierce-looking rider cut off Downing's head, had been shocked and appalled by the savage quickness of it. One moment the handsome captain had been leading his men forward – bravely, it had to be said – and the next moment he was a headless corpse. She had been struck by a strange thought, that it was entirely possible that Captain Downing's child was being born at the same moment its father was being killed. But then she had recognized a beautiful black stallion and the man, the killer, on its back viciously exacting vengeance on the transgressors. She had cast aside the musket that had bruised her shoulder and the match that had burned her fingers, scooped her baby from Winifred's cradled arms, and hurried out to greet the conquering hero. Her brother.

'What news from Emmanuel?' she asked now, her patience worn through, cracked like the thin crust of ice on a shallow puddle. She, Mun and their mother had withdrawn to the parlour and had stood in awkward silence, watching Isaac set a fire, the swaddled baby sleeping soundly in Bess's arms. Now the servant had gone and the flames cracked and popped as though joyful to be given life again after four cold, dark, damp weeks. 'And Father, too,' she added. 'You must have so much to tell us, Mun. Are they in Oxford with the King?' Mun took up the fire iron and prodded at the logs, raising a swarm of excited sparks, and Bess reflected that he seemed much changed. His jaw was grim-set, almost cruel-looking. His eyes were different too. Harder.

He did not look at her but leant the poker back against the hearth and picked up the cup of hot hippocras MacColla had brought him. 'We fought a battle near a village called Kineton,' he said eventually, then closed his eyes and inhaled the spiced wine's perfume. *He is not yet used to the stench of death that fills the house*, she thought, yet she herself hardly noticed it now.

Then those steely eyes fastened on hers. 'There have been other fights. Skirmishes. But this was . . .' He shook his head. 'This was a contest between two great armies. A deafening hell of pike-divisions and cavalry and regiments of musketeers.' From the corner of her eye Bess saw her mother sit down and she felt in her own aching belly a sharper pain bloom, as though a length of icy rope was inside her, tying itself into a knot. She rocked the babe in her arms though it was fast asleep. 'It went very hard for us in the heat of it,' Mun said, 'but His Majesty is fortunate to have such men of honour as would not quit the field and give the day to the traitors.' There was a tremor in his voice.

Please, God, no! she beseeched in the dark maelstrom of her mind. *I beg you!*

Mun's eyes glazed. 'Men who would not yield even though they stared into the abyss,' he said. 'And we would have lost without such as they.'

'They're dead,' her mother said flatly. Bess did not look at her, instead glaring at her brother, waiting for the words that would contradict Lady Mary. And yet she knew those words would never come, and Mun's eyes suddenly thawed, so that she saw the pity in them and hated it.

'No. No, it's not true,' Bess heard herself say. She stared at her baby, at his eyelashes that were dark against his white skin. 'They are alive. They are coming home, aren't they, Mun?'

'They gave their lives fighting to protect the Royal Standard,' Mun said. 'They saw the colours were threatened and they rode into the hottest part of it to save the King's honour.' The words were encased in steel, ill-fitting armour that was coming loose. 'I was nearby but could not get to them.'

'If you had you would be dead too,' their mother said. Still, Bess could not look at her, could not bear that weight as well as her own burden.

'Bess, there was no braver man in England than Emmanuel,' Mun said, the muscle in his jaw bouncing, his eyes tear-brimmed. 'And I know he would have been so proud of you. He would have been proud of his son.'

Bess swallowed hard, fighting back her own tears, fearing that if she let them come she might never stop them. Somewhere within, her soul shuddered, like a great door straining to hold against the onslaught of an inexorable foe. She clung to the bundle in her arms and looked upon the sleeping child's face, so perfect and innocent and unknowing.

And inside, she wept like a river in spate for all that would now never be.

CHAPTER THIRTY-ONE

TOM WAS COLD. BEFORE HE HAD SET OFF FROM KINETON,
Margaret had given him a pair of breeches and two
shirts that had belonged to her son David.

'David is broad like you,' she had said, holding up
a shirt against his chest and giving a satisfied nod.
'Strong as an ox is our David.' Then she had given him
an old moth-holed doublet of her husband's and a pair
of worn shoes that Edward had taken from a corpse
before throwing their owner into the dead-crammed
pit. Edward had given him flint and steel and tried to
make Tom take his everyday cloak too, but Tom would
not hear of it.

'You have already given too much,' he had said and
they had known he was not simply talking about the
clothes. For the King's soldiers had ransacked the
Dunnes' house in their search for Parliament soldiers.
They had taken their food too, accusing the folk of
Kineton of being sympathetic to the rebels' cause and
claiming that the requisition of provender was the least
they could expect if they did not mend their treacherous ways. They had even molested Anne, plucking at

her hair and skirts and suggesting what she might do to put her family in His Majesty's good graces, and in his dark hiding place Tom had listened helplessly. He had burned with fury and shame but he had not come down, had barely breathed, for his being caught there would have made things even worse for the Dunnes. Eventually, the soldiers had left and he had thanked the family for all their kindnesses and been on his way.

But now he wished he'd taken the cloak. He was shivering uncontrollably and feared his teeth would rattle themselves out of his jaw. 'I will repay you,' he had promised them, and Edward had nodded as though he expected as much. Now, as he sat in the freezing dark beneath a shelter he had made from the boughs of a fir, Tom realized that his promise meant more to him than almost anything. Somehow, he would repay the Dunnes for bringing him back from the dead, for making him strong again and for the clothes on his back. And in doing so he would see Anne again, too. If he did not freeze to death.

He poked the small fire he had made and it crackled and flared, promising more warmth than it yet gave, but without it Tom knew the raw night would tear into his flesh like a bear's claws.

Somewhere above him rooks haggled boisterously. A savage gust blew down from Parbold Hill, foraging through the trees, rattling bare branches and stirring creaks of complaint from larger boughs. Tom huffed hot breath into cold hands, rubbing them together then tucking them under his arms and squeezing his elbows into his sides, trying to make himself smaller, trying to hide from the callous dusk. The sweet smell of decay, of damp wood and rotting leaves, was the same as it ever was in the beech woods behind Shear House. It was a powerful, bewitching scent that sought to trick Tom into thinking he was a child again, squandering the short days away amongst the trees. And yet this place no longer felt safe as it had done when he was a child. It was the same, but different. It is I who have changed, he thought.

Another bleak draught brought water to his eyes and carried the faint murmur of folk making merry, but the sound was as fleeting as a bat through the branches, so that Tom could not be certain he had heard it at all. This was his third night in the beech woods and he was freezing and starving and no longer trusted his own senses. He had walked north more than one hundred miles in a dead man's shoes, sleeping under hedges and in hay barns, lighting fires when he thought it was safe, shivering through the night when it was not.

'You are not strong enough yet,' Anne had said when he had told her he was leaving. It had been a crisp, cold day and they had been walking along the north bank of the Dene. Tom had been fascinated by the way those errant strands of golden hair that escaped her linen coif seemed to turn to flame with the low winter sun behind her. Light to Martha's shade. 'Stay with us until your wounds are healed. The King's soldiers have gone now. You will be safe here, Thomas.'

'I am grateful for your kindness,' he had said, 'and indebted to you and your family. But I must go.' He had told her that his conscience demanded he return to his regiment and take up the fight once more, and whilst this was true, what he did not say was that he would go north first. Ever since he had lain amongst the stiffening corpses, almost one of the dead himself on the plain below Edgehill, he had felt the pull of an invisible tide, an undertow drawing him home if not in body then in spirit.

And yet now, with Shear House, his home, lying before him, Tom found himself lacking the courage to take the final step, to walk through the lion-guarded gates and face his family.

That first morning, shocked to see the evidence of a siege and soldiers manning the boundary wall, he had skirted west, following his and Mun's old trails up towards the higher ground, keeping the house in sight where he could. At midday he had seen a troop of horse ride out of the gates and it had struck him that perhaps they were Parliament soldiers and that Shear House had fallen. But there was no way of knowing and so he had crossed Old Gore meadow and taken refuge in the beech wood north of the house and now he wondered if he would freeze to death before he could summon the mettle to go down there.

At last the fire began to throw off some heat and so he moved the nearby pile of damp sticks closer to the flames to dry them. Somewhere an owl hooted and he looked up through the skeletal, wind-stirred branches at the darkening sky. It was a sombre, starless evening. But at least it was not raining.

He climbed to his feet, stamping them, feeling the vibration through the thin leather soles of the dead man's shoes but not feeling the feet themselves. Then he left the spitting fire and set off towards the bluff at the edge of the woods that overlooked the house in which he was born.

*

Mun had been glad to see Osmyn Hooker and his men ride away. They had done their job, done it well, too, annihilating the besieging rebel force, all but smiting them from the face of the earth, like God's avenging hand, as Hooker himself had put it. But Mun could rest easier knowing that the mercenaries were gone.

'There is little to like about a man whose only allegiance is to silver,' he had said to Bess as the two of them had watched Hooker's column funnel out of the gate.

'He did not have the look of a trustworthy man,' she had said and suddenly Mun was struck by the notion that he had been duped. He had given Hooker silver plate amounting to some fifty pounds, which Lady Mary had brought out from what she called the last reserves – though Mun knew his mother well enough to suppose there were last reserves and *last reserves*. Hooker had cursed, growling that a parson's salary was poor reward for giving a knight his estate back.

'It is all we have,' Mun had said with a shrug and been surprised when Hooker had nodded and ordered his men to distribute the silver amongst the column. Now, though, Mun was almost certain that the Prince had already agreed to pay Hooker for his services before they had even left Oxford, which was why Hooker had taken the fifty pounds with but little fuss. After all, the destruction of a rebel force was as conducive to furthering the King's cause as it was to furthering the Rivers family's own. But no matter now. Hooker had been right. Fifty pounds *was* a small price to pay to see the traitorous devils dead and in the ground and since then Mun had thrown himself into the task of repairing and improving Shear House's defences, for they could not be sure there weren't other Parliamentary forces in Lancashire that might move against the estate. His estate. Furthermore, at the news of Sir Francis's death, Major Radcliffe had volunteered to stay on with a permanent garrison and hold Shear House in the name of Sir Edmund Rivers, His Majesty the King, and the demi-cannon that sat in its emplacement like a beast waiting to spew wrathful fire on any foolish enough to come with ill-intent. Mun would have to ride back to rejoin his regiment but he would not leave until he was satisfied that Shear House could be defended.

Now, after an exhausting day and a welcome dinner of roasted capons, parsnips and beetroot, they had withdrawn to the parlour with a jug of Madeira which MacColla had fetched up from the cellar, the wine as dark as the night outside. The parlour was dusky too, the gloom relieved by a few globes of candlelight and the spreading fire in the hearth.

'I don't understand how they were not found. Father and Emmanuel,' Bess said, the words arriving with a potency that suggested they had long brewed on the tongue. Mun recognized the question in the statement, too, had suspected Bess's reticence over dinner was down to her having things to say: raw, tender words that prefer darker places than dinner tables. 'I cannot imagine how it is possible that no one discovered them where they had fallen,' she pushed on, clutching the swaddled babe to her bosom.

Mun glanced at O'Brien, whose lip curled within his red beard at the grisly memory of it. 'There were so many bodies, Bess,' Mun said, knowing that only the truth would do. 'You cannot imagine what it was like.' And I am pleased for that, he thought, looking at her. 'I scoured the field, walked amongst them all, but by then it was getting dark. Folk from nearby villages came, joined the crows and dogs to pick at the dead. Stripped them. Took everything they could get their filthy hands on. You would have mistaken it for Hell, sister.' His stomach soured at the pictures his mind conjured. 'At dawn they started to cart the dead away.'

He looked from his sister to his mother who was sitting by the window, staring out at the snow that had begun to fall in goosedown clumps against the black. She had said barely a word since she had heard about her husband and by the fire's glow she looked ashen and drawn, as though she had not slept for days. Likely she had not.

'It must have been terrible,' Bess said, shaking her head. Her eyes glistened. 'You must have been very afraid.' She kissed her baby's forehead, holding her nose there, inhaling his scent. Remembering his father. And her own.

'The only time I have been more afraid was when I read that you were besieged,' Mun said truthfully, turning away to stare into the flames that roared in the hearth. The large parlour had become their retreat, a rare place of privacy in the busy house, and now it filled with silence. Mun felt it growing, spreading, but did nothing to dispel it.

'What are you going to name the little man?' O'Brien asked, his bold, lilting voice turning the mood three shades lighter.

Mun turned back round and watched his sister present her swaddled babe for the big Irishman's inspection. Mun would not have thought his friend, so savage in battle, would be comfortable around gentlewomen and newborns, but O'Brien grinned wildly and bent to look into the child's face, scratching his beard thoughtfully.

'He's a handsome cub so he is. Looks like a Clancy to me,' he said, and Mun laughed in spite of himself as O'Brien turned his palms up as though to ask what was so funny. 'It's a fine name, you ask my ma.'

'I'm going to call him Francis,' Bess said, and Lady Mary's head came round slowly, her gaze settling on the baby. 'Aye, well that's a grand name, too,' O'Brien admitted, a thick finger tickling little Francis under his chin. 'Well, young Francis, may you have the health of a salmon. A strong heart and a wet mouth.' And with that he raised his Madeira in the baby's honour and Mun did the same, ferocious pride blooming in his chest, for his sister had given the boy life in the heat of battle and possessed courage that could put any soldier to shame. Bess's heart was broken. Yet it beat still and would grow strong again with the new life in her arms.

'He is out there, you know.' They all looked at Lady Mary who had turned back to the window, her breath fogging the glass. 'He is out there in the freezing dark. All alone. Watching.'

'Who is out there?' O'Brien asked, frowning and glancing Mun's way.

'My son. Thomas.'

Mun bristled at the mention of his brother. He had said nothing of their meeting, had not seen what good it would do. His brother was a rebel. A traitor. Better for them all to forget about him. 'Tom will be in London by now with the rest of the damned rebels,' he said. 'If he still lives,' he added, regretting that cruelness as soon as it was out.

'He is alive, Edmund,' his mother said calmly. 'I can feel him. As can you.'

Bess looked at Mun, her brows arched above anguish-filled eyes. Mun gave an almost imperceptible shake of his head.

'You are tired, Mother,' Bess said. 'We are all so tired.'

Lady Mary ignored her, turning back to Mun, her proud features besieged by unspeakable sorrow. 'Find him, Edmund,' she said. 'He will perish out there in this weather.'

'There is no one out there, Mother,' Mun said, walking over and putting his hands on her shoulders. But she stepped back, shrugging him off.

'Find him,' she said again, eyes boring into his.

'Tom has turned his back on us,' Mun said, anger flaring in his chest like powder in the pan as he turned to Bess. 'On all of us! He rode against us at Kineton Fight. He is not who he once was. He is our enemy.'

'He is my son!' Lady Mary snapped, eyes suddenly ablaze, and Mun remembered his father saying those same words the night before he died. Then the fire in her eyes receded and she took Mun's hands in hers, thumbs white, squeezing. 'My children are all I have. And one of them is out there in the snow. My boy is out there. Go to him, Mun.'

Mun did not know what to say. Part of him wanted to tell her that Tom had changed, that he was no longer the boy she had known. But his mother's grief had clouded her mind and to disperse the fog he would have to hurt her more, which he could not bear to do.

'My lady, I will take a turn of the grounds,' O'Brien said. 'Don't feel the cold, a big Irish lump like me. If we can't drink it or punch it God knows we ignore it.'

'No, Clancy,' Mun said, stepping back from his mother but still holding her eye, 'I'll go.'

'Then I'll come with you,' his friend said.

Mun shook his head. 'There is no point in us both freezing. If he is out there, I will know where to look,' he said, sharing a knowing glance with Bess. 'Make sure Isaac keeps the fire blazing. And don't let that Irish troll drink all the Madeira,' he said, pointing a finger at O'Brien.

'Be careful,' Bess said. Mun nodded, then left them to the warm parlour and, rather than wait for Isaac to tell one of the grooms to ready Hector, he threw on his fur-lined cloak and went out into the night.

After the relative warmth of the house the frigid air struck him like a blow, its savage fingers clawing at the vulnerable parts of his body – his eyes and ears, hands and feet – as he walked across to the stables. It was early in the season for snow but there it was, beginning to settle on the lawns, hiding the scars of battle like a shroud over a torn corpse. Making it clean again. Sentries stood hunched at their posts, cupped hands to mouths, feet stamping. Some shielded match-cords inside spare hats to keep them dry, the ends glowing sullenly in the white-flecked gloom. Those that recognized Mun touched their hat brims or called greetings, no doubt wondering what could bring the master of the house out into the grim night, though none asked, and when he came to the stables three young men jumped up from the brazier beside which they had been huddled.

'Sir Edmund,' one of them spluttered, eyes wide, 'no one told me you would be needing a mount.'

'Be at your ease, Vincent,' Mun said, raising a palm, then gesturing at the inviting fire. 'I'm taking Hector for a turn round the grounds. I'd wager the sentries are busier trying to keep warm than looking out for rebels. But we can't take chances on those hedgeborn curs sneaking up on us in this snow, can we?' Vincent frowned, clearly doubtful that any such thing was likely, and though Mun did not need to explain himself, he smiled, adding, 'The truth is, Vincent, it has been a few days now and I didn't want old Hector to think I had forgotten about him. We have been through much together.'

Now Vincent grinned, for the boy loved horses more than he loved his own mother. 'He misses Achilles, too,' he said, then blanched suddenly because mentioning Achilles was a mane's hair away from mentioning Tom.

Mun forced a smile. 'At your ease, lad. I'll saddle him myself,' he said. In the Prince's Regiment of Horse he had grown used to doing such things himself and had not slipped back into the routine of letting servants attend his every need. 'And don't worry, I'll have him back in his stall soon enough.'

Hector nickered softly, as though he really had missed his master, and Mun put his face against the stallion's muzzle, their breath coalescing in short-lived clouds. 'Hello, boy. I've missed you, Hector,' he said in a low voice. 'Do you want to come with me? Up to the woods like we used to?' Hector nickered again and Mun rubbed his muzzle and patted his heavily muscled neck. 'Good boy,' he said, then fetched his saddle from the rack.

He wore a wool skullcap beneath his broad hat whose

brim was catching the snow. Beneath his thick cloak he had strapped on his back- and breastplate and he had brought his two pistols and his Irish hilt, for in days like these only a fool would go anywhere unarmed. Though he had left his carbine behind. In truth he was certain that the woods behind the house would be empty and silent. Even the creatures that lived there, the deer and the foxes, the badgers, polecats and weasels, would be lying low, sheltering where they could. But although the night air was biting on his face, the rest of him felt relatively comfortable, for he could feel Hector's body warmth seeping into his legs, even through the saddle, and he was glad to be in the stallion's company once more. Together they had been to Hell. And come out again.

'Sir Edmund! Is there something I can do for you?' A shrouded figure loomed out of the snow, tramping up on his right, and Mun recognized Major Radcliffe.

'Good evening, Major,' Mun said, touching his hat's brim. 'Thank you but no. I needed some air.'

The old veteran nodded, rubbing Hector's glossy black shoulder, his breath pluming. 'It can be hard,' he said, 'coming home to loved ones after seeing the things you've seen. Doing the things you've done.' His one eye was wide beneath his snow-covered hat. 'Battle leaves its stain on a man and no amount of scrubbing will get it out.'

'I haven't thanked you properly, Major,' Mun said, deflecting the man's concern. 'Without you the house would have fallen.'

Radcliffe batted the praise away with a big hand. 'The rebels were a bloody shambles. Their young officer had the makings of something but he'd have been better off with Essex and the rest of them instead of with the misguided shower that thought to take your father's house.' He grinned. 'Truth be told, Sir Edmund, your mother didn't need me. M'lady could have scattered that rabble like bloody chaff in the wind. She's a formidable woman. Brave as any man I've ever served with. Your sister, too. And talking of such things, I hear that you saved the King's own colours no less. If I may say so, good to know one apple did not fall far from the tree. Your father would have been proud.'

The mention of his father was like a knife in Mun's heart but he dipped his head in thanks for the words. 'We are lucky to have you at Shear House, Major,' he said. 'I will make sure you are provisioned, that your garrison has match, powder and ball enough to keep the damned rebels from our door.' Then he flicked the reins and touched his heels to Hector's flanks. 'Good evening, Major,' he said, moving off into the snow-muted gloom, feeling the veteran's one-eyed gaze on his back.

By the time they had climbed the old paths between the rocky, gorse-covered ground and ridden into the beech wood behind the house, the cold was beginning to touch his bones. Half memories of simpler times touched him too, but with ghost fingers, and he shrugged them off, giving them no purchase. He would not indulge things that were dead.

'We'll turn back soon, boy,' he said to Hector, making fists of his gloved hands then opening them again, doing similarly with his toes, clenching and un-clenching. Even the lower slopes of Parbold Hill were no place to be on such a night. 'Just a little further, that's all. Then we'll go back before we freeze.' The wood was eerily quiet, made more so by the snow that was settling on the ground and along branches and piling up in the crooks between bough and trunk. Mun could not recall such silence. These days his world was filled with the boisterous cacophony of army life, of camps and soldiers, of cannon, musket and drum. But here there was just silence, as there must have been before God created the animals. Before He created men to tear the world apart with their wars.

They cut east, the house on their right now below the ridge where the treeline thinned. And after what would have been two hundred paces on foot Mun had decided to end the charade and turn round. When he heard it. The crack and spit of a fire somewhere on his left. He could smell it too, now that he knew it was out there, though he could not see it, nor even its glow, and supposed it must be behind some rock that he could not make out for the snow.

Hector tossed his head and whinnied, then nickered, a foreleg pawing the snowy ground.

'Easy, boy,' Mun soothed, pulling a pistol from its saddle holster. Then his blood froze.

'Hello, brother,' said a voice in the darkness. He pulled Hector round and pointed the pistol at the figure that had materialized like an apparition. The man was dishevelled and thin and sick-looking. His arms were crossed over his chest, hands clawed, and his head was pulled in and to the side, giving him the look of a starving London beggar.

'Tom?' Mun holstered the firelock and dismounted, holding Hector's reins in his left hand.

'I'm cold, brother,' Tom mumbled, and even in the gloom Mun could see that his lips were blue. Dropping

484

the reins, he took off his cloak and stepped up, throwing it around Tom, followed by an arm that invited him to mount Hector.

'Can you ride?' Mun asked.

'I said I was cold, not dead,' Tom said, blue lips pulling back from his teeth. And with that Mun helped his brother up into the saddle, then climbed up behind him, putting his arms around Tom to grip the reins.

Then he turned the stallion round and began back the way he had come.

CHAPTER THIRTY-TWO

TO AVOID BEING SEEN BY THE SENTRIES MUN HAD TAKEN them down a steep, dangerous track that brought them out in the orchards north of the house. Then they had crossed the rear lawns, skirting the walled rose garden, where Tom knew a handful of men were stationed for he had watched them playing cards and heard their pipe music on the breeze. He could not see them now, though, through the heavy snow, and only the smell of their tobacco smoke gave them away. And neither were he and Mun challenged as they came to the north-west edge of the house and entered through the dairy. There he waited, wretchedly cold, unable to stop his shivering, as Mun asked a young girl Tom did not know to fetch Jacob. When eventually the boy appeared, he did not seem to recognize Tom, and Mun made no introductions before telling the lad to take Hector back to the stables.

'You have forgotten me already, Jacob,' Tom said, sniffing and cuffing his nose, still unable to stretch himself out, as though his tendons had shrunk in the cold.

'Master Tom!' Beneath the shock of copper hair Jacob

looked amazed and appalled in equal measure. Then Mun nodded for the boy to be on his way, warning him not to breathe a word of who he had seen, and as Jacob opened the dairy door he took one last look at Tom before disappearing into the night.

'Smells of death,' Tom said when they had passed through the kitchen and the buttery.

'The last of the bodies was taken to the village yesterday. As for the traitors who killed them,' Mun added pointedly, 'we flung them in a ditch, may the Devil take their souls.' They were in the dark corridor that would come out in the hall across from the parlour and Mun stopped and turned, eyes like shards of flint. 'Father was killed at Kineton Fight. Emmanuel too. They died trying to protect the King's standard.'

Tom felt his legs buckle. His right shoulder scuffed against the oak panelling but he kept his feet, glaring at Mun, who did not move to help him.

'You were there?' Mun asked, unfastening the shoulder strap of his back- and breastplate.

Tom nodded. 'I was there.' Memories of that bloody day slashed like a blade through his mind's eye. Mun gave an almost imperceptible shake of his head, but the disgust in his eyes was loud and clear and Tom thought he was about to say more, when he turned his back on him and strode into the hall, handing his armour to Isaac who stared wide-eyed at Tom. And suddenly, Tom wanted to be anywhere but where he was, would rather stumble back out into the bitter dark than face his mother and Bess, knowing now what they had lost. But it was too late to run even if his legs could have carried him, as Mun opened the parlour door. So Tom followed him in.

When Bess saw him her eyes filled with tears and she hurried over, throwing her arms around him, and the smell of her hair made him feel, for the first time in perhaps a year, safe. Yet it was a scent that wrenched his heart.

Over her shoulder he saw his mother, hands clasped beneath her chin, sad, tired eyes absorbing the scene.

'You're shivering,' Bess said, 'come by the fire.' He let himself be led, saw Mun grimace at Bess's helping him, then noticed another man in the room, sitting on a chair, cradling a mug. He was a big man with red hair and a burning bush of a red beard and he stood, draining the mug and dragging a hand across his mouth.

'I'll be leaving you to it, then,' the stranger said in an Irish lilt, bidding the ladies a good night with a respectful nod. The door closed behind him, leaving the four of them in the deafening silence of unspoken words.

Then Bess opened the door again and called for Isaac to bring a plate of hot food and some hippocras.

'Why have you come back?' Mun asked. 'Why now?'

'Let him warm his bones, Mun,' Bess chided, then turned back to Tom. 'You look so thin,' she said, shaking her head sadly. 'And you need a bath.' Tom looked down at himself. She was right, he was filthy. And now that the fire's warmth was seeping into his flesh he was aware of his terrible hunger and the pain in his shoulder, which all those nights of sleeping under hedges had done nothing to ease.

'This is my house, Bess,' Mun said, 'and I would know what a rebel is doing here.'

'Edmund, he is your brother,' Lady Mary said, though she had not taken a step towards Tom since he had come into the room.

'He is a traitor, Mother,' Mun said. 'To his king and his family.'

'Stop, Mun,' Bess implored him, but Tom cut her short with a raised hand and shake of his head.

'Well, brother?' Mun pressed, *brother* the rasp of a sword from a scabbard. 'Why are you here? Are you the Trojan Horse come to deliver Shear House to your masters?'

Tom felt his teeth trying to clamp together, yet forced the words out. 'I lay amongst the dead at Edgehill. I *was* dead.' He held up his hand with its missing finger and Bess put a hand to her mouth. 'But God did not want me.' He let that hang in the air that was sweetened by the birch logs blazing in the hearth. 'I cannot say what made me come back.' He shrugged. 'Perhaps I should have stayed away.'

Now Lady Mary came from the window and, taking Tom's mutilated hand in her own, looked up into his eyes. 'You are home, my son,' she said in a low voice, 'and for now that is the only thing that matters.'

Tom pulled his hand away, glancing at Bess. 'I will not stay long.'

'But surely you will join the King now?' Bess said. 'We need you here, Tom. I have a baby now. Little Francis.' Her eyes lit at the child's name. 'He is sleeping but you will meet him tomorrow.'

Tom heard the words but they did not penetrate, instead rolling off him like raindrops from a lanolin-soaked cloak.

'I mean to kill Lord Denton and his maggot of a son,' he said, anger flaring in his chest at the thought of those devils. 'They have taken everything from me and I will see them dead for it. I can never join the King.'

'I will not stand here and listen to this,' Mun said, then raised a finger at Tom. 'It is as well we did not meet on the field, brother.' The threat was clear and Tom held Mun's eye a long moment, wondering if his brother really would have killed him if they had met beneath the Edgehill escarpment on that grim and savage day. Then Mun shook his head and left the room, bitter gall, almost a tangible thing, billowing in his wake.

'I knew you were out there, my son,' Lady Mary said, gesturing towards the window beyond which the snow still fell, though the flakes were smaller now. There was a smile on her lips that was not even close to reaching her eyes.

'My course is set, Mother,' Tom heard himself say, then saw fresh tears sheen his mother's eyes.

'Come on, Tom,' Bess said, 'let us get you clean and into some of your old clothes.'

He nodded and followed her out, leaving his mother standing alone as the fire spat angrily.

He got up when it was still dark. His breath plumed in the inky gloom of the parlour where he had slept in blankets on the floor beside the fire, and he spent a moment rubbing some life back into his limbs. The hearth was piled with grey ash from which smoke still rose lazily, tainting the air. His bones ached and the wound in his shoulder, which had knitted well, nevertheless smarted. At least his belly was full, though the spiced wine had left it sour, so that he thought he might vomit, for he had not drunk anything so strong for a long time. He dressed quietly, finding some comfort in his own familiar breeches, silk stockings, shirt, doublet and a sleeveless jerkin for extra warmth. Over this he fastened a cloak and lastly pulled on a pair of tall bucket-top boots, relieved to be rid of the dead man's shoes in which he had walked more than a hundred miles. Then he went to the kitchen and quietly opened the door, breathing out a curse as he came face to face with Prudence the house cook, who gasped at the sight of him, her hands up to the wrists in dough.

'Master Thomas,' she said, blinking at the vision.

He put a finger to his lips and she nodded dumbly as he went about filling a linen sack with bread and cheese and some parsnips that lay on the sideboard ready to be washed. Then he lifted a cured leg of mutton off a hook in the ceiling, putting that in the sack too and pulling the drawstring tight. He gestured for Prudence to carry on kneading the bread, then left without a word, closing the door softly behind him. He wanted to look for a weapon or two, preferably a firelock and a sword, but he could hear folk stirring now, hear voices in more than one of the rooms. He had no time and cursed himself for a fool for not thinking of weapons sooner.

But he had clothes on his back and food to eat. All he need do now was get to the stables, take a horse and ride away. For it had been a mistake to come home. There had been a look in his mother's eyes that had managed to hurt him more deeply than any wound. That look was disappointment, and it cut him to the quick. She might have welcomed him back, might have wanted him to stay, but she would never forgive him for taking Parliament's side, for fighting with those who had slaughtered her husband. With Bess it was different. When he had looked at her he had felt guilt, and that sickened him. Because she *would* forgive him.

He knew her heart and knew that she would never turn her back on him, and yet he could not rest until his blood-lust was sated with the deaths of his enemies. That was no way to repay Bess's forgiveness. Besides which, he would never fight for the King. Not now. Not after all that had happened. And Mun – Sir Edmund Rivers – wanted him gone. That was clear as a war banner in a stiff breeze and loud as a drum. So Tom would leave.

Someone was coming down the corridor and though it was unlikely to be his mother or Bess he could not chance it, so he turned and made for the front door, crossing the dark hall and all but stepping on Crab who opened one eye lazily, his head on his paws. 'Good boy, Crab. Easy, boy, it's just me,' Tom murmured, drawing the bolt on the door and opening it. Crab climbed to his feet, wagging his tail at the prospect of going out, but Tom eased the door shut behind him and stepped into the biting pre-dawn, his first breath of the cold air short and sharp as a knife and sending a shudder up his spine. He descended the steps and there in front of him, cast in the copper glow of a small crackling fire, sat the demi-cannon and a canvas shelter under which some soldiers hunched, swaddled in cloaks against the night. A fire near all that black powder was not the best idea, but then neither was freezing to death, Tom supposed, turning his back on them to make his way across the white-mantled lawn to the stables.

This was my home, he thought. Once.

'Who goes there?' a voice in the darkness challenged. Tom did not stop. 'You there! State your business.'

'My business is not your affair,' Tom said over his

shoulder, not slowing, but then he heard boots crunching through the snow. Several pairs of boots.

'Stand where youar, yo' damned scoundrel,' a big man in an ancient helmet said and Tom turned to face four men armed with muskets and blades, though they looked too cold to use them. 'Who are yo'?' the big man asked.

'Who are *you*?' Tom replied, dropping the food sack to the snow. One of the others spat a curse and came at him, reversing his matchlock and swinging it like a club, but Tom stepped in and grabbed the weapon, ripping it from the man's grasp and punching his right arm forward, smashing the musket's butt into the soldier's temple and dropping him. Then something brutally hard cracked against the back of Tom's head and he stumbled forward, into the big man who hammered a fist down, driving him to the ground.

'Do you know who I am, boy?' the newcomer growled and, blurry-eyed, Tom looked up to see an older man, whose one hard, knowing eye glared at him from beneath his broad hat's rim. The other eye was patched.

'I do not care who you are,' Tom said. His head was spinning and he could feel hot blood working its way through his long hair.

'Well I know you, Thomas,' the man said. 'Know you're a worthless bloody traitor and God-damned disgrace to your father. Sir Francis gave his life for his king. Your brother saved the King's colours. And you? I don't know what you're doing back here, rebel, but you're a damned canker.'

'Bastard,' spat another man. 'This is for my brother.' For a heartbeat Tom wondered if the man's brother was the soldier sitting in the snow holding his head, or one of the garrison killed in the siege – as a boot slammed into his ribs. Then another foot, poorly aimed from behind, scuffed his head, prompting cold laughter from the others. And more garrison men were coming.

'Shouldn't we fetch Sir Edmund, Major?' someone asked.

'We'll let the lads work some warmth into their bones first, Cawley,' the older man replied.

It was Edward Radcliffe, his father's friend, Tom realized. The old bastard.

'Besides,' Major Radcliffe went on, 'how were we supposed to know this cur was Master Thomas? My sight's not what it used to be.'

'Radcliffe,' Tom snarled, 'I'll spill your rancid old guts—' Another boot flew in. And another, slamming into his left shoulder, so that Tom felt the wound rip open again.

'So you do remember me, lad?' the major said. ''Tis a shame you did not remember your damned duty.'

Got to get on your feet, Tom, his benumbed mind warned. *Before they kick you to death.*

'Give the dog a proper beating!' someone called. Tom was aware of more garrison men trudging towards them, shapes shambling through the murk. Like a crowd to a bear-baiting.

'Bloody rebel!' another man growled, launching a kick. But Tom threw up his hands and grasped the boot aimed at his head, and hauled back, pulling the man down into the snow. Then he pitched forward, slamming clasped hands into the man's face, crushing his nose in a spray of hot blood. Some amongst the crowd cheered to see the bear fight back, and Tom clambered to his feet, turning this way and that, looking for the next threat. Which was the big man who had first challenged him. In he came, swinging his fists, and Tom blocked one of them with both arms, and slammed a boot into the man's groin, doubling him over. Then he hauled the knife from the man's belt and slammed it down between his shoulder blades, though the blade snagged in cloak and buff-leather and the big man screamed and the crowd bayed like hounds and rushed in, hammering Tom with fists. He lashed out blindly but could not fight them off, could not have even in full health, and his right leg gave way and he fell to one knee. A fist slammed into his cheek, exploding white light in his skull, but still he tried to rise.

Then a firelock cracked in the dawn like thunder.

'Get back! All of you, get back. You, too, Major, or I'll kill you where you stand!'

There was blood in Tom's eyes but the eastern sky was wan with the breaking day and by that sickly light he saw Mun running through the snow. Behind him came Bess and his mother. And Jacob too.

'I said get back!' Mun roared at the garrison men, who reluctantly retreated from their wounded prey, two of them helping the big man away, the knife hilt still sticking from his back. Mun sent Jacob running off across the lawn, then came forward and faced Radcliffe and the largest group. 'How dare you lay a finger on him?' he snarled.

'He's a bastard rebel!' a man yelled. 'We should bloody well 'ang 'im!'

Mun strode up to him, clutched the man by his cloak and yanked him forward, slamming his head into the soldier's face, then shoved him off and the man fell in a heap on the snow. 'Anyone else want to test me?' he challenged, glaring at Major Radcliffe. None did. Then he turned to Tom and offered his hand and Tom took it, rising on legs that felt too weak to stand.

'Bring him into the house, Mun,' Bess said. Beneath a woollen cloak she was still in her night clothes and shivering.

'Leave, Thomas,' Mun said, their eyes locking for a moment.

Tom felt a smile pull his swollen, pain-filled face. 'That's what I was trying to do, brother,' he said.

Then over Mun's shoulder he saw Jacob, and the boy was leading a saddled mare. A good horse by the looks. Tom nodded, understanding, and Mun beckoned Jacob forward.

'He needs to stay!' Bess exclaimed, running over as Tom mounted the horse, determined not to show the pain he was in. 'Stay, Tom. Please stay,' she begged him, her eyes filling with tears. Tom glanced over at his mother, who stood back from the rest, her eyes unreadable in the half light.

'I need to go, Bess,' Tom said, trying to smile. He leant over, his ribs screaming agony, and Bess put her hands on his cheeks and kissed him and he felt her tears. Then he straightened in the saddle and nodded to her, glanced once more at his mother, then looked at Mun, whose face was hard as granite.

Mun stepped up and handed him one of his pistols. 'You'll find powder and ball in the knapsack,' he said, gesturing at the canvas sack tied behind the saddle, as Jacob reached up to give Tom the food sack he had dropped. It was cold and wet now.

'Thank you, Jacob.'

Then Tom turned the mare around and flicked the reins, not looking back at those who watched him walk the horse through the snow.

And in the east, the sun broke free of the horizon.

AUTHOR'S NOTE

There is no getting away from it. The period of great upheaval, of political, religious and social turmoil that we now call the English Civil War (though some historians would rather, and with some valid argument, term it the British civil wars) was a messy business. The inferno of strife that wreaked havoc in England in the mid-seventeenth century was kindled from many flames, but the result was singularly devastating. Families, villages and towns were destroyed. Almost a quarter of a million lives were lost as King and Parliament went to war for their religious and political ideals. In the end, the monarchy and the House of Lords were abolished, replaced by a republic and personal military rule under Oliver Cromwell; a rule that was in the event perhaps as contentious as that of the man he had executed. The traditional authority of Church and state was overthrown and in their place novel philosophies were given breath. New ideas about religion, politics and society grew and flourished. We even saw the birth of a free press. And, crucially, for the first time all these things were accessible to the lower or middling sorts, the tradesmen and tenant farmers and all those ordinary folk who had previously been more or less voiceless. Indeed, the period of conflict that blighted the years between 1642 and 1651, touching every part of the British Isles, has been described as the bloody battle for the soul of the nation. But what caused the conflict in the first place? What made men and women, highborn and low, take up arms against their fellow countrymen? Why did they mass in the fields with pike and musket, or lay siege to great houses with cannon and shot?

Well, frankly, this is the really messy part. The reasons are many and complicated.

The public, especially the Puritans, didn't like having a Catholic queen and thought Charles sympathetic towards her faith. Some even believed Charles was himself secretly Catholic, and the fear of a Catholic uprising *was* very real. Another contributing factor was the ever-increasing friction between King and a Parliament he would rather have done without. Many resented their king levying taxes without Parliamentary consent, saw Ship Money and the Forced Loan as harshly oppressive amongst divers unlawful revenue-raising designs. Particularly worthy of note (and the climax of years of tension) are the events of 4 January 1642, when Charles entered the Commons to arrest five MPs whom he accused of treason. Though the members in question were not present (the King is recorded as saying 'I see the birds have flown'), this action turned most of Parliament against Charles because it was held to be a breach of Parliamentary privilege. Soon after this King Charles fled the capital and seven months later the country was at war with itself, a conflict unique in British history.

But I'm not an historian and I'm not here to discuss the causes of the English Civil War. There is an abundance of non-fiction that does that superbly well. From Diane Purkiss's breathtakingly touching people's history of the English Civil War, to Trevor Royle's vivid and masterly account in *Civil War: The Wars of the Three Kingdoms*, there is no shortage of excellent material on the subject. For me though, when it comes to this extraordinary conflict, the family is where the drama is. There are many accounts of families being ripped apart, of brother against brother and of father against son, the most famous example being the Verneys, from whom many thousands of letters survive, giving us an insight into their trials and tribulations. One of the ideas that I wanted to explore was the complexity of familial duty (and love) set against the pull of ideology, social pressures, or darker motives such as revenge. How far would my characters be prepared to go for a cause, for each other, for survival itself? How strong are bonds of blood amidst what must seem like the chaotic collapse of civilization, or even, as some believed at the time, the end of days as brought about by Man's sin? To my mind, the English Civil War provides the most perfectly dramatic backcloth against which to explore these issues, particularly because what has been somewhat lacking on the bookshelves, in my humble opinion, is real gut-wrenching English Civil War fiction; tales that pull you back to those turbulent days by the scruff of your neck and throw you into the massed ranks. I find this surprising, not only because the subject is surely fertile ground for the adventure fiction writer, but also because the period was so pivotal in this nation's history. And yet whilst watching the TV quiz show *QI*

I was amazed and horrified to learn that 90 per cent of Britons cannot name a single battle in the English Civil War, 80 per cent do not know which English king was executed by Parliament, and 67 per cent of schoolchildren have never heard of Oliver Cromwell! If anything, though, these alarming statistics made me even more convinced of the validity of the story I was writing, despite my subject choice no doubt surprising some of my readers. After all, it's quite a leap from Vikings! Nevertheless, when I told Bill, my agent, and my editor, Simon, that I wanted to 'do' the English Civil War next they were both so enthusiastic about the idea that I could not wait to get into the thick of it.

However, a lifelong interest in the period and events had not prepared me for the challenges and rewards of writing a tale about them. As I have already mentioned, the English Civil War is an unwieldy subject, which is perhaps why historical adventure novelists have, in the main, left it alone. Perhaps it was inevitable, but I soon found that I was never going to be able to cover as much ground in the first book as I had initially planned. This was because the three main characters, from whose perspectives we view the events, demanded to be heard. Whereas I had thought to march from battle to battle, from the bloodbath of Edgehill to the cut and dash of Brentford, I found that Edmund, Tom and Elizabeth Rivers had their own ideas and, for better or worse, depending on what type of book you were hoping for, I allowed them the space they sought. I found myself moved when writing of their struggles, admittedly a new experience for me. Some of this is perhaps down to being a father myself these days, the arrival of my little girl, Freyja, having no doubt softened me up.

Moreover, sometimes when writing a particularly gruesome scene (the hanging, drawing and quartering in this book springs to mind!), I even horrified myself, thinking, *gosh, this is just appalling, I hope Freyja never reads it*! But perhaps an even stronger reason for my own empathy, even sympathy, towards my characters is again due in part to the contrast between this book and those making up my *Raven* saga. The Viking books come with a certain level of expectation. That is to say, the protagonists are Vikings and so you expect them to wilfully pillage and slaughter. Acts of sudden violence are a prerequisite, all part of the job (and yes, remember that Viking is a job description, not the name of a people). In short, with that lot you expect bad behaviour – indeed it may be why you bought the books. In this novel, though, the principal characters are by comparison civilized, normal people (if you can consider a family of Lancashire gentry normal). They are victims of events beyond their control. They become caught up in a terrible war that sees them – Tom and Mun at least – all of a sudden having to shoot dead other human beings, or hack into them with cold, sharp steel. Because the violence is not casual, when it does come it is all the more shocking. And by that token it has a more discernible effect on those suddenly engaged in it. Of course, when it comes to the battles I have taken certain liberties for dramatic effect. For instance, in reality a person's entire experience of the wars might have been a brief (yet no doubt terrifying) skirmish along some nameless country lane. Tom and Mun on the other hand are subject to what I call the 'Sharpe effect', that is of always being in the wrong place at the wrong time. Unluckily for them, but for the sake of the drama in the tale, they will experience many of the major battles that serve as markers throughout this series. However, having said that that is stretching reality a little, there is no doubt that the likes of Cromwell and Prince Rupert were themselves present at numerous fights and survived very many potentially life-threatening actions, so perhaps Mun and Tom's involvement is not so unbelievable after all.

There were other marked differences in writing this book, one being the language itself. In the *Raven* saga I very purposefully chose language that would 'feel' right for the period and the people. Its quality had to be at times quite harsh and abrasive, to give at least an impression of Old Norse or Anglo Saxon. Often the obvious word would, in the writing, look incongruous, its very sense seeming anachronistic. Even though no Viking ever uttered a single word that you'll find in the novels, I chose the language carefully to weave a certain impression. In this novel I was suddenly presented with an infinitely broader palette with which to paint; the vocabulary bag was much deeper. I'm not saying there was no poetry in the *Raven* prose – there certainly was – but in *The Bleeding Land* I was given relatively free rein and it was thrilling.

Well, I say free rein but it's rarely as straightforward as that. When writing historical fiction one very often has to make difficult choices regarding terminology. Let me give you an example. My copy-editor said that, to her, some of the spellings I had used felt too self-consciously archaic. My use of 'pott' (helmet) was one such, and so we agreed to stick with 'pot'. She did let me get away with 'poll-axe' (though with added hyphen), but noted that, according to the *Oxford*

English Dictionary, 'pole-axe' had taken over as the most common spelling by 1625. However, I've seen the word in contemporary texts written 'poll axe', 'pole-axe' and 'pollaxe'. Another case in point was 'snapsack.' Now, then, if you were to go to a re-enactment event you would see the soldiers equipped with a simple tube of canvas or leather that is secured at each end and carried across the back by a stout leather strap. In this bag the soldier carries everything he needs on the march, including spare clothing, money, flint, steel and charcloth, a wooden bowl and spoon, leather bottle, blanket, etc. Generally, a soldier was to carry three days' provisions in his 'snapsack'. However, according to *OED*, the word 'snapsack' only came into common (written) usage about a decade after the events of this book. The suggestion was that since 'knapsack' is the older word for the same object and still current, it seemed preferable. I didn't disagree (though still admit to being curiously fond of 'snapsack').

As you can see, there are occasions when the author has to decide whether he or she wants to please the period expert by using the lingo in which he or she is immersed, or the general reader who might find unfamiliar terms awkward or confusing. I hope I have struck an acceptable balance.

What else? Well, the environment and the landscape itself was a marked contrast. Charles I's London is a far cry from the pastoral, agrarian world of ninth-century Mercia or Frankia. In fact, my agent told me that in this book London itself is almost a character. I know what he means. Of course, this often complicated matters for the author. The seventeenth-century urban environment is sufficiently familiar to us to let us think we can picture it, but it has changed more than enough to make the research somewhat of a headache. Let us not forget that some twenty-four years after the bulk of this novel is set, the Great Fire gutted London, specifically the central parts of the city within the old Roman wall, all but obliterating the medieval city. Sometimes one has to dig a little beneath the ashes for answers.

Which leads me to a confession or three. Whilst I have tried to convey the events in this book as we understand them today, at least in historical terms, I have at times exercised a novelist's prerogative and am guilty of a little conflation of events for dramatic purposes. The Grand Remonstrance was passed in November, but the Root and Branch petition and Colonel Lunsford's intervention were December. I closed this gap to have them happen more or less concurrently. Also, the Wormleighton skirmish actually happened the night before the Battle of Edgehill rather than four or five days earlier as in my narrative. As for the battle itself, my telling of it might not fit squarely with the traditional assumptions and indeed your own understanding of what happened on that October day in 1642. That is because after reading numerous accounts of the battle I decided to base my own version on Malcolm Wanklyn's study in his book *Decisive Battles of the English Civil War*. Using contemporary accounts and, importantly, by methodically examining the terrain over which the battle was fought, Wanklyn has reassessed the Battle of Edgehill. And whilst his evaluation is perhaps slightly controversial, his new viewpoint questioning the perceived understanding of events, I found his account compelling. It just seemed to me to ring true and so I have followed in his boot prints to a large extent.

As for Shear House, it did not exist. However, the idea for the siege in this story is loosely inspired by the very real siege of Lathom House near Ormskirk in Lancashire in April of 1643. The episode and the defiant stand of Charlotte de la Tremoille, Countess of Derby, is one of the most celebrated of the war. For me, the proposition of writing strong, brave women was too tempting to ignore and Lady Mary's rejection of terms for surrender is based on Lady Derby's actual morale-boosting and elaborate speech of defiance delivered to the Parliamentarian Colonel Rigby. However, I don't see much point in going through and saying which parts of the novel are based on real events and which are made up, which of the characters really existed and which are invention. An historical novel is by necessity a blending of truth (or a version of truth as it has been passed down to us) and the author's own imagination. We have the luxury of taking real events and making them the skeleton of a story upon which we then place the flesh and, hopefully, a human face that the modern reader can recognize. That is what makes it, to my mind at least, such a rich and rewarding genre. An historical novel is an invitation to you to join the author on his or her journey to the past as it might have been. Assuming you are adhering to convention and reading this note after having read the story (my mother, frustratingly, often reads the last pages of a novel first!) I am truly honoured you accepted my invitation.

When all is said and done, this is simply a story, a tall tale and nothing more. My very greatest hope is that you have enjoyed it.

One final pleasure remains and that is to thank some very important people. Firstly I want to acknowledge

Mr Transworld himself, Larry Finlay, for wholeheartedly backing this book even before my first novel, *Raven: Blood Eye* had been published in mass-market paperback. Since the very beginning, Larry has shown me unstinting support, giving me the freedom and confidence to get on with the job, and for that I'm tremendously grateful. Likewise, I want to say a huge thank you to my editor, Simon Taylor, whose brisk enthusiasm is only matched by his astute understanding of the craft. He is also great fun to work with, all of which makes my job the easier. My agent, Bill Hamilton, deserves wholehearted thanks for putting up with me. Bill, you know all that sensible and well-considered advice? Well, keep it coming! And while I'm at it I must tip my three-bar pot helmet at Stephen Mulcahey who designs my covers. Steve, if I hadn't written them, I'd buy them for the covers alone. That's good enough for me.

I'd also like to thank a good friend and film director with whom I've twice had the privilege of working, first for a short film and book trailer for my *Raven* saga, and recently for the trailer to the *Bleeding Land* series. Phil Stevens and the fantastically talented team at Urban Apache Films have gone above and beyond to produce two stunning pieces of work that, in my opinion, put even some Hollywood multi-million-dollar movies to shame. Talent always rises to the top, and my heartfelt gratitude goes to Phil and the team for all their support.

As I have mentioned, this novel presented its own set of challenges, particularly the research side of things. Fortunate for me then that in 2010 at English Heritage's Festival of History at Kelmarsh Hall I met a group who have been only too happy to share with me their passion for keeping history alive. The Fairfax

Battalia of the English Civil War Society have invited me into their ranks, put me in full kit, and given us fantastic photo opportunities. Ken Clayton deserves special mention for being incredibly helpful and for introducing me to Fairfax Battalia's CO, Simon Frame. Simon very kindly agreed to read this novel in draft form and share with me his prodigious knowledge of the period. Many of my original errors are not present in this book as a result of Simon's eagle eye. Thanks, Simon! Any remaining mistakes are of course entirely my own.

I would also like to mention re-enactment societies in general. Groups such as the English Civil War Society and the Sealed Knot campaign tirelessly, sharing their passions with the general public at events up and down the land. I don't think I'm overstating it when I say that these men and women provide an essential public service by educating, entertaining and bringing the past back to life in all its noise and glory. If you get the chance this year, do yourself a favour and go along to a re-enactment event. I promise that you'll come away with a whole new level of understanding as to how our ancestors lived and died.

As ever, I would be floundering without the support of my inspirational wife, Sally, and the love of my little girl, Freyja. Thank you both, you are wondrous beings.

Finally, I want to thank you for reading this novel, for galloping into the fray with me. I have said it before but without your imagination this book is just so much printed paper. I'm enormously grateful that you choose to immerse yourself in my tales. If you have any comments or questions about my books, stop by my website www.gileskristian.com or my Facebook group, which is often buzzing with banter. You can find me on Twitter too: @gileskristian.

So, until next time, keep your powder dry. We'll be marching together again before long, you and I.

Giles Kristian
Thurcaston
February 2012

Want to know what happens next
to the Rivers family?

Turn the page to read
the first chapter of

BROTHERS' FURY

*The next exciting instalment
in* The Bleeding Land *trilogy*

COMING SOON

CHAPTER ONE

14th January 1643. Lancashire

GOD ALMIGHTY, IT WAS COLD. A LITTLE AFTER MIDDAY, yet the pallid sun clung to the horizon throwing the riders' shadows far ahead of them in spindly misshapen caricatures that seemed to gush across the ground like black water. The night's frost still held the land in its frigid grip, whitening tussocks and heather, sheathing leafless branches and making a hoary-haired old man of the peat moor. It was a white, silent, frozen world, and it was empty.

But for the passing of a small troop of horses.

Mun twisted in the saddle, blinking watery eyes against the biting air. Cocooned in cloaks and hunched into themselves as though protecting some feeble flame that yet flickered within their chests, the men of the column resembled corpses swathed for burial and lashed to saddles. But for a slight sway as their mounts trudged on, they barely seemed to move, all flesh trussed up leaving only the eyes visible, and even these were slitted defensively, so that Mun could not read their thoughts. Not that he needed to see their eyes to know their minds. He supposed they resented him for leading them across the empty, bitter-cold moorland when all sensible folk were inside by their hearths. Even the great armies of Parliament and King had, for the most part, settled in for the winter, Essex's force at Windsor and Charles's at Oxford, that city having become for all intents and purposes the seat of his Court and the Royalist capital. And yet not all had sheathed their blades and let their match burn out, and Lancashire remained a battle-ground upon which Parliament was seeming to press the advantage. There were still powerful men waging the King's war here in the northwest, Mun knew. Men such as Richard Lord Molyneux, the wealthy Thomas Tyldesley, and the most powerful of all, James Stanley the earl of Derby. But the earl had been deprived of his best regiments for service with the King elsewhere and had been forced to abandon his siege of Parliament-held Manchester the previous October. Now his forces had consolidated around Preston and Wigan and had made their headquarters in Warrington just twenty miles south of Shear House.

Meanwhile the rebels were growing bold. They were recruiting.

And Mun was hunting.

'Winter either bites with its teeth or lashes with its tail, my da used to say,' O'Brien riding beside him muffled into the cloak covering the lower part of his face, 'but this whore-hearted bitch has had us with her claws too as she's walked across our backs.' The big Irishman pulled the cloak down and dragged a sleeve beneath his nose, breath pluming in the cutting air. 'No bugger's daft enough to be out in this.'

Mun would have wagered that every trooper in the thirty-six strong column was thinking the same, but only O'Brien had the nerve to say it.

'*We're* out in it,' he said, watching rooks and jackdaws rise and dip across the heath, foraging amongst the frosted clumps of bilberry and heather, feeding if they could, making the most of the scant daylight hours.

'Aye and what does that make us?' O'Brien muttered to himself.

'Would you rather be a lapdog or a wolf?' Mun asked, the cold air hurting his teeth.

'On a day like this I'd be a bloody cat,' O'Brien said, 'all curled up on some pretty wench's lap by the fire.'

Mun smiled grimly at that image, for O'Brien was a giant of a man, red-haired, red-bearded and in battle as savage as this long winter's claws. Twice as dangerous too. But the Irishman was right about the cold and Mun had not known a harsher winter. He recalled something his own father had once said, that in winter every mile is two, and watching the scavenging birds he decided not to range too many miles more before turning for home. Perhaps an hour had passed since they had skirted the town of Longridge above the Ribble river, eight miles north-east of Preston, and now they were at the fringes of the Forest of Bowland, and the fells were no place to be after dark, especially in weather like this. Mun knew the black moor could swallow their whole column, freezing man and beast as solid as the rocky outcrops and gritstone boulders that tore through the wild heath, and no one might ever find them.

We'll turn back at Deerleap crag, he thought, if we have caught no sight of the enemy by then. But the damned traitors were out there somewhere and he hungered to find them, would have that rather than all the warmth and comfort Shear House could offer.

'Just a little further,' he called over his shoulder, receiving no answer but for a loud snort from one of the horses – eloquent testimony as to what they felt about being out on such a day.

'As much as I enjoy giving the rebel turds a good hiding, this should be down to Derby, not us,' O'Brien said, hawking and spitting a thick gobbet into the snow. 'We can't be more than nine, ten miles from Preston. It's those buggers should be out here freezing their balls off instead of sitting around scratching their arses.'

'True enough,' Mun said, 'but the earl and the other commanders are more concerned about the lightness of their purses and the gaps in their ranks than they are about waging proper war. And while they fret, the rebels recruit. They reinforce. Get stronger. Our lads were given a good kicking on Hinfield Moor, booted out of Leigh, and then earned a bloody nose for their troubles when Sir Gilbert Houghton tried to re-take Blackburn.'

'Aye, well that was a wet fart of a thing,' O'Brien said. 'I heard Sir Gilbert gave up the siege so that his men could eat their Christmas pies at home by their own hearths.'

Mun could not tell from his tone whether the Irishman thought that was deplorable or admirable. He suspected the latter. 'Whatever the reason, they're not fighting,' he said. 'And if they're not fighting they're not winning. But I promise you this, Clancy, the rebels are not safe. Not even in this Godforsaken weather. Not from us. Not from me.' Gloved fingers instinctively caressed the curved butt of the twenty-six inch-long firelock pistol holstered on the right of his saddle's cantle. The weapon's twin nestled snug in its leather sheath on the saddle's other side against his left thigh. 'We're going to find them,' Mun said, watery eyes ranging across the frosted land, 'and we're going to kill them.'

'Aye, I suppose that would be agreeable. There's nothing like a bit of a fight to stir some heat into the blood,' O'Brien said, 'and the boys will play the part, won't you, lads?' He called over his shoulder, his helmeted head wreathed in his own fogging breath. A few mumbled *ayes* rose from the column but most of the swaddled troopers kept their hot breath inside their chests, shoulders hunched, heads pulled in. The column comprised the best riders and most capable men from Shear House's garrison, and though most were relatively inexperienced, they were fit, healthy and strong.

'Men learn quickly in war, My Lady,' Major Radcliffe had assured Mun's mother when she had voiced concern at Mun leading them out into winter's savage maw to track and kill rebels. 'Sir Edmund is proof of that.'

'We have all been changed by this war, Major,' Lady Mary had said, and Mun had avoided her eyes then, not wanting to see the sorrow in them.

'They may be miserable as bloody Puritans in a brothel, but they'll sing loud enough when the shooting starts,' O'Brien assured Mun now, snuffling back down into his cloak.

'Like avenging angels,' Mun muttered, remembering the day he and Captain Smith – now Sir John Smith

– had brazenly ridden back onto the killing field at Edgehill and wrested the King's colours from a well-armed knot of roundhead soldiers. A Catholic and not shy to admit it, Smith had announced to a group of dragoons that he and Mun were two of Saint Michael the Archangel's soldiers come with swords of fire to smite God's enemies.

And smite Mun would, for the rebels had destroyed his family. His father was dead, slain at Edgehill, as was Mun's good friend, his sister Bess's husband Emmanuel. Then the traitors had besieged Shear House and killed many of its defenders before Mun could break the siege, the scars carved into the house by their demi-cannon serving as a constant reminder of that desperate episode. Added to all this the feckless enemy had recruited his brother Tom, meaning that Tom and he were now enemies, ripping the heart out of their once-proud family. It was a wound that would not – could not – heal. And for all this the rebels would pay in blood. Which was why Mun had not returned to his regiment, despite having given his word to Prince Rupert that he would join him as soon as he and the mercenary Osmyn Hooker had raised the Siege of Shear House.

Be sure to return to us with news of the rebels' movements in the north-west. Had those not been the Prince's words? So rather than sit idle in Oxford with the King's army watching the enemy grow stronger and letting the edge of his sword dull, Mun would hunt. He would kill. Surely a child of war like the Prince would understand his reasons for remaining in Lancashire, would rather Mun remained a thorn in his enemy's side than becoming a swaggering wine skin like most of the Gentlemen Cavaliers in Oxford.

'You don't have much faith in the peace negotiations I take it?' O'Brien said, one bushy red eyebrow hoisted. Tack and armour jangled and clinked and horses snorted; those sounds and the occasional raucous *caw* of a crow the only interruptions to the frozen fells.

'There's more chance of you taking holy orders and ending up the Bishop of bloody Bath than there is of his majesty going along with Parliament's demands,' Mun replied. O'Brien cocked his head thoughtfully, as though the scenario Mun had suggested was not entirely inconceivable. 'The concessions they demand of him are unrealistic,' Mun went on. 'Just think it through.' He doubted the Irishman would. 'The King will not relinquish his sovereign control of the militia. Honour prevents him handing over those whom Parliament would scourge. His religion will not let him put an end to bishops, and only a fool would disband a growing army that shows signs of being useful.' Mun clapped his hands together and pumped his fists, trying to get some warmth into them. 'No, the negotiations will come to nothing, mark my words, and if I know the Prince he'll be stalking around Oxford like a caged animal.' Mun thought about the Prince and his seemingly boundless energy for war. 'Actually, I'd wager he is ignoring the sham of peace entirely. He'll be up to the same as us, trying to further our political advantages by means of steel and shot,' he said, patting the pistol's butt, 'for he knows better than anyone that our failure to take London has cost us dear.'

O'Brien sniffed loudly. 'Well let's hope the royal fellow doesn't decide to use his steel and shot on us for not re-joining the regiment.'

'You're free to leave. Bugger off back to Ireland if

you want. I won't make you stay,' Mun said, looking straight ahead, feeling a stab of irritation. Or rather disappointment to think the Irishman might want to leave. Yet he knew it was unfair to expect O'Brien to risk punishment for Mun's own dereliction.

'I'll freeze my arse off awhile longer if it's all the same to you.' O'Brien looked off across the frost-hardened heath. 'You need me to look after you. Besides, Little Francis would miss me something terrible if I buggered off now.'

Mun felt the cold air bite into the cracks in his lips, for who would believe that, aside from their friendship, a baby was truthfully the main reason why O'Brien had not turned his mare south and ridden to Oxford. Mun knew the big man had grown fond of little Francis, of Bess and their mother too. Though how the infant did not wail with terror at the sight of the red-haired giant was a constant surprise to Mun.

'It's all the same to me but Prudence will be happy to hear of it,' Mun said, watching from the corner of his eye for O'Brien's reaction. Which was a great shiver and beard-splitting grimace. The cook did not boast looks that Anthony van Dyck would have got his brushes wet for, but she clearly thought the Irishman did and her ears and cheeks would flush red whenever she saw him.

'The way she leers at me . . .' O'Brien growled, 'as though she'd put me in one of her pies and wolf me down with a wash of ale.'

Mun laughed, his breath fogging around his face, blending with Hector's breath. Then the stallion neighed, the bit in his mouth jangling against his teeth, and Mun knew Hector well enough to follow the beast's gaze into what little breeze prevailed against them from the east.

And that was when he saw it. A faint stain on a ridge of ground thirty paces off his right shoulder, where the frost had been knocked off the heather.

'Come on, boy,' he said, clicking his tongue and pressing his right knee against Hector's warm flank, 'let's take a look, shall we?'

O'Brien flicked his reins and made to follow. 'Good idea. It won't be so damned cold if we get off the high ground,' he called, thinking that Mun would lead them over the swell and down into one of the many deep river valleys that cut through the moorland. But Mun did not answer, because he did not know yet what he was looking at.

'Could be deer,' O'Brien said, drawing alongside, looking down at the disturbed clump of heather. 'Or a sheep that has wandered off.' Behind them the rest of the column had halted in a cloud of their own fog, some of the men slapping their upper arms for warmth, others sitting their mounts as though they had already frozen to death. 'Mary Mother of God!' he said then, seeing what held Mun's eye; a column of infantry down in the valley trudging towards a copse of skeletal oak, ash and alder. There were several horsemen too, one of whom had evidently scouted up the valley's steep side and left his tracks in the frost; tracks which now lead all the way back to the column. 'Do you think he saw us?'

'I'd wager a half crown on it,' Mun said, twisting and gesturing for his troopers to join them. 'That's why they're heading for the trees.'

'So we know the buggers aren't ours then,' O'Brien

said, 'else they wouldn't be scarpering like mice back to their little hole.'

'You're assuming that scout knew who we were,' Mun said, sweeping out an arm towards the men and horses that were bunching around them. 'We're not the Prince's horse now.'

O'Brien frowned, casting an eye over the Shear House men who had become Sir Edmund Rivers's cavalry troop. 'Aye, you'd think us a horde of starving cutthroats,' he said. None of the men disagreed, their liquid eyes fixed on the column of foot below.

'Not cutthroats. Not with these horses,' Mun said, 'yet the sight of us was enough to curdle that scout's blood and put his whole company to flight. All, what, forty of them?'

O'Brien grinned wickedly. 'Horses put the fear of God into infantry.'

'That's part of it,' Mun said, 'but there's another reason they're wetting their breeches.'

The Irishman's gloved fingers raked the thick red bristles on his cheek until the answer struck him. 'They're bloody recruits!' he said. 'Not even proper soldiers, but for those officers sitting nice warm beasts, boots out of the frost.'

Mun nodded. 'Those officers have come north-east. From Blackburn.' He gestured at the handful of riders who were corralling those on foot towards the trees, which were still four or five hundred yards away by Mun's reckoning. 'They've come looking for wool traders and farm boys to turn into soldiers, those who were not in the villages when the sergeants came banging the drum.'

'To give the traitorous fellows their due it looks like they've found some,' O'Brien admitted.

That was true enough, Mun thought. The rebels knew Derby was holed-up forty miles south in Warrington and they'd guessed correctly that the Preston garrison would be keeping their bones warm. So here they were, out in the freezing cold. Recruiting. Mun felt the blood begin to tremble in his limbs. It was the battle thrill coming on him.

'The brazen bastards,' trooper Lawrence said, winding his wheellock. Many of the others were doing likewise, slipping spanners over the square section of their weapon's wheel shafts and filling the still morning with a salvo of clicks, before priming the pans with powder and pulling the pan covers shut.

'We're going to tear them to shreds,' Mun said, checking that his own weapons – the two firelocks and his carbine – were secure. His heavy sword was snug in its scabbard on his saddle behind his left hip. He still wore the old back and breast he had bought from a trooper in Nehemiah Boone's company whose place he had taken after breaking the man's leg, but beneath it he now wore a fine buff-coat stripped from the dead captain who had led the assault on Shear House. Downing had been the man's name and his leather coat – so fine that it could not have cost the captain less than eleven pounds – fitted Mun perfectly, providing not only protection but much-needed warmth.

'If we let those men live they and others like them will be at the gates of Shear House before spring,' he announced to the troop, taking off his gloves. 'They will threaten our families. They will try to kill us.'

'Whoresons can try,' a hard-looking man with a weathered face said. His name was John Cole and from what Major Radcliff had told Mun, and from what

Mun had since seen for himself, Cole was a useful man to have with you in a fight.

'They will spread their sedition and we shall never be rid of this war,' Mun went on, tying his helmet's leather thong beneath his chin then shoving cold hands back into the gloves. 'So we kill them before they get to those trees.'

'Do we offer quarter?' a wide-eyed lad named Godfrey asked, pushing his wheellock back into its saddle holster with a trembling hand.

'You can offer by all means, lad, but kill them first,' O'Brien gnarred, pushing his own helmet down snug over his thick red tresses.

'Kill them,' Mun said, holding Godfrey's eye with enough steel in the gaze to make the young trooper more afraid of him than of the enemy below. And with that he gave Hector a touch of heel and urged him over the frost-stiffened tussocks of the ridge, his eyes riveted on the enemy below, whose formation had disintegrated now in their panic to get to cover.

Mun knew it was unwise to ride at any sort of speed down such a slope, but he also knew that if they descended at a walk the rebels would gain the trees and they would lose their advantage. So they went at the trot, hooves thudding against the iron-hard ground, armour and tack clinking and jangling. Mun felt the icy wind bite into his face, blurring his vision and dragging tears from the corners of his eyes. The bitterly cold air scorched his throat and lungs but he relished it, his whole body thrumming now with the excitement that always flooded his veins before mortal danger. And now he could hear the men in the gully below shouting, could discern fragments of commands mostly lost amongst the wind gushing past his face and eking into the gaps between helmet-steel and ears.

'For England and King Charles!' he roared, and that's when the first muskets cracked in the valley, etching a grimace between Mun's lips, for this all but confirmed that the men below were Parliament men and in truth Mun had not been utterly certain before. 'England and King Charles!' he yelled again, and this time several others repeated the war cry as they followed Mun's lead and gave the spur, breaking into a gallop, the fear of flying lead hunching shoulders and pulling in heads.

O'Brien, no great admirer of the king but a sworn devotee of killing men who pointed muskets at him, gave his own cry of 'Kill them all,' as a stuttering volley of musketry shredded the crisp afternoon and Mun felt a ball whir past his left cheek, and his troopers' horses beat their frantic rhythm against the ground.

They galloped down onto the valley floor, men folding forward and grunting with the impact of coming onto flatter ground, and now Mun could make out the faces of his enemies one hundred feet away, their eyes wide with terror as their freezing hands fumbled at powder flasks, scouring sticks and glowing match cords. He saw one man drop his musket and another turn and run, but Mun's prey was a buff-coated officer sitting a chestnut mare, who was screaming at his recruits to form a line and for the love of God load and give fire.

Forty feet away.

Taking the reins in his left hand Mun reached behind him with his right and hauled his carbine round on its belt, though he did not fire because the weapon was jolting wildly.

Twenty feet.

The rebel officer must have fired his pistol already for now he drew his sword, but Mun gripped with his knees and brought his left hand up to steady the carbine's barrel and the rebel threw his other arm across his face in vain as Mun squeezed the trigger. The carbine roared and its ball punched a hole through buff leather, skin and breastbone, and through the rebel's heart, spraying gore-flecked bone and slivers of glistening meat out of the ruin of his back, and then Mun was flown past him.

A callow-faced young rebel raised his matchlock and Mun cursed, thinking himself a dead man. But in his fear or inexperience the musketeer had misjudged the length of match clamped in the serpent's jaws and the tip of the burning match missed the priming-pan, or else he had forgotten to open the pan, and Mun spurred Hector forward so that the stallion's chest slammed into the man, catapulting him backwards with the sound of bones snapping. 'King Charles!' Mun clamoured, drawing a pistol and shooting a rebel between the eyes. The man collapsed, a dark stain blooming on the crotch of his breeches, his brains spread across the frosted tussocks like spilled porridge.

Mun twisted and saw O'Brien bury his pollaxe into another mounted officer's shoulder, heard the rebel scream like a vixen before the Irishman leant across and shoved his pistol into the man's belly and gave fire, erupting gobbets of flesh and spine from a vulgar void in the officer's back.

Some rebels were still running for the trees and so Mun hauled on the reins and kicked back with the spurs that had once been fastened to the boots of the King of England himself, and he yelled at the stallion to run, breaking away from the chaos to cut down the fugitives.

'Wait for me, you greedy bastard! Sir!' O'Brien yelled, and pulling his own mount round, galloped after Mun. Who was already pulling his heavy sword out of its scabbard and into the raw, death-filled day.